# LIARS DICE

# LIARS DICE

*Bob Gust*

SYREN BOOK COMPANY
*Saint Paul*

Most Syren Books are available at special quantity discounts for bulk purchases for sales promotions, premiums, fundraising, and educational needs. For details, write

Syren Book Company
Special Sales Department
2402 University Avenue West, Suite 206
Saint Paul, Minnesota 55114

Published by
Syren Book Company LLC
2402 University Avenue West, Suite 206
Saint Paul, Minnesota 55114

Printed in Canada on acid-free paper

ISBN 0-929636-36-8

LCCN 2004113993

Cover design by Kyle G. Hunter
Book design by Wendy Holdman

To order additional copies of this book see the order form
at the back of this book or go to www.itascabooks.com

To Cary Johnson:

The truest test of character is a person's ability to deal with adversity. You've proved your character in ways beyond belief, but it's time for you to **STOP SHOWING OFF!**

♦

# ACKNOWLEDGMENTS

First and foremost, I want to acknowledge my parents and my family for always giving me whatever was needed in terms of love and support. The only thing absent from my all-too-functional upbringing is the ability to claim to be a self-made man.

Second, I want to thank everybody who gave me input or other help with the manuscript. In no particular order, the nonprofessional assistance came from Cary Johnson, Paul Maahs, Jolene Gust, Jim Gust, Vern Gust, Aras Vebra, Shelley Furer, John Crane, Wade and Barb Salisbury, and Todd Holtan. I also appreciate the professional assistance I received from William Greenleaf and Nadene Mattson. Special thanks goes to my dad for slaving over an early manuscript and circling the swear words.

Finally, I want to thank all of the clients that I have represented in more than twenty years of private practice. The fact that you entrusted me with your legal needs has brought me tremendous professional satisfaction. From simple contracts to "you bet your company" litigation, your confidence has sustained me. Service to others is a privilege, and I am deeply thankful to those who have given me the opportunity to serve them.

# PREFACE

Elements of this book are based on actual events that are a matter of public record. The characters and the other elements of the story are fictional, and any similarity to actual people or events is not intended

# PROLOGUE

KOOCHICHING COUNTY SHERIFF'S DEPARTMENT

Transcript of 911 Call

DISPATCHER: Sheriff's 911.

CALLER: Yes, uh—(heavy breathing). This is Les Krueller. (Inaudible) Duke MacKenzie just shot me. Send an ambulance.

DISPATCHER: Okay. Was the shooting at MacKenzie's place?

CALLER: Yeah.

DISPATCHER: And where are—

CALLER: I caught him fuckin' my wife!

DISPATCHER: Okay. But you must be on a cell phone 'cause I can't locate you. Where are you now?

CALLER: I'm layin'—I'm—uhh, them sons-a-bitches wouldn't even call an ambulance.

DISPATCHER: Okay, but where are you?

CALLER: I'm at Duke MacKenzie's out on Way Lake Road. Or —

DISPATCHER: Moose Lake Way?

CALLER: Moose Way Road.

DISPATCHER: I think that's Moose Lake Way.

CALLER: (Woman's voice—inaudible)

CALLER: Yeah, get an ambulance out here. I'm sure as hell not going to die for that son of a bitch.

1

DISPATCHER: Is Duke still there?

CALLER: (Woman's voice) I hope you die Les! You had no business being here.

CALLER: My fuckin' wife. She was fuckin' MacKenzie, now she wants me to die.

DISPATCHER: Is Duke still there?

CALLER: No, he took off.

DISPATCHER: Okay, we're gettin' the ambulance going. What'd he—what did he shoot you with?

CALLER: (No response—heavy breathing)

DISPATCHER: Do you know what kind of gun?

CALLER: I caught him fuckin' my wife!

DISPATCHER: Was it a handgun or a shotgun or—

CALLER: Handgun.

DISPATCHER: Are you bleedin' pretty bad? Where'd he shoot you?

CALLER: Stomach. Hard for me to tell how much blood.

DISPATCHER: Okay. Hang in there. We're trying to figure out exactly where you're at.

CALLER: (Woman's voice) You're an asshole Les.

DISPATCHER: MacKenzie's place. Isn't that north of the dump?

CALLER: Goddamnit! I'm bleeding and you fucking idiots can't read a map. Get an ambulance out here now!

DISPATCHER: Take it easy—take it easy Les, the deputies are on the way.

CALLER: Those bastards wouldn't even call 911 for me. MacKenzie shot me and left me for dead.

CALLER: (Woman's voice) Don't drive too fast getting here.

CALLER: I'm not going to die for that ... hey, you bitch, get away from ...

(Telephone hangs up.)

LIARS DICE

# CHAPTER 1

"IT'S GENETICS. All that bullshit about a person's upbringing affecting their personality will someday be scoffed at as medieval." This was Dixon Donnelly's credo and he would happily spar with anyone on the subject.

Sandy Swanson frowned and shook his head. "You gotta be kidding me. Everyone knows that lying is a learned skill and people growing up in certain circumstances learn how to lie as a survival mechanism."

Dixon wasn't yielding. "I'm not saying the way a person is raised is irrelevant, but its impact is overrated. A bad family situation might help hone someone's deception skills, but a conscience and basic ability to know right from wrong are things people have since birth. I tell you, when I'm in court and I'm trying to decide if a witness is going to lie, analyzing life histories just doesn't cut it."

"So you want witnesses to give DNA so you can search for the dishonesty gene?"

"Sounds good to me," Dixon responded. "Look, remember when we were in college and everybody thought gay men must have had overbearing mothers?" Dixon didn't wait long for a response. "Now everybody claims to be enlightened on this issue. You know damn well that you and everybody you knew believed homosexuality was the result of something that happened during childhood. I was one of the first to say it's genetic or at least congenital and I'm telling you, we'll be coming to that conclusion about a lot more personality traits as the studies continue."

Sandy gave Dixon a patronizing look. "I think it might be a little early in the morning for your philosophizing."

It was 5:30 A.M. and the unblemished sky and exuberant sun made it one of those perfect spring mornings that used to be experienced only by farmers and paperboys. Now it seemed half of Minneapolis was out for early morning exercise. While Dixon was a regular on the morning workout circuit, Sandy wasn't a morning person and had only grudgingly agreed to the run.

Dixon persisted. "Even people who grow up in affluent households can turn out to be bums, but sociologists explain that away by saying their parents didn't pay enough attention to them. On the other hand, if someone in the same situation turns out to be normal, it's because of the advantages they had while growing up. I think most of those traits are determined when people leave the womb."

Dixon Donnelly had a name that suggested he'd been born to such affluence, but a bank account that indicated otherwise. "Donnelly" was an aristocratic name in that Ignatius Donnelly was one of Minnesota's founding fathers, having been the second Lieutenant Governor and a Congressman during the Civil War. Dixon might have been a shirttail relative, but his mother wanted people to think more. She named him Dixon Ulysses Donnelly because "Dixon" was more of a last name "as the rich are known to do," and "Ulysses" because she mistakenly thought that was the name of the famous statesman.

There were few subjects about which Dixon didn't have opinions, and he relished the role of contrarian. Along with strong opinions, he carried a general disdain for those who, in his words, "stood for nothing and fell for anything." The politically minded who declined to take positions were, in many respects, more infuriating to Dixon than those who could provide a spirited opposition.

Sandy, on the other hand, was a charmer in all senses of the word. He was bright and could discuss the hot issues of the day, but savvy enough to know when not to. It was, perhaps, indicative of Sandy's consummate political skills that he could be a political navigator and still be friends with Dixon.

They had met in law school ten years earlier, but took seemingly different paths. Sandy was a big-firm, mergers and acquisitions lawyer, whose good looks, interpersonal skills, and perennial tan took him right to the top. Dixon was not short on character or physical appeal, but his iconoclastic nature had eventually required him to establish his own law practice. The pay was sometimes sporadic, but for once he didn't think his boss was an asshole.

They were about halfway through their morning run around the chain of lakes south of downtown. Minneapolis, which translated from Sioux and Greek means "water city," was as attractive an urban area as one could find—at least in the summer. The three lakes south of downtown were the best known and most used. Bikers, skaters, and pedestrians orbited in both directions, with a street carrying automobiles counterclockwise, a bike path on which anything else on wheels went clockwise, a pedestrian path that was multidirectional, and, finally, a dirt cow path that runners had worn into the ground, defying city planners who thought three routes should suffice.

Dixon had grown up with these lakes. He learned to swim at the Queen Avenue beach. When he was in junior high, his posse would bike to the Lake Harriet bandshell every summer night, even if the entertainment du jour was an Oompah band. He had kissed his first girl in a car parked by the rose gardens. Still, when he was young, he was sure he was destined for a bigger city and a faster lifestyle. In the end, the city and the lakes kept pulling him back. He was living proof of an adage among headhunters that "Minneapolis was the hardest place to recruit people to and the hardest place to recruit people from."

The pair ran under a canopy of green formed by the trees lining the path. As they rounded the west side of Lake Calhoun, the trees gave way to a magnificent view of the downtown skyline rising above the trees at the opposite end of the lake. Sandy had stopped responding to Dixon's hypothesizing, but finally broke the silence. "I have to admit, I probably won't ever get up again this early in my life, but it's pretty cool to be out here at this time of day."

"Well, the workout will certainly do you some good," Dixon replied.

"What are you talking about?" Sandy said with mock indignation.

"All that fat-cat lawyering is giving you a bit of a gut."

Sandy grabbed the small roll around his waistline. "I can't lose this. That would ruin my dating life."

"How do you figure?" Dixon asked.

"Hey, it's the flaw that makes me appear attainable. Without this, women would think they didn't stand a chance."

Dixon shook his head. "Y'know, as stupid as that sounds you're probably right."

As they neared the north beach, they spotted a young woman running toward them wearing the standard uniform of spandex shorts and a tank top. She looked awfully good for the time of morning, but it didn't appear she had to work at it. As she drew closer, a broad smile crossed her face and she shouted, "Hey Sandy, how're you doing?"

Sandy exchanged the greeting. After she passed he turned to Dixon, "By the way, that's three."

"Three what?" Dixon asked.

"Three hot women that've said 'hi' to me this morning as opposed to one old guy that you knew who wanted to show you the fish that he'd caught."

Now it was Dixon's turn for mock indignation. "Do you really think I'm interested in having lots of superficial relationships with beautiful women?"

"I think you're interested in having relationships with lots of beautiful women and superficial is a good place to start."

Dixon was not giving in. "That's the difference between you and me. You love the hunt, the conquest, the not-calling-her-back-even-though-you-promised. I've never done particularly well in that mode and, for that matter, never really enjoyed it."

"You talk about my life like it's a bad thing. Maybe you should learn to embrace your essential nature the way I do."

Dixon could only smile.

They crossed under the bridge toward Lake of the Isles, which was old-money country. The northern tip was within a mile of downtown and was the destination of the moneyed class as Minneapolis had grown. There were no beaches to speak of, as the denizens of the area did their swimming at "the club." This was an area where Dixon hadn't spent any time during his youth.

"What's your trial about?" Sandy was normally the type to gloat about his prowess, but he mercifully changed the topic.

"It's a little involved and not particularly sexy."

"Business litigation rarely is," Sandy said.

"It's part securities fraud and part breach of fiduciary duty. My client syndicated several limited partnerships in order to start a chain of Scandinavian fast-food restaurants."

"You're kidding, right?" Sandy interjected. "Lefse wraps and lutefisk tacos?"

"Well, that might have been part of the problem. Things didn't always go great, and my client occasionally had to make loans between the partnerships. Then the market for investor capital went south, and they were caught in the middle of some big projects with nowhere to go. One thing led to another and now all the investors are suing him. Among other things, they're claiming the concept was destined to fail because the food is completely unappetizing to the general public and Scandinavians are too cheap to eat out."

"The six Norwegians on the Minnesota jury might have a different opinion," Sandy said.

"I think that's how the lawsuit ended up here. The partnerships were set up in Delaware, but a lot of the investors were from here. I'm a little worried my out-of-town defendant won't get a fair shake."

Sandy started to respond, but a tall brunette leaning over the drinking fountain distracted him. "Melissa," he shouted.

"Hi, Sandy," came the eager reply.

He turned toward Dixon and announced, "Four! I'm rethinking what I said a minute ago. I may have to do this with you more often." Sandy raised his head and pumped out his chest as if he were responding to an audience that was cheering his accomplishments. After a few moments of basking in it, he returned to the topic of the trial. "What's your defense?"

Dixon shrugged his shoulders. "All the transactions were on the up-and-up, everything was documented, and several of the loans have already been repaid. Unfortunately, the investors will pretend they had no idea that investing involves some element of risk. Also unfortunate is the fact that my guy continued to pay himself pretty well while the businesses were faltering."

Dixon and Sandy picked up the pace as they headed into the last mile. Up ahead, Dixon spotted redemption. Rachel Anderson worked for an ad agency and could have been a supermodel. Dixon had met her at a Happy Hour and, while he didn't really know her well, a superficial acquaintance was all that was necessary for his purpose. As she drew closer, Dixon fixated on her in an effort to attract her attention. He raised his hand in a wave until he caught her eye.

"Dixon!" she hollered, a big smile lighting her face. "I didn't know that you were a friend of Sandy's!"

# CHAPTER 2

THE HENNEPIN COUNTY COURTHOUSE would never be in style again. Constructed in the seventies, it was cursed with the same color scheme generally seen in kitchen appliances of that era: harvest gold chairs, avocado carpet, and chocolate floor tile. The wood paneling in the courtrooms was better quality than the plywood people used to finish their basements, but not by much. Plans were constantly made for updating, but renovation of the courthouse always got lost in the budget shuffle. Politicians could claim great victory for new construction, but championing the remodeling of the courthouse wasn't likely to be the basis of an election platform.

The building housed the other essential government offices for licensing, property taxes, and whatnot. As a result, it was the closest thing to a melting pot for the area. The atrium was always overflowing with citizens clutching little paper numbers waiting for their turn to be called. Today was no exception.

Dixon met his client outside the courtroom to discuss the expected events of the day. Bennie Fosnick's ethnicity could best be described as "New York." He could have been Italian or Jewish or something else, but his demeanor and countenance were decidedly out of Brooklyn or Queens. He was a slicked-back, paunchy fifty-year-old who, despite his attorney's sound advice, insisted on wearing gold chains to every event, including his trial. His attitude matched his appearance, as he was convinced the jurors were already on his side and the only way he could lose was if any of the female jurors turned out to be "vagi-tarians," Bennie's graphic term for lesbians.

The first two days of trial had consisted of the investors explaining how they'd been misled as to the nature of their investments and the operation of the businesses. All of them expressed shock that Bennie would draw any salary, much less the exorbitant amount he'd provided for himself in the various partnership documents. While many of the investors in the ventures were probably very sophisticated, Plaintiffs' attorneys had used care to select the least sophisticated individuals as representatives of the class. Each had a Scandinavian surname and each could have lived across the alley from any of the jurors.

Today was likely to focus on the operational side of the business. The first scheduled witness was Jennifer Harper, Bennie's former bookkeeper and business manager. Both sides had listed her as a witness, and it appeared the plaintiffs would take the first shot at her. Dixon had interviewed her prior to trial, but her position was fairly administrative. Furthermore, Fosnick said they'd once been romantically involved, and that she wouldn't say anything to jeopardize her already thin possibility of getting back together with him.

Dixon pulled a notepad from his briefcase. "Tell me again what Ms. Harper will be able to testify to?"

"Nothin' but the up-and-up. Money was loaned back and forth, but everything was written down and paid back. And that's not all, my pay was spelled out in detail in the documents."

"Well there must be something else," Dixon replied, "otherwise I don't think the other side would be calling her."

"Don't worry," Bennie insisted. "She still wants my schwantz, if you know what I mean."

Dixon didn't take much comfort in that response. Nonetheless, lawyer and client headed into the courtroom.

Dixon had thought he knew what Jennifer Harper's testimony would be, but her presence as a Plaintiffs' witness cast considerable doubt on whether she would tell the story he'd anticipated. The cardinal rule of cross-examination is never ask a question to which you don't know the answer. More specifically, never ask a question to which you don't know the witness's answer. Unfortunately, this turn of events made such an analysis difficult.

Jennifer Harper was a striking woman. How or why she'd ended up in a romantic relationship with Bennie Fosnick was the real mystery. On this day she was smartly dressed in a blue business suit with a pleated white blouse. As she took the stand she appeared confident and businesslike. In short, she possessed all of the attributes one would expect to be absent from one of Fosnick's girlfriends.

Plaintiffs' counsel had a reputation for thoroughness to the point of tedium. The testimony sped through the usual formalities of name, education, and current occupation, but quickly bogged down in the relevant areas. Ms. Harper wanted to appear neutral, but it soon became apparent she'd met with Plaintiffs' counsel to prepare her testimony. This wasn't good news for Bennie Fosnick.

Jennifer Harper was quick to point out that money raised by each new partnership was used to provide funds to the existing entities. This smacked of a classic Ponzi scheme in which investors are promised high returns, but the payments come from money raised from subsequent investors rather than business operations. That wouldn't be a problem if there were an unlimited supply of new investors. Unfortunately, there never was.

When asked about Fosnick in particular, Harper pointed out his compensation never declined and he made a big chunk of money every time a new partnership was formed. Furthermore, while the empire collapsed, he appeared to do nothing to stop the demise. In fact, all actions he'd taken seemed to protect himself to the detriment of his investors. Nothing about her testimony suggested Jennifer Harper still wanted Bennie's "schwantz."

The testimony, while highly unflattering, wasn't necessarily fatal. The loans were documented and it may have been more a case of greed than fraud. Still, there was no reason for the jury to doubt the testimony as it stood, and every reason to believe the jury would react negatively if the testimony went unchallenged. Hell hath no fury like a woman scorned, and Jennifer Harper was proving that point in a big way.

After several hours, Plaintiffs' counsel finished and turned the witness over to the defense. Dixon introduced himself to her and did what he could to establish some rapport. It didn't seem to be working.

"Ms. Harper," Dixon said, "take a look at Exhibit 4. Please confirm for me that it is the partnership agreement for Uff da Partners I."

"Yes, it is."

"Now turn to page eighteen." After pausing for her to find the reference, Dixon continued. "Doesn't it disclose the fact that Mr. Fosnick will receive compensation and how it will be calculated?"

"If it says that, it says that," she responded matter-of-factly. "I never read those documents, and I don't know what was said about that subject."

"Weren't you responsible for cutting the checks to Mr. Fosnick?"

"Yeah, but I just did it based on what he told me. I never looked at the partnership agreements."

That answer didn't correspond with Dixon's recollection of his pretrial discussion with her, but that didn't do him much good now. "Okay," Dixon said, "so you're saying your job was more on the operational side once the partnerships were formed?"

"Yes."

"Take a look at Exhibit 11, which should be a promissory note from Uff da Partners I to Uff da Partners II, do you see that?"

"Yes."

"It shows that the money moving from partnership number two to partnership number one was documented, doesn't it?"

She shrugged her indifference. "There's no way to prove when the note was signed. It could have been prepared after the fact."

"But part of your job was preparing the documentation," Dixon protested. "Are you saying you don't remember documenting this at the time it happened?"

"That's what I'm telling you."

Efforts to get her to acknowledge that loans were repaid were equally unsuccessful. Her answers were vague, and she conveyed a sudden inattention to detail in all areas that could have been helpful to Bennie. She clearly had an axe to grind. Dixon finally decided it was time her pettiness over having been spurned needed to be revealed.

"It's true, isn't it, Ms. Harper, that you had a romantic relationship with Mr. Fosnick?"

There was some stirring in the jury box that could have been explained as either shock or admiration over Fosnick's conquest. At least physically, Fosnick and Harper went together about as well as bacon and chocolate.

"Yes," she responded with some hesitation.

Dixon smiled as he realized he'd struck a nerve. He felt a mild surge of adrenaline as he moved in for the kill. "When did that relationship begin?"

"About two years ago."

He paused to emphasize the importance of the testimony he was eliciting. "And when did it end?"

Jennifer Harper looked at Dixon and paused as well. After a moment, she threw back her shoulders and turned to face the jury. "It ended one year at Christmas dinner when he called me a 'cunt' in front of my parents."

Several jurors sputtered as they tried to hold in their laughter at this surprise turn of events. Harper tried to look nonchalant, but it was clear this was testimony she'd longed to give. Opposing counsel smiled slyly, and it was apparent the ploy had worked exactly as hoped.

The blood rushed out of Dixon's face. "Move to strike the testimony as nonresponsive." When he looked up, he could see he was in trouble. The judge had turned his back away from the jury, but his 250-pound frame shook from his attempt to hide his laughter.

Dixon glared at his client in disbelief that this tidbit hadn't been mentioned. Fosnick responded with a puppy dog look that suggested the testimony was completely true, but that he really didn't think it was a big deal or that anyone would be offended by it. Talking crudely was apparently part of what he found charming about himself.

Dixon scrambled some more. This was damage that might be irreparable. The jury now saw Fosnick as utterly classless, in addition to greedy and perhaps dishonest. Worst of all, most of the damage had come from his own lawyer.

"Move to strike the testimony as nonresponsive," Dixon pleaded again. "I was seeking a date and she gave a reason. The testimony is character evidence and the rules are clear that evidence of an unrelated bad act cannot be admitted because it might cause a jury to rule against someone for the wrong reason."

The judge struggled to compose himself. "I know it wasn't the response you expected and you'd be right if the other side had tried to put it in. But I'm afraid you asked the question and the answer does follow from the question as asked. It is character evidence, but there isn't much we can do now that you've brought it out."

Dixon was at a loss for words. For her part, Jennifer Harper tipped her head back as if waiting in anticipation to knock the next question as far out of the ballpark as she'd drilled the last one. She was in control and wanted no doubt to exist on that point.

The trial had gone reasonably well up to that point, but a surprise witness turning state's evidence always captures the imagination of a jury. Dixon thought of asking for a recess or taking a moment to confer with his client. The problem was that he might still be left without an explanation and that might look even worse in the eyes of the jury. Dixon paused a moment longer while instinct took control.

The second unwritten rule of cross-examination is never ask open-ended questions. Skillfully asked questions suggest their own answer and are generally only susceptible to "yes" or "no" answers. Dixon wouldn't flaunt the rules anymore.

"That made you angry, didn't it?" he asked.

"Of course it did."

Dixon nodded his head to suggest he was in agreement with her response. "In fact, there's really nothing more offensive than what he said."

"Absolutely nothing. I've never been treated so poorly in all my life. Can you imagine such a thing? I'd never put up with someone calling me that, but what kind of a person would do it in those circumstances?"

"It caused you to develop an animosity toward Mr. Fosnick?"

"That would be an understatement."

Dixon again nodded his understanding. "Then you ended the relationship?"

"Absolutely, I demanded he leave immediately. I broke up with him and promptly quit working for him."

"That didn't give you much comfort though, did it?"

"Not really. He disgusts me and those feelings have never subsided."

"So you'd like nothing better than to see him suffer?"

"He should burn in hell as far as I'm concerned."

Plaintiff's counsel fidgeted at the turn the testimony was taking. For her part, Jennifer Harper was enjoying the opportunity to explain how much she'd been wronged, but she was oblivious to the extent she was undermining her own testimony.

"So it's fair to say, isn't it, that you would do anything in your power to punish Mr. Fosnick for the terrible thing he did to you?"

"Absolutely. He is the lowest of low. I hope they lock him up."

"No more questions," Dixon announced. He'd save the rest for closing arguments. Harper's attempt to discredit Fosnick had collapsed under its own weight. Jennifer Harper was not just a woman scorned. She was a woman with a vendetta. She may have had a right to her vendetta, but she had no right to try and mislead the jury. Ultimately, because she had all but admitted her goal was to harm Fosnick, the jury would be hard pressed to accept her testimony. What at first appeared to be the most damaging testimony was, in fact, the testimony that most undermined the Plaintiffs' case.

# CHAPTER 3

NIGHT HAD FALLEN over the city, and the view from Dixon's office resembled that from a plane just descending below cloud cover for landing. The building air conditioning had been shut down hours earlier and the air in the office was heavy from a lack of circulation. Still, a few hours without a ringing phone should provide ample opportunity to catch up on the work he'd put off because of trial.

Dixon sat with his feet propped up on his office desk and the phone cradled under his chin. Sandy was on the other end of the line, and Dixon was recounting every detail of the trial. "You know how these things go. The jurors probably didn't pay attention to a single thing until that bomb dropped. I admit that it took me by surprise, but, once I recovered, I *owned* that courtroom."

"So what was the end result?"

"We settled during lunch," Dixon said. "After being hoisted on their own petard, they were willing to make a more reasonable demand."

"You're an animal," Sandy replied sarcastically. "Talk about making lemons into lemonade."

"You know what I always say, 'God is apparently on the side of the just,' because every case I'm in involves some revelation or late development that helps justice prevail."

"So, do you think the ex-girlfriend prevaricated on the stand?"

Dixon sat silent for a moment. Vocabulary created a running contest between the two of them. "Prevaricated?" Dixon finally said with contempt. "Look, vocabulary boy, the idea behind having a big vocabulary is word economy and the ability to choose a word that conveys the meaning of many. 'Prevaricated' just means 'lied.' There's nothing impressive about using a sesquipedalian word to express the same thing that can be expressed in one four-letter, one-syllable word."

"All right, Professor Know-it-all," Sandy responded. "I'm not even going to give you the satisfaction of asking you what sesquipedalian means. Just tell me whether you think that she lied."

"She didn't lie outright, but she gave testimony that implied things she knew were not true."

"So you don't feel at all bad about all the innocent investors who lost money on account of your client?"

"No. Should I?"

"I know we swore an oath to zealously represent clients," Sandy said, "but doesn't it bother you when the bad guy wins?"

Dixon cleared his throat as though he were about to make a speech. "It doesn't bother me because my job isn't about good or bad."

"It's not? Then what is it about?"

"Truth. Truth is an absolute. Good and bad, on the other hand, are subjective concepts that exist as points on a continuum. Juries aren't supposed to decide good or bad or even right or wrong. They're supposed to decide the truth. The truth is, the entire case was about sour grapes. The investors were aware of the risks and they didn't care that my client was a little greasy when they thought that would help them."

"Yeah, I guess you're right," Sandy said. "But where's the truth in a settlement?"

"I wanted to take it to the jury, but that's not my decision. My job is to drive the train to the truth and my clients can get off anywhere along the way. That's what he wanted to do, and it's not my job to prevent it."

"Fair enough. By the way, speaking of getting at the truth, I just referred you a potential doozie. I have a client up in Hibbing that I helped with a small business matter. He has some litigation and we have a conflict."

"I appreciate that," Dixon said. "What's his story?"

"His name is Hank MacKenzie, and he has an insurance dispute.

I don't know all of the details, because he just called this morning, but I think he has quite a predicament on his hands."

"Will I get to spend some time in heavenly Hibbing?"

"Maybe. Would you consider that a benefit?"

"I don't know. I've never been there."

Hibbing was one of the towns that grew with the development of what is known as the "Iron Range." Northern Minnesota had originally been the domain of lumber barons, but the discovery of iron ore had generated a development boom starting in the north-central portion of the state and extending east to Lake Superior. Serious mining ended decades ago, and the latest generation of "Rangers" had mostly migrated to the Twin Cities. Nonetheless, the area retained the moniker and the legacy.

"Well, whether I get to spend time on the Range or not, I appreciate the referral," Dixon responded. "Drinks are on me next time we're out."

"I'll hold you to that."

Dixon hung up and returned to the piles on his desk.

The Law Offices of Dixon Donnelly consisted of low-rent furnishings in the high-rent district: two offices, a conference room, and a cubicle/reception area for his assistant. The furnishings were adequate, but lacked the rich, cherrywood elegance of the big firms.

On the wall facing him was a framed document stating: "Challenge Assumptions; Question Authority; Defy Convention." He didn't know where he'd heard it, but he liked the sentiment. Each command was, in his opinion, the obligation of every thinking person.

Behind him hung a replica of the Rosetta Stone. This was Dixon's private joke. The jagged-edged carbon rock contained identical text transcribed in three sets of characters—Egyptian, Greek, and hieroglyphics—and its discovery in 1799 was the key to deciphering hieroglyphics. He considered it a metaphor for virtually every case he handled: two sides appearing to say completely different things, but a latent discovery that reconciles the conflict.

As soon as he'd gotten comfortable, the telephone rang. "Dixon Donnelly," he said into the mouthpiece.

"Hi honey pie, it's me." The "me" was Sharon Veckner, a woman who had no cause to refer to him as "honey pie."

When Dixon had first met her, he was less than bowled over. A client had wanted to set them up. Sharon was a friend of the client's new wife and, given the client's lecherous tastes, it seemed likely Sharon would be more attractive than the typical "My wife's got a friend that she wants you to meet," because that phrase invariably means "My wife has a friend who can't get a date and my wife thinks she'll be doing her friend a big favor by setting her up with the likes of you."

Sharon had potential because she had the endorsement of both a woman and a man. The new wife was an outgoing, attractive, and physically fit woman who made a pitch on all the female levels: "smart, good sense of humor, fun to be with." The husband's endorsement was more direct—"I'd do her in an instant if I wasn't married. In fact, if I knew my wife wouldn't find out, I might do her anyway."

Dixon had agreed to meet Sharon, but didn't want an actual set-up. In his mind, a mere introduction was closer to fate than having someone else plan his romantic life. The venue for the encounter was a party the matchmakers gave at their new house. Prior to agreeing to come, Dixon got commitments the meeting would not be apparent to others in attendance. Specifically, he obtained assurances the party wouldn't be ten couples and the two who were to be "coupled." Furthermore, it would be their secret and the other guests—especially Dixon's acquaintances—wouldn't be gawking at his every move.

Dixon had made it a point to show up late and then decided to enhance his anonymity by not announcing his arrival with the doorbell. He was still wiping his feet when the hostess rushed across the room to greet him. Before he could camouflage himself among the masses, the entire party seemed to separate like the Red Sea, with all eyes fixed to the center. Through the resulting gap walked a small brunette with a purpose. The hostess announced—in a voice far louder than necessary under the circumstances—"Sharon, I'd like you to meet Dixon; Dixon, I'd like you to meet Sharon." Dixon was in hell.

Sharon wasn't a bad looking woman, but there was no warmth

about her. She had black hair and pale white skin that would later cause Dixon to mumble the chorus from "Ebony and Ivory" as a tease. Her thin, unsmiling lips, coupled with hair that seemed chopped too short, resulted in a look best described as "hard." She was height-weight proportionate, but held little womanly allure. Dixon decided that, for once, he wouldn't rely on the lack of an initial thunderbolt as a reason not to proceed. Besides, he'd convinced himself, the circumstances might have made him resistant to Cupid's arrow.

Four months had now passed and he was starting to believe first instincts were the basis for relationships. The spark had never really ignited, so their time together did little to fan the semblance of any flame.

"Oh, hi," Dixon said without much enthusiasm.

"What are you doing at the office?"

"Just trying to catch up on things that slipped while I was in trial."

"I was just thinking that you should come over. We could open a bottle of wine and go from there." Then, in her best baby talk, she said, "Sha-won misses her man and needs some lovin'."

"Sorry," Dixon said, "but I've been busy and I've got too much to do."

Baby talk continued. "My big impo-tant man needs to take a bwake sometime. Why don't you come over and let Sha-won help you with your briefs?"

Dixon found it difficult to imagine he'd be the person in a relationship who wasn't interested in sex. Despite his professional training, he didn't like conflict in his personal life. Breaking up was destined to be acrimonious, and he hoped that somehow, if he delayed enough, he would either die or she'd find a reason to break up with him.

"Listen," Dixon said, trying to change the subject. "I was talking to Sandy Swanson earlier. He has tickets to the touring production of some off-Broadway show and asked if we wanted to go. I said I'd talk to you about it."

"What's it about?"

"I don't really know," he responded. "I know it's a musical, and the creator died of AIDS before it made it to Broadway. Anyway, I told him I'd think about it, but here's the thing: You know how I hate it when you insist on talking in the movies. I don't want to take you to an expensive production if you can't enjoy it by just watching."

Sharon shot back, "Well, who would you bring instead?"

"Nobody. I just wouldn't go. It's like I said, we don't have to go, but I thought I should ask."

"No, I'd like to go," Sharon implored.

"Do you understand what I'm saying about the talking? I think it's really annoying and I don't want to go if you insist on giving a commentary."

"Can I talk before the show?" she said impudently.

"You just have to agree not to embarrass me."

"Listen to you. Don't worry, Mr. Holier-than-thou, I won't embarrass you."

Dixon had no confidence in her answer, but agreed to go. He promised to call her later, but was careful not to make any specific commitments. He hung up and resumed his assault on the mountain of paper on his desk.

# CHAPTER 4

DIXON'S ASSISTANT announced Hank MacKenzie's arrival on the intercom and, at Dixon's request, led him into the office. As MacKenzie entered, Dixon stood and extended his hand. "I'm Dixon Donnelly. It's a pleasure to meet you."

"How she go?" MacKenzie responded as he took Dixon's hand.

Dixon wasn't even sure what that meant, but did what he could to conceal his disappointment. He generally preferred to meet with business executives or clients who were otherwise sophisticated. He had chosen business law specifically so as to avoid dealing with the everyday problems of the common man.

Hank MacKenzie was not a man who looked comfortable in a law office located in a skyscraper in a major metropolitan area. His red flannel shirt, faded blue jeans, and work boots made it evident he preferred the outdoors. He sported red hair and a beard, with the fair complexion that generally accompanies such features. His eyes were small and wrinkled by fifty-some years of squinting out the effects of the sun. He was diminutive, to say the least, and resembled a sort of mini-lumberjack. In short, he held little promise of satisfying Dixon's standard.

MacKenzie wasted little time with pleasantries. "I's referred to you by Sandy Swanson. I need a lawyer, and I need the best money can buy."

"That's very flattering, but I can assure you there are plenty of good lawyers in this town and many of them charge substantially more than I do." Privately Dixon pondered why every unsophisticated client with insignificant problems believed their circumstances warranted "the best lawyer money could buy."

"Well, Sandy says yer top shelf."

"That's great, but I thought you had a dispute over insurance coverage. That's usually pretty straightforward."

"Well, it might seem that way for you, but I t'ink it's confusing as all hell." Iron Rangers had an accent and a vernacular all their own. Among the older generation, the "h" was frequently dropped out of the pronunciation of "think" and various other words that began with "th."

Dixon motioned for MacKenzie to sit and retook his own seat. "Understood. Why don't you tell me what this is about?"

"I'm not sure where to start. My brother got hisself into a little trouble. I told him he was playin' a dangerous game messin' with someone's wife, but he wouldn't listen. I guess the best t'ing is for you to look at this." MacKenzie pushed a redrope file toward Dixon.

Dixon held up a hand to indicate that he didn't want the file. "First things first," he said. "Before I look at that, why don't you tell me why you're here instead of your brother?"

"He's dead. Accordin' to the sheriff, he committed suicide." There was no sorrow in Hank's voice, but his eyes conveyed a profound sense of loss.

"You say 'according to the sheriff.' Do you think something else happened?"

MacKenzie shrugged his shoulders. "That's what I want you for. I need somebody to look at this whole t'ing for me."

"Okay," Dixon nodded. "Start at the beginning and tell me your understanding."

"All right. My brother Duke started sniffing around after this married gal named Debi Krueller. But he wasn't so much chasing her as protecting her. Y'see, she's married to this guy Les Krueller, and the two of 'em fight like cats and dogs. Anyway, one t'ing leads to another and Duke starts spending time with her. One night Duke and Debi are at Duke's house doin' the nasty when Les climbs up to the second floor balcony, smashes the sliding glass door with a shovel, and runs down the hall to the bedroom. Well, apparently Duke shot him in the stomach and then Duke went out in the woods and offed hisself. Now this bastard Krueller is suing

Duke's estate and I'm the Executor so I need to hire an attorney to represent it."

As Dixon jotted down the information, he couldn't help but think this wasn't, in fact, a routine insurance coverage dispute. "Okay, let's look at the documents."

Hank handed Dixon the first document, a Summons and Complaint in a civil lawsuit entitled *Lester Krueller v. The Estate of Duane MacKenzie by and through His Personal Representative Henry MacKenzie.* The caption on top of the first page indicated it was filed in the Koochiching County District Court, Hibbing Division. The document totaled a mere five pages and was substantially less after the boilerplate was removed.

"The lawsuit is against Duane MacKenzie, but you keep saying 'Duke' MacKenzie. I assume they're the same person."

"Yeah. Duke was his nickname. Y'know, in small towns you tend to get nicknames when you're young and they stay with you forever."

Dixon had little interest in small talk and continued his review. After identifying the parties and their counties of residence, the Complaint told a brief story. Mr. Krueller was shot and injured by Duane MacKenzie while Krueller was in MacKenzie's house. The Complaint stated the shooting was intentional or, in the alternative, negligent. Alternative pleading was commonplace in the state. If Krueller could show intentional wrongdoing, there was the possibility of recovering punitive damages, and that meant more money. This was not, however, an all or nothing proposition. If Krueller could merely show negligence, he could still recover for his injuries and there was usually an insurance company to make sure payment was made. On the last page, the signature block indicated that "Earl McGuckin" of the "McGuckin Law Office" represented Krueller.

"This Complaint says it was served last March," Dixon said. "Please tell me someone has put in a response."

"I don't know," MacKenzie responded. "I t'ink they got some sort of extension."

"Well, maybe there's something else in the file. What can you tell me about Earl McGuckin?"

"Nothin' good," Hank said with contempt. "Earl was a few years behind me in high school, and he's been a character as long as I can remember. His clients aren't really the cream of the crop. He handles mostly criminal stuff, divorces, and injuries."

"That's a fairly common combination," Dixon replied. "Clients with one of those problems tend to eventually have the others. I think alcohol might be a likely common denominator, but some people just seem to be born to have problems and they have lawyers to match."

"Well, Earl likes to act like he's above it all. He talks like he's a southerner and always says that he 'went to law school down south,' even though that means he went to a night law school in St. Paul. I don't know who he t'inks he's fooling."

"Sounds like a class act."

"That's just part of it. When he first started as a lawyer, he wanted to be known as 'Earl the Pearl.' Guess he thought that was a name folks would remember and that 'Earl the Pearl' would make people think he was smooth."

"Well, it's nice to know what I'd be up against," Dixon said with mild amusement.

"The t'ing is, he's a son of a bitch. He'll do or say anyt'ing for a buck and he usually wins."

"We'll see about that," Dixon said.

"I got a question about that there document," Hank said. "It says he wants an amount in excess of $50,000. What I need to know is how much he can get."

"That's a hard question to answer," Dixon said. "Putting a value on pain and suffering can vary depending on the jury. Furthermore, punitive damages is a wild card. If the jury is sympathetic to Krueller, it could be millions."

"That's what I was afraid of," Hank said.

"Well, what are we talking about anyway?" Dixon asked. "Is there money in the estate?"

"There's a couple million dollars. Duke and I inherited a little money from a great-uncle. I used my share to raise a family, but Duke made a buncha dough investing in real estate."

"Did Duke have a wife or kids?"

"Just a daughter. And that's why I need your help."

Dixon was puzzled. "Perhaps you better explain that to me."

"Duke got a girl pregnant when he was young. He didn't want to get married just because of that, but that made the girl mad. She said if he wouldn't marry her, he couldn't have nothin' to do with the baby."

Dixon watched Hank in earnest, but was having trouble following the point of the story.

"Anyway," Hank continued, "Duke never did get married and it wasn't long before he started to regret the deal he made. After Sarah—that's his daughter—turned eighteen, Duke was able to contact her and tried to start a relationship with her. It wasn't easy at first, but they finally got something going."

"I'm sorry," Dixon interrupted, "but I'm not sure I'm following you."

"Sorry about that. I'll try and get to the point. Duke always felt really bad that he wasn't there for Sarah growing up. He spent most of his life trying to figure out how to make it up to her. Now that he's gone, there's only one thing he can do for her and that's pass on his money. It wasn't that easy for Sarah growing up, but Duke's money will let her live comfortably from now on—at least so long as McGuckin doesn't get it."

"Is she the sole beneficiary?"

"Basically, yeah. There's a few other things, but she gets the majority. She doesn't expect nothin', but I feel like it's my duty to make sure Duke's intentions are followed."

Dixon was being drawn into Hank's plight. This wasn't what he went to law school for, but he didn't know how he could say no to someone who appeared so desperate. After a moment, he said, "Okay, what else do you have in the file?"

"You should probably hear this," Hank said. "It's a copy of the 911 call from the night of the incident."

Dixon took the mini-cassette from MacKenzie, popped it into his Dictaphone, and pushed the "Play" button. The sound quality was marginal, but the operator's voice was discernible. "Sheriff's 911."

The next voice indicated the person speaking was Les Krueller and he needed an ambulance.

Dixon was jotting notes when a voice on the tape screamed: "I caught him fuckin' my wife!" Dixon smiled at the frankness and wondered how a woman could not be enamored with a husband of such high character.

As the tape played, Hank fidgeted and squinted at the Rosetta Stone as if it were merely his eyesight that kept him from recognizing it. The tape was either old news to him or it was making him uncomfortable. They continued listening until the call ended with the sound of a telephone hanging up.

"That's quite a tale," Dixon said. "Tell me, how did Duke and Debi manage to meet?"

"One of the t'ings Duke and me inherited from our great-uncle was a mobile home park. That's where the Kruellers live. There's sort of a caretaker's office with a bedroom and sometimes when Duke was in town drinking, he'd stay there instead of driving home. When the maintenance guy moved, Duke started doing some of the upkeep hisself."

"All right. So Duke lived out of town somewhere?"

"Yeah."

"And the mobile home park was in town?"

"More or less."

"Okay," Dixon nodded. "Did Duke ever tell you his version of events on the night in question?"

"Never saw him again."

"What do we know about the alleged suicide?" Dixon asked.

"The sheriff said that he put the gun in his mouth and pulled the trigger."

"Where did they find the body?"

"The better question is: where didn't they find the body? Y'see, his body parts was scattered all over because he was eaten by bears." Hank was matter-of-fact in telling these details. A lifetime of hunting had apparently created some sort of circle-of-life mentality that found an animal's consumption of human flesh to be well within the range of normal.

"Were they able to make a positive identification?"

"They looked at the dental records for the top jaw and said it was him. They didn't find the lower jaw, but the upper jaw was enough."

"Did they do any DNA testing?"

"I'm afraid our law enforcement isn't quite in this century. The whole deal was pretty gruesome, and even the sheriff's office wanted to close it as soon as possible."

"This must be awfully hard for you to deal with."

"It's always tough to lose a family member, but losing family in this situation is really tough. Duke made some bad choices, but he didn't deserve what happened. The fact that this bastard is suing is what really kills me. He's the one who's responsible, and he should be held to pay for the fact that Duke's dead."

"Let me ask you," Dixon said, "have there been any criminal charges filed against this Krueller fellow in connection with this incident?"

"Yeah, but I'm not sure I really understand them, and that's part of what you're going to help me with. I know the criminal trial is next month."

"Well, let's see what else is in the file," Dixon said, extending his hand.

The majority of the documents appeared to be the criminal file from the case *State of Minnesota v. Lester Krueller*. The first document was an "Investigation Report" written by a sheriff's deputy named Halvorsen, and it indicated that he was the first person on the scene on the night of the incident.

Dixon scanned it. "According to this, the wife says she wasn't having sex with Duke. She says she'd been fighting with her husband, that Duke just offered her a place to stay, and that she was afraid to go home because the husband kept threatening Duke."

"Keep reading," Hank suggested.

Dixon found another report that looked like the first, but had a different date. "Oh, I see. Later on she admits that she had sex with Duke, but claims it happened just once." Dixon held up the two reports side by side. "Do you think the second version is accurate?"

"I doubt it. Debi Krueller has round heels, if you know what I mean."

Dixon pondered the statement in the same way Hank had eyed the Rosetta Stone. "Actually, I'm afraid I don't know what you mean."

"I mean, you don't have to push her very hard to get her on her back."

Dixon smiled at what he assumed was a regional expression. "Well, regardless of which version we use, she has nothing good to say about her husband. That has to help us."

"You won't find many people with good t'ings to say about Les Krueller," Hank responded.

Dixon paged through the papers again. "All of these documents quote her as saying Les threatened to 'blow Duke's fucking head off.' Do you think he made good on that threat?"

Hank shrugged his shoulders. "I'm not sure. I know Krueller is a lowlife, and it wouldn't surprise me if he'd try, but Duke was pretty handy with a gun. He used to sit on his porch and shoot turtles off of logs at thirty yards."

To this point, the case seemed simple. Even in northern Minnesota, women were not chattel. Lester Krueller had no right to forcibly prevent his wife from having sexual relations with another man. He should be convicted for burglary and assault and the civil case should be thrown out because there is no basis to sue somebody whose only transgression is declining to allow an intruder to cause great bodily harm.

"So, you submitted this to Duke's insurance company?" Dixon asked.

"Yeah. Look toward the back of the file. There's a letter denying coverage. We just got it about a week ago."

Dixon's quick perusal of that letter indicated the insurance company admitted the policy was in force, but claimed that shooting a gun fit the policy exclusion for any "action taken with intent to harm." It was the insurance company's position that there was no insurance coverage regardless of whether the act was done in self-defense.

As Dixon read, MacKenzie interjected, "The lawyer helping me with Duke's estate told me to submit the first lawsuit to the insurance company. They initially hired a lawyer for us, but then changed their mind and sent this letter. I called Sandy, but his firm wasn't able to help us because one of the lawyers there has done work for the insurance company."

"So let me get this straight," Dixon said with a hint of sarcasm. "You suffer one of the worst tragedies any family can experience. The perpetrator of that tragedy then files a lawsuit in an effort to profit from his own wrongdoing, and then the insurance company, who you thought was supposed to protect you from such frivolous lawsuits, abandons you?"

"You summed that up nice. Now you know why I need your help."

"Let me make sure I've got my arms around everything. First, there's a criminal trial for Krueller that's scheduled for June 20?"

"Right."

"And then this personal injury lawsuit was filed by Krueller in March, and the insurance company hired a lawyer for you but, as far as you know, he hasn't entered a formal response to the lawsuit and now he's withdrawing?"

"Right again."

"And you just got the letter from the insurance company denying coverage?"

"Yup."

"And you want me to sue the insurance company?"

"For starters, but I'd also like you to represent me in the other matters."

"Well, there isn't that much I can do in the criminal case. That's the responsibility of the County Attorney."

"Well, he's a nice guy, but I'm afraid McGuckin will beat the pants off him. I need to hire the best to handle the criminal claim against Krueller."

"I'm sorry, Mr. MacKenzie, but there's nothing I can do about the criminal matter."

Hank looked frustrated. "Mr. Donnelly, I really need your help."

Dixon furrowed his brow as he pondered the issue. "Unless, maybe . . ."

"Unless what?" Hank asked.

"Well, I suppose I could schedule the depositions of the Kruellers. We've got almost a month until the criminal trial, so I could get their testimony and give it to the County Attorney to help him out."

Hank looked puzzled. "I'm not sure that I know what a deposition is."

"It's a procedure where you take testimony under oath. It's like being in court except there's no judge to rule on objections. There really isn't such a procedure in criminal law, but it's almost always used in civil litigation. By filing the personal injury suit when he did, Krueller opened himself up for some unwelcome discovery. I can send subpoenas for both Les and Debi Krueller. That should be quite the interesting time."

Hank nodded with enthusiasm. "What about a countersuit against Krueller?"

"You mean for the property damage?"

"Not just that. If it wasn't for Krueller breaking in, Duke would still be alive."

"You're saying that Krueller killed Duke?"

"Maybe. Or maybe indirectly."

"I know that if a person commits a crime and causes someone to have a heart attack, there might be liability, but proving that the crime caused someone to commit suicide might be a bit of a stretch."

"Well, let's make that stretch," MacKenzie said.

"I guess I'm willing to give it a shot. I'll make a generic claim that Krueller's actions caused Duke's death, but don't bank on a recovery on the Counterclaim."

"That sounds fair to me," MacKenzie responded. "Sandy said you'd probably require a retainer to get started." MacKenzie tossed a checkbook onto the desk and pulled out a pen. "Just tell me how much and I'll give it to you right now."

This was suddenly starting to sound more and more palatable to Dixon. Hank MacKenzie needed his help, and, while Dixon might not have been the best lawyer money could buy, he realized he might be the best lawyer for the situation. "Your credit is good with me. You'll get monthly invoices detailing the charges and all I ask is that you pay them promptly. I need to spend some time reviewing your files so I can understand the legal actions that are pending. After I've done that, I'll let you know how I intend to proceed."

"T'ank you, Mr. Donnelly," MacKenzie said, rising from his chair. "I'm starting to feel better about this already."

# CHAPTER 5

D IXON FOLLOWED THROUGH on his plan and was soon greeted by his first communication from Earl McGuckin. "Motion to Quash Subpoenas" was the heading on the document. "PLEASE TAKE NOTICE," the document continued, "that Plaintiff Lester Krueller will move the Court, the Honorable Rexford Stockman presiding, for an Order quashing the subpoenas served on Lester and Debi Krueller." *Quash* is a legal term that essentially means the same thing as the colloquialism that had been adopted by many in the business—"squash."

Other than the signature of Earl McGuckin of the McGuckin Law Office, that was it. In the Twin Cities, memoranda explaining and arguing the position generally accompanied such motions. Apparently the courts in greater Minnesota followed a different practice.

Dixon couldn't imagine a basis for the motion. If someone files a lawsuit, they are subject to having their deposition taken. Krueller should have waited to file his lawsuit until after the criminal trial, but he didn't. This was Krueller's fault or, more specifically, the fault of his lawyer.

Perhaps it was for the best, Dixon thought. The hearing would give him a chance to visit the courthouse, interact with the judge, and meet opposing counsel. On the other hand, he feared being "home-towned," and wished he understood the basis for the motion. Dixon was already prepared to brand Stockman as "Judge Huckleberry" in the event the motion to quash was granted.

On the day of the hearing, Dixon loaded his briefcase in his Volvo and set out for the Koochiching County Courthouse. Unfortunately, it was a three-and-a-half-hour drive. The Court had accommodated him by scheduling the hearing in the early afternoon. That way, Dixon could drive up and back on the same day. Not the most enviable duty, but better than using up two days. The judge probably would have let him appear by telephone, but Dixon felt like he would be even more of an outsider if the judge didn't have a face to put with the name.

The drive gave Dixon ample time to rehearse his arguments. As it happened, he had little to rehearse. Any right against self-incrimination would have to be waived by the filing of the lawsuit and the same reasoning should apply to Debi Krueller. That was it.

Dixon opted for the scenic route up Central Avenue and then Highway 65. It would probably be slower, but the drive would be more interesting. As he headed north he was struck by the fact that every few miles he saw an establishment called "The Sportsmen's Bar." This wasn't a chain, and the logos bore no similarity. Rather, every one of these establishments fancied itself as the destination for hunters and fishermen and apparently thought the name would draw them in.

As he traveled north, he entered the lakes country, which was the destination of the "sportsmen." The rugged hills and lakes had been tamed by Indian casinos and high-end golf courses. Nonetheless, the farther north he went, the farther back in time it felt.

Dixon arrived in Hibbing with an hour to spare. He'd left room for car trouble, heavy traffic, or an inability to find the courthouse. None had happened and, in fact, those things never seemed to happen to Dixon. Just the same, it made the trip more enjoyable because he didn't have to worry about something causing him to miss the hearing.

The Koochiching County Courthouse was older, but much more elegant than the one in Hennepin County. It was a Brooks Brothers suit compared to Hennepin County's Nehru jacket. Koochiching was a classic and would never really go out of style.

Dixon parked his car, retrieved his navy blue suit coat from the backseat, and set out to find the courtroom. He was still an hour early, but he wanted to find it and confirm the timing before looking for lunch. He entered through a side door and found the building empty. As he walked, his shoes clapped the marble floor and the sound ran down the hallway and echoed back. Apparently the legal problems in Koochiching County were somewhat less than in Minneapolis.

He found the District Court Administrator's counter and stopped to ask directions. There were a half dozen or so people sitting at desks in a big, open room. Dixon couldn't help but feel they were all looking at him, but no one made a move to help him.

Finally, a middle-aged woman got up from her desk and approached the counter. She had a warm look, but a constellation of moles on her face that could have earned her the nickname "Ursa." She glanced past Dixon and asked, "Who's next?"

Even though he was the only one waiting, Dixon looked around as though seeking the consent of the ghosts the clerk was apparently seeing. "I guess I am."

"You didn't get that suit in town did you?" the clerk asked.

"Well no, but what makes you say that?"

"Because I don't think anyplace in town sells anything that nice."

Dixon smiled politely and thanked her for the compliment. "Could you tell me where I can find Judge Stockman's courtroom and a copy of his calendar?"

"Up the stairs and it's Courtroom Number Two. As for his calendar, I'm his scheduling clerk and the only thing on it this afternoon is a discovery motion in Krueller v. MacKenzie at one. I take it that's what you're here for?"

"That's correct. I'm Dixon Donnelly, attorney for the MacKenzie estate."

"That was my guess. Sometimes we get lawyers from Duluth, and they have nicer suits than the locals, but they're still a far cry from that."

"Thank you again," Dixon said, feigning graciousness. "How about Earl McGuckin? How does he dress?"

"He looks out of place too, but mostly because he dresses like he's from the South."

"Well, he must be doing something right to land the nickname Earl the Pearl."

"Who told you that?"

"I guess my client. Why? Isn't that his nickname?"

"You have to understand that Earl is hated by pretty much everybody in the criminal justice system in Koochiching and all of the other counties around here."

"Really. Why's that?"

"Just about every deputy has been attacked by Earl on the witness stand, and his antics are known to everyone from us clerks to the district chief judge."

"Sounds like quite a character."

She nodded her head in response. "That's one way of puttin' it."

"So, you don't refer to him as Earl the Pearl?"

"Not hardly," she said with a chuckle. "Everybody I know refers to him as 'that fuckin' McGuckin.'"

Dixon smiled and shook his head. "Well, on that note, I guess I'll grab lunch while I'm waiting."

◆

At ten minutes to one Dixon was waiting outside the courtroom door. He didn't want to be in the wrong place in case there was a last minute courtroom change or for some reason the judge wanted to start early. The door was locked, however, so he paced back and forth while waiting.

At a few minutes before one, "Ursa" appeared and unlocked the door. Dixon smiled at her and walked into the courtroom. He stopped two steps in and looked around with surprise. He was standing amid pews that were obviously for the spectators. Unlike most courtrooms where the onlookers sat in back and the jurors sat on one side, here the spectators had sideline views with the judge and witness in the end zone on the right side of the field, the jury in the end zone on the left-hand side, and the attorneys on the fifty yard line facing the judge and the witness.

"Excuse me, is that the jury box?" he asked while pointing to the twelve-tiered seats in the back of the courtroom.

"Yes, it is."

"You mean the lawyers sit with their backs to the jury."

"That's right. Lawyers were always jockeying to see who could get the table closest to the jury. One time we had lawyers lining up at the doors in the middle of the night like Rolling Stones tickets were going on sale. Finally, the chief judge made them rebuild the interior of the courtroom so neither side would be any closer to the jury."

"Are all the courtrooms in this building like that?"

"This is the only courtroom where jury trials are held," the clerk responded. "The other courtrooms are only used for motions or bench trials."

"Interesting." Dixon took a seat at one of the tables that was equidistant from judge and jury.

"Let me know when McGuckin gets here and we'll get started," the clerk said as she disappeared through a door behind the judge's bench.

Dixon sat, staring at nothing in particular. The clock ticked past one without an appearance by anyone. Apparently Mr. McGuckin didn't have the same sense of punctuality that infected Dixon. At 1:04, Dixon started to imagine a default in his favor as his reward for driving seven hours round trip. At 1:07, the courtroom door burst open and a slightly frazzled man in his late twenties appeared.

Dixon rose and extended his hand. "Mr. McGuckin?"

"No, I'm an associate with his firm," he said, thrusting out his hand. "My name is Ron Farmer. You must be Dixon Donnelly."

"I am. Nice to meet you."

"Sorry I'm late, but up here the judges and the lawyers sort of ride a circuit. I had a pretrial in Grand Rapids at ten and it went longer than expected."

"Mr. McGuckin couldn't make it?"

"No. He's in trial up in I Falls."

"Excuse me?" Dixon asked.

"International Falls. You know, the nation's icebox."

"Oh, I'm familiar with the town. It's the main border crossing into Canada. I just never heard it called I Falls."

"Well, I didn't make it up. That's pretty much what everyone on the Range calls it." Farmer struggled to straighten his tie, but the non-Windsor knots that were the style in rural America never really looked straight. "Should we let them know I'm here?"

"Be my guest," Dixon responded.

The disheveled Farmer plopped his papers and briefcase on the other counsel table and walked to the same door through which the clerk had exited. He opened it half way, exchanged a few words, and came back into the courtroom to take a seat.

After a few minutes the door opened and the lawyers instinctively rose. "All rise," bellowed the clerk. Behind her walked Judge Stockman. He wasn't the rugged, silver-haired jurist Dixon had expected. Rather, he was a somewhat gangly man in his mid-forties with brown curly hair.

"Be seated," the judge announced in a voice that suggested he was embarrassed by the pomp and circumstance associated with a judicial entrance. After arranging himself and his papers, he looked to the court reporter and, after getting a nod, he began. "Now on for hearing is the case of Lester Krueller versus The Estate of Duane MacKenzie. This matter comes before the court on Plaintiff's motion to quash subpoenas. Counsel, please state your appearances."

Rising to his feet, the disheveled lawyer announced, "Ron Farmer on behalf of Plaintiff."

Dixon went next. "Your honor, I'm Dixon Donnelly and I represent the Estate of Duane MacKenzie."

Judge Stockman acknowledged them both and stated, "Mr. Farmer, I believe it's your motion."

"Thank you, your honor," Farmer began. "We are here asking that the Court quash the subpoenas served on Mr. and Mrs. Krueller in this case. Mr. Krueller is facing criminal charges and it would violate his rights against self-incrimination to require him to testify at a deposition."

"Doesn't he waive those rights by filing a personal injury lawsuit?" the judge asked, beating Dixon to his main argument.

"Your honor, it's not uncommon for insurance policies to have provisions requiring that the homeowner give notice of a claim within a particular period of time. One year is typical, but sometimes it's six months. We filed the lawsuit when we did to make sure the Estate would have insurance coverage. We don't think we should be penalized considering that we only did what we felt might be necessary and, quite frankly, the Estate should be glad that we have raised the issue in order to preserve coverage."

"Mr. Donnelly," the judge queried, "what do you think of that?"

Dixon sat in shock. That argument hadn't even occurred to him and he wondered whether he'd asked for trouble by straying from his usual practice area. Dixon rose to his feet and made some introductory remarks while the other part of his brain raced for a response. "I think it's entirely speculative. They could have sent a letter saying 'hey you guys, notify your insurance carrier we might be suing' and they could have accomplished the same thing. To now claim they thought the insurance policy might have required something different is just an after-the-fact rationalization."

"I tend to agree with you, Mr. Donnelly," the judge said, "but my first commitment is to the Constitution and the criminal proceeding. If I allow you to take depositions, I might jeopardize the criminal trial. In other words, if Mr. Krueller is convicted, it may be grounds for reversal if I have allowed your depositions to proceed. Normally, defendants in criminal cases are not subject to depositions before trial, and I don't want Mr. Krueller to be treated any differently. I know you'd like to take the deposition, but I'll bet if there is a conviction in the criminal trial, you wouldn't want the specter of a Constitutional argument as a basis for appeal."

Dixon was somewhat taken aback by the Solomonic wisdom coming from the judge. As much as he thought he would win the motion with a slam dunk, he now realized that winning the motion might be the worst thing that could happen.

"Your point is well taken, your honor. But what about Mrs. Krueller?"

Turning to Farmer, the judge asked, "What's your position on that?"

Farmer, who looked relieved that he appeared to be on the winning side, said, "Minnesota law provides for a clear spousal immunity. The statute states: 'A person cannot be compelled to testify against a spouse in any court proceeding.'"

"Mr. Donnelly?" the Court asked.

"Your honor, first of all, my understanding is she is the estranged wife, so there is probably no marital relationship to protect, and second, one of the explicit exceptions to spousal immunity is when the spouse is a victim of domestic abuse, and that is clearly the case here."

Judge Stockman flipped through some pages in the file. "Well, on the first issue, I think the test is whether they were married at the time of the communication. I'm not sure about that, but I don't think being estranged is enough. On the second issue, I understand your point, but the defendant is not being charged with domestic abuse."

"That's not because it didn't occur; it's only because Mrs. Krueller is so terrified of her husband she won't press charges," Dixon protested.

"That may or may not be true," Judge Stockman replied, "but I think that is the concern of the County Attorney. Mr. Donnelly, I know you've driven a long way to be here, and the Court wants to indulge you and give you an opportunity to make a record for appeal. I'm going to grant the motion to postpone the depositions until after the criminal trial, but feel free to state anything further so you may have an adequate record."

"Thank you, your honor. I think you've given me that opportunity, and I respect your judgment on this matter. I do not need to make a record." And with that, Dixon had a newfound respect for the man he had been prepared to label a hick.

# CHAPTER 6

SATURDAY NIGHT was date night. Despite the fact that he apparently had a girlfriend, Dixon was in the habit of spending Fridays, and sometimes Thursdays, with his buddies. He justified his actions as a need to network and by the fact that, once he was married, he wouldn't have the opportunity. The implication to Sharon was that he meant, "once the two of them were married." While Dixon never stated as much, he felt like his nights out were driven by the possibility he would meet someone new.

Dixon had made it to thirty-five years of age without ever being married or even particularly close. He believed he'd been in love, but never with someone he perceived as a life mate. There had been girlfriends with whom he had experienced meaningful relationships, and he always persuaded himself the emotional bond was strong enough that he was prepared to deal with a birth control failure. He apparently only convinced himself superficially, however, because each coital climax was filled with the mixed emotions of triumph and trepidation.

There had never been much intensity to his relationship with Sharon. There had been moments when he thought they might be approaching something, and he did like the idea of being in a relationship for a change. He just wasn't that crazy about this particular relationship.

Dixon arrived at Sharon's apartment at six, having built in a cushion for Sharon's inevitable inability to be on time. After having to push the doorbell a second time, Sharon came on the intercom yelling "C'mon up," while activating the release on the security door.

On their first date, he'd been pleased that she showed a comfort level by inviting him up. On the second date, he made the mistake of leaving the car running. He had now resigned himself to the fact that she would never be ready on time, but he had come to hope for the "I'll be down in a minute," instead of the I-wish-I'd-brought-the-newspaper dread of "C'mon up."

He knocked on the apartment door and then let himself in. He could hear the whir of the blow dryer coming from the bathroom of the one-bedroom condo. This wasn't standing around time. It was take off your jacket and get comfortable time. Mockingly, he yelled, "Where do you keep the video of the *Star Wars* trilogy?"

"Whaaat?" came the reply.

He ignored the question, as he didn't think she'd understand or appreciate the joke.

After a few minutes, Sharon emerged wearing only underclothes. She scurried across the room and gave him a hurried Hollywood kiss—no actual contact.

"That's it?" Dixon groaned.

"I don't want to smear my make-up," was the excuse.

Another ten minutes passed before she announced that she was ready. Halfway down the hall she remembered something and had to go back. Still, the time cushion had been sufficient.

The theater-bound eightsome included Dixon's friends and their wives or girlfriends. The men were all lawyers and had known each other since law school. The other women had known each other from such events in the past, but Sharon was a relative newcomer and not particularly comfortable among them.

The group assembled at a small bistro to grab something to drink prior to the show. Dixon renewed introductions for Sharon's benefit and they ordered cocktails. The conversation soon turned to the show, past touring shows, and the resurrection of the Minneapolis theater district. After a while, there was a lull and Sandy got everybody's attention. "Who wants to hear about Dixon's new case? It's a doozy."

Dixon shook his head with a smile. He wanted to tell the story, but pretended they'd have to drag it out of him. "It's a simple matter,"

Dixon said. "Do you think a person has a right to use deadly force against an intruder in his home?"

"Did he know the intruder?" asked Marlin, the intellectual property lawyer.

"Shouldn't matter," responded Dixon.

"What was the intruder doing in the house?" asked the wife of the employee benefits attorney.

Dixon paused for effect. "The intruder wasn't happy that his wife was banging the guy who owned the house."

"Dixon," Sharon snapped, "where are your manners?"

"I guess I left them at home. Or I lost them when I finished my first drink."

"That might be a relevant fact," Marlin said.

Dixon smiled, "Well, putting aside the moral judgments, if you're in your bedroom having sex with a willing participant and an objecting party interjects themselves, do you think it's reasonable to shoot the son of a bitch."

"I'm not sure it is," commented Sandy's date Melody.

"Okay," Dixon said, unwilling to accept defeat, "do you think it's okay to shoot the person if he had a shovel in his hand and had just smashed a sliding glass door to break into your house?"

Put in those terms, no disagreement could be found at the table. "I don't know if you'll win," Marlin said, "but I think juries tend to favor the right to self-protection."

"Here's the problem," Dixon continued. "My guy was so distraught that he blew his own brains out. I don't have anyone who can tell his side of the story."

"What about the unfaithful wife?" Melody asked.

"That's not as easy as it sounds," Dixon said. "The wife declined to press charges and I think she's too afraid to voluntarily do anything. I think she is someone with either very low self esteem, a chemical dependency problem, or both, and with her husband being an Olympic-caliber wife beater, I don't know if I can count on her."

The employee benefits attorney asked, "So you might have to try and prove your case without any living witnesses who support your version of events?"

"Unfortunately, you're probably right on the money," Dixon said. "Furthermore, this won't be a jury of our peers. The case is venued up on the Iron Range, and who knows what the average juror up there is thinking."

"You don't think they'll have an even greater belief in the right of self-protection?" Sandy asked.

"Oh I do, but I'm a little worried. I mean I think my clients are hillbillies, but they appear to be the veritable aristocracy up there. I'm afraid the jury might side with the downtrodden husband who took matters into his own hands."

"How much money does a hillbilly slash aristocrat have to lose anyway?" Marlin asked.

"I'm afraid that's privileged information," Dixon said, "but, whatever the amount, there's an illegitimate daughter who could put the money to much better use. My client didn't have any contact with her when she was growing up, and his last will and testament provided that his estate was to go to her to try and compensate a little for what he didn't give her when she was young."

"That's gotta put a little pressure on you," Melody said.

"Yeah, and don't think I don't feel it," Dixon replied. "There's a pot of money and I need to protect it from a wife-beating lowlife and his shyster attorney. As it happens, the criminal trial against the intruder is next week and if the state can get a conviction, it might undermine his lawsuit considerably."

"Perhaps we could find a more pleasant topic," Sharon interjected.

Dixon assumed the philosophical debate was beyond her capacity and that she wanted to talk about something more in her league, like who was on the cover of the supermarket tabloids that week. Nonetheless, he decided to comply. "Good thought," he said. "Besides, I feel as if I'm constantly rehearsing a closing argument for a case that is months away."

The conversation soon turned to golf for the men and movies for the women. Dixon couldn't help but notice that Sharon didn't seem to get involved in either conversation. Fortunately, show time was fast approaching and the group exited the restaurant.

The crowd for the show was a little more Bohemian than typical for a Broadway show at the Orpheum Theatre. As the band of lawyers and dates made their way through the lobby, they noticed an extra dose of face piercings. Furthermore, there were a lot of same-sex couples being more openly affectionate than normal for such a venue.

"Look at all the dikes and queers," Sharon said in a voice not nearly soft enough.

The rest of the group stared straight ahead so as not to be associated with the person making the remark. Dixon just looked at his shoes and tried to pretend it didn't happen; the way polite people treat a fart hanging in the air.

The group found their seats and Dixon scored the aisle. Sharon sat to his right, and Melody and Sandy followed. The other two couples occupied the four seats directly in front. "Great seats," Dixon exclaimed, sending a look of appreciation toward Sandy. The others joined in the sentiment.

Sharon and Melody were talking away. As the lights dimmed, Sharon droned on about her father or her father's business. As the overture began, their conversation continued. The murmurs in the audience generally faded, but Sharon apparently felt the overture was basically just practice and didn't require her attention. Dixon shook his head, silently wondering what had possessed him to bring her. Finally, Melody gave her a look like "it's time to watch," and Sharon stopped her narrative. For the moment.

It didn't take long for Sharon to decide others would be entertained by her opinions of the proceedings. She sarcastically cooed over the clothing worn by a cross-dressing character. She blurted out "what a waste," when two particularly buff-looking men embraced, making it clear their characters were lovers. Even as the story unfolded and tragedy played out, two glasses of wine kept Sharon thinking her comments were the only thing saving the show. None of the rest of the group responded to her comments, but she didn't seem to need encouragement.

♦

Dixon was silent on the drive home.

"Well, that was nice," Sharon announced in a voice that bordered on sincere.

"Yeah," was all Dixon could muster.

After a couple more miles of silence, Sharon asked, "Is something wrong?"

Dixon paused and reflected upon whether he really wanted to get into it. He shook his head and said nothing.

"Why won't you tell me? I think I have a right to know."

He shook his head again and slowly the words came. "We had a deal. I asked you whether you'd talk during the show and you promised that you wouldn't. I specifically said we didn't have to go and I didn't want to go if you couldn't keep quiet. Do you have no sense of honor? Much less, no sense of consideration for those around us?"

"What is that supposed to mean?" she shot back. "Nobody cared. What's the big deal? The only people who heard me were those in our group."

"It's not just about hearing the show," Dixon replied. "It's about making an agreement and then going back on your word."

"It's a woman's prerogative to change her mind," Sharon insisted.

Dixon rolled his eyes. "That's an expression that got its start in an era before women had the right to vote, serve on juries, or enter into contracts. Is that what you really think? In today's day and age, women aren't responsible for their actions?"

"I think this is a stupid argument and I'm not going to discuss it anymore."

They drove the rest of the way in silence. When they arrived at Sharon's, Dixon pulled up at the door with the motor running. "Aren't you coming up?" she asked.

"No, I'm afraid I'd rather just go home."

Sharon stared blankly. "Why don't you come in and we can talk about it?"

"I'm tired. Maybe we can talk about it later."

"But you're leaving Monday for the trial in Hibbing and then the next week I'm going to the cabin with my parents. I don't want to leave it this way."

"Maybe some time apart will be good. We can talk about it when you get back."

Sharon leaned over and kissed Dixon with as much passion as she could muster. Unfortunately, Sharon thought there was a direct correlation between tongue and passion, and Dixon found nothing about the kiss to be sensual.

After a moment Dixon pulled back. "Goodnight. We'll talk about it later."

With a hurt look Sharon gathered her purse and opened the door. She looked back at Dixon hoping for a reprieve, but it was not to be. She said a soft "goodnight" and got out of the car.

Dixon waited until she cleared the security door and then drove off. He felt a sense of relief that he wouldn't have to deal with Sharon for the immediate future. Perhaps some time apart would help.

# CHAPTER 7

Dixon drove to Hibbing on Sunday afternoon so he'd be ready for the trial the following morning. He thought he should call Sharon, but it was really the last thing he wanted to do. His solution was to call when he thought she wouldn't be by a phone. After praying through four rings, he was delighted to hear the click of the answering machine. He listened to her greeting and pondered how even the sound of her voice made him cringe. After the beep, he said, "Hey there, I guess you're not home. We're going out for dinner and I thought I'd try to reach you beforehand. I'm not really working tomorrow, so we might be out late and I probably won't be able to call back at a reasonable hour. Catch you later." After he hung up, he could only think, *Catch you later? If that's the best you can do, you are in the wrong relationship.*

With that, Dixon was out of his hotel and on his way to dinner with his clients. They were meeting at the Side Lake Supper Club. Dixon amused himself as he drove, pondering whether the dinner special would be broasted chicken or an all-you-can-eat fish fry. Either way, he was sure that any establishment elegant enough to be called a supper club would be adorned by a neon sign in the shape of a martini glass with neon bubbles appearing to effervesce out of it. He proved to be right.

Hank and his wife Margie were already at the restaurant when Dixon arrived. The hostess wasted no time when Dixon walked in. "Honey, you must be the big-shot lawyer here to dine with the MacKenzies."

"What gave it away?" Dixon asked. "The starched shirt or the arrogant smirk?"

"Oh heavens no," she chuckled. "I heard you were a right fine looking specimen, and it's pretty obvious you don't live in these parts."

"Well, I'll take at least the first part of that as a compliment," he said, flashing her a smile.

Hank and Margie each had a highball going when Dixon arrived at the table. Duke had gotten into a little trouble with alcohol, and it was apparent the "thirst" ran in the family. The waitress descended upon him as he took his seat. "Well, look's like I've got some catching up to do," Dixon said. "Bring me a Maker's Mark Manhattan."

"Good luck," cracked the waitress. "This is the Side Lake Supper Club, not the Waldorf Astoria. I think I can come up with a Crown Royal Manhattan if that would do the trick."

"That would be perfect." Dixon felt a little embarrassed for not assessing his surroundings better.

"I's just telling Mother how nervous I am about this whole t'ing," Hank said. "I have a bad feeling about this trial. Isn't there somet'ing you can do?"

"I'm sorry, Hank," Dixon said, "but criminal trials are the responsibility of the County Attorney. Y'know, I'm not a criminal lawyer anyway. There are a lot of procedural rules and other unique things about which I don't know the first thing."

"Tell me this," Hank continued, "there's no doubt in my mind that Les Krueller is responsible for Duke bein' dead. If Les hadn't broke in and Duke hadn't shot him, Duke would be alive today. How come Krueller isn't bein' charged with murder?"

"In a word—'intent.' I think a jury would have to conclude that Krueller intended that Duke would commit suicide as a result of the break-in. I don't know for sure, but it's hard to charge someone with an outcome that wasn't at all obvious in advance. Under the circumstances, the only way to convict Krueller for murder would be to find evidence that Duke didn't actually commit suicide, but was shot by Krueller."

"I thought we filed a wrongful death Counterclaim against Krueller," Hank said.

"Yes, but civil liability and criminal responsibility are two different things. Criminal trials focus on the act and the intent of the defendant, while a tort claim like ours is more focused on the injury to the victim. Furthermore, civil proceedings require a lower level of proof."

"What do you mean?"

"In the criminal action, the state has to prove its case beyond a reasonable doubt. We only need to prove it by a preponderance of the evidence."

"What's the difference?"

"In rough terms, beyond a reasonable doubt usually equates to about ninety percent sure. Preponderance of the evidence is like fifty-one percent sure."

"Got it."

"Furthermore, I don't really expect to win the wrongful death claim. I only agreed to make the claim because you were so adamant and because I didn't mind putting a little fear in the Kruellers' hearts by creating the risk that they have something to lose."

"Why don't they just charge him with murder anyway?" Hank asked. "Can't the state charge Krueller with murder and let the jury decide?"

"Not really. The County Attorney is ethically prohibited from pursuing a charge that he doesn't believe is supported by the facts."

"But lots of people are found innocent. How can that happen if the County Attorney can only bring claims where he believes there's enough evidence?"

"That's a good question," Dixon responded. "The County Attorney doesn't need to have proof beyond a reasonable doubt to bring the case. He just can't have evidence that he knows proves the defendant's innocence."

"What if I swear to facts that show Krueller's guilt?" MacKenzie persisted.

"Still no good. If you have to testify and lie, you are subject to perjury charges and, furthermore, Krueller could get a new trial or get out of jail if he could later show your testimony was false."

"So, how will tomorrow's case affect ours?" Hank asked.

"That remains to be seen. In our case, we want to prove that Duke acted in self-defense. Minnesota statutes say you can use deadly force against an intruder who is in the act of committing a felony in your home. Ordinarily, self-defense requires you to attempt to avoid a confrontation, but there is no duty to retreat in your own home."

"That's good for us, right?" Hank said.

"Basically yes, but there's a catch. You've heard the term *judicial activism*. It refers to situations where judges decide they don't like the laws made by the legislature so they make their own. As you may know, most judges at the appellate level are political hacks who want to make laws but lack the charisma to get elected, so they get appointed to the courts instead. Well, there's a Minnesota Court of Appeals decision that ignores the plain language of the statute and says the homeowner has to prove he reasonably feared his life was in danger. Now that's all well and good if the homeowner is alive to tell about it, but you can imagine it creates an issue for us."

"I see yer point," Hank replied. "Everyone knows Lester Krueller is the kinda guy who beats up women, and I don't t'ink Duke would have ordinarily been afraid of him. Anytime anyone breaks in with a shovel, though, that seems pretty clear."

"I agree. And here's the interesting part. For us to show self-defense, we'll have to show Krueller was trying to commit a felony when he broke in and that Duke reasonably feared for his life. If the State convicts Krueller of a felony during tomorrow's trial, we've basically won on that issue because the jury in our trial will be instructed that Krueller was committing a felony in Duke's house. The only issue then would be whether Duke reasonably feared for his safety or the safety of others. In my opinion, deadly force was justified."

"I don't understand," Margie piped in. "Why do you talk about deadly force when Duke didn't kill Krueller?"

"Deadly force refers to force that has the potential to be deadly. Shooting a gun always qualifies, and it's referred to as deadly force because it describes the level of force and not the consequences. I believe the situation warranted the use of deadly force, and the

County Attorney can make my job a whole lot easier if he proves that Krueller was in the act of committing a felony."

"Well," Hank responded with a sigh, "there ain't nothin' we can do at this point, so let's just hope for the best." With that, he raised his glass and the three of them made an air toast before imbibing.

# CHAPTER 8

Hank and Dixon arrived at the courthouse well before the proceedings were scheduled to begin. They would have no role in the trial, but they wanted to witness everything. Furthermore, Hank was fairly well known around town, and they hoped his presence might influence some of the jurors.

On this day, Earl McGuckin would be in his element. He was appearing at a criminal trial that arose from a domestic dispute that resulted in a personal injury—the triad of his practice united into one dispute. Who could be better versed and better able to represent a defendant who had so many diverse issues?

More was at stake than simply a finding of guilt or innocence on the criminal charges. The testimony and the potential for adverse findings could have a negative impact on Krueller's other pending disputes. A finding that he was guilty of a crime at the time of the incident had the potential to derail his personal injury litigation. A victory in the criminal trial was important, therefore, because it assured Earl Fuckin' McGuckin of at least one more lawsuit.

The ramifications for McGuckin's practice were equally great. This was high profile. The MacKenzies were among the leading citizens of the area, and sordid details brought out the curiosity in everybody. The small courtroom gallery was expected to be overflowing with spectators, and the local news was sure to cover the proceedings.

To top it off, the case played directly to McGuckin's strengths. He was representing the poor downtrodden husband whose wife was stolen away by a local rich boy. McGuckin postured himself as the champion of the purported underdog or underachiever and this was his opportunity to shine.

McGuckin's wardrobe lived up to its billing. He wore a white linen suit and a pair of braided leather suspenders that, unfortunately for him, only accentuated his ample stomach. He was tall enough that most people wouldn't see his balding pate, but he combed over several greasy strands of graying hair to make sure.

Krueller wore a coat from a chocolate brown leisure suit that might have fit him at about the time leisure suits were considered acceptable. The two of them made quite a pair sitting at the defense table: Colonel Sanders meets the Brady Bunch.

The bailiff pounded the gavel and called the court to order. The gallery became quiet and rose to its feet. McGuckin, in his inimitable style, rose, but continued to confer with his client. McGuckin's actions seemed designed to demonstrate that different rules applied to him.

Judge Stockman entered from a door behind the bench, walked to his seat, and ordered that everyone be seated. He looked around in disbelief at the size of the crowd, and, with all the formality that usually occurs during the first few minutes of any legal proceeding, announced, "Now before this Honorable Court is the case of the State of Minnesota versus Lester Wayne Krueller, Criminal File No. 00-7734. Counsel, please state your appearance."

While it was customary for the County Attorney to be the first to note his appearance because he would ultimately be the first to present evidence, McGuckin had his own thoughts in the matter. Without a pause or a look, he sprang to his feet and announced with a drawl that he was "Ear-r-r-l McGuckin, appearing on behalf of the wrongly accused Lester Krueller."

Judge Stockman, in even but stern tones replied, "Mr. McGuckin, you will have ample opportunity to argue your case at the appropriate time, so I ask that you wait until then."

"As you wish, your honor." Rather than appearing to have been rebuked, McGuckin acted as though he and the learned judge had just reviewed a novel point of procedure known only to them.

Judge Stockman turned to the County Attorney and nodded for him to proceed.

"Perry Passieux for the State of Minnesota." Passieux appeared to be in his forties. He had short black hair that accentuated an already oversized head. The top button of his shirt looked as if it hadn't reached the top buttonhole for years, so he relied on an ill-fitting tie to hold it together. All in all, he didn't present the picture of intimidation.

Jury trials begin with the selection of a jury through a process called "voir dire," which is generally pronounced "vwa dear" by all attorneys other than McGuckin, who referred to it as "voy-eur dyer." The original purpose of the process was to determine whether prospective jurors could act as fair and impartial judges of the facts. That purpose had been all but forgotten in modern proceedings. Now, the primary function was to begin arguing the case or to ascertain obscure facts to determine whether a potential juror had the traits that a jury consultant thinks would favor one side or the other. In Hibbing, Minnesota, jury consultants were all but unheard of, so the main purpose seemed to be persuasion.

"Ladies and gentleman," Judge Stockman began, "you have been selected as potential jurors in the case of the State of Minnesota versus Lester Wayne Krueller. I will ask you a series of questions to determine whether you are suitable to act as fair and impartial jurors in this case, and then I will give the attorneys an opportunity to ask you some additional questions for the same purpose. Please understand that if you are dismissed, it is not because anyone believes that you would not faithfully discharge your duties, but, for reasons that do not always need to be spoken, there is a determination that something about your background, experience, or relationships might make it more difficult for you to discharge your duties. Those of you who are dismissed will be asked to report back to the court administrator to determine whether to appear for a future trial."

The juror prospects sat attentively. Keeping their attention as the trial progressed was usually the difficult part.

Judge Stockman continued, "This case involves a charge of burglary and aggravated assault. The defendant is accused of breaking into the home of Duane MacKenzie, with the intent of causing bodily harm to Mr. MacKenzie, and further that he did in fact try to attack Mr. MacKenzie. Now, did any of you know Duke MacKenzie?"

A few prospects raised their hands.

Stockman asked follow-up questions to determine whether the jurors in question might still otherwise be suitable to serve. After exhausting that issue, he changed topics. "Do any of you know Lester Krueller?"

Predictably, the least desirable miscreants in the crowd were the ones who had run with Krueller. Some had worked with him and others just knew him from "hanging out." Personal acquaintances were pretty much always forbidden and this group quickly became rejects in another sense of the word.

"Have any of you heard about this incident prior to today? Please indicate by raising your hands."

Eight of the twenty remaining prospects raised their hands.

"Of those of you who raised your hands, how many of you heard about it only as a result of reading the newspaper?"

Seven of the hands remained raised.

"The gentleman who did not hear about it through the newspaper, without telling us what you heard, could you tell us what your source of information was?"

"My wife works for Duke MacKenzie's company and she told me about it."

Judge Stockman nodded and said, "In a small community such as ours, it is often difficult to find jurors with no knowledge of the events giving rise to trials. Prior knowledge does not necessarily disqualify a juror, but, because the substantial majority of the other juror prospects have no outside knowledge, I am going to dismiss you. Thank you for your willingness to serve. As for the others who read about it in the newspaper, I will leave it to the attorneys to explore the issue further so they can determine whether they believe you can be impartial notwithstanding your prior knowledge."

The judge continued with his standard litany and the pool narrowed. After screening the clearly unacceptable, Stockman directed his clerk to call names and fill in the jury box with prospects. The process was then turned over to the attorneys.

Perry Passieux followed a script that was not much different from the inquiries made by the judge. He then questioned each juror prospect individually and asked whether they would follow the Court's instructions regardless of their personal feelings about the law, whether they had any objection to incarceration for felons, and a variety of other questions about being good Americans. The goal of such an approach was to give the impression that any right-minded person would find in the State's favor. Ultimately, he did not ask to strike any jurors for cause, but he did gather information to help him make "peremptory challenges," which allow a lawyer to dismiss a specified number of jurors without an explanation. By that time, the panel needs to be weeded down anyway, so jurors rarely take offense or read much into such decisions.

This process had been going for nearly two hours, and it showed in the dissipating attention of the panel. That fact was not lost on Judge Stockman, who announced, "We'll recess for fifteen minutes to allow everyone to stretch and use the restroom and then Mr. McGuckin will have some questions for you."

The judge took his leave. McGuckin stood smiling at the prospective jurors as they filed out of the room.

Dixon turned to Hank, "Pretty exciting, huh? This is the part they don't show you on the lawyer programs on TV." In fact, the real show was about to begin.

After about ten minutes, the juror prospects filed back in. McGuckin sat on the edge of the counsel table as though he was a ninth grade civics teacher about to give a lesson to his students. While the process had eliminated the lowest rung, i.e., Krueller's cronies, it had also eliminated the only people with college educations. McGuckin's pedantic style was likely to be effective with those willing to be educated but not smart enough to doubt the teacher.

Once court was back in session, McGuckin wasted no time. "How many of you have ever been wronged in a way that you felt you had to take matters into your own hands?" While a few hands went up, McGuckin didn't really care. He was laying his theme and what he really wanted was people to think about what they would or might do if such a situation occurred.

"Would you be willing to listen to the explanation of an otherwise law-abiding citizen if he committed one indiscretion, but he had a good reason?" The men and women in the audience looked puzzled and unclear as to whether they were still supposed to raise their hands or just listen.

McGuckin apparently thought that using the word "indiscretion" might have been asking too much and rephrased. "Would you be willing to give a fair shake to a simple mine worker even though he's up against a wealthy and prominent citizen of this community, if the simple mine worker had a good explanation?"

"Your honor," yelled Passieux as he jumped from his chair. "What Mr. McGuckin is doing is not voir dire. It's not even an opening statement. Mr. McGuckin has jumped all the way to closing arguments."

"I'm afraid I have to agree," replied the judge. "Mr. McGuckin, you appear to be asking only rhetorical questions and voir dire is designed for actual questions."

"My apologies, your honor. Let's start with juror number one. Sir, do you think you could give a fair trial to a simple mine worker even though he was up against a wealthy and prominent citizen of this community?" And so it went. McGuckin proceeded to build his theme one laborious person at a time. By the phrasing of his questions, he rivaled Aristotle in his ability to get the juror candidates to reach a conclusion without telling them the answer. As McGuckin took control, Hank MacKenzie's head drooped lower and lower.

The lunch hour had long since passed, but Judge Stockman had not shown any inclination to interrupt McGuckin. The rest of the gallery began fidgeting and looking at their watches. Finally, McGuckin seemed to be past his subtle mind bend and into his standard litany.

Turning to one of the remaining prospects, he said, "Ms. Murphy, you've told me many things about your background and beliefs. Do you know of any reason why you might not be able to judge my client impartially?"

The young woman raised her eyebrows and clenched her teeth. She rocked her head back and forth as though she was in the school principal's office and knew she had to come across with the information. "Remember, I didn't say that I knew Lester Krueller," she said, "but isn't he the same guy you always hear about who goes out, gets drunk, and beats up his wife?"

Hank MacKenzie's head popped up, and a smile crossed Dixon's face. McGuckin was in trouble. His credibility would suffer if he failed to be honest in responding or refused to respond, but the truth would do him no better. With pleading eyes he turned to Judge Stockman who, albeit hesitantly, came to his rescue. "I think we should take a lunch recess. Ladies and gentlemen, please do not talk about the case or what just transpired during that time and be back here at 2:15."

McGuckin was in a bind. He had romanced the entire jury pool magnificently, but now had to consider asking that the entire panel be dismissed. After the prospective jurors filed out, Stockman turned to McGuckin and said, "I guess I should have asked the preliminary questions a little more broadly. Ultimately, I think it's a matter of public record that your client has a record of domestic abuse and that fact might come out anyway. What do you want to do?"

McGuckin's further problem was of the "speak now or forever hold your peace" variety. If he did not request a new jury panel he could not later claim that Krueller had been unfairly prejudiced by the information the jury had just heard. The best possible result for him would be to make the request but have it denied. That way, he could keep the otherwise favorable jury but preserve the appeal if something went wrong.

"Your honor," McGuckin began, "I'm afraid we have no choice but to request that the entire panel be dismissed and that we start over. As we established at the pretrial hearing, Rule 404 of the Minnesota Rules of Evidence explicitly states that evidence of a person's unrelated bad acts cannot be admitted to prove the character of that person or to prove he acted in conformity with such prior acts. The rule exists so that a person will not be convicted simply because there is evidence of other conduct a jury might find objectionable. Now, your honor, you agreed when you granted our motion to prohibit the prosecution from eliciting such testimony, and allowing the jury to hear it in this situation is just as bad."

"Your honor," the District Attorney chimed in, "we've spent more than half a day at this and I think it would be sufficient for you to admonish the jury that they can only consider evidence that is received from the witness stand and to disregard the comment. Mr. McGuckin can challenge the juror for cause and we can move on."

"I'll think about it over lunch," and with that Stockman pounded his gavel and dismissed the proceedings.

Hank and Dixon shuffled out of the courtroom. "What do you think?" Dixon asked.

"I t'ink we're going to get hammered. I know Perry will give it his best, but I t'ink McGuckin will get the better of him."

"No argument," Dixon replied. "But that last incident was sure something."

◆

The gallery was less crowded in the afternoon. Either the curious had realized the trial would be a slow process, or they had satisfied their curiosity with the antics of the morning. Still, Dixon and Hank had to ask the bailiff to make room so as to not appear too pushy. Dixon was happy about the smaller crowd, as he would have to try a similar case in the same courtroom and he didn't want everyone in town disqualified because of information learned as a result of the criminal trial.

Judge Stockman promptly denied the motion to dismiss the jury. He reasoned that the prosecution had done nothing to cause the disclosure and that he could give a curative instruction. McGuckin acted indignant, but he had to know that it was the best possible outcome. After resolving those issues and dismissing the juror in question, the parties proceeded with the peremptory strikes until they were left with twelve jurors and two alternates.

Judge Stockman thanked those who were dismissed and invited the State to begin its case with its opening statement. Passieux was methodical, and not particularly engaging. He made attempts at theatrics, but, because he was largely reading from his notes, he wasn't very effective. After about fifteen minutes he announced: "My case is simple. Lester Krueller does not deny that he broke in with a shovel and with the intent of separating Duke MacKenzie and Debi Krueller through any means necessary. Those are the facts, and that is all you need to know to convict on both the burglary and assault charges." While Passieux was right that those facts standing alone were sufficient, he didn't do anything to anticipate the arguments to be made on Krueller's behalf.

McGuckin was a bit more animated, to say the least. His opening statement had the histrionics of a religious revival but the intricate storytelling of a Boy Scout campfire. The jurors hung on every word. Passieux had focused on the physical acts, which the law refers to as "actus reus." McGuckin focused almost exclusively on the "mens rea," or the state of mind. A conviction required both the wrongful act and the intent to commit such a wrongful act. McGuckin was relying on the fact that his client was a pathetic soul who was powerless in the face of what was happening. The key, of course, was keeping the jury from focusing on his wife-beating history.

McGuckin stood at the lectern but never lost eye contact with the jury. "Debi Krueller was a woman without hope when she met Lester Krueller. She had been in an abusive relationship for years in her first marriage and the results had been devastating. As for Lester Krueller, he is a hard-working miner who rescued her from that life. But as much as he loved her, she was still a woman with problems—a woman suffering from chemical dependency and low self-esteem. Duke MacKenzie, on the other hand, was nothing but an opportunist. He saw this vulnerable young thing and decided to have his way with her. Oh sure, I'm sure if he were here today he'd claim he was just trying to help her, but, if that were true, why couldn't he help her without helping himself to the pleasures of her womanhood?"

Dixon glanced sideways at Hank, who rolled his eyes in disgust.

McGuckin continued, "There will be no dispute that Les and Debi had gotten into a disagreement. There will be no dispute that Debi left and Les took some of her belongings and put them in the yard. There will be no dispute that Les became very concerned about his wife and the things that might happen to her. There will be no dispute that Les tried to intervene and get his wife away from Duke MacKenzie on more than one occasion, and there will be no dispute that Lester Krueller did, in fact, break into the MacKenzie house— while Duke MacKenzie was having sexual relations with Debi—in an attempt to stop what was going on. Those facts, ladies and gentle-men of the jury, will not be subject to any serious dispute."

McGuckin walked out from behind the lectern for effect. Now standing in front of the jury, he said, "The issue for you to decide will not be whether it was Les Krueller who broke in. The issue for you to decide is whether he was justified in taking the actions he took. You will hear testimony from Mr. Krueller about how broken up he was that his marriage seemed to be falling apart. You will hear testimony from Mr. Krueller about how concerned he was about the emotional well-being of his wife, who was being used by Duke MacKenzie for his own sordid pleasure. You will hear testimony from Mr. Krueller about how he was concerned for his wife's physi-cal safety because he knew Duke MacKenzie had a wild side."

Hank leaned close to Dixon and whispered, "Do they really get to drag Duke through the mud like this?"

"I think it's going a little far," Dixon responded, "but the best thing to do is to ignore it."

The jurors were at attention. Whether they were agreeing with McGuckin was far from clear, but they seemed to appreciate his ability to spin a yarn.

McGuckin retreated to the lectern for his notes. Putting on read-ing glasses, he said, "Let me tell you precisely what testimony you are likely to hear." With that, he began clicking through the names of the prosecution's witnesses and giving a short report on each witness's role and expected testimony. When he finished the list he said, "The only relevant witness is Mr. Lester Krueller. The prosecution's wit-nesses will tell you what they saw and who they talked to, but none of them can tell you what was going on in the mind and heart of Lester Krueller. So, I invite you to be attentive to the prosecution's case, but I'm telling you now, the only thing that will matter is what you will hear from Mr. Krueller himself. In the end, I'll be asking you to render a verdict in Mr. Krueller's favor." After a short pause, he concluded with "Thank you," and sat down.

Judge Stockman sat forward and looked at the jury. "Ladies and gentlemen, we will recess for the day. Please do not discuss the case with anybody, and return tomorrow at 8:30."

# CHAPTER 9

SANDY PICKED DIXON up at 5:30 for a five o'clock wedding. They relied on the fact that the bride and groom would, by and large, be facing away from those in the pews and, as a result, would not likely notice their absence at the church. Sandy had convinced Dixon that "the big day with the white dress" was for the women and, since they were going stag, there was no reason to attend.

As soon as Dixon got in the car, Sandy asked, "How'd the trial go?"

"Like nothing you'd ever believe."

"Oh-oh. This sounds good. Don't keep me waiting."

"Gladly," Dixon responded. "I've seen the gruesome underbelly of American jurisprudence and it ain't pretty. I saw a greaseball defendant, represented by a greaseball attorney, get basically exonerated even though he admitted to basically every element of the charge. I don't know if it was a failure of advocacy or a testimonial to the shortcomings of the jurors or the jury system."

"You're not telling me Krueller was acquitted on all charges are you?"

"Fortunately, not quite. Krueller was acquitted of the burglary charge, but convicted of the assault charge."

"How can that be?" Sandy asked. "Burglary is unlawfully entering a dwelling with the intent of committing a crime. There's no question that smashing a sliding glass door with a shovel is an unlawful entry, and the fact that he was convicted of assault would seem to satisfy the second element."

"Now you understand what I was saying about the gruesome underbelly. Either the jury disregarded the instructions because in

65

their minds they thought burglary involved stealing, or they thought Krueller broke in with a shovel because he wanted to chat about the weather. Either way, it was a pitiful display."

"What's he looking at for a sentence?"

"I don't really know, but it's probably workhouse time or something minimal. Furthermore, he's appealing the conviction he did receive and, the way the rest of it went, I wouldn't be surprised if he walked."

"What's the basis for the appeal?"

"As I understand it, the main thrust will be an incident that occurred during jury selection. After the jury was all but seated, a woman piped in with, 'I don't recognize the defendant, but is he the same Lester Krueller that always gets drunk and beats up his wife.'"

"Hah!" Sandy let out a yell. "You've got to be kidding," he wheezed between belly laughs. "What did the judge do?"

"I think he did exactly what Fuckin' McGuckin hoped he'd do. He cautioned the jury, but decided not to start the process over from scratch. Thus, he gave McGuckin the jury pool he had charmed, but left him grounds for appeal."

"What happens if it's reversed?"

"I suppose they'll try him again."

"They can't retry him on the burglary can they?"

"No. Once acquitted always acquitted. Although a reversal of the assault charge might permit further charges."

"What do you mean?"

"Well, a person can only be tried once based on a certain set of facts, so ordinarily you cannot charge someone with assault and later try them for murder based on the same facts."

"I've heard of that," Sandy said. "That's why defendants sometimes hurry and plead guilty to assault before their victim dies."

"Exactly, so if the assault conviction is vacated the prosecution might be able to enhance the charges the next time. For example, if Madame Krueller gets the courage to press charges against the Marquis de Krueller, he could be charged with two counts of assault or some sort of domestic assault. That might draw a longer sentence."

Sandy shook his head in disbelief. "How does it affect your case?"

"The assault conviction definitely helps my theory that my guy was trying to prevent the commission of a felony in his home and was justified in using deadly force. The problem is, it might not hold up on appeal."

"What's your next step?" Sandy asked.

"I'm going to proceed with discovery. I think the Constitutional issues are behind us and, anyway, I think they want to get on with it."

"What kind of discovery will you need?"

"I need to prove my case without any witnesses to help me. The battered wife should be helpful, but I'm not sure I can rely on her. As for the rest, 'Dead men tell no tales.' I'm going back up next week to take the depositions of the cuckold and Mrs. Krueller."

Sandy shook his head. "That should be fun."

"Yeah, they're quite a couple. Speaking of which, perhaps we should conduct an investigation of tonight's wedding and figure out how the groom managed to marry someone so far outside of his class."

"Class," Sandy responded, "she's outside of his species."

"Well, if you want to be technically accurate," Dixon shot back, "his bride is in a whole different phylum." Dixon smiled an erudite smile.

Sandy matched him in pretentiousness by laughing heartily at a reference he also knew was reserved for those who studied and remembered biology.

"Of course, maybe we shouldn't be mocking somebody who's managed to find somebody," Dixon said. "At least he seems happy."

"That's his nature. Guys like you and I just aren't suited for that."

"You don't think there's somebody out there who could cause you to give it all up?" Dixon asked.

"I suppose I might if I could find a woman who meets my criteria."

Dixon rolled his eyes. "This should be good. What are your criteria?"

"Don't you think that's kind of personal?"

"Come on," Dixon prodded. "Give me a hint of what you're look-ing for in case I happen to come across her."

"Well," Sandy started, "I've actually given this some thought and

I've boiled it down to three things. The first thing is I want a woman who is so stunning that when we walk into a party or a restaurant together, all of the men and about ninety percent of the women wish they could sleep with her."

"Good idea to set your sights low," Dixon chided. "Nice to know someone else who wants to date outside his phylum."

Sandy gave him an evil eye before continuing. "Second, I want a woman who laughs at my jokes. I don't mean she laughs out of respect, fear, or something else. I mean she gets my jokes."

"How about if she gets your jokes but doesn't think they're funny?" Dixon asked.

"That's a hard call. If she never laughs at anything, forget it. If she simply disparages the more risqué part of my shtick, that might be okay."

"I'm dying, oh marvelous one. What is the third criterion?"

Sandy hesitated while pretending to give it some thought. "She can't make a yuck face after oral sex. I don't care if she was giving or receiving, there's nothing more annoying than a yuck face after oral sex."

Dixon laughed. "Just put that in a personal ad. I'm sure you'll find plenty of enlightened prospects who would be flattered to be considered."

"Well, you asked," Sandy said. "How about you? What are you waiting for?"

"I'm afraid I was hoping to just let it happen. I don't have a recipe for it."

"Maybe I'm just being more pragmatic. Think about it. You must have something in mind."

Dixon thought this was a debate he should probably avoid, but he couldn't help himself. "Y'know, when I was young I thought it would be a matter of finding someone who was always there for me. I mean, whether it was literally or emotionally, she would always be there for me, and I would always be there for her. Now, I think I'd settle for someone who could just be on time."

Chuckling, Sandy asked, "This wouldn't be Sharon-related would it?"

"Sharon's issues go deeper. It's getting to the point where I don't even want to talk to her. I guess I just don't think interesting conversation consists of interrupting, answering a question with a question, or an endless supply of worn-out clichés."

Sandy put a hand on Dixon's shoulder as though he was a mentor educating his charge. "You should take my approach. That way, you're less likely to be disappointed."

◆

The wedding was a yuppie classic. The ceremony was at the Basilica of St. Mary and the reception was at the Glen Hills Country Club. There was a time when Catholics and Glen Hills didn't mix, but the club members eventually concluded that it was the most acceptable "integration" into their club.

The reception was filled with familiar faces. Dixon and Sandy scouted out Matt Colter, who was the best man. Matt was an accountant slash tax lawyer and they knew they could get the skinny on what happened, if anything, during the ceremony.

"Mattster, my man," Sandy said, with a slap on the back. "I'm sure you can appreciate how a couple of unromantic boobs like us decided to skip the ceremony, but we'd like to make sure that we appear to have been there weeping with the parents. Did we miss anything? Did anybody pass out, throw up, make an ass of themselves, or anything like that?"

"Don't worry," Matt replied. "I'm sure the big screwup will come when I try to give the toast. I'm a tax lawyer for a reason. I hate public speaking."

"Mattster! Where's your confidence. I'm sure you'll be great," Dixon said. "What are you going to say?"

"That's the problem," Matt confided. "I don't really know. Maybe I'll just say: 'May they always be as happy as they are today.' What do you think?"

"Not bad," Dixon mused, "but I think you can do better."

"Well, it has to be short," Matt protested. "The longer I'm up there the greater the margin for error."

"How about this," Dixon said, "I heard it at my cousin's wedding:

'Pete, Vickie, you've both set high standards in your lives and you've always had good, but now you have the best.'"

"I like it," Matt replied. "You've both had good," he said, rehearsing to himself, "but now you have the best."

"Good luck!" Dixon and Sandy chorused as they set their sights on the champagne girl. They worked their way through the crowd, stopping to greet their friends and colleagues.

Dixon stopped and scanned the crowd. After a moment, his gaze became fixed and his jaw dropped ever so slightly. "Holy shit, who's that?"

At the opposite side of the room was a face he had never seen. Dark hair and deep blue eyes that projected like high beams across the room. "She certainly meets your first criterion," Dixon said in a half whisper. "Have you ever seen eyes so blue?"

"Blue eyes, my ass," Sandy responded. "Let's talk about her big boobs and thin arms."

Just then she looked toward the gawking pair and turned a half smile at having caught them in the act.

"Busted!" Sandy joked.

"Christ, the girl of my dreams and now she thinks I'm a rutting school boy. Let's go get that drink so I can feign indifference for a while."

"Fair enough." Sandy led the way through the crowd to the bar.

"Now I just need an excuse to talk to her other than, 'I suppose you noticed me gawking at your blue eyes and big boobs,'" Dixon complained.

"Do you want me to spill a drink on her?" Sandy offered.

"Thanks, but I'm hoping for something better. Call me a hopeless romantic, but I'd like to think an assault isn't a prerequisite to meeting women."

"Wow, you are a hopeless romantic."

As they returned from the bar, Dixon saw the Mattster talking to the vixen. Actually, the more he observed the situation, the more the two appeared to be dates. This could not be. On the other hand, this might be a benefit. If she was actually dating Matt, she must not have as much on the ball as it seemed, and Dixon wouldn't need to waste his time. If they were not dating, however, Matt would be an instant best friend.

"Mattster! How's the toast coming?" Dixon exclaimed with all the enthusiasm and sincerity of a used car salesman. Before Matt could respond, Dixon continued. "Why haven't you introduced us to your girlfriend?" As Dixon turned to look at her, the false bravado that he had been affecting left him and he felt a little light-headed.

"I'm a girl and I'm his friend," she said, "but I'm afraid 'girlfriend' carries a connotation that isn't accurate." She smiled at Dixon and extended her hand. "I'm Jessica Palmer. Matt and my brother were in the same fraternity in college."

As Dixon took her hand he felt a softness not characteristic of a hand. In fact, it was skin like he had never felt before. "So you must be Tom Palmer's sister."

"You know my brother?"

"Only by reputation," Dixon replied. "I'm not sure I ever actually met him."

Jessica let out a sigh. "That's a pretty common response."

Tom Palmer was renowned for his parties. Few people actually knew him, but everyone claimed to have been at one of his events.

Dixon was in awe. Jessica's dark hair and blue eyes were a stunning combination. Her hair looked completely natural, but completely undisciplined, as there was no discernible part and a randomness to the waves. The skin on her face matched the skin on her hands—flawless. Despite appearing to be in her mid-thirties, she had no crow's-feet or wrinkles. In fact, she didn't even appear to have pores.

Oblivious to the connection that seemed to exist between Jessica and Dixon, Sandy jumped in to introduce himself. Jessica graciously shook his hand, but declined to fawn over him in the manner to which he had become accustomed. The way Dixon saw it, this was getting better and better.

"So what do you guys do?" she asked.

"I'm an alumismith," Sandy interjected. "Had I lived in an earlier time, I would have been a blacksmith. But, with all the technological advances, the money now is in aluminum."

"Really," Jessica remarked with a roll of her eyes.

Dixon smiled, having participated in this ruse before. "And I'm an entomologist." After a pause he said, "You know, someone who studies words and their roots."

Jessica paused for a moment and a smile came across her face. "An entomologist studies insects. A person who studies words is an etymologist. But if you were a person who studied words, you'd know the difference between etymologist and entomologist."

Dixon drew back. Of all his inside cerebral jokes, only Sandy had ever figured this one out. Dixon's heart was starting to pound.

Matt broke Dixon's trance. "Jess, I think they want us at the head table."

"Excuse me," Jessica said. "As much as I'd like to stay here and discuss insects, words, or the words that insects use, I need to join the wedding party. It was nice meeting you and I'd like to hear more about your professions later, but I really must go." With that, Jessica took her leave.

"Pretty and smart," Dixon said with admiration. "What more could anyone ask for?"

The receiving line had dwindled, and the guests began taking their seats. As if on cue, glasses began clinking in an effort to quiet the crowd for the toast. "You're the man, Mattster," Dixon cheered silently.

Matt rose from the head table with a feigned look of confidence. Sweat beads were already building. "As most of you know, I'm not really a public speaker. I will not belabor the matter, therefore. I'd just like to say to the bride and groom, you have high standards and expectations in everything. I've known you both for a long time and I'd just like to say, Vickie, you've had good . . . and Pete, you've had better . . . So here's to you!"

Matt raised his glass in a toast, but the crowd sat dumbstruck. He looked around, searching for someone to join the toast. He sat down and frantically conferred with Jessica. "Wait!" Matt jumped back to his feet. "You know I was nervous, but I want to get this right. Pete and Vickie, you've both had good and now you both have the best."

The crowd joined the toast and the evening was spared further awkwardness.

After dinner Dixon sought out Jessica. She didn't seem to know anybody, but appeared comfortable either standing alone or being gracious to those who were introduced to her. Dixon approached from the side and she did not see him coming. "That Matt's quite a catch. Are you sure you don't want to claim him as your boyfriend?"

"Let's see," she pondered, "I could have Matt the successful tax lawyer or I could hold out for the alumismith or the dyslexic etymologist. The choice is just so difficult."

"I'm sorry about that," Dixon offered. "Sandy started it and I just kind of went with the flow."

"And if Sandy decided to jump off a bridge?"

"That would be just fine with me." He waited for a laugh, but none was forthcoming. "I'm afraid in the excitement we never found out what you do."

"Astronaut," she responded. "I'll probably be on the next space shuttle."

"Really," Dixon replied. "I would have guessed Olympic figure skater."

Jessica smiled but stared away from him as though she were bored with him. "I thought you meant what do I do for a living? I'm also an Olympic figure skater, but I don't make any money at it. That's why I said astronaut."

"Well, are you in training for either a mission or the Olympics or can I buy you a drink?" Dixon asked.

"White wine would be nice, thank you."

Dixon hurried off to the bar to fill the request. When he returned, Sandy was again trying to steal his action. Jessica didn't look particularly engaged, but was too polite to blow him off.

"Here's your drink," Dixon said with a smile. Turning to Sandy he said, "I would have gotten you something, but then you wouldn't have had a gracious exit from this conversation." Dixon glared at Sandy and raised his eyebrows high in a nonverbal attempt to emphasize what he had just verbalized.

"I guess maybe I'll go get in line in case there's a dollar dance," Sandy blurted out as he left.

"Now, where were we?" Dixon asked.

"No place that I'm eager to go back to," she said.

"Let's start over," Dixon suggested. "What do you really do?"

"You don't think I'm an astronaut?"

"I think you could be, I just don't think you actually are one. Look, I said I was sorry."

"I guess you're right. I'm a systems analyst for a consulting firm in Atlanta. I'm here on a project that will probably last until the end of the year."

"Really. So you have a house or an apartment in Atlanta, but now you're here for six months?"

"Basically. I sublet my place in Atlanta and the company pays for my place here."

"Still, that's got to be inconvenient."

"It is, but part of the reason I took the assignment was to be nearer my family for a while."

"Where do they live?"

"My dad lives in LaCrosse, which is where I grew up. My mom now lives in Minneapolis."

"Oh, they're divorced."

"Yes," she responded. "Since I was little. I'm afraid neither is doing that well health-wise and I thought it would be good to spend some time with them."

Dixon was now feeling even more sheepish about the vocational prank. "So what's up with you and Matt?"

"Nothing. He said he needed a date and I don't know many people in town, so I was looking for something to do. It's not the high point of the social season, but it's nice to get out and meet interesting people with fascinating careers. By the way, do you plan to tell me what you really do?"

"Trial lawyer."

Jessica drew back a little at the sound of his words.

"Now you understand why I make up other occupations," he said with a grin.

"No, I have nothing against lawyers. It's just that my dad was a trial lawyer and that seemed to consume him. That, and the stress helped him to consume his share of alcohol."

"I'm sorry to hear that," Dixon said. "Is he still drinking?"

"No, he's been dry for about ten years."

As much as Dixon wanted to ask her out, the tone just seemed too somber. Furthermore, it felt as though many eyes were upon them and breaking out the pen and paper would give the gossips more chum than necessary. So Dixon and Jessica just continued with their small talk. Finally, Matt came to ask her to dance. As she started toward the dance floor she turned and, with a smile, said, "It was nice chatting with you." And with that, Dixon had missed another opportunity.

# CHAPTER 10

Dixon waited until Tuesday to begin his pursuit of Jessica Palmer. With Sharon out of town, Dixon found himself regularly distracted by thoughts of Jessica. The chances of a random encounter were remote, so he took matters into his own hands. He called Matt.

"Matt Colter," announced the voice on the other end.

"Matt, it's Dixon. How're you doin'?"

"Not bad, thanks. Did you call to give me more grief for the way I massacred your simple toast?"

Dixon responded, "Matt, I can assure you that was one of the most memorable toasts ever."

"Thanks. I hope that isn't the only reason for your call."

"No, not at all. I don't want to be a hound dog, but I'm wondering what you can tell me about your friend Jessica."

"Now you're going after my date!"

"That's part of what I'm asking. Is there something going on between the two of you or between her and somebody else?"

"There's nothing going on between us, and I don't really know if she has anything else going on. Considering she came to live here by herself for six months, I doubt there's anything serious."

"That was my take on it," Dixon said. "I'm wondering about baggage, though. Has she been married? If not, why not? Those types of things."

"Well, I hate to talk out of school, especially about someone I'm fond of. I was good friends with her brother in college and, as you may know, he liked to drink—a lot. She has always seemed a little more straight-laced. She is sweet, smart, and funny, but I think she has a little bit of an edge. She gets asked out a lot, but I don't really remember her being that involved with anybody. Her brother once told me she had a boyfriend in high school who broke up with her, and she more or less vowed no guy would ever hurt her again."

"Wow. That's definitely out of school."

"Look," Matt came back, "I think she's terrific and she did ask me about you on the way home from the wedding. So if you're interested, I think there's an opportunity. I just want you to proceed with caution."

"I appreciate that."

"Do you want me to set something up," Matt asked. "I'm supposed to have lunch with her tomorrow, so I can ask her about it."

"No. If you give me her number, I'll just call her." Dixon could afford the confidence with which he declined assistance. He was certain Matt would mention their discussion to Jessica so that when Dixon did call, they would be able to avoid the awkwardness often associated with "the first call."

◆

Dixon had written Jessica's number on a yellow stickie on the desk in his bedroom. It sat next to the phone, daring Dixon to make the call. Every time he walked in the bedroom, the stickie ridiculed him for his delay. After two days, he mustered the courage and beat a path toward the phone. When he got there, he turned and walked back to the living room. *Wasn't this supposed to get easier after high school?* He walked back into the bedroom and picked up the phone. He dialed the prefix, but then hung up. *Maybe I should check the news first.*

He finally picked up the phone and dialed. As it began ringing, he thought about how terrific it would be to talk to an answering machine. He could listen to her voice and leave a message to alert her that he would call. On the other hand, Matt probably mentioned Dixon's interest to her, and Matt would have alerted him if she had expressed horror at the thought of dating him.

Just when he thought he was in the clear, the phone clicked and a female voice stated a melodic "hello."

"Hi, is this Jessica?" Dixon managed.

"Yes it is. Who's calling?"

"It's Dixon, from the wedding."

"Oh, the wordsmith. Or are you an insect guy, I forgot?"

"Well, because I'm a lawyer, I guess some people would perceive me as both."

She chuckled.

Dixon continued. "Is it fair to assume that you're never going to forgive me for our little prank at the wedding?"

"No, that's not fair to assume. You did already apologize, and I was just having a little fun."

"Speaking of which, did you have a good time at the wedding?" He realized it wasn't a penetrating question, but it was about the only common ground they had.

"All things considered, it was okay. If nothing else, Matt's little slip should provide a good story for years to come. How about you?"

"It was all right. Sandy got a little impatient because we were about the only people there without dates, so we didn't stay very long after the dancing started."

"Matt and I stayed as long as seemed proper for the best man, but, because I didn't know anybody, he was kind enough to not make it last all night."

Dixon struggled through some additional small talk. He soon found himself moving past the pleasantries to the purpose. "So, the reason I'm calling is . . . I was wondering . . . if you're in any sort of a relationship." The words sounded a little too formal after Dixon spoke them, but there was no taking them back.

"Why do you want to know?"

*Why do I want to know? Is she kidding? What could be more obvious?* Somewhat put off by her response, Dixon recoiled. "I'm sorry, you're right. It's none of my business and I'm sorry I invaded your privacy."

"I didn't say you invaded my privacy, I just asked why you wanted to know."

Not mollified by her response, Dixon said, "Well, I wasn't completely honest when I said I was a lawyer. Actually, I'm trained as a lawyer but I'm in the insurance business. I wanted to know if you were in a relationship because I can get you some great rates on dual, whole-life, single-premium insurance policies." He deliberately tried not to sound sarcastic because, in his mind, his matter-of-fact tone provided even greater sarcasm.

She hesitated before responding. "I'm sorry, I guess answering your question with a question was rude. I know I'm a little too defensive at times, but you've made the effort to call me and I didn't make the effort to make it very comfortable for you."

Dixon stayed on the line, but didn't say anything.

"Look," Jessica continued, "if the reason you asked was because you'd like to ask me out, I'm not in a relationship and I would like to go out with you."

Dixon was impressed with the way she grabbed the reins of vulnerability and relieved with the direction the conversation had turned. "Great. I'm out of town next week, but how about the following weekend?"

"That sounds great," she responded. "What day?"

"I don't have a preference. Maybe I should call you from the road next week and we can firm something up."

"That sounds fine. Where will you be?"

"I'm going up to Hibbing. I have a case up there and I'm taking some depositions. Some very unusual depositions at that."

"How so?"

"Well, I represent a guy who was having sex with the neighbor's wife and when the neighbor broke in, my guy shot him. I have to prove self-defense or some reasonable facsimile thereof, and the thrust of my case—if you'll excuse the pun—is showing that my guy could not have been lying in wait because he was too busy with the neighbor lady. As a result, I'm going to be asking her all sorts of questions about exactly what they were doing at the time of the break-in."

"Can't you just ask your client what happened?"

"That's the tricky part. My client committed suicide. I have to prove my case through adverse witnesses."

"Well, do me a favor and spare me the lurid details," she said.

"Fair enough. Well ... I guess I'll just call you next week then."

"That would be great."

Dixon said goodnight and hung up. As soon as the phone hit the cradle he jumped in the air with his arms raised. He proceeded to dance around the room doing the lawn mower pull-start motion as if he had just hit a home run to win the World Series.

Jessica had displayed an attitude, but had also displayed empathy. The attitude aroused excitement, while the empathy evoked respect. Dixon had only one problem. He didn't want to two-time Jessica and, notwithstanding his recent feelings about Sharon, he felt obliged not to lead her on any further. In short, he needed to find a way to do what he had been putting off. He needed to break up with Sharon.

# CHAPTER 11

D IXON SPENT SEVERAL days pondering how he would break up with Sharon, but couldn't come up with a strategy with which he felt comfortable. He'd never really had to dump anybody. Either he just stopped calling, one of them moved away, or there was some sort of mutuality. On reflection, he realized he'd never really been dumped either. There were plenty of relationships that had ended, but none that required the desire to be verbalized.

He had no desire to hurt Sharon, and that made matters worse. As he continued to suffer through the relationship, he became increasingly resentful of the whole situation. He had been displaying substantial indifference and hoped she would pick up on it and they could have a calm conversation about the fact that the relationship was no longer meeting expectations. With any luck, Sharon would claim she was equally unsatisfied and it would look as if it was at least part her idea. Dixon wanted to give her an out, but she just wasn't recognizing it.

They never spoke about the night of the Broadway show. When Sharon returned from her parents' cabin, she had called and acted as though nothing had happened. Dixon showed no enthusiasm, but took the path of least resistance. Ultimately, he had promised to go to a dinner party with her, and he thought the fair thing would be to wait until afterwards because otherwise she wouldn't have a date for the party. Furthermore, she'd probably be forced to spend the party telling everyone that she got dumped.

Dixon lived halfway between Sharon and the party, so the plan was for her to pick him up. Oblivious to Dixon's plan, Sharon announced she was bringing "a little surprise for afterwards." The responsibility of packing an overnight bag and driving were two additional impediments to Sharon's punctuality. Dixon was ready to go at the appointed time, but he had reading material available that would last at least a half hour. Every bit of it was necessary. Because the party was with Sharon's friends, Dixon wasn't concerned.

Sharon called from her cell phone when she was a few blocks away, and Dixon was on the street when she pulled up. Dixon climbed in and said "Hi," but made no attempt to kiss her.

"You don't have a little kiss for me?" Sharon implored.

"Sure. I thought you'd be concerned about your makeup." With that Dixon leaned over and gave her a quick peck.

The drive to St. Paul was uneventful. Dixon asked her a variety of questions about her day and about some problem she'd been having at work. Dixon didn't really listen; he just tried to keep her going to avoid the awkward silence. She didn't ask him about the depositions or the trip to Hibbing. Without prompting, she talked about herself, an argument she'd had with her hair stylist, and a variety of other things about which Dixon couldn't get excited.

The party was at the home of Sharon's best friend Judy. She was an outgoing but sometimes overbearing woman who worked with Sharon. She was pleasant looking and lucky to have snagged her husband before her ass began its geometric expansion. The rest of her body remained normal sized, but her butt had ballooned into—well, balloons.

Her husband, Steve, was a dentist, and he had all the humor and mirth usually associated with his chosen profession. On the other hand, at least Dixon knew him, which was more than he could say about most of the other guests.

The cocktail hour was nearly over when Dixon and Sharon arrived. They found drinks and offered the obligatory compliments about Judy's decorating skills. Before long, a buffet table was set up and everyone got in line. Sharon and Dixon filled their plates and found seats in the den. They were joined by two couples that Dixon didn't know. Still, he had little trouble getting a conversation started.

They exchanged a variety of stories about best restaurants, worst restaurants, best vacations, worst boss. Dixon was somewhat accomplished as a raconteur and prided himself on his ability to tell a story. Sharon followed everyone else's story with an anecdote that she announced was "even better." Almost invariably, just before the punch line she would pause when she remembered leaving out an essential fact and say something like: "Did I mention they were on a deserted island?" and the story would fall far short of its billing.

As the night wore on, Dixon took note of the couples around him. A pair in the corner held hands once they'd finished eating. Another couple was expecting their first child and both had the glow usually associated only with expectant mothers. Even Steve and Judy seemed to exchange tender looks as they put the food on the table. It dawned on Dixon that such feelings had never been part of his and Sharon's relationship. She was merely a companion, and not even a very good one.

After dinner, the guests reconfigured, with the men staking out the kitchen and the women taking the den. The women all worked together, and had a tendency to talk shop—complete with specialized jargon and personal references that were foreign to everyone else. Thus, not only did they talk about things no one else was interested in, they spoke in a language that prevented an outsider from understanding even if they wanted to. Dixon tried to strike up conversations with some of the other "significant others." There wasn't much common ground in terms of careers, background, or political philosophies, so the talk turned to sports and the Minnesota Twins.

Dixon loved to talk baseball because it could be easily broken down into components and analyzed. "Baseball involves a series of specific decisions that any fan can scrutinize," Dixon explained. "In football, most fans don't understand the nuance of different plays or strategies, and the only coaching decision subject to much analysis is whether to run or pass or whether to go for it on fourth down. Basketball and hockey are similar. The coaches may be making dozens of decisions on an ongoing basis, but few are evident to the spectators. Baseball, on the other hand, is filled with strategic decisions and, as a result, lends itself to cocktail party debates. The rampant second-guessing is what led to the maxim "There are three things every man thinks he can do better than any other man: run a restaurant, manage a baseball team, and make love to a woman." Dixon also enjoyed the baseball debates because you could have dramatically different opinions, but nobody seemed to go home with hurt feelings.

Apparently not content with her own conversation, Sharon yelled in to interrupt the one between the men. "Are you guys talking sports again?"

"Don't take that as a sign we found your conversation dull," Dixon responded. "We just didn't feel like we could intelligently participate in your discussion so we went for a lower common denominator."

"Very funny," Sharon responded.

All Dixon could think was, *it won't be long now.*

The party broke up at about 10:30 and Dixon and Sharon headed for home. Sharon asked Dixon to drive her car, and he was only too happy to oblige. Sharon believed she needed to make eye contact with people she was talking to in the car, and it annoyed Dixon to no end. Sharon would routinely turn around to look at people riding in the backseat, even when she was driving in rush-hour traffic.

Dixon was quiet as he thought about the mission ahead. He'd hoped his silence would prompt a "what's wrong?" or similar inquiry. Either Sharon was oblivious to the problem or was completely aware of it and was too afraid of the outcome to pursue it. When they got to Dixon's place, Sharon grabbed her overnight bag out of the trunk. Dixon wanted to say, "don't bother," but he didn't want to start the process in public.

When they got inside his apartment, Dixon went for the living room. Sharon told him to wait there and disappeared into his bedroom with her overnight bag. *Oh shit,* was all Dixon could think. *How could he break up with her while she was wearing something slinky?* It had nothing to do with the fact that he would be aroused. Instead, it just seemed like a ridiculous amount of rejection to tell a half-naked woman that you don't want to be with her even though she is in such a state of readiness.

Suddenly the bedroom door swung open and a fully clothed Sharon marched out clutching a yellow Post-it note she'd found on Dixon's desk. "Who's Jessica Palmer?" Sharon demanded. "Is that your new cleaning lady?"

*Omigod,* Dixon thought to himself. *How could I have left that note out?*

"Are you going to answer me?" Sharon demanded again.

Dixon was never one for deceit and couldn't see any benefit in lying even if he had been good at it. But still, this wasn't the way he'd wanted it to go. "What were you doing going through my personal stuff?"

"Are you going to answer me or not? Who is Jessica Palmer?"

Dixon stared at her with a look of helplessness. Not finding a response that would short-circuit the dispute, he said, "That's a woman that I just met that I'm going to start dating."

Sharon was momentarily dumbstruck by the answer. She'd apparently been prepared to deal with a denial, but the admission seemed to knock the wind out of her. She searched without success for an appropriate response. Finally, she said, "Who is she? Where did you meet her?"

It occurred to Dixon that Sharon's reaction might be appropriate upon the discovery of infidelity after twenty years of marriage and three children, but it was out of place in a relationship that was only a few months old and which had never really generated any emotional pledges of any significance. Furthermore, Sharon acted as if she'd been two-timed when, as she was finding out, she was being replaced.

"I don't see why any of that matters," Dixon said.

Sharon's rage was not abating. "Well, what does this mean?"

Frustrated by her continuing inability to grasp the obvious, Dixon finally said, "Well, I can tell you with pretty much absolute certainty that you and I are not going to be dating anymore."

"Well, I can say that too!" Sharon snapped.

Now frustrated by her childish behavior, Dixon responded in kind. "Well—I said it first." Dixon didn't really care who broke up with whom, but he couldn't help but lash out. He would never be able to have an adult conversation with Sharon, so he might as well try and communicate on her level.

After a long silence, Sharon pleaded, "Was it something I did?"

"Sharon, this just hasn't been working for me for a long time. I tried to give it a chance, but that made me even more unhappy."

Sharon was crying now, but tried to hide the tears. "Can't we talk about it?"

"I don't think there's anything to say. I don't want to be mean about it. I just want to be done."

Sharon's voice got higher as she tried to talk through her tears. "You don't know how hard this has been for me. You have these walls you've built around yourself and you won't let anyone get close to you."

"It's probably fair to say that I've been holding you at arm's length, but I didn't want to lead you on. This isn't going anywhere, and I've known that for a while.

"That's it then? Four months and then 'poof' without a hint?"

"Sharon, I gave the best hints I could. The mere fact that I haven't wanted to have sex with you for the last several weeks should have been a hint. I'm looking for something else and, y'know, I might never find it. All I know is I'm not happy now."

"Fine," she said. "Don't come crying back to me when you change your mind."

Dixon saw her last statement as an attempt to get the last word. He was happy to give her that if it would give her some dignity and otherwise end the ordeal. "Okay," he said with a graveness that didn't match his feelings.

Dixon followed her out but didn't speak. As they approached her car, he dropped back so he could watch her get in, but wouldn't be so close as to tempt a final embrace. "Good-bye," Dixon said.

"Bye," she said curtly.

As Dixon returned to his apartment, he pondered what had just happened. He wasn't happy about the way it had transpired, but he felt as if a heavy burden had been lifted. He had no reason to believe he would want to date Sharon again, so he wasn't concerned about the finality she tried to impose. Still, he was saddened that another relationship had ended.

# CHAPTER 12

Aᴼᵀᴇʀ ᴛʜᴇ ᴊᴜᴅɢᴇ had quashed the subpoenas, Dixon sent amended notices rescheduling the depositions for a couple weeks after the criminal trial. Judge Stockman had only stayed discovery in the MacKenzie matter through the criminal trial and, considering the outcome, Dixon felt comfortable proceeding. McGuckin hadn't objected. Whether the Constitutional issue remained was unclear. Dixon assumed, however, that McGuckin was counting on a recovery in the personal injury matter in order to pay the bills in the criminal matter. As with most lawyers, the most important right was the lawyer's right to get paid.

Debi Krueller hadn't testified at the criminal trial. Immediately after the incident, she had seemed ready to do anything to implicate her husband. Time had passed, however, and there was no telling what her testimony would be. One thing for certain, Dixon would get her under oath to avoid the surprise he had during the Bennie Fosnick trial.

Dixon had heard Lester's story at the trial: He loved his wife, but couldn't control her and got in a fight over her drinking; she took a fancy to the local rich guy and Les was so consumed with jealousy that he had to stop her at all costs; he broke in to stop the adultery, but was shot before he could do anything. Dixon wanted to ask Les some follow-up questions, but the main purpose of the depositions was to get Debi Krueller's testimony. She was scheduled for the afternoon, and Lester would be the witness the next day.

Hank had asked to attend, but Dixon discouraged it. A party to a lawsuit has an absolute right to attend depositions, but it is not that common for the right to be exercised. Depositions are potentially tedious, and it is usually preferable to get the summary afterward. Hank was persistent, but Dixon had convinced him his presence might inhibit Debi's testimony. After all, part of the subject matter was going to be her sexual relations with Hank's brother. Even someone like Debi might fail to give the detail desired out of a newly discovered sense of shame or decorum. If the goal of the deposition was information, Hank would just have to wait for the box scores.

The Court Reporter had arranged for the use of a conference room at the courthouse. The depositions would be basically devoid of the normal creature comforts available when conducted at law firms, but the price was right. Besides, an overabundance of pop and coffee generally resulted in too many bathroom breaks.

A few minutes after the appointed time, Debi, Lester, and McGuckin made their entrance. Dixon was a little stunned to see them enter together. The estranged wife appeared to be no longer estranged, and that was not good news. Dixon had anticipated she might not be cooperative, but it now appeared likely she was actually cooperating with the other side.

McGuckin sported the same suit he'd worn the first day of trial. Debi wore a dress, but also wore a waist-length jean jacket that undercut any formality or class that the dress might have otherwise conveyed. Lester was out of his leisure suit, but wore gray slacks that tried to pass for flannel and a black leather motorcycle jacket. He was still badly dressed, but he was now badly dressed from the eighties, as opposed to the seventies look he had at the trial.

Dixon rose from his chair and extended his hand, "Mr. McGuckin, we didn't have a chance to meet before, I'm Dixon Donnelly."

"Pleased to make your acquaintance," he drawled while extending his hand for a shake. "These are my clients, Lester and Debi Krueller."

"How do you do?" Dixon stated with an extended hand.

Lester and Debi both shook his hand, but were silent. It may have been out of a sense that Dixon was the enemy, but it seemed more likely that they were just unfamiliar with basic social graces.

Dixon had hoped Lester was just dropping Debi off, but he promptly removed his jacket and took a seat. Watching her humilia-

tion under oath was apparently either a part of the retribution he
wanted to inflict or part of the mental abuse she was regularly made
to endure.

After a few more pleasantries, Dixon nodded to the court reporter
and said, "Why don't you go ahead and swear the witness." The
reporter obliged and the process began.

"Mrs. Krueller, as you just found out, my name is Dixon Donnelly
and I'll be taking your deposition today. I trust that Mr. McGuckin
has explained this process, but I want to go over a few things for the
record. As an initial matter, is Mr. McGuckin acting as your lawyer
today?"

She hesitated and looked at McGuckin for help. His raised eyebrows and slow nods apparently helped her. "Mr. McGuckin is my
husband's lawyer in this lawsuit and I guess he's my attorney as
well."

"Okay, fine. As he may have told you, this is a process where I ask
you questions and you are answering under oath. The court reporter
will take down everything that is said, but she doesn't record anything else. As a result, you cannot answer questions by nodding your
head or shrugging your shoulders. In fact, you should avoid using
'uh-huh' and 'uh-uh' in order to make for a clear record. Do you
understand that?"

"Uh-huh," she responded.

Dixon, trying to be patient upon realizing what a long day he was
in for, responded, "See, that's what you're not supposed to do. Did
you mean 'yes'?"

"Uh-huh, I mean yes," she said nervously.

"Furthermore," Dixon continued, "the court reporter can only
record one person at a time, so please wait until I finish my questions before answering. I sometimes ask long questions and, even
if you think you know what I'm going to ask, please wait until I'm
done. Okay?"

"Yeah, I mean yes."

"If you don't understand my question, please ask me to clarify
it. I'm not trying to trick you. I'm only trying to find out what
you know. Also, if you need to take a break, just say so and, unless

there's a question pending, we can probably accommodate you. Fair enough?"

"Okay."

"And before I forget, I referred to you earlier as Mrs. Krueller. Do you prefer Mrs. or Ms.?"

"I guess I prefer Debi."

"Well, for the sake of decorum, I'll probably use a title, so which do you prefer?"

"Either is fine. I guess I go by Mrs. more than Ms." The dialogue seemed to help her get comfortable.

Debi Krueller wasn't a classy woman, but she had a decided sex appeal. Dixon could see how Duke might have been taken by her. She had delicate features, gently curled brown hair, and a trim but shapely physique. Furthermore, she had an air of vulnerability, and was the perfect fit for somebody who was looking for someone to rescue.

"Mrs. Krueller," Dixon began, "have you ever given testimony before, either in a trial or in a deposition?"

"Yes."

"How many times?"

"Well," she said, "let's see. I testified in my divorce, and I've testified in connection with some restraining orders. So I think two or three times."

"Tell me about the divorce trial. Who was your ex-husband and how long ago was it?"

"Objection!" McGuckin barked. "That's a multiple question, or should I say questions."

"I'm sorry," Dixon replied. "I was trying to expedite things, but I'm afraid you're right. Mrs. Krueller, give me a brief synopsis of your first marriage starting with when you were married, to whom, and concluding with the date of the divorce." The new question was substantially more burdensome than the one that had drawn the objection, but the phraseology was better.

"I was married to Nick Thurber. We got married in 1988, we had two kids, he abused me from the honeymoon on, and we got divorced in 1995. That's about all there is to say about that."

Dixon tried to look as though he wasn't interested in the sordid details. "What were the issues requiring testimony? Was there a dispute about custody, money, or something else?"

"Mostly custody. I had been through alcohol treatment and he thought I was unfit."

"Where was that court proceeding held?" Dixon continued.

"Grand Rapids, Minnesota," she responded. "I think that's Itasca County."

"How about the restraining order proceedings, were they filed here?"

"That's right. The proceedings were right upstairs."

Dixon continued to fill in the available details that would enable him to search the court files if necessary to review the prior cases. He didn't want to antagonize her any more than he had to, but he wanted access to as much information as possible.

"Where do you currently live?"

"The Chateau."

"The Chateau. What's that?"

"It's the mobile home park south of town."

"That's the name of it?"

"The full name is 'The Chateau Le Blanc Camelot.' Most people just call it The Chateau or Camelot."

Dixon smiled. "That's quite a name. What is it—a gated trailer park?"

"No, I don't know why it's called that. I mean, it's nicer than most mobile home parks because it's all double-wides and each has its own yard. But I don't know why it's called that."

"Well, I guess that's not really important. Why don't you tell me when you first met Duke MacKenzie?"

"I guess it was about May of last year.

"So, about three or four months before his death?"

"That's right," she responded.

"How did you meet him?"

"The guy who used to run the trailer park left town, so Duke started handling some of the maintenance. One day I seen him working at the park and I walked over and introduced myself."

Dixon was armed with some information Duke had shared with Hank. "Were you sunbathing at the time?"

"I don't remember. I might have been."

"And is it true that you sometimes sunbathe topless?"

"No, I don't know where you got that idea. I might unstrap my top to avoid tan lines while I'm on my stomach, just like everybody else." Debi's initial nervousness was giving way to defiance.

"Well, if you're all alone and figure nobody's around, isn't it fair to say you might not pay much attention to whether your top was on when, for example, you got up to answer the phone?"

"Objection!" McGuckin bellowed. "What difference does it make?"

"Sir," Dixon replied with a false showing of respect, "I saw the way you conned the jury in the criminal case into believing that Mr. MacKenzie seduced Mrs. Krueller, and, expecting that you'll continue to sing the same tune, I think it's my prerogative to explore the circumstances leading to the relationship."

McGuckin gave Dixon an angry stare before shaking his head dismissively. "I don't like your characterization of my trial strategy, and I don't see how this is relevant, but if it appeals to your prurient interest I guess I can't stop you." You could always tell that someone was a lawyer, because no one else used the word "prurient" except those who had studied the Supreme Court's attempt to define pornography.

Dixon turned back to the witness. "Can you answer the question please?"

With a smirk, Debi responded, "If someone wanted to spy on me, they probably would have seen my titties, if that's what you're asking."

According to Dixon's information, Debi had walked over to Duke while topless and struck up a casual conversation. Unfortunately, the only other witness to the event was now dead.

"When did you first have physical relations with Duke MacKenzie?" Dixon inquired.

"The night of the shooting," she replied.

"So, are you telling me you didn't have sex with Duke MacKenzie while your husband was away on a fishing trip?" This one caught

Debi and Lester by surprise. Suddenly, Lester sat up as though he was hearing something for the first time.

"That's what I'm telling you," she said in an unconvincing voice.

"So you don't recall an incident during which you snuck into the caretaker's house in the middle of the night, slipped into Duke's bed, and began performing oral sex while he was still sleeping?"

Lester was now fidgeting and staring at his wife. Dixon realized he might have given Lester an excuse for more spousal abuse, but there wasn't really anything he could do.

"Who told you that!" she snapped. "Just like a man to have a fantasy and drag an innocent woman through it."

"So, that's a 'no?'" Dixon asked.

"Your goddamn right it's a no," she responded.

Dixon continued to probe the subject, but tried not to stray too far from his purpose. He asked about additional contacts between the first meeting and the weekend of the incident, but her memory was conveniently short. Considering she had once claimed to want Lester dead, she was telling a decidedly different story.

Dixon proceeded methodically for the next couple hours, eliciting more details. Liars can generally remember the big lies in order to keep their story straight, but the details usually cause a problem. Dixon asked as many questions as relevance and time would allow. While she might manage to keep her story consistent on this day, he would run her through the drill again at trial and see if her story could withstand such scrutiny.

Having covered the background chronology in detail, Dixon was ready to cover the weekend of the incident. "Tell me about the night your husband threw you out of the house."

"He never threw me out of the house," she replied.

"I'm sorry," Dixon said, feigning confusion, "wasn't there an incident where Lester threw all of your clothes out in the front yard of your house?"

"That doesn't mean he threw me out of the house. I don't know what he was doing, but just because he took my things out of the bedroom doesn't mean he wanted me out of the house." Here was an answer that smacked of coaching from McGuckin.

"So, you really don't know what message he intended to send when he put your clothes on the front lawn?"

"That's right," she replied.

"Well, what did you do when that happened?"

"I went into town to see what was going on."

"Did you go to a bar?"

"Eventually. I ran some errands and then went to The Boondocks."

"That's a bar?"

"Yes."

"Is that where you encountered Duke MacKenzie?"

"Yes."

"Tell me what happened then?"

"I told Duke that Lester and I had a fight and I wasn't sure I wanted to go home. Duke bought me a few drinks, and we sat and talked for a while. Finally, he said he was leaving, but if I needed a place to sleep he had an extra bed at his place."

"Was this the place in the trailer park?" Dixon interrupted.

"No, his regular house on Moose Lake."

"What did you say to his invitation?"

"I said, 'Great. I don't want to go home and it's cheaper than a hotel.'" Her anger had subsided and her tone became breathy, like a Hollywood starlet from the fifties.

"What were the sleeping arrangements when you got there?"

"He slept upstairs in his bedroom and I slept on the rollout in the den on the main floor."

"Was there any physical intimacy at all?"

"No. I might have hugged him and thanked him for helping me out, but there was nothing intimate."

"Did you have drinks at the house, sit and talk, watch a video, or what?"

"Pretty much just went to bed. I think Duke was looking for something more, but he respected me as a lady."

Dixon watched her as she answered and couldn't help but visualize her naked. He decided if she were staying in his house he would probably be interested in sex, so there was every reason to believe her when she said Duke had such an interest. On the other hand, her denial that they had sex was not believable. Duke had confided in Hank that the sex was frequent, good, and often unusual. Unfortunately for Dixon's own prurient interest, Duke had not provided many other details.

"Tell me what happened the next day," Dixon continued.

"Well, I woke up first and decided to make breakfast." This seemed to catch Lester's attention as another thing that Debi didn't do for him but was happy to do for another man. "After a while, Duke got up and we ate and had coffee."

"According to your previous statement, Lester showed up at Duke's house."

"That's right," she responded, with a bat of her eyes. "While we were still drinking coffee."

"So, what happened?"

"Les came to the door and walked in and wanted to know what I'd been doing and why I didn't come home. I told him I didn't know if I was welcome there, so I stayed at Duke's place."

"Well, Mrs. Krueller, according to your statement to the sheriff, Lester accused you of having had sexual relations with Duke. Are you changing your story?"

"No. Les did say something like, 'what's going on, are you guys having an affair?'"

Dixon shuffled some papers to find the sheriff's report. "Isn't it true that you previously told the sheriff that your husband said words to the effect of: 'I know you're banging my wife and when I catch you I'm going to blow your fucking head off!'"

She was nonchalant in her response. "Well, I was drunk when I gave that report to the sheriff."

"But you gave two reports to the sheriff, they both say the same thing, and the second one was done at nine in the morning," Dixon said incredulously.

"Well, at the time, I was mad at Les, so I woulda said anything to get him in trouble."

"Okay," Dixon responded with a disbelieving sigh. "What happened next?"

"That's about it. Duke said 'no, no, don't worry, I just gave her a place to stay,' and Les took off."

Dixon plodded through a few more questions to tie up some

loose ends. He scanned his notes and continued, "What happened that night?"

"Well, I didn't want Les to know where I was, so Duke and I decided to go to Duluth to go dancing."

"What time did you go?"

"About six or seven, I guess," she replied.

Dixon had her fill in some more details before getting to the essentials. "Where did you spend the night?"

"At a Best Western or something like that. I don't really know. I was pretty drunk."

While hesitant to show his hand, Dixon asked, "If I told you Duke's credit card records show he paid for a room at the Edgewater, would that refresh your recollection?"

She paused, suddenly realizing that third-party evidence could be her undoing. "Yeah, that could be. I think it might be called the Best Western Edgewater."

"So, the two of you shared one room?"

"Yes."

"And one bed?"

Debi paused and it was unclear who she wanted to deceive—Dixon or Lester. "How do you know there wasn't two beds?"

"Well, I'm sure the hotel can tell us, but right now I'm asking you about it."

Having not found refuge in that answer, she said, "I slept on the floor. I tried to lay on the bed, but I had the spins so I slept on the floor."

"Where did Duke sleep?"

"On the bed. At first he was going to sleep on the floor, but we switched when I felt sick."

"Did you have sex either on the floor or in the bed?"

"No."

"How about in the car on the way there?"

A seductive smile crossed her face. "Like, what do you think, that we're in high school?"

"If you don't mind, I'm the one asking the questions here. Just tell me, did you have sex in the car either on the way to Duluth or on the way from the bar to the hotel?"

"Absolutely not."

"So if the police lab found your pubic hairs on the seat of the car, that would just be a coincidence, is that your position?"

"Objection!" bellowed McGuckin. "Not only am I unaware of such evidence, I'm quite certain Hibbing's finest don't even have the capability to conduct such an analysis."

Dixon had bluffed, in part. There was no police report, but Duke had reported it to Hank. Apparently not content with performing a "mobile hummer," Debi had actually tried to mount Duke while he was driving.

"What's your objection, and are you instructing her not to answer?" Dixon inquired.

"Assumes facts not in evidence," McGuckin responded. "I'm not instructing her, but I think it's a waste of time."

Turning to Mrs. Krueller, Dixon stated, "Please answer the question."

"What question?"

"If the police report shows your pubic hair on the seat, how would you explain it?" Dixon grimaced to himself upon realizing what a poor question he had asked.

"How would I know?" she said with a shrug. "I was wearing shorts part of the time and it could have just got there."

As the questioning continued, Debi fixed her gaze on Dixon. She answered in matter-of-fact tones, but she looked at him in a decidedly flirtatious way. The exchange appeared to be oblivious to everyone except Dixon, and he found himself mildly aroused by the secret communications apparently passing between them. There was a distinct possibility that she was just toying with him, but he didn't really care.

"So, what did you do on Sunday when you got back?" Dixon continued.

"I went home."

"Was your husband there?"

"Yes."

"Did the two of you talk?"

"Not really," she replied.

"Then what?"

"Not much. Les went out to get something and I might have watched TV. I think the Vikings might have been on."

"When did Les get back?"

"Couple hours later, maybe three," she said.

"What happened?"

"We started arguing again, so I left."

Dixon paused to reflect on whether he had missed anything up to that point. "When did you next see Duke MacKenzie?"

"Later that afternoon. We had a barbecue at his place. Duke, me, my daughter and her boyfriend."

"Did your husband show up?'

"Yes."

"Was he invited?"

"Of course not."

Dixon didn't want to look directly at Les or McGuckin, but turned his head to his notepad so he could catch a glance. "What did he say?"

"He wanted to know whether I was coming home that night. I told him it was none of his business."

"Did he say anything threatening to Duke MacKenzie?"

"No, not that I remember," she replied.

"Are you aware that both your daughter and her boyfriend told the sheriff's deputy that Les told Duke if he caught the two of you having sex he would 'blow Duke's fucking head off'?"

"I don't know what they heard, or whether they would tell the truth. They don't like Les very much, so there's no telling what they were thinking."

"Anything else happen while Les was there?"

"Not that I remember."

"How long was he there?"

"Five, ten minutes tops."

"What time did your daughter and her boyfriend leave?"

"Probably around eight or nine."

Dixon was ready to get to the heart of the matter. "So, when did you and Duke first have sex?"

"That night."

Dixon glanced again at Les and noticed he was at least pretending to believe her. "So, after all that time together over the weekend, staying in the same rooms, drinking in excess, and everything else, why do you all of a sudden decide to have sex that night?"

"Well, Lester was accusing me of it all along. So, I figured, if my husband is going to think that way I might as well go ahead and do it. I mean, if someone you loved didn't trust you, wouldn't you want to do something about it?"

Dixon paused. "So, are you saying after Lester removed your belongings from your bedroom and you spent two nights with Duke MacKenzie, you thought your husband should have believed you weren't having sex with MacKenzie?"

"Well I wasn't!" she snapped. "Just 'cause I was mad and wanted to get even, he shoulda known I wouldn't throw it all away for nothing."

Dixon resisted the urge to ask "throw what away?" Instead, he asked, "What did you do after your daughter left?"

"Nothing. Made a drink I guess."

"What were you drinking?"

"Who cares what I was drinking?"

"Please answer the question," he implored.

"Windsor Coke," she said in a patronizing voice.

"How many did you have that night—all totaled?"

"One. Maybe I'd made the second one when Duke came at me and wanted to mess around."

"And after the shooting, did you have anymore?"

"Of course not, what do you think I am." In her zeal to defend her honor, Debi had now contradicted her earlier claim that she was drunk when she gave the first police report.

"How about drugs, were you on any?"

"No."

"Okay, you testified a minute ago that 'Duke came at you.' Could you expand on that and tell me exactly what happened?"

"Just that. He kinda grabbed me in the kitchen and said he couldn't stand having to hold off because he thought I was a beautiful woman and he wanted to have me. I thought, 'what the hell, Lester thinks I'm doin' him anyway, why fight it.'"

Dixon's thoughts drifted to a fantasy of such a willing participant, but he caught himself before anyone noticed. "Did you say anything, either 'oh, okay,' or 'no, we better not,' or anything like that?"

"Not that I remember. He just started kissing me and there wasn't nothin' to say."

"Where did this start?"

"I don't know. Kitchen I guess."

"Did you discuss what would happen if Lester showed up?"

"Not really. I guess I suggested that we go upstairs and turn off the lights so he couldn't see in if he showed up."

"Did one of you lock the doors?"

"Yeah. I think Duke did that as soon as we went inside."

Nodding, Dixon continued, "So you went upstairs and had sex?"

"Yes."

"On the bed?" he asked.

"What is it with you? Don't you get it enough?"

Dixon responded with exasperation. "I can assure you madam that I do not, in fact, get it enough, but that is not the reason for my question. And while I have no obligation to tell you the reason for my questions, I will indulge you this once and tell you that the precise sequence of events in the bedroom may be critical to this case. I will, therefore, be asking you about a lot of details." He shook his head and repeated, "Were you on the bed?"

"Yes." She rolled her eyes.

"About how long was it from the time you went upstairs until the time your husband broke in?"

"It was about six inches long the whole time," she said with a smirk.

"Let me rephrase," Dixon replied, with his patience slipping away. "How much time passed between the time the two of you went upstairs and the time of the break-in?"

"I don't know, half hour."

"Did you have sex more than once during that time?"

"I don't know. We switched around a lot. I don't know if Duke came or not. Maybe he's on Viagra and it just stays up."

"At some point, did you think you heard a noise outside?"

"Yes," she replied.

"What kind of a noise was it?"

"Kind of a clanking. Like somebody running into something."

"Were you having sex when you heard the noise?"

"How would I remember that?"

"Well, for some people sex is kind of loud. If that was the case that night, I would think it would have been hard to hear anything going on outside."

"I don't remember. I think we were just laying in the bed smoking."

"So, what did you or Duke do when you heard the noise?"

"Duke got out of bed and looked out the window. We both got real quiet and tried to listen for some noise."

"Did either of you see anything?"

"No. I told Duke he was just being paranoid."

"What happened then?"

"Duke pulled a pistol out of his nightstand and set it on top. I said, 'keep that thing away from me,' and he said, 'don't worry, I'll point it the other way.'"

"Then what happened?" Dixon continued.

"Nothin.' We just laid there and listened for a while."

"Did you eventually start having sex again?"

"I don't remember."

"Ma'am, this is very important. At the time your husband broke in, were the two of you having sexual intercourse?"

"We started fooling around again because Duke hadn't seen nothin' and we figured it was safe."

"Okay, but was Duke MacKenzie inside of you at the time of the break-in?"

"Inside me! Do you mean was his dick in my vagina? No, it wasn't."

"I'm sorry, ma'am, but I don't mean to limit this to your vagina. Was he inside of you?"

Debi's face became flush and her eyes got wider. "Can we take a break?" she pleaded.

"As soon as you answer that question," Dixon responded.

She looked at McGuckin, but he was not stepping in to help her. "Yes, he was inside me! There, are you happy!"

Dixon nodded his head slowly. "Thank you. Let's take a short break."

As the witness and her husband departed with their attorney, Dixon thought again about whether Lester's attendance was part of Debi's humiliation or simply a way to garner information to justify more abuse. Dixon wasn't happy about contributing to either, but he had to prove self-defense and the less time Duke MacKenzie had to react the better. If he otherwise had to "disengage" at the time of the break-in, it could only help his case.

The court reporter shook her head after the Kruellers were out of earshot. "This is certainly one for the books."

"Yeah," Dixon responded. "This has to be a lot more interesting than most of your cases. You should be paying me to be here."

She smiled in agreement and excused herself to freshen up.

After ten minutes the parties returned and the proceeding continued. Dixon resumed his questioning. "Did you hear any sounds before the break-in?"

"Only what I told you about before," she said.

"What did you hear when the break-in occurred?"

"Just a huge crash and then glass hitting the floor."

"Could you tell where it was coming from?"

"Only that it was close," she said. "It wasn't in the bedroom, but you could tell it wasn't far away."

"What did you do?"

"I rolled off the side of the bed and covered my head."

"What happened next?"

"I saw Duke reach for the gun and I yelled 'don't shoot, it's Lester.'"

"How did you know it was Lester?"

"I just figured it had to be."

"And how did you know Duke reached for the gun if you covered your head?"

"I was laying on my side with my hand over the side of my head and I could see him above me and I yelled 'don't shoot, it's Les.'"

"What happened next?"

"Duke shot. Then there was all sorts of commotion with Duke running at Les and then running downstairs and out of the house."

"Did Les have a shovel with him when he came in the room?"

"I don't know. I told you I was behind the bed."

"Well, when you eventually got up, did you notice a shovel next to him?"

"I don't remember."

"Under the circumstances, Duke really didn't have a choice, did he?"

"I don't know about that. He could have fired a warning shot, or he could have yelled that he had a gun, or he could have blocked the door instead of relying on his gun." McGuckin had clearly coached her on this subject. The testimony was unfavorable, but the purpose of a deposition is to find out what someone is going to say—regardless of whether it is favorable.

Dixon continued to explore the details. He asked her about the 911 call and the subsequent police reports. In the end, he wasn't sure exactly what to believe. Reports around the time of an event usually are better remembered, but calm reflection might also contribute to a better account. The main problem was that she was now telling a story that differed substantially from her prior reports to the sheriff.

# CHAPTER 13

Dixon checked into the Lakeview Motel. There was a distant view of a lake—on the other side of the highway. "In-Room Coffee" and "Free HBO" made up for the disappointing view. The standards of luxury were apparently a little different on the Iron Range.

He laid out his notes and exhibits on the spare bed to study them. He really didn't have that much to prepare. Krueller had already testified at the criminal trial, so Dixon's main goal was to see if his story had changed. Furthermore, he hoped his cross-examination might be a little more revealing than Perry Passieux's.

He turned on the television to watch the local news. Small markets like Duluth were sort of the minor leagues for TV news people. Bright young faces hoping to be noticed and promoted. If any of the on-air personalities were approaching middle age, it was apparent they had been labeled "minor-league lifers." They had the distinction of being celebrities, just not very important ones. The news team announcing on this night appeared to be one of each.

Dixon soon grew bored, but lacked any other diversion. With nothing else to do, he undressed and went to bed. He closed his eyes and thought about Jessica. He imagined her next to him, but in his mind's eye they were not in a clapboard motel in the middle of nowhere.

He lay there for what seemed like an eternity. The encounter with Debi Krueller had apparently spiked his adrenaline level, and he couldn't seem to turn down the jets. He heard the fire door at the end of the hall creak open and then slam with the thud mandated by the local fire code. Two voices could be heard drawing nearer and then passing and fading away. The nearness of their voices and the thinness of the walls left Dixon feeling a little vulnerable.

Dixon reverted to his thoughts of Jessica. He imagined them walking hand-in-hand discussing anything and everything. He saw them dining in some waterfront restaurant in any one of a number of places around the world. They hadn't even been on a date, but something about it just seemed right.

Just when he was fading off, the fire door thumped shut again. Dixon could hear footsteps, but no voices. The steps got closer, but then stopped. Dixon rolled onto his elbow to listen. It was quiet for a long moment and then Dixon heard someone trying the doorknob. The blood rushed out of his face and he sat up on the bed. He heard the sound of a key card being inserted into the security slot.

"Who's there?" Dixon barked while praying to himself that he had remembered to chain the door.

It became quiet. "Who's there?" Dixon said again.

Dixon scurried across the room to locate his pants. Once he found them, he slipped them on and turned on a light. He tiptoed toward the door, using care to stay to the side of the peephole. He was relieved to find he had, in fact, chained the door.

He was trembling beyond what he would have expected under the circumstances. Leaving the chain on, he jerked the door open to see who was there. He saw nothing. After a long pause and an attempt to listen for a heartbeat or a breath other than his own, he mustered the courage to close the door, unlatch the chain, and throw the door wide open. Again, nothing. He poked his head out into the hall and peered in each direction. Nothing.

Dixon closed and chained the door. He walked back and sat on the edge of the bed. He decided it must have just sounded like someone at his door, but was instead one of the nearby guests retiring for the evening. *That was it,* he thought, *the cheap construction in this place carries sound vibrations like two cans connected by a string.* While he was sure that had to be the explanation, his inability to fall asleep became more acute.

# CHAPTER 14

THE DEPOSITION OF Lester Krueller was destined to be less eventful than that of his wife. He had already given testimony, so his story was known. He claimed to have been in an uncontrollable rage and also tried to claim he was justified in committing a crime to prevent another crime.

While there was no apparent need or right for Debi Krueller to attend, she was there. In all likelihood, Les wanted her there so he could berate her under oath. Dixon considered asking McGuckin to excuse her, but didn't want to be indebted to McGuckin in any way.

Dixon dispensed with the formalities and merely said, "Mr. Krueller, you were here yesterday, do you understand the process and procedures?"

"I think so."

Today, Dixon would be facing Les Krueller all day, and he wasn't looking forward to it. From a distance, Les was just out of style. Up close, he was much worse. He had black curly hair, small eyes, a recessed chin with a dimple in the middle, and teeth that alternated white and yellow like bi-colored corn on the cob.

Dixon started with the usual background questions. "Where did you grow up?"

Krueller sat with a blank stare.

After a moment, Dixon said, "You know, the questions get harder later on."

"I know, I know," Krueller responded. "I just wasn't sure how to answer. Y'see, the area I grew up in used to be called 'Squaw Lake,' but it isn't called that anymore."

"Why not?"

"Well, you mighta heard about it. I guess 'squaw' doesn't mean Indian woman like we always thought. Apparently it means an Indian woman's private parts."

"Oh yeah," Dixon said with a nod. "I did see something about that. Even though everyone understood it to mean 'Indian woman,' they want to change the names because they're offensive."

"Now you know why I had a hard time answering."

"Fair enough. What do they call your hometown now?"

Les paused for another moment. With a devious smile, he responded, "I think they call it 'Lake Tomahawk Wound.'"

Dixon let out an involuntary laugh from deep in his gut. He had to admit that he found the response humorous, but didn't want to sink to Krueller's level. He had tolerated Bennie Fosnick's degenerate remarks because Bennie was his client, but he saw no reason to encourage Krueller.

Dixon resumed his questioning. Krueller testified about his vo-tech education and subsequent employment in the mining business. He had dabbled in other things to offset the layoffs inherent in that business, but he was always seduced back by the high wages being paid when there was work.

He had his share of experience with the local law enforcement authorities, as the police had been called for more than one disturbance at his house. His domestic violence issues weren't allowed into evidence at the prior trial because evidence of prior bad acts is not generally allowed to prove someone is simply a bad person who is likely to engage in bad behavior. Furthermore, while a witness who has previously committed crimes involving dishonesty can have their credibility challenged with evidence of such crimes, domestic abuse did not fit that standard.

Dixon was in luck, however, because Les Krueller had sued for loss of consortium. While the literal definition of loss of consortium is the loss of a spouse's affection, the legal understanding is generally considered to be the loss of or damage to the ability to have sexual relations. That distinction was once learned the hard way by a new lawyer suing over his client's loss of a dog when the lawyer claimed, among other things, that his client's damages included loss of consortium.

The reason Dixon was in luck was because the claim opened up the issue of the Kruellers' personal life and whether it had actually been damaged. If Dixon could prove Les Krueller really didn't have much of a personal and intimate life with his wife and he just abused her, there wouldn't likely be an award of damages. After all, how would a jury value the loss of the pleasure of beating your wife? Ultimately, Dixon didn't really need the evidence for damages. That would be the justification, however, to allow the jury to hear about Krueller's propensity for spousal abuse.

"When did you first meet your wife?" Dixon asked.

"About six years ago. She moved here from over in Ely to get away from an abusive husband."

"So, you understood she had been in an abusive relationship before you met her?"

"Yes."

"How did that affect your feelings toward her?"

Les paused and reflected as though he were going to explain something difficult. "I guess I felt sorry for her. Wanted to protect her."

"How long did you know her before the two of you had your first physical altercation?"

"You mean when did we first have sex?"

"I'm sorry," Dixon responded. "Let me try again. When was the first time you and Debi had an argument or a fight that you can remember?"

"I don't really know. I love her so much, but I can't control her drinking and carrying on and I try to be strict, but it doesn't help."

"I understand, but could you focus on my question. I'm not currently asking *why* you fight, I'm just asking the *when* part of it."

"Well, I know we had some problems before we were married because she talked about going back to her ex-husband even though she said he abused her, and that got me mad and then she went all crazy and started throwing things around my house."

"Did you ever strike her?"

"Absolutely not."

"Ever choke her?"

"No."

"Ever touch her in any way during any of your disputes?"

"I'm sure I touched her a lot to calm her down or to restrain her."

"Are you aware there are police reports in which she accuses you of hitting her and choking her?" Dixon persisted.

"I know that's what she said at the time, but she was usually drunk and just trying to get me in trouble."

"Well, are you aware the County Court has, on more than one occasion, found probable cause to believe you were physically harming her and ordered you to stay away from her?"

"Am I aware? I don't really know what the courts do. I know my lawyer has told me after the court proceedings to stay away from her for a while."

"As these incidents continued to occur, did you get frustrated with the constant battle?"

"Yeah, I guess. I mean, I tried to be calm and everything, but she just gets out of control."

"Well," Dixon paused, "in reading the reports, you seem to get crueler in terms of the things she alleges you did."

"What do you mean?" Les asked.

"Well, in the early reports it appears you just yelled, while in the later reports she accuses you of a variety of acts of physical and emotional abuse. Is there a reason for that?"

"Only that she learned to play the system and didn't think she'd get any attention unless she made up bigger and bigger lies."

Ignoring his response, Dixon said, "Looking back, do you think it might have helped the situation if you had been less crueler?"

"What? I don't understand. I am Les Krueller."

McGuckin stirred from his near-sleep. "Ignore that question, sir. Mr. Donnelly is just trying to make a pun. While it's borderline clever, it doesn't quite fit."

Dixon could not deny either statement. He'd asked the question for his own amusement, but now it was time to move on to other subjects. "When did you first meet Duke MacKenzie?"

"That's hard to say. I think I met him in a bar a long time ago, but we didn't really know each other until he started doing some work around the Chateau," Krueller responded.

"That's the Chateau Le Blanc Camelot?"

"That's right."

"Do you have any idea why it has such a fancy name?"

"No idea."

"So, when did you first meet him after he started doing that work?"

"I don't remember for sure. Probably a couple months before he shot me."

"How did you come to meet Duke MacKenzie?" Dixon asked.

"I think probably just seein' each other outside and then one of us went over and introduced themself to the other."

"Do you know whether your wife had already met him by the time you did?" Dixon grimaced at his own sentence structure, but realized he wasn't interrogating *The Chicago Manual of Style* and let the question stand.

"I think maybe she had, 'cause I think I already knew who he was when we met."

"Thereafter, how often would you see him?"

"It was real irregular," Krueller responded. "Sometimes he'd be there working for days and sometimes weeks would go by and he wouldn't be around."

"Did he ever come into your house?"

"Not when I was there, but I came home once and found him visiting with my wife."

"Visiting?"

"They were sitting drinking coffee. He claimed he needed to use the phone, but it seemed pretty suspicious to me."

"Did you raise that issue with either of them? I mean, did you say, 'hey, what's going on here?' or something like that?"

"After he left I asked Debi. She just said it was nothing and she couldn't help it if men were attracted to her."

"Did you accept that?" Dixon asked.

"I don't mind if other men wish they could have sex with my wife.

I only mind when they actually try to have sex with my wife. Debi's not a slut, but she's weak-willed and has a drinking problem so I was afraid a snake like MacKenzie would take advantage of her."

Dixon reflected that Les's answer was more articulate than he would have expected. "Anything else happen that made you suspicious?"

"Yeah. He seemed to hang around more when he found out I was going to Canada to go fishing."

"Hang around your house, or spend more time working in the park?"

"Both, I guess."

"Mr. Krueller, to your knowledge, has your wife ever been unfaithful before?"

"Not as far as I know. We've been separated a couple times, so I can't really say what happened then or if you would consider it unfaithful since we weren't together."

"Well, was her fidelity ever a cause for arguments between the two of you?"

"Her what?" Krueller asked with furrowed brow.

"I'm sorry, did the fact that she might be unfaithful or might have been unfaithful ever cause arguments between the two of you."

"Maybe, I dunno. Actually, it was usually the reverse. We'd have an argument and she'd say she was going to sleep with someone else who would let her get away with her bullshit." Krueller looked from side to side with embarrassment. "I guess I should say 'let her get away with her crap.'"

"A couple days before the shooting, the two of you had an argument, is that right?"

"Yeah," Krueller said.

"What was that about?"

"The same as usual. She was spending all her time and money on clothes and booze and not doing the housework. I told her that and she got mad and started throwing things."

"What happened then?" Dixon asked.

"She left."

"What did you do?"

"Nothing."

Dixon shuffled some papers in order to give the impression he had evidence to the contrary. "Isn't that when you removed all of her belongings from the bedroom and put them in the front yard?"

"I did that later on. I was going to bed and I wanted to lock the door, but I thought she might come back and need something."

"So, are you saying you didn't feel comfortable picking out what she might wear, so you put her entire wardrobe in the yard?"

"Yeah, I guess that's about right."

Dixon was poised to move on, but decided to close the loop. "So that goes for all of her jewelry and makeup too? You didn't know what she might need so you put it all in the yard?"

"Yup."

"And you don't think your acts demonstrate you were kicking her out of the house?"

"I can't do that. She owns half of it."

Dixon nodded as though what Krueller was saying made sense. "Okay, when was the next time you saw your wife?"

"The next day. At MacKenzie's place."

"How did you find out she was there?"

"I thought she would have gone to her sister's. I called there in the morning and she told me she hadn't seen her."

"What gave you the idea she was at MacKenzie's?"

"Part hunch and part a tip-off from a bartender who'd seen them together that night."

"Did you try calling her?"

"No. I didn't want to accuse her of something if it wasn't true, so I wanted to go out to Duke's place to see for myself."

"And did you?"

"Yeah. She was there all right."

"Tell me what you did when you got there."

"Okay. I parked down on the road and walked halfway up the driveway. Then I cut through the woods so I could get close without being seen. I seen 'em through the window, so I walked in."

"Did you knock?" Dixon asked.

"No, they seen me and the door was open so I just walked in."

"The door of the house was just hanging open?"

"No, the inside door was open. I opened the screen door and walked in."

"What did you say to them?"

"I don't remember. Something like, 'what's going on, why didn't you come home?'"

"What was her response?"

"She said she thought she wasn't welcome."

"So," Dixon continued, "she didn't come home because she thought you had kicked her out."

"I object," interjected McGuckin. "That question calls for the witness to speculate as to what someone else was thinking."

"You can answer," Dixon said to the witness.

"I don't know. She probably didn't have a key and realized I'd locked the door."

Shaking his head in disbelief, Dixon said, "So, that's your story and you're sticking to it."

"Objection," McGuckin stated. "Argumentative."

"I'll withdraw the question," Dixon announced.

"Do you recall speaking to Mr. MacKenzie at that time?"

"Not directly."

Dixon persisted. "Do you recall saying words to the effect of 'if I catch you banging my wife I'll blow your fucking head off'?"

"No."

"Are you aware that your wife, your stepdaughter, and your step-daughter's boyfriend all told the sheriff's deputy you made such a statement?"

"They weren't there, how would they know?" Krueller responded.

"Perhaps I'm getting a little ahead of myself," Dixon said apologetically. "Are you aware that your stepdaughter and her boyfriend testified you came to the MacKenzie house the next day and made those same threats?"

"I don't know what they said or why they'd tell a lie like that."

"Your testimony is that you never said anything at all like that to Duke MacKenzie?"

"I might have said something like 'you must be out of your head to hang out with my wife' or something like that."

*Perfect,* Dixon thought. Liars who try to rationalize or explain their lies invariably dig themselves a deeper hole. Krueller would have been better off sticking with a simple denial. Dixon considered challenging the ridiculousness of the statement, but thought better of it. There was little point in making someone look foolish during a deposition because, on paper, they never appear as dishonest. Rather than trap him in a lie now, Dixon wanted to focus on having him tell more lies so he could expose them later on.

"What happened next?" Dixon asked.

"Nothing much. They denied anything was going on. I looked around a little more and left."

"Did your wife come home that day?"

"Not while I was there. Somebody came by and picked up a bunch of her clothes and stuff from the lawn, but I wasn't there, so I don't know who it was."

"Did you talk to her anymore that day?"

"No, I don't think so."

Dixon proceeded to cover what Krueller had done that day. It was probably of no relevance, but it would test the witness's recall. Also, by being thorough it would make it difficult for Krueller to surprise him at trial with the revelation of something else relevant happening that day. In the end, there was little of significance.

"You didn't go out to MacKenzie's house again that night?"

"Nope."

"What did you do that night?" Dixon asked.

"I went to a bar with some guys I work with."

"What was the name of the bar?"

"Dirty Dick's."

"Does the name refer to the proprietor or the clientele?"

McGuckin let out a sigh. "Could we please focus on the facts of this case?"

Dixon smiled. "Let me rephrase that. Who is the owner?"

"Dick Lundy is the guy who originally owned it. I'm not sure if he still does."

"What did you guys do? Eat, shoot pool, chase women?"

"What does that matter?" he asked, suddenly on the defensive.

"Well, I may need to verify your story, so I'd like to know what it is," Dixon replied.

"Hung out, told stories. That's about it."

"Was part of your goal to be unfaithful to your wife in order to get even for the fact that you thought she was being unfaithful to you?"

Krueller hesitated. "Yeah, I guess."

"And did you succeed?"

"None of your business."

Dixon glanced at McGuckin to see if he would intercede. When he didn't, Dixon continued, "Mr. Krueller, you don't really have the option of not answering questions. Now, I don't need details the way I did yesterday with your wife, but I'm entitled to know what you did that evening and who you did it with."

McGuckin nodded. "You should answer the question, Les."

This course of events was apparently not previously known by Mrs. Krueller, as she sat staring, more anxious for the answer than anyone else.

Dixon repeated the question. "Did you succeed in being unfaithful?"

"Yes," Krueller responded sheepishly.

"With whom?"

"Does she have to be part of this?" Krueller pleaded. "It was just a lark."

"Tell me her name and then we'll move on," Dixon compromised.

Les lowered his eyes and his voice. "Dawn Engelbrecht."

"What!" Debi screamed. "You fucked my sister?"

"No, no, I didn't say that. I just said I was with her."

Debi continued, "What the hell does that mean?"

"Wait a minute, wait a minute!" McGuckin interjected, raising a hand as though he were a referee separating boxers. "Debi, this is Mr. Donnelly's deposition. You can do your interrogating at home."

Dixon spoke up. "Mr. Krueller, I know I told you I would move on, but I'm not sure I understood your testimony in light of the colloquy that just occurred between you and your wife. Are you now saying you didn't have sexual relations with Ms ..." Dixon glanced at his notes, "Engelbrecht?"

With a smirk, Krueller responded, "We didn't have sex in the same way Bill Clinton didn't have sex with that Monica girl."

"So, you had oral sex?" Dixon asked.

"Yes."

Debi Krueller shook her head in disgust.

"Mr. Krueller, would you like to take a break?" Dixon asked.

"Not really. I'd rather answer your questions than my wife's."

"Fair enough," Dixon responded. "Let's talk about the next day. Did Debi come home at all?"

"Yes."

"What time was that?"

"Around noon, I guess."

"What happened? Did you talk?"

"We did. I asked her where she'd been and she just said 'none of your business.' Stuff like that."

"Well, had she come to pick something up, was she coming home, or what?"

Krueller shrugged his shoulders. "I think she was coming home. I mean she plopped down on the couch like she was just coming home from work."

"Did the two of you argue?'

"Not then. I just wanted things to calm down a little, so I didn't really say anything for a while."

"What happened then?" Dixon asked.

"I left to get a part for my truck. So, I was gone for a coupla hours."

"Was your wife still at home when you got back?"

"Yes."

"What happened then?" Dixon asked.

"She was drinkin' and it was the middle of the afternoon, so we got in an argument about it."

"What happened then?"

"She started hollerin' and then she said something about wanting to be with a real man and left."

"Did you try and stop her?"

"No."

"Did you know where she was going?"

"Not for sure, but I had a pretty good idea she was going to MacKenzie's," Krueller replied.

"So what did you do?"

"At that time? Nothing."

"Did you call Dawn?"

"No."

"Did you think about it?" Dixon persisted.

"I don't remember."

"When was the next time you saw your wife?"

"That night at MacKenzie's."

"Prior to going to MacKenzie's, did you have anything to drink?"

"No."

"What time did you go?"

"Well," Krueller began, "the first time I went was about six."

"What happened during that visit?"

"Nothing much. I told them I didn't believe they were just friends."

"Who else was there, anybody?"

"Debi's daughter and her boyfriend."

"How long were you there?"

"Five minutes."

"Did you threaten Duke or Debi?"

"No."

"Then what happened?"

"I got in my car and left."

"What did you do then?"

"Just drove around. It was a nice night, so I drove around and tried to clear my head."

"Did you stop anywhere?" Dixon asked.

"No. Well, maybe for gas."

"What time did you arrive at the MacKenzie place for the second time?"

"I s'pose around ten," Krueller answered.

"What did you do when you arrived?"

"Well, I did pretty much the same thing as the first time I told you about. I parked on the road and walked up the driveway and cut through the woods."

"What did you see? Were the lights on?"

"I saw 'em, my wife and Duke, sitting downstairs having a drink. I crouched in the woods and watched for a while and then they turned off the lights and went upstairs."

"How do you know they went upstairs if they turned out the lights first?"

"Because they turned on lights upstairs."

"So, what did you do?"

"I went around to the back of the house to try and see in."

"And could you see in?" Dixon asked.

"Not really. In order to get high enough up I had to move away from the house and up a hill. I could see people in there, but I couldn't see what they were doing. And then they turned out the lights anyway."

"So, what did you do then?" Dixon asked.

"Started to cry."

Dixon thought to himself, *That's an easy lie with no one around to testify otherwise.* He pondered whether to bother, but couldn't help himself. "What was the reason you were crying?"

"Because my wife was in there having sex with another man, and it looked like my marriage was over."

"How did you know they were having sex?"

"I could hear 'em. One of the windows was open."

"What happened next?"

"I went to see if the doors were locked. Then I started looking for a way to get in a window or something else."

"What did you do next?"

"I found a ladder and leaned it up against the balcony. I went up the ladder and checked to see if the sliding glass door was locked."

"And was it?" Dixon asked.

"Yeah."

"So what did you do then?"

"Climbed down the ladder and looked for something to break in with."

"Keep going," Dixon prodded.

"I found a shovel by the woodshed. I carried it up the ladder and tried to pry the sliding glass door open."

"Any luck?" Dixon asked.

"Not really."

"So then what?"

"I grabbed the shovel like a baseball bat and smashed the sliding glass door."

"What sort of a sound did it make?"

"Really loud."

"Then what?" Dixon asked.

"I walked through the big hole I had just made."

"And?"

"I walked through that room and down the hall. I came to a door and I opened it."

"During this time did you say anything or otherwise announce your presence?"

"I didn't say anything," Krueller responded. "The shovel made the announcement."

"Okay, when you opened the bedroom door, what happened?"

"I yelled 'ah-hah,' and then I heard a loud bang. I fell to the ground and realized I'd been shot."

"Did you still have the shovel with you when you opened the door?"

"No, I dropped it on the deck after I broke the window."

"Did you have a gun or any other weapon on you?"

"No."

"Did you turn the light on when you opened the door?"

"No."

"How much time elapsed between the time you opened the door and the time you were shot?"

"Very little," Krueller responded. "It was almost instantly."

"So then what happened?"

"Duke MacKenzie walked across the room and stuck the gun in my face and yelled 'you son of a bitch, you son of a bitch, what are you doing here?'"

"Did you respond?"

"No."

"So what happened next?" Dixon asked.

"Duke left. I yelled for Debi to call 911 and she ignored me. Finally, I went to the phone and called myself."

"Did you ever see Duke MacKenzie again?"

"Nope."

Dixon studied some of the police reports he had from the incident. "Mr. Krueller, let's take a break for lunch. I think I have about an hour left, but I'm getting hungry, so let's stop for now."

"Fine," was the response from both Krueller and McGuckin.

♦

The afternoon session focused mainly on damages. The medical bills were mostly paid by insurance, and had been about $50,000. Krueller had missed several weeks of work and claimed a lot of pain and suffering. He also said the relationship with his wife had been damaged both by the affair and by the pain and suffering from the wound. Of course, he also wanted punitive damages, but he didn't have any way to establish the amount he thought was necessary.

Dixon was still waiting to get all of the medical records and didn't need to discredit Krueller on the issues at this juncture. Rather, the point was to get Krueller to articulate all of his claimed damages in order to keep him from making something up at a later date. In the end, the injuries were not terrible, but the prospect of punitive damages was frightening because the standard was so ill-defined.

After an hour or so Dixon announced he was finished, subject to a possible recall if the medical records raised new issues. McGuckin nodded his agreement as he collected his things and shuffled his clients out of the room. Satisfied with the day's events, Dixon packed his briefcase and headed for home.

# CHAPTER 15

JESSICA HAD RENTED a house in the Linden Hills neighborhood of south Minneapolis. The area had been built during the first half of the twentieth century and construction had proceeded in fits and starts through the depression and two world wars. As a result, it was a patchwork of grand residences and small bungalows. The families that grew up in the neighborhood covered the economic spectrum, and the ethnicities ranged all the way from German to Swedish. Now the area was occupied primarily by young singles or others who could make do with a one-car garage.

Dixon made reservations at the nearby El Gatto Pronto, which he was told was Italian for The Quick Cat. The name amused Dixon because shortly before it came into existence he was frequently heard to say: "You can't swing a dead cat in this town without hitting a new northern Italian restaurant." Just the same, it had gotten good reviews and seemed like the right touch for their first date.

Dixon arrived at Jessica's at 7:15. Actually, he was a block away by 7:05, but drove around awhile. He told himself he wanted to look around the neighborhood, but he just wanted to collect himself. Satisfied that he was ready, he parked the car and proceeded up the walk. He rang the bell and, within a few seconds, Jessica appeared.

"Hi," she said with a big smile. "Come on in a second while I grab my purse." He liked that. She was ready on time, but if she hadn't let him in he would have wondered what she was hiding.

Dixon surveyed the living room and as far as he could see beyond it. "Nice place. I realize you're just renting, but you've managed to make it look awfully homey."

"Thanks," she yelled from the kitchen. "Part of my deal in coming here was that I didn't want to be in a hotel. I'm pretty happy with this house and the neighborhood."

As Jessica reentered the room, Dixon couldn't help but look her up and down. It was evident she'd spent some time preparing for their date, and Dixon was gratified she wanted to make the effort. On the other hand, she was a picture of self-assurance. Her hair, her lipstick, her nails, and her clothes were elegant but understated. The only things flashy about Jessica Palmer were her eyes and her smile.

"I hope you like Italian," Dixon said.

"I think everybody likes Italian, don't they?"

"I guess you're right. That's kind of why I chose it. I figured it wouldn't be much of a first date if I had to watch you make yuck faces over sushi."

"Well, that's thoughtful of you, but I'm usually able to find something. I pretty much always like eating when someone else has done the cooking."

"So, you don't cook?" Dixon asked.

"Actually I do, I just don't have the time."

"Really. Well, I guess I can understand that," Dixon replied. Then, with a gesture toward the door, he said, "Let's be off."

The restaurant was typical of the trend to convert "something" into a restaurant. What had started as a trend to convert warehouse space to restaurants had progressed beyond its logical extreme. Soon, dress shops, doctors' offices, and even pharmacies were following the trend. El Gatto Pronto was located in a building that had once been a gas station.

When they arrived, there were several people waiting by the host stand. Dixon was assured their table was being prepared and it would just be a minute. Dixon was confident he and Jessica would have a lot to talk about once they sat down but, in the meantime, the circumstances didn't seem very conducive to anything other than small talk. They had already covered the weather and the Minnesota Twins in the car, so Dixon was hoping to find a bridge before rolling out his heavy material. For her part, Jessica seemed to take it in stride.

After a few minutes, the host appeared and led them to their table. Dixon glanced around the restaurant as they walked through and observed more than one male diner turning his head as Jessica walked by. She had a regal quality Dixon couldn't quite define. She was shapely, but the black shorts and sleeveless blouse she was wearing didn't reveal the curves that had been apparent at the wedding. Her bare legs were tan and black pumps completed the ensemble. She was, if such a thing is possible, beautiful in a way that didn't necessarily evoke thoughts of sex. Dixon was starting to appreciate Sandy's fascination with being seen with the most beautiful woman in the place.

A waiter appeared and asked about drinks. "What do you think about getting a bottle of wine?" Dixon asked.

"Wine would be nice, but I'll only have a glass or so," she responded.

"Well, we may as well get a bottle. If we don't finish it we've probably still made the value decision. Would you like to pick something out?" he asked while extending the wine list to her.

"What do you like?" she asked.

"I'm pretty flexible with maybe just one exception."

"Let me guess," she smiled. "No white zinfandel."

Dixon chuckled. "You hit that nail right on the head. In fact, spare me the white merlots as well. I'll take a white burgundy, but nothing that's supposed to taste like a wine cooler."

"How about a sauvignon blanc?" she asked.

"That would be terrific," he sighed with relief.

Jessica pointed out a Napa Valley vintage to the waiter and he departed with the customary "very good madam."

After he left, Dixon asked, "Do you drink much wine?"

"Usually just when I go out or there's a special occasion. I like it, but I don't want to get in the habit of liking it too often," she said.

Alcoholism seemed like too heavy of a topic for that point in the evening, so Dixon quickly tried to shift gears. "Tell me about your job. Most people know what lawyers do, or at least think they know, but I don't really know what a systems analyst does or why someone would hire a consultant."

"Prepare to be bored," she announced. "There's a reason why

there aren't any TV shows about system analysts, or consultants for that matter."

Dixon became virtually oblivious to everything she said. On some level he was absorbing the information, but his conscious mind was focused on everything about her other than her words. As she spoke he noticed her teeth were white without looking bleached and straight without looking straightened. When she gestured, he noticed delicate hands with medium length nails not obscured by anything other than a clear polish. Most of all, he noticed the over-sized cerulean eyes sitting on top of her high cheekbones. He smiled and nodded as she spoke and even managed a question or a chuckle at the appropriate times. He wasn't, however, particularly focused on the content of the conversation.

The wine came and it was perfect. After a couple sips, Jessica said, "I think I've told you more than you want to know about what I do. I'd like to hear a little more about your practice and how you came to be on your own."

Dixon was pleased that the entomologist prank hadn't come up. Jessica had accepted his apology, and it was clear she was ready to move past it. Dixon gave her a short employment history and explained that his primary mission was solving business people's problems. He told her he'd spent time working in law firms, but that he liked the flexibility of having his own practice because he could work on cases without worrying about whether the client could pay right away. Dixon's clients frequently had problems beyond their financial means, and he had garnered significant loyalty by finding ways to help.

The vocational conversation continued until the two had worked backwards chronologically to college. That then became the next topic of conversation. Dixon had gone to the University of Wisconsin at Madison, and he was unapologetic in admitting that he went there for the partying. Jessica, on the other hand, had attended Tufts as a sociology major.

"So, what happened with the sociology degree?" Dixon asked.

"Well, I hate to admit it," she replied, "but for all my desire to make a difference in society, I went for something that pays better."

"What would you have wanted to do to better the world?" Dixon asked.

"Oh, I don't know," she replied.

"Well, you must have had something in mind. Just give me an example," he pleaded.

She hesitated out of an apparent sense of humility. "Well, I think as Americans we still have a long way to go before we are truly an integrated society. We've eliminated some of the barriers, but we still have a lot further to go."

"And you think that's the responsibility of sociologists?"

"If not them, then who?" she asked.

"I don't know if I think any sort of social engineering is a good idea. It creates unrealistic expectations and may have unforeseen and undesirable results."

"Like what, for example?"

Dixon pondered whether the discussion was heading out of the "safe" zone, but was too in love with the sound of his own voice to hold his tongue. "I have a pro bono client who sort of typifies it. You know how they're getting rid of all public housing, and they want to buy property all over the metro area to disperse people on public assistance?"

"Sure," Jessica said, "I've read about that."

"I don't understand the theory. Do they think poor people will feel better about their lot in life if they can live nearer people who are better off than them?"

"I think it's a diversity issue to eliminate the concentration of minority groups and I think it's a great idea," she replied.

"I think you're right that it's a diversity issue, but I'm not sure if I agree it's a great idea. Think about it. If you were in a minority group that was otherwise disadvantaged, would you want to be spread out so you were always outnumbered, or would you want to be in a community with people you could identify with and be part of the majority at least within that community?"

"I'm not following you. Who's your client?"

"I've got a guy who is one of the leaders in the local Vietnamese community. They are really upset about being dispersed around the metropolitan area because they are already a small community and, because some of the older ones don't speak much English, the community is a vital part of their existence. Their position is that the housing projects are kind of crummy, but they'd rather live in bad housing so long as they can be together."

"Well, that's different because of the language issue."

"That's true, but I, for one, believe there are cultural differences between all ethnic groups, and those cultural differences will be marginalized and eventually eliminated if we insist that every neighborhood and institution become a microcosm of the overall population."

"So you think we should go back to segregation?"

"Not by any means. I'm saying people and neighborhoods should be allowed to develop on their own without the intrusion of social engineers."

"Don't you think that's kind of racist?"

"To the contrary, I think anyone who feels the need for such policies to be racist."

"Would you be willing to make that into a campaign platform?" Jessica asked.

"I guess I'm already regretting having said it to you. I can see that if you're a B. F. Skinner fan we aren't going very far together."

"What do you mean by that?" she asked.

"Look, I can see I've carried this conversation to a level of seriousness well beyond where it should be. Let me give you a more common example and I hope I don't offend you."

"That might be difficult," she said with a wry smile.

"Okay," Dixon began. "You told me before that your father had a bit of an alcohol problem. Now, when you were young, you probably heard statistics that indicated a person who grew up in a home with an alcoholic parent had a much greater chance of becoming an alcoholic, am I right?"

"Yeah."

"Okay, but now there's all kinds of evidence that alcoholism is genetic. Thus, while it may be true that people who grow up with alcoholic parents are more likely to become alcoholics, that may have very little to do with the environment because they are already genetically predisposed to alcoholism."

"So, what's your point?" she asked.

"I guess my point is that I think modern sociology overstates the significance of environment in claiming everything is learned behavior and, as a result, it may be doing more harm than good."

"I think I see what you're saying. I'm not agreeing with you, but I'm willing to accept your position as one that at least has been thought out," she said.

"Well, I can't ask for more than that," Dixon replied.

Just then the food came and Dixon had a welcome transition.

"This is terrific," Jessica commented after a few mouthfuls of food. "For a little neighborhood place, they really do a good job."

"No argument," Dixon responded. "It's nice to know you don't have to go downtown to get a *something-crusted* piece of meat served in a *something-or-other* reduction."

She smiled at his amateur restaurant review.

After a few more bites, Dixon cleared his throat to ask the more serious question. "I guess the thing I'm wondering more than anything is how someone as desirable as you made it to thirty-five without getting married."

"How did you know I was thirty-five?"

"Well, I know how many years behind Matt you were in school, so I figured you had to be about that old."

"Oh," was all she said.

After a brief silence, Dixon said, "Are you trying to avoid the question?"

"In a way. I get that a lot and I don't see what the big deal is. I've just never met anyone I wanted to be married to."

"Well, have you ever been close?"

"I've had some relationships that lasted for a couple years and I guess there was some talk about it a couple times, but it's not like I've ever been engaged. Is that pretty much what you expected to hear?"

"I don't know that I expected anything in particular," Dixon responded. "I thought, you know, maybe you had a long-term relationship and something tragic happened or something like that."

"And if that had happened, you think it would be a good idea to bring it up the way you just did?"

"No, not at all," Dixon said. "But your answer pretty much ruled that out."

"How about you?" she returned the volley. "You must be about my age and as near as I can tell you've never been married. Did your college sweetheart die in a tragic accident?"

"No. Although I'll be honest, I've considered inventing such a story to ward off any suspicions that I'm gay."

"Are you kidding," she laughed. "You'd tell people you had a dead girlfriend just to avoid having them think you're gay?"

"I didn't say I'd do it, only that the thought occurred to me."

"So what's your explanation of your bachelorhood?"

"I don't really have one. I'm not against being married, but I only want to do it once, and I was never comfortable that I'd found someone I thought I wanted to be with for the rest of my life. In retrospect, if I'd married some of my former girlfriends, I would probably be perfectly happy. At the moment of truth, however, I always thought there was someone else out there and that I'd wonder about it forever."

"So, what is it you're looking for?" she said. "Do you know?"

"I think I do, but I don't know if I can explain it. Furthermore, I don't think I want to try and explain it at this juncture."

"That's fair," she said. "I think we have in common the fact that neither of us has been willing to settle for less than what we envision, and neither of us is overly concerned about bucking a societal norm."

"It's nice to know we have things in common."

"I wouldn't make too much out of that if I were you," she cautioned. "Remember, a minute ago you pretty much maligned all of my beliefs when it comes to sociology."

"I think that's an overstatement," Dixon protested. "I didn't purport to know any answers. I merely pointed out I thought there were some questions that needed to be asked and that traditional assumptions should be challenged." Without waiting for her reply, Dixon continued. "Why don't we move to something less controversial, like . . . abortion?"

She chuckled and the conversation moved to more lighthearted topics. Jessica had opinions about almost everything. She wasn't critical for the sake of being critical, but she certainly wasn't a Pollyanna. Furthermore, she didn't hesitate to challenge things Dixon said or to roll her eyes to express her incredulity at things he would say. All of that suited Dixon just fine.

The busboy came and cleared their plates. "Are you thinking about dessert?" Dixon asked.

"I don't know. Why?"

"Well, if you wanted, I thought maybe we could go over to the Linden Hills Creamery for ice cream and then maybe walk around the lake."

"That would be nice," she replied with a smile.

When the bill came, Dixon took it from the waiter. "What's my share?" Jessica asked.

"Thank you for offering," Dixon replied, "but I'll get this."

"Well, thank you for dinner. Can I buy the ice cream?"

"Absolutely."

The line for ice cream was relatively long. What had been a quaint neighborhood ice cream parlor had managed to draw crowds from all over. Jessica opted for the raspberry chocolate chip, while Dixon splurged on her nickel and got a scoop of banana walnut topped by a scoop of raspberry chocolate chip.

They walked the block and a half to Lake Harriet. "This is amazing ice cream," Jessica remarked.

"I agree," Dixon said. "Ice cream is one of my real weaknesses and it doesn't get any better than this."

"It's not just that, but did you smell it?"

"What do you mean?"

Jessica moved a little closer. "Smell the ice cream."

Dixon raised the cone to his nose to take a whiff. Just when he got it close, Jessica slapped the underside of his elbow and pushed the cone into Dixon's face. "Oops," she said with a giggle.

Dixon couldn't help but laugh. "What was that for?" he asked.

"Nothing in particular. I'm just paying you back in advance for some childish prank I'm sure you'll pull in the future."

He wiped his face. "So you're basically giving me carte blanche to retaliate."

"If that's what you think is appropriate," she said as if she were talking to a child.

Dixon clenched his lips together and nodded. "Well, we'll just have to see when the time comes."

They finished their cones and began a loop around Lake Harriet. It was only a few weeks after the summer solstice and it was still light out. The Minneapolitans were out in force to take advantage of it.

As they walked, Jessica would occasionally move close as if to make a point. When that happened, their shoulders would touch. Dixon took that as a sign and took her hand in his. She clasped back, and Dixon was confident that he'd interpreted things correctly.

They continued to walk hand in hand as the sun began to disappear below the trees. The conversation flowed. At times there would be pauses, but they weren't uncomfortable. Dixon occasionally shifted from the reverse-handshake grip to an interlocking grip and back again. He sometimes would put his free hand on the back of hers, and kept thinking that he didn't want to let go.

As they drove home, Dixon wondered what he should do when they got to her house. This was their first date and, if the relationship continued, what happened on the first date could be the subject of future derision. If he walked her to the door, she might later tell others that he "expected it" on the first date. If he didn't walk her in, she might later tell everybody how inconsiderate he had been on their first date. He decided to err on the side of chivalry.

He threw the car into park and turned off the key before she could say goodnight. As they strolled up the walk, he slowed his gait in an effort to signal that he was nearing his end. He felt a nervousness in the pit of his stomach while he thought about the awkwardness that might follow. He stood on the bottom step while Jessica unlocked the door. If she invited him in, he wasn't likely to fight it, but he didn't want to look too eager.

"I had a really nice time tonight," Jessica said.

"So did I," Dixon replied. "Can we do it again?"

"Absolutely," she said with a smile. She didn't turn away.

After a moment, Dixon took her right hand in his and pulled himself up the step that separated them. He looked for a moment in her eyes and leaned forward to kiss her. She leaned in and kissed him back. It was not a peck, but it wasn't tongue wrestling either. They stood, lips slowly exploring each other, for several seconds before Dixon broke the embrace. He pulled back, looked at her with a smile, and said a quiet "goodnight."

"Goodnight," she responded with a bat of her eyes. Dixon squeezed her hand before letting go. He smiled again, turned, and started down the walk.

"Thanks again for dinner," she called after him.

He turned slowly. "Thanks for the ice cream. In particular the part that made it to my stomach and didn't end up on my face."

"You're welcome," she giggled.

# CHAPTER 16

SANDY WAS WAITING when Dixon pulled into the Lake Calhoun parking lot. "This is a little more civilized," he said as Dixon got out of his car. "That 5 A.M. stuff is for the birds."

"I don't dispute that my first choice is sleeping a little later, but during the week the only time to run seems to be early morning," Dixon replied. "Give me a couple minutes. I didn't get time to stretch."

"This is so unlike you, Dixon. You're always on time and always ready to go. Something happen last night you want to tell me about?"

Dixon looked up from his hurdler's stretch. "I have a ton to tell you. I think we better run three lakes today if I'm going to get it all in."

"All right!" Sandy exclaimed. "Our little boy's finally becoming a man."

"Well, if you're hoping to hear about sex, the only story is my case on the Iron Range. If you want to hear about fireworks, I'll tell you about Sharon and my new female interest. If you want to hear me debunk Stephen Hawking's theories, well, I just won't have the time."

"I feel like a kid in a candy store," Sandy smirked.

Dixon finished limbering up and the pair started to trot along the pedestrian path. "Of course, if I do all the talking, you'll run me into the ground," Dixon said. "Maybe you should guess what happened and I'll just nod or shake my head."

"No deal. You come walking up here with that coprophagous smile and expect me to simply let it slide," Sandy scolded.

"My what smile?"

"You heard me—coprophagous."

"Are you going to tell me what that means?"

"Whoa, score one for Sandy," he replied. "I might tell you what it means, but not until you spill the beans."

"No deal. You're Mr. Vocabulary for the day. What does it mean?"

"You've heard of coprophagy. It refers to organisms that eat dung."

"And?"

"Well, a coprophagous smile is a more genteel way of saying . . ."

"Shit-eating grin," Dixon finished the sentence.

"Very good, grasshopper. Of course, I'm not really sure of the derivation of the expression 'shit-eating grin,' but that's for another day."

"I think I know that one, smart guy. It's when you're happy about something, and you can't wait to tell it. But just like you'd be eager to get shit out of your mouth, you're eager to get the story out, but you can't just spit it anywhere."

"Makes sense to me," Sandy replied. "But let's get back to the important stuff."

"Well, the easiest place to start is that I dumped Sharon. I didn't want to dump her per se, but I really wanted to be rid of her."

"What are the chances that you'll get back together with her later on?" Sandy asked.

"Absolutely zero."

"In that case, I can only say it's about time. She was really starting to annoy me."

"Hey, try sleeping in the same bed with her. You think she's Ptolemaic ordinarily, try being intimate with her."

"She's what?" Sandy asked.

"You heard me—Ptolemaic."

"Wow. That was the shortest reign as Mr. Vocabulary that I've ever experienced. I'm afraid you'll have to define that for me," Sandy said.

"I'll give you a hint," Dixon said. "It's spelled with a pt, as in Ptolemy."

"I'm afraid that doesn't help."

"Ptolemy was the astronomer who believed the universe revolved around the earth. Hence, Ptolemaic, as far as I can tell, is someone who believes the universe revolves around them."

"I like it," Sandy replied. "Not as good as coprophagous smile, but respectable. So tell me, how did you dump Sharon?"

"It was basically the 'it's not you it's me' routine. I said, 'Sharon, it's not you, it's me; I'm the type of person who just can't stand being with people like you.'"

Sandy pretended to stumble from the laughter. "Smooth," he said. "How'd that go over?"

"Actually, that's not how it happened. I was holding off and holding off because I didn't want to hurt her, and I kept thinking I'd get lucky and get hit by a bus instead. Finally, I was set to do it when she discovered a Post-it note with Jessica's phone number on it—you remember Jessica from the wedding. Well, Sharon went ballistic and I finally couldn't hold off any longer. She said 'who's Jessica Palmer?' and I said that was the woman I was going to start dating."

"You're kidding. You just told her that?"

"Yes. And it went downhill from there."

Sandy tried to extol the virtues of little white lies, but Dixon wasn't persuaded. "I didn't want to hurt her, but, in the end, maybe I did want to hurt her," Dixon confessed.

They reached the cutoff to Lake Harriet, jogged in place waiting for the light to change, and then bounded up the hill. "How're you doin'?" Dixon asked.

"I'm fine. I haven't decided if I have three lakes in me, but I'll keep going as long as the stories are as good as that one. What's next?"

"Well, to stay in theme, I guess I should tell you about my date last night with Jessica. Did I tell you I called her?"

"No. You told me you were going to call Matt to find out about her, but I haven't talked to you since. Let's hear it."

"Well, first of all, Matt says she's great, but can't really explain why she's never been married. He thinks her parents' divorce may have had an impact. So I call her and she's very friendly, but when I ask her if she's seeing anyone, she wants to know why I'm asking. So I'm a little concerned. Remember when we used to say that dating divorced women was a problem because they would have baggage? I'm starting to think that a woman in her mid-thirties who has never been married has more baggage."

"Well you're mid-thirties, don't you think you must have some baggage?"

"It's different for guys," Dixon responded.

"Whatever you say," Sandy said sarcastically.

"Anyway, we went out to dinner at El Gatto Pronto and had a fabulous time. Everything about it: the food, the wine, the conversation."

"The sex," Sandy interjected.

"Hopefully that will be part of next week's report," Dixon said with a smile. "She has a very strong personality. I like that. I overpower most women and that doesn't make for a very fulfilling relationship."

Sandy signaled for a stop at the water pump. After taking a drink, he said, "I assume you're seeing her again?"

"That's the plan. I've got tickets to a concert next weekend, and I thought I'd see if she wanted to go. Ordinarily I'd wait until next week to call again, but I'll probably call her tomorrow to make sure she doesn't make plans."

"Dangerous," Sandy said in a haunting voice. "Established convention requires you to wait awhile after the first date before calling. You don't want her to think she owns you, do you?"

"I'm aware of standard operating procedure, but this is not a standard situation. Besides, she might be levelheaded enough that I can skip the shenanigans."

"Heretic!" Sandy yelled in jest. "How dare you defy the Code."

"Sorry, but my judgment tells me these are special circumstances. If it'll make you feel better, I'll act a little indifferent on the phone."

Sandy lowered his voice and tried to sound professorial. "It's not my feelings, my son. It's the Code that I'm worried about."

Dixon and Sandy came upon the main beach. At thirty feet deep by a hundred feet long, anyone who'd ever been to either coast would laugh wondering about the size of the beaches that were too small to be considered the "main" beach. It was early in the day, so the sunbathers and swimmers were not in force. Still, the pair had to split apart for a while to avoid the people on or crossing the path.

"Let's hear about Hibbing," Sandy said.

"I'm not sure I could do it justice. Can you imagine having to ask a woman about her sexual liaisons with the neighbor, much less doing so when her husband is sitting there?"

"You're kidding," Sandy chuckled.

"No. And what's worse, the sex was not exactly missionary style. There was a little backdoor action, lots of oral, and who knows what I could find out if my guy had lived to tell about it."

"So, how did the . . . what did you call him . . . the cuckold, respond to all of this?" Sandy asked.

"Some of it seemed like it might have been new to him, as he kind of sat up and took notice. I also think it came as a surprise to McGuckin, because he either would have prepared her better or arranged for Lester the Molester to be out of the room. I can't imagine McGuckin would have let things transpire the way they did if he had known what was going on."

"What do you think will happen now that everybody knows the gory details?"

"I don't know," Dixon responded. "I originally thought Lester attended the deposition because publicly humiliating his wife was either part of her penance or part of his pleasure. I couldn't help but think that Les has more ammunition for his next round of physical or emotional abuse."

"Well, there's not much you can do about that."

"I know," replied Dixon, "but I feel bad for her because it seems like she's really got a shitty deal. Not to mention, if you could give her a self-esteem transplant, she'd be pretty hot."

"So, how do you explain her lot in life?"

"Good question," Dixon responded. "I don't believe that boys growing up in abusive households become abusive husbands for that reason alone. I think their thug fathers passed their thug genes on to the kids. The battered wife syndrome is a little harder. It seems as if abused wives go from one abusive relationship to the next and that daughters of abused women follow in their mother's footsteps.

The question is whether some women are genetically predisposed to being in abusive relationships, and I think there's something to that."

"Do you think that if you put a normal, high self-esteem girl in an abusive household, she'll come out fine?" Sandy asked.

"I'm not saying she'd be fine, I'm just not surrendering to the idea that she's definitely screwed up."

"I hope you shared your enlightened thoughts with Jessica last night," Sandy said sarcastically.

"Worse, I told her about my opposition to dispersing public housing throughout the metro area."

"Well, just tell her you were drunk and maybe she'll ignore it," Sandy chided.

"You know, I think I was born in the wrong time. I miss the day when you could have a provocative discussion without being labeled a Nazi."

"Dixon," Sandy said. "You've got to stop caring. The world is the world and you need to focus on your life."

"You might be right," he said.

They jogged on in silence for a while. "So, let's get back to Hibbing. What's your next step?" Sandy asked.

"I'm at a bit of a loss. Usually my cases involve two sides saying different things and I have to persuade the judge or jury why our version is correct. Here the opposing versions come primarily from the same witness."

"That's unique," Sandy said.

"I thought I'd go back up in a month or so and interview some of the sheriff's deputies and see if I can find anything to support Debi Krueller's first version of the events.

"Are you thinking about hiring a jury consultant?"

"I'm not sure it would do any good. The population is pretty homogenous—white, blue collar, Lutheran, simple . . ."

"Just the same," Sandy said, "maybe you need to learn how to speak the language."

"I'm not sure this case justifies it."

"You don't think so? How much is at stake?"

"That's the problem. You can't really quantify it. Krueller wants something for pain and suffering, but there's no real standard. Furthermore, McGuckin will ask for punitive damages, and that's just a crap shoot as to how much a jury thinks is necessary to punish someone."

"How do you punish someone who is dead?" Sandy asked.

"Indirectly. I guess you punish his heirs."

"How's Duke's daughter doing?"

"Okay I guess, but the outcome may affect that. Not only for the money. I think vindicating her father may be important."

"Can you put her on the stand to show she's more deserving of the money?"

"I'm afraid not. The jury will be asked to evaluate Duke's conduct, and the heirs can only hope."

"Well, they have you to rely on."

"That's true, so I hope I'm up to the task."

"Aren't you glad I referred this case to you?" Sandy said.

"Y'know, I always wanted to avoid the areas of law that involved too much emotion. That's why I don't want to do divorce or criminal work. The fact of the matter, though, is that in some ways the stakes in this are higher than most anything else. I mean, in a divorce or a criminal situation, the client usually had at least some responsibility for creating the situation. Here, Hank and the daughter had nothing to do with what happened, but they're counting on me to protect them."

"You need to take the pressure off yourself. I thought you were the one who was indifferent to the problems of the common man."

"I'm not sure I ever said that. I admit that I don't want to deal with the problems of the common man, but I think that's different from saying I don't care about those problems."

"So, you don't want to do anything to help, but you're willing to feel bad about it?"

"Sandy, I don't think anyone whose charitable deeds are limited to donating his used clothes to the Goodwill should be lecturing me about being my brother's keeper." Dixon's tone indicated he wanted the subject to be closed.

Sandy hesitated. "At least the clothes I donate are stylish."

Dixon accepted that as the last word. They jogged on as the sun rose higher and the day got warmer. In the end, it was ten miles in an hour and twenty-five minutes. Sandy was declared Vocabulary King for the day for his deft use of "jingoism."

# CHAPTER 17

Dixon called Jessica on Sunday as he'd planned. She said she'd thought of him while reading an article in the newspaper about the effects of nature and nurture on intelligence. Dixon didn't really care whether the article supported his views, but he was pleased to know she was the kind of person who read the paper and even more pleased to know she had thought about him while they were apart.

Dixon told her about the concert tickets. She'd never heard of the band, but accepted the offer with enthusiasm. Perhaps that was good, Dixon thought, because she wanted to be with him even though the show might not have otherwise interested her.

It occurred to Dixon that he wouldn't have a good excuse to talk to her again until Friday. He didn't think he could wait that long, so he concocted a story about not knowing for sure when the show started. That gave him an excuse to call again on Wednesday.

On Friday he picked her up as scheduled. She greeted him at the door, and he felt a rush of exhilaration at the sight of her. "You look great," he said. And he wasn't lying. Her hair was pulled back with a barrette and the result was better exposure of her face and her long lustrous neck.

"Thank you," she said, blushing.

Dixon had a hard time keeping his eyes off her as they drove to the show. It wasn't just that he liked her look. Jessica had an air of strength about her that he found captivating.

When they arrived, Dixon scurried around the back of the car a moment too late to assist Jessica. He shut the door and took her hand as they began to walk. They strolled along the park across the street from the theater. As they approached the crowd surrounding the entrance, Jessica removed her hand from Dixon's. He glanced to see if she had needed to reach into her purse or something else, but she had her hands by her sides. Dixon opened the door and put his hand on her back to guide her through. She accepted the courtesy, but seemed to deflect the affectionate touch.

Once inside, Dixon suggested they get something from the bar. "I'll have a 7 Up," she said. Dixon raised his eyebrows in surprise, but ordered her soft drink and a glass of red wine for himself.

They made their way into the theater. The usher walked them down the aisle and pointed to two seats on the end. Dixon stood back to let Jessica in. She stopped and looked at him. "I like the aisle," she said.

"Of course. Everybody likes the aisle, but I'm bigger than you so I'd be uncomfortable in the inside seat."

"I'll let you lean toward me," she said without a hint of giving ground.

Dixon hesitated while thinking about the dilemma. Jessica didn't seem angry, but she did seem less at ease than a few minutes earlier. Dixon replayed the events of the evening and couldn't identify anything that seemed out of the ordinary or that would cause the apparent discord. Just then the house lights came down, so Dixon relented and took the inside seat.

As the show progressed, Dixon kept peeking at her hands through the corner of his eye. He wanted to hold her hand but didn't want to reach too far and be rebuffed. Finally, she put her elbow on the armrest, and Dixon slid his hand inside hers.

When the lights came on, Jessica broke the embrace. They replayed the same scene after the intermission. Public displays of affection were apparently regulated. As they walked to the car, Dixon remained shoulder to shoulder with her, but didn't reach for her hand or put his arm around her.

Dixon decided he'd be a little more forward when they got to her house. He walked her to the door with the expectation that she'd invite him in. When she didn't say anything one way or the other, Dixon prompted her, "Are you going to invite me in?"

"Well, I s'pose for a little while."

Once inside, Jessica offered a pop and got herself a glass of ice water. Dixon volunteered to turn on the stereo and then lingered there while Jessica was in the kitchen. He hesitated to sit on the couch first for fear she'd take the side chair. His plan was to let her sit down first and hope she went to the couch so he could sit beside her. He wasn't sure what he'd do if she went for the chair.

Fortunately, he didn't have to come up with a contingency plan. She handed him the can of pop and settled into the couch. Dixon wasted little time taking the seat next to her. He made small talk for a while until he reached across her to set his pop on the end table. With his body draped across hers, he paused until their eyes met and he leaned in for the kiss.

Jessica responded in kind. She wrapped her hands around his back and ran her fingers through the hair on the back of his head. After a short time, Dixon tipped her back so that they were lying on the couch. Dixon, perched on his elbows over her, traced his nose over her cheek. He kissed her eyebrows, kissed her cheek, and then their mouths rejoined. Dixon stroked her back in a way that caused her sweater to ride up. He put his hand on the bare skin of her back and began caressing.

After a while, they lay still, side by side, with their limbs intertwined. Dixon's nose was back on her cheek, and he moved it in small circles. He lifted his head and then propped himself on his elbows next to her.

Jessica opened her eyes. "What are you looking at?"

"You. I'm just admiring what a nice face you have."

Jessica blushed and raised her hand in an attempt to manually close his eyes.

Dixon bobbed his head back to keep her from reaching him. "I have a right to look, don't I?"

"I guess. But what's the smiling all about?"

"I'm just thinking how happy I am that we met."

Jessica smiled, but didn't say anything. She seemed to be as taken with the situation as Dixon, but he lay there with the discomfort of having rendered himself vulnerable with a statement of his feelings that was not reciprocated. It wasn't like someone ignoring an "I love you," but in a way it was worse because it really wouldn't have taken much to return the sentiment.

After a while, Dixon said, "Y'know, you're very unique looking. The blue-eyed brunette thing is really captivating."

"I think that's because I'm half Lithuanian. I'm told there are a lot of blue-eyed brunettes in the Baltic countries."

"I don't remember learning about Lithuania in high school history class."

"That's probably because it wasn't a country then. It was part of the Soviet Union, but regained independence after the fall of communism."

"You seem to know a lot about it."

"Well, my dad was actually born in Lithuania and next month he and I are going there on vacation so he can see the 'old country.'"

"Really. I'm afraid I don't even know where Lithuania is."

"It would be easier to show you on a map," she replied. "Essentially, if you're in Sweden you would go southeast across the Baltic Sea and you'd be there."

"That sounds interesting. Will you just go, or do you have relatives there?"

"We're going with some sort of travel group. We may hook up with some relatives, but I don't know the details."

Dixon pondered the adventure to be undertaken. "I never would have thought that Palmer was a Lithuanian name."

"It's not," she replied. His name was Paulus, but it got changed along the way."

"So your name should actually be Jessica Paulus?"

"Not really. I think that's why he changed it. In Lithuanian the names are all patronymic, so my name would be Paulaite, which means 'the daughter of Paulus.' My mother would have had a different name as well to signify that she was the wife of Paulus. All in all, I guess Palmer just seemed easier."

"So, what's your mother's nationality?"

"Mostly Norwegian and a little German."

They grew quiet and Dixon leaned closer. He dropped his mouth on hers and they resumed kissing. They lay together for a few more minutes, with Dixon alternately staring and kissing. Jessica then announced that it was late and it was time for bed.

Dixon pondered her statement. "I'm guessing that's a statement of your intentions and not an invitation to me."

"No wonder you're such a good lawyer," she responded. "You pick right up on these things."

Dixon got up, straightened his clothing, and prepared to leave. Jessica carried the glasses into the kitchen and returned about the time Dixon was reaching the front door. "Thanks for going to the show with me," Dixon said.

"Thanks for asking me. I had a good time."

They exchanged a last kiss before Dixon was out the door.

As he drove home, he replayed the events of the evening. There had been moments when her companionship seemed the most natural thing in the world. Yet, at other times, she seemed uncomfortable with the intimacy. Dixon was intrigued, but he was also puzzled.

# CHAPTER 18

"KEEP THE TIP UP!" Hank shouted from the stern of the little fishing boat. "She's liable to run on ya," he said, feigning seriousness.

Dixon reeled as fast as could. He encountered some resistance, but nothing that could be labeled as fighting back.

"Do ya t'ink we got a big enough net?" Hank chided.

At that moment, the fish broke the surface. It was a perch about the size of a banana. Hank chuckled.

Bewildered, Dixon asked, "How did you know it was so small? I didn't think it was a lunker, but how could you tell?"

"Your pole was barely bent, there wasn't any real fight, and the fish didn't change directions to try and get away," Hank answered.

"Well Mr. Smart Aleck, you're the guide here. I can't help it if I put my line in and the only thing there to take it is a baby perch."

"Try to get your rig lower," Hank responded. "I caught that nice walleye a few minutes ago because I was only a few feet off the bottom. Sometimes ya need to get the bait right in front of their nose for them to see it." He unhooked Dixon's perch and set it free. "I'm afraid ya lost your minnow," Hank said, tossing the lure toward Dixon.

Dixon sat for a moment to take in his surroundings. Lake Winnibigoshish was a huge man-made lake that resulted from a dam constructed on the Mississippi River. The sun's reflection off the lapping waves created a glimmering path that extended to the horizon, at which point the lake met the sky. "This is what they mean by the 'land of sky blue waters,'" Dixon said, paraphrasing the English translation of Minnesota. "It doesn't get any better than this."

"Actually it does," Hank responded. "In another hour or so I'll break out the beer and then we'll really be living."

"All we'd need then is girls," Dixon said over his shoulder.

"You t'ink fishing is more fun with nagging?"

"Well, I didn't mean just any girls. Maybe like a couple Indian girls who didn't speak the language, so all they'd do is bait our hooks, cook our shore lunch, and massage our tired shoulders."

Shaking his head, Hank said, "I guess I'll keep my expectations a little more in line with reality. Once we pop the beers, it will be as good as it gets."

"I guess I'll have to defer to your judgment." Dixon rebaited and dropped his line in the water. He let out some slack until he felt his lure hit something and then reeled it in a little in an attempt to be a couple feet off the bottom. As they trolled, Dixon imagined a fish eyeing the bait, so he alternately released slack or jerked the line in an effort to make the minnow more visible and more realistic. Dixon thought if there were a fish lurking, a minnow would naturally try to swim away, so he jerked the line to simulate that effect. Of course, it was equally likely that he was jerking it toward a fish. Ultimately, he figured the fish weren't smart enough to know people were trying to catch them, so it didn't really matter.

After a few more attempts to make his minnow dance, he asked, "How often do you go fishing?"

"That's hard to say," Hank replied. "I don't fish much around here anymore, so it depends on whether we can get a trip together. Usually a couple times a year."

"How about hunting?"

"Well, in the past we usually hunted during the season here and went to Montana or somewhere else for a hunting trip. I s'pose that will all change now that Duke's gone. He was my huntin' partner ever since we were kids."

"That's gotta be tough," Dixon sympathized. "I guess you guys were pretty close."

"That's for sure. On the other hand, if we were so close I would've thought he'd come to me before doing something crazy like killing hisself." Hank paused and shook his head. "You'd have liked Duke.

He was a lot like you. Real outgoing. We had some wild times together. At least I have the memories."

Dixon thought this kind of conversation might dampen the mood, but then realized it would probably have some therapeutic value. "Like what kind of stuff? Do you remember any of the stories?"

"Oh sure." Hank had a faraway look.

"Let's hear it."

"I guess my favorite was when we were still young and single. We didn't really have much money and were scraping to get by. One night we went to a dance up in Eveleth, which was quite a ways north of where we lived. Duke was always kind of a ladies man and sure enough he picked up this gal. Well, he danced with her a little bit and of course he had to offer to take her home. We all piled into my truck, but Duke wasn't ready to end the night so he started asking about some place we could get another drink. This gal said she worked part time at a nearby bar and the owner would let us drink after hours. Well, I was driving and I wasn't crazy about the idea, but back then people didn't t'ink that much about drinking and driving."

Hank paused and took a pull from his beer. "Anyway, we go to this little roadside place called The Hilltop Bar or something like that. We go in and Duke has to look like a big shot so he pulls out a twenty-dollar bill, which was pretty much all we had to last us until the end of the month. He and I order beers and this gal orders some kind of mixed drink. After the bartender sets 'em up, Duke looks down to the end of the bar and there's these two old miners drinking quarter beers, so Duke, Mr. Bigshot, says 'buy those boys a round as well.' After the bartender drops those off he comes back and Duke says, 'buy one for yourself.' So the twenty-dollar bill is still laying on the bar and all of a sudden Duke says to the guy, 'How much you want for this place?' 'Are you kidding?' the owner says. 'No,' Duke tells him, 'I've spent a lot of time on this side of the bar, and I always thought it would be cheaper to be on the other side.'"

Hank raised his eyes as though addressing someone above. "I have to say, by the way, that truer words were never spoken." Hank redirected his focus back to Dixon. "Anyway, this gets the owner all excited on account of I think he was just getting a little too old to run a bar. So the owner says he wants to go in back and look over some things. He leaves without picking up the twenty, so Duke puts it in his pocket."

"What are you doing during all this?"

"I wasn't really sure what to do. After a while I joined in. I went out to the truck and got a tape measure and started pretending we were going to do some remodeling. Anyway, the guy comes back and says something like $15,000, plus all of the stock at cost. Duke says that sounds pretty fair, but that we should probably count the inventory so we'd know exactly what would be required. That was just fine with the owner and pretty soon he's got all the liquor out on the bar and we're counting and calculating. The whole time he's giving us free drinks and then he even gave us something to eat. Finally, we get through it all and it's like $1,800 worth of booze. Duke says 'fine, but how will we know what's left at the closing on the sale?' Well they talk about it back and forth and agree that $16,500 would be a fair total price, so the guy would get that amount regardless of how much stock was left. So we all shook hands, the guy told Duke to come back on Wednesday, and we were out the door with full stomachs and more drinks than we had needed. All without payin' anything."

"That's a great story," Dixon said with amusement.

"No, that's an okay story. The great part is what happened afterwards. That Sunday we were at the bowlin' alley when a bunch of our buddies came in. They'd been up at Rainy Lake fishing for the weekend, and the first t'ing they said was what a mistake we'd made by not going with them. We said 'fishing was that good, huh?' 'No, the fishin' sucked,' they said. 'The reason you should have gone was because on the way back we stopped at some place called The Hilltop Bar, and the owner was selling out so it was free drinks for everybody all night long. The place was packed and it was just a madhouse.'"

Dixon laughed out loud at the punch line. Hank smiled, savoring the moment. Finally Dixon spoke, "Anything ever happen after that?"

"Not that I remember. Y'know Duke never actually said he'd buy the place, but I think he felt a little bad about it."

"That is a good story," Dixon said.

"That's just the way Duke was. He was a character. I remember another time when I was first dating Margie, I took her to Duluth for a nice dinner at the Pfister Hotel. Duke got wind of it and showed up. He bribed a busboy and put on an apron so he could walk over and hear what we were talking about. Margie didn't know him at the time, so he always tried to stand behind me when he cleared the dishes. Finally, near the end he stepped out from behind me to ask how the dinner had been and I almost shit my pants."

"That's hysterical," Dixon said with a laugh.

"Not only that," Hank continued, "Duke was better at finding the fish than I am."

"Don't give it another thought," Dixon replied. "I like the out-doors. I'd be enjoying myself even if we didn't have lines in the water. As far as I'm concerned, just being here is fishing."

"Well, August is sort of the dog days. You shoulda been here in June." As he finished speaking, Hank jerked his pole and began reeling. His pole was bent like a horseshoe, and he rushed to adjust the drag.

"Big perch?" Dixon asked.

"I'm afraid not," Hank replied. "Big northern."

"How do you know that?"

"Because walleyes don't fight much. They tap twice and you reel 'em in. A northern will fight you even if it's just a little thing." Hank put the engine in neutral so he wouldn't have to worry about the line getting in the propeller. The fish ran ahead of the bow and Hank stood to hold the line over Dixon's head. Dixon reeled in his line and crouched in the bow so as not to be in the way.

"What're ya doin' catching northerns?" Dixon teased. "I thought you knew right where to put the line to catch walleyes."

"Well, a sonofabitch of this size probably feeds on the same size walleyes we're hopin' to catch."

"Holy shit," Dixon joked, "will we need a gun to land it?"

"You just have the net ready, okay, wise guy?"

"Aye aye," Dixon responded.

After ten more minutes of battle, the great fish was growing weary and splashed alongside the boat. Dixon moved to the middle of the boat and stood straddling the center seat. He leaned over the edge of the boat with a firm grip on the net. As he thrust the net toward the water, the fish found the energy to flip up and slap its tail on the water. The water splashed with a loud "thwack" and Dixon, who had no fishing instincts, flinched and almost dropped the net.

Hank started laughing almost beyond control. "Did ya t'ink it was going to jump up and bite your neck?"

"It just surprised me a little. I'll try and do better."

"Just get it over his head and you've got it. Northerns can't back up, so if you get it started you're done."

"Really," Dixon said. "Can other fish back up?"

Hank paused to ponder the issue. "That's a good question. I don't know. The only ones we ever talk about are northerns and muskies because everyt'ing else is pretty easy to net."

The fish came alongside the boat again and Dixon didn't miss it this time. He got the net over the head and swept it up. Dixon hoisted the beast into the boat and plopped it at Hank's feet. "Keep the net taut," Hank said. "If he gets loose and starts flipping around in the boat, we're likely to all go in the drink."

Hank reached in with a needlenose pliers to reclaim his tackle. Hank spoke to the fish as if he were a dentist, "Hold still now, this will just take a minute, take deep breaths." Within seconds, the rig was removed from the lip of the fish. "I reckon that one's about fifteen pounds," Hank announced. With that, he grabbed the metal hoop of the net with one hand and put the other hand under the netting. With a quick, effortless motion, he catapulted the fish back into the water.

"Why did you do that?"

"Why not?" Hank replied. "A fish that size isn't good eatin' 'cause it's too old, and northerns are too bony anyway."

"Couldn't you have had it mounted?"

"Sure, but I need another mounted fish like a moose needs a

hat rack. Besides, that was barely trophy size. By throwing it back, maybe someone else will catch it in a couple years."

"I guess that makes sense," Dixon replied. "I'm really getting an education up here on the Range."

"Come back in a few months and I'll take ya huntin'. That, my friend, will be an education."

"I'll have to think about that one," Dixon answered. "In the meantime, I think all this excitement justifies moving happy hour up a little. How about some beer?"

"Good plan."

The pair retook their positions and resumed the hunt. After they got comfortable, Hank asked, "What's your plan for the rest of the week?"

"Interview the sheriff, talk to the deputies, visit the scene, that sort of thing."

"What do you expect to find?"

"To be honest, nothing. This case seems pretty straightforward. We need to show that Duke wasn't lying in wait and was given no opportunity to do anything but shoot the son of a bitch."

"That seems pretty obvious," Hank replied.

"Well, it'd be easier if we had a witness on our side. As it currently stands, about the only thing we can do is discredit Debi Krueller, because her story doesn't match what she initially told the authorities."

"That's pretty much because of McGuckin, isn't it?"

"I don't give McGuckin much credit," Dixon said, "but it is unethical to help clients make up lies."

"Then how do people come up with defenses in court?" Hank asked. "I thought the idea was to hire a creative lawyer to help you make up an alibi or an explanation."

"You're not necessarily far off, but the lawyers have to be more clever in order to protect themselves. They say something to their clients like 'the only defense is if we can show such and such, so you go think about it and let me know if that's what happened.'"

"I'm not sure I follow you."

"Here's an example," Dixon said. "A guy gets drunk one night and drives over to his ex-wife's house. He passes out in the car and when the cops find him it turns out he's violating a restraining order because he's supposed to stay away from the ex-wife. The guy goes to his lawyer, tells him the story, and the lawyer says: 'I think the only defense is if you can find the old friend that you ran into in the bar and have him testify that he didn't know you had gotten divorced and that, because you had too much to drink, he drove you to your old house and left you in the car in the driveway.' With that, the client goes and finds a buddy who is willing to tell that story on the stand even though it's a complete lie. The attorney can claim that he or she didn't tell the client to lie and didn't know the testimony was false, but it's pretty questionable behavior."

"Are there lawyers who do that?" Hank asked.

"Absolutely. Furthermore, I would expect something like that from McGuckin, but his clients may not be smart enough to take the hint."

"That's probably a safe assumption. Let me make sure I got this straight. A lawyer doesn't get in trouble if his client lies so long as the lawyer didn't help him or tell him to lie. Do I have that right?"

"Basically, yes. If the lawyer knows the client is lying or the evidence is false, the lawyer is not supposed to do anything at all to help. So, instead of asking the client a lot of questions while on the witness stand, the lawyer would just say something like 'tell us your version,' and let the client take it from there."

"What if the lawyer finds out after the fact that the client lied?" Hank persisted.

"I don't think there's generally a problem with that. It's kind of a pure-heart test."

"So, even though the client has done somethin' wrong, the lawyer doesn't have to turn him in?"

"Well, keep in mind that what you're talking about is the foundation of our justice system. Attorneys often know or at least believe their clients are guilty of a crime, but they still are allowed to provide a zealous defense."

"I guess I'm getting an education here, too," Hank said as he scratched his head.

The duo made a few more passes before Hank announced that his big fish must have driven the walleyes somewhere else. They reeled in and moved to another part of the lake. Dixon drained the last of his can of beer before locating the cooler and cracking another one. He sat back, put his feet up, and enjoyed watching the pine-lined shoreline race by. *Hank was right,* Dixon thought to himself. *It doesn't get any better than this.*

They stopped in an area Hank described as a reef. "Walleyes like structure," Hank said. "If a fish just sits there, the current will push it downstream. If a fish wants to rest, it gets behind rocks or some other structure to break the current."

"Current?" Dixon said in a confused voice. "In a lake?"

"Absolutely. Every body of water has a current of some sort, and the ability to figure it out is what makes some guides better than others."

"So are you saying that was one of Duke's skills?"

"Among others."

They switched from "Little Joe" rigs to fluorescent jigs with minnows. They dropped in their lines and did what they could to attract the attention of the walleyes.

After a while, the discussion turned more personal. Hank was interested in where Dixon had grown up, gone to school, and things like that. Dixon was equally intrigued by the lore of Hibbing and the Iron Range. Hank couldn't help but ask about Dixon's love life, and Dixon couldn't help but rant on about Jessica. The two came from different backgrounds and lived in different worlds, but they were developing a kinship of sorts.

Hank had started to turn the boat when Dixon's line went taut and the tip of his pole bent to point to the expected visitor below. The line ran out for several feet before Dixon began cranking it back.

"Y'got a northern on there?" Hank asked.

"Well, I'm not the expert, but I'd say it's either a northern or a nonconformist walleye."

The fight, ultimately, wasn't long. After a couple minutes, they landed a five-pound northern. Hank pronounced it very "keepable," but promptly threw it back saying he was confident they'd catch enough walleye.

Ultimately, they caught one limit between them. Hank cleaned the fish and said he'd freeze them for Dixon to take when he left.

"Sorry I can't join you for dinner tomorrow," Hank said as they were loading the boat on the trailer. "Mother made a commitment for us at church and I can't get out of it."

"Don't give it another thought," Dixon assured him. "I like doing a little exploring on my own."

"Good enough. Well, give my regards to José tomorrow."

"Who?" Dixon asked.

"The sheriff. His name is José."

"Really," Dixon said, perplexed. The documents had referred to a Sheriff Langaard, and he couldn't imagine a José Langaard. It sounded like one of those Mexican-Irish theme restaurants, but he couldn't place the nationality of Langaard.

"Will do," Dixon responded. "I'll touch base later in the week and let you know how it's going."

# CHAPTER 19

"I'M HERE TO SEE José Langaard," Dixon announced to the receptionist. "My name is Dixon Donnelly and I have an appointment."

The receptionist smirked and punched some buttons on the telephone console in front of her. In between snaps of her gum she said, "Mr. Donnelly is here to see you." After a few more snaps she said, "Okay," before turning to Dixon and saying, "he'll be right out. You can take a seat over there."

Dixon moved across the reception area and planted himself on the couch. He scanned the outdated *Rod and Gun* and *Today's Hunter* magazines on the end table and decided to simply wait. After a few minutes a big, burly blond man was standing over him extending a large paw. "I'm Sheriff Langaard."

Struggling to his feet, Dixon extended his hand and exchanged the courtesy. Dixon followed the sheriff into a back office. After they were seated Dixon said, "Are you the same sheriff they call 'José'?"

"That's me."

Dixon paused to ponder whether his next question would be considered too personal. He decided to proceed. "Could you explain how your parents came to name you José?"

"Oh, that's not my given name. My real name is Richard. They call me José because when I was growing up my family went on a vacation to Mexico. Back then, that wasn't very common for people from around here. Some of the kids started calling me José and it just stuck. Part of being in a small town I guess."

"Seems like nobody around here goes by their real name," Dixon said.

"Well, your friend McGuckin sort of goes by his real name. I mean, whether you call him Earl the Pearl or that Fuckin' McGuckin, at least it uses his given name."

Dixon smiled an acknowledgment.

"But I'm sure you didn't drive all the way up here for that," the sheriff continued. "What can I do you for?"

Dixon pulled out a yellow notepad. "Well, I have to get prepared for the Krueller civil trial, and while the facts are similar to the criminal case, there's obviously a little different slant. When you guys were working up the case against Krueller, there were certain facts that were important, but the facts that are important in my case are a little different. I'm not so much focused on what Les Krueller did, but rather what Duke MacKenzie did. So I need to kind of reconstruct some things and ask some questions. Okay?"

"Seems all right, but you should probably talk to Deputy Halvorsen on account of I didn't have much to do with the investigation," the sheriff replied.

"Oh, I plan to, but I thought I would talk to you first to get an overview of your operation and then I'd go to the next level."

"Fire away," Langaard replied.

"Tell me what standard operating procedure is when your department responds to a homicide."

"What's that got to do with anything?" Langaard asked defensively.

"Well, I'd like to just get an overview of the process and then ask more specific questions."

"But this wasn't a homicide," Langaard replied. "It was just a shooting, and we didn't find out Duke had killed himself until about a week later."

"All right," Dixon replied. "What is the standard procedure when responding to a call like the one received in this case?"

"Dispatcher sends out a deputy. On the way, they try and figure out if the situation presents a danger and get a backup if necessary. The officer will approach if he deems it safe and will secure the premises. Once he or she believes the situation is under control, the officer will make any decisions about the need for additional personnel, emergency medical teams, and whatnot."

"Okay. Then what?"

"Well, once an incident is over, the job is to find out who or what caused it. That would involve interviewing the people at the scene and otherwise taking an inventory of things. You know, gathering the weapon, taking pictures, things like that."

"So there's no standard protocol?" Dixon asked. "The deputy just shows up and asks questions and looks around?"

Sheriff Langaard glared at Dixon. "The standard protocol is to evaluate the situation and then make a determination as to the best way to proceed. If there are witnesses available, that's usually the best place to start. That's what happened here."

Dixon nodded his understanding. "I've seen the reports of Deputy Halvorsen. Would they contain everything that he did?"

"Basically. Obviously, he only records things if he thinks they are material. No sense in writing down when he went to the bathroom, things like that."

"Fair enough," Dixon responded. "I haven't seen anything indicating there was any incident reconstruction. Was one done?"

"No."

"Why not?"

"Why would we?" the sheriff snapped. "We had witnesses who told us exactly what happened."

Without adequately concealing his disbelief, Dixon said, "So, nobody ever did any sort of reconstruction of the events to determine whether the objective evidence supported the story?"

"Are you questioning my authority?" Sheriff Langaard bristled. "I think you are. You're questioning my authority."

"Sir, you're the authority around here and I'm questioning you, but I'm not questioning your authority. I'm just trying to find out what was and wasn't done and the reasons that go along with that."

"We did what we needed to do. There was a shooting and a suicide and I'm as sad as anybody that Duke's gone, but he's dead 'cause of what he did and not what the sheriff's office did." Langaard pulled some files off his desk and perused them. "Look, I've got other things to do. Halvorsen can tell you everything he did and what everybody else did. Let me take you to him."

The sheriff led the way down the hall, where he unenthusiastically introduced Dixon to Deputy Halvorsen. Dixon mustered all the sincerity he could in thanking Langaard and decided a different approach might be needed with Halvorsen.

"Thanks for meeting with me, Deputy Halvorsen. I've read your reports and I watched the criminal trial, but there are some things I don't completely understand. Furthermore, my case focuses on some different issues so I need to reconstruct the incident from a different perspective."

"That's fine," Halvorsen responded.

"Your reports are pretty thorough, but I'm wondering if we could talk about the incident, because there might have been things that are relevant to my case, but weren't important to yours. Sound fair?"

"Sounds fine. I can't really think of anything that I would have left out, but we can talk it through." As Dixon pulled out the reports, Halvorsen said, "Actually, I can think of one thing I might have left out. Originally, Debi tried to claim she hadn't been upstairs having sex with Duke. I asked her several times, and it seemed logical because Les was hollerin' about catching her in the act, but she kept denying it."

"Yeah, I saw that she gave different versions at different times," Dixon said.

Halvorsen proceeded to walk Dixon through the details of the exchanges with Debi Krueller and her ultimate admission that she and Duke were having sex at the time of the break-in.

"Any reason you didn't put all of that in your report?" Dixon asked.

"I guess once she admitted she was having sex with Duke it didn't seem to matter how she came to admit it. In your case it might be relevant because it looked like the sex was pretty spontaneous."

"Thank you, Deputy Halvorsen," Dixon said. "You've figured out exactly the type of information I need." With that, Dixon began to work through the chronology in the reports. Each time new information was contained in a report, Dixon would ask a series of questions designed to elicit additional details or memories.

After a half hour or so, Dixon said he thought he understood everything Deputy Halvorsen had done and seen, but he wanted to explore some things that weren't done. "Did anyone ever examine Krueller's wound to see if it was consistent with the story?"

"What do you mean?" Halvorsen asked.

"Well, was there a powder burn or something else to indicate he was shot at close range? Was the angle of entry consistent with the story? Those types of things."

"Krueller said he was shot by Duke and there wasn't any real mystery. So I guess the answer is no, we didn't do anything to verify that version of events."

"Okay, there was some blood on the carpet. Was it ever tested?"

"For what?"

"To make sure it was Krueller's," Dixon responded.

"Well, the blood was still wet when we got there and Krueller was bleeding. That seemed like a pretty safe assumption."

"I'm not doubting the assumption, I just want to know what was done. Did you do any tests to look for traces of other blood that might have been cleaned up?"

"Like whose?"

"Nobody in particular. I just want to know what else was done."

"No," Halvorsen responded.

"Did anyone do any fingerprinting?"

"We did check the gun after it was recovered. We didn't find anything on it."

"Isn't that unusual? Shouldn't Duke's prints have been on it?"

"Not necessarily," the deputy responded. "The gun wasn't found for about a week."

"Were you part of the search for Duke?"

"Yes sir."

"When was that?"

"Mostly the next day and thereafter. The night of the incident we called out into the woods and asked Duke to surrender, but we didn't want to go looking for him in the dark because as far as we were concerned he had just shot a man and might be a threat to us."

"Fair enough," Dixon nodded. "That next day, did you try and track footprints or use a bloodhound or anything like that?"

"No, not really. We just fanned out and looked in the woods for anything that might help."

"Do you remember ever seeing footprints?"

"Yeah. Some."

"What do you remember about that?" Dixon asked.

"Well, there were a couple low spots that could get muddy, and we found a lot of footprints, but we couldn't really tell if they were anything. There were different types of shoe prints, so we figured most of the prints were old."

Dixon scratched his chin in a thinly veiled effort to make his interrogation seem as nonchalant as possible. "Did you check the shoes of either of the Kruellers to see if they had mud on them?"

"No. In fact, Debi was barefoot when I arrived."

"Were any of the footprints in the mud of bare feet?" Dixon asked.

"Not that I remember, but we didn't really study it."

"Any evidence that anyone had washed mud off their shoes."

"I don't remember noticing anything out of the ordinary," Halvorsen said.

"How about fingerprints on the shovel? I forgot to ask you that before."

"We didn't check it, why?"

"Well, Krueller says he dropped it on the deck and Duke moved it into the bedroom."

"Gotcha," Halvorsen replied. "But it was Duke's shovel, so his prints might be on it anyway."

"Good point." Dixon flipped through his notepad. "Any forensic testing done on Duke's remains?"

"Some. They needed to confirm it was him."

"How did they determine it was suicide?"

"The injury was consistent with somebody putting a gun in their mouth and shooting through their upper palate into their brain. That, along with the testimony from the Kruellers seemed to make it clear to the coroner."

"But I thought the upper jaw was recovered intact?"

"I guess you're right," Halvorsen responded. "Come to think of it, the shot was more through the back of his head."

"Going which direction?" Dixon asked.

"You'd have to ask the coroner for sure, but my understanding was they could tell by the hole which way the bullet was going and it exited out the back of the skull."

"Nobody reported hearing a second gunshot, is that right?" Dixon continued.

"Right," Halvorsen said with a nod.

"And from the time you arrived until early the next morning, you or someone with law enforcement was present, is that right?"

"Yes."

"So Duke either pulled the trigger before you got there and the Kruellers just didn't hear it, or Duke waited until later the next day or after."

Halvorsen leaned forward, having apparently not considered the issue. "I think it would be hard for the Kruellers not to have heard a shot, because we ultimately found body parts and the gun only about fifty yards away from the house. On the other hand, the way they fight there's no telling how much hollering was going on."

"Well, Deputy Halvorsen, in your experience, isn't suicide an impulsive act and wouldn't it seem less likely that Duke would have hung out in the woods for a day and then offed himself after the authorities were gone?"

"That makes sense to me, but I'm not a mental-health expert so I don't really want to say," he responded.

"Tell me, Deputy, you made a variety of assumptions based upon what you saw and were told and those things led you to suspect suicide. It's accurate, isn't it, that suicide is just a best guess and there is no evidence that establishes that conclusively?"

"I don't know how to answer that. We gave Doc Richardson our findings and he made the call. We don't have anybody who witnessed Duke's death so there's always a doubt, but Doc makes his determination based on the best information available, and I think he made the right call."

"Fair enough," Dixon said. "I appreciate your time and I may call you again if I have more questions." The men shook hands and Dixon found his way out.

Dixon grabbed lunch and spent the afternoon reviewing court files, arrest records, and incident reports involving Les and Debi Krueller. Some of the documents he had seen before. Others were new and shed new light on some of the issues. Dixon took a variety of notes and then arranged for photocopies. He also took down information so he could obtain hearing transcripts if necessary. All in all, the afternoon was more productive than the morning.

# CHAPTER 20

Dixon called Hank to tell him about the day's events—the hostility from the sheriff's office and the fact that the previous investigation was pretty minimal. He also shared some of the information he'd found while perusing files in the afternoon. Finally, he asked if Hank would take him out to the property the next day. Hank obliged and they arranged to meet for breakfast.

Dixon then headed out to spend a night on the town by himself. He had changed into his most modest apparel, but he still wasn't likely to blend in. He found a fairly authentic southern Italian restaurant for dinner, but neglected to bring reading material with him, so he passed the time waiting for his food by reading a local shoppers' guide.

After dinner, he decided to try a neighborhood bar to sample the local color. There was a remote possibility he'd meet someone with good information about Duke, the Kruellers, or something else. Worst case scenario: he'd have a couple drinks and unwind.

He drove toward the main street, with no idea what he was looking for. The buildings in the area were old, and Dixon imagined things probably hadn't changed since the fifties. He spotted a Grain Belt beer bar sign with "The Boondocks" written in plain block letters at the bottom. Once upon a time a beer executive had come up with the brilliant idea of giving bar owners their signage and appending that signage to something bearing the beer company's name and logo. The signs weren't classy, but they were free and they were everywhere.

Dixon parked up the street. Volvos weren't unheard of in these parts, but they usually signaled "out-of-towner." He hoped to blend in at least a little, so he thought he'd park out of sight. As he approached the bar, he realized it didn't really matter because, like most small town bars, there were no windows to speak of and the only thing allowing light in or out were a few glass blocks mounted where a window might otherwise be. Whether that architectural choice was driven by the patrons' desire for anonymity or was a practical response to the inevitable bar fights was never clear.

Dixon grabbed the door handle and pushed the thumb release to unlatch the door. As he pushed the door in, the smell of stale beer and long-since-smoked cigarettes pushed its way out. This was an establishment dedicated to vices.

Dixon stopped and surveyed the setting—on the left, a couple of wooden booths; on the right a long bar fronted by bar stools with metal legs and worn-out red vinyl coverings proclaiming homage to "The King of Beers." There was a coin-operated pool table in the back with a low-hanging Pabst Blue Ribbon light. On the wall was a clock with "Leinenkugel's" spread across the face. Dixon wondered whether bar owners actually had to buy anything to furnish their premises.

He walked almost the entire length of the bar before finding an empty stool. The bar was only about half full, but the seats at the bar were apparently at a premium. Dixon saddled up and waited for service.

A jukebox was playing Johnny Cash. The twangs of the music were regularly interrupted by the slamming of dice on the far end of the bar and the occasional holler when a particularly good roll came about. Behind the bar were the culinary delights of the house: pickled eggs, pickled pig's feet, and some unspecified kind of jerky. For the sake of authenticity there was a long mirror, but it was covered by more beer paraphernalia and a prominently posted schedule for the upcoming Vikings season.

The bartender was a heavyset woman with thinning hair who stood talking to patrons while joining them in a cigarette. After a moment she noticed Dixon and strolled down to him. Before she reached him she stopped and put the cigarette in an ashtray on the back bar as if doing so would actually grant Dixon some refuge from the smoke. "What'll ya have, sweetie?" she cooed in a gravelly voice.

"Grain Belt Premium would be great."

"Tap or bottle?" she asked.

Imagining that the beer lines had probably last been cleaned for the Bicentennial, Dixon opted for the bottle.

The bartender fished a bottle from a refrigerated enclosure, snapped the cap off in a bottle opener mounted under the bar, and put the beer in front of Dixon. "Do you want to pay cash or shake for it?" she asked.

"At the risk of sounding naive and basically giving you license to screw me, why don't you tell me what you mean by 'shake for it.'"

"The name of the game is 'Liars Dice.' If you win, the beer's free. If I win, you pay double."

"I guess you better educate me on the official rules of the game."

"I'm afraid I can only tell ya the Boondocks' rules. I don't know if they're official."

"Fair enough," Dixon said with a nod.

"Whoever goes first rolls five dice, but doesn't let the other one see them. The idea is to make a poker hand. The first roller says what he's got and the second guy has to beat it. Then, the first roller goes again and you keep going back and forth having to beat the other guy."

"Where does the 'liar' part come in?"

"The roller doesn't have to tell the truth. In fact, even if they have a good roll, they can say something completely different. If you catch the other guy lying, you win. So, if you don't think you can beat the roll as it stands, you might as well challenge it."

"I think I'm following you," Dixon said. "When I roll, I need to either beat what you said you had, or lie well enough to make you think that I did?"

"That's the gist of it."

"So, if I'm not a good liar, I'm in trouble?"

"Not necessarily. It depends on what the dice say. If you roll good enough, you don't need to be a good liar."

"Something about this sounds like my job."

"Which is?"

"Lawyer."

"Then you should be good at lying."

"Some lawyers are, but I'm afraid I'm not."

"Then you better be good at figuring out when the others are lying."

"I can't tell you how right you are about that," he said. "But let's get back to what we're doing here. Just so I know what I'm getting into, how much is the beer normally?"

"A buck."

"Well that seems like a risk I can afford. Do you think we can borrow the dice from those guys?" he said, pointing.

"No need," she said, pulling another dice cup from under the bar. "Do you want to go first or second?"

"I guess I'll let you go first so I can make sure I know what I'm doing."

"Fine." She slammed the cup upside down on the bar and lifted it to take a peak. "Two 3s" she said.

Dixon put the dice in the cup, shook it twice and dumped it on the bar. He was relieved to spy two 5s and promptly announced them.

The bartender smirked, but didn't challenge him. She slammed the cup on the bar and took a long look. "Three 2s," she declared.

Her pause had been too long, as if trying to convince Dixon she was having to make something up. While beating that roll would be difficult, Dixon didn't want to be taken in by her ruse. He swept the dice into the cup, covered the opening, and spun it around his head in the hope of instilling some spiritual influence. He slammed the cup down and gingerly lifted it to reveal a 1-2-4-5-6. He realized that he should have prepared a bogus claim in advance so that he could announce something with confidence, but it was now too late. Meekly, he said, "How about a flush? Does a flush count?"

"Maybe on the reservation," she smirked, "but here at the Boon-docks you owe two bucks."

"Fair enough," Dixon said, slapping two singles on the bar. "Just don't let me try and roll for any of that pickled stuff on the back counter."

"It's a deal," the bartender said as she retrieved her cigarette and returned to her perch on the other end of the bar.

Dixon took a long drink from his beer. There was a small TV in a corner, but it was not on and, even if it were, it wouldn't be particularly visible from where Dixon sat. With virtually no food and minimal entertainment, the only real diversion the Boondocks had to offer was drinking and, to the regular customers, that was the purpose and not the diversion.

Dixon swung around on the stool to face the open area of the bar. There was nothing in particular to look at, but it allowed him to use the bar as a backrest. He just sat, drinking his beer, while trying to blend in. He occasionally eavesdropped on neighboring conversations, but none of them held much interest. Eventually, he swung back around and rested his elbows on the bar. Maybe this wasn't the best idea he'd ever had.

He was studying a sign taped to the mirror that listed all the recent pull-tab winners from the Boondocks when a woman's voice spoke from directly behind him. "Mr. Donnelly, you're taking a liking to our lifestyle."

Dixon spun his chair around and found himself nose to nose with Debi Krueller. Upon realizing who she was, he leaned back against the bar to provide a comfortable distance. "Well, when in Rome . . ." Dixon said, while looking around nervously.

"Oh, don't worry. Les isn't here."

"I wasn't worried. I just thought that if he was I should say hi."

"No, he's working the night shift over in Hoyt Lakes. I'm all by my lonesome."

Debi Krueller was dressed like someone on the prowl. Her hair had received a recent visit from the curling iron, and her makeup was clearly the result of a protracted effort. Her clothes weren't fancy, but, compared to the blue jeans and tee shirts populating the bar, she looked like she could have just come from a wedding, albeit an Iron Range wedding.

"Buy me a drink?" she asked.

"Well, ordinarily I would never refuse such a request, but it's considered improper for a lawyer to speak directly to an opposing party who is represented by an attorney."

"I'm not an opposing party. Les is. I'm just his wife," she protested.

"Well, actually, you are essentially a party, because of the claim for loss of consortium."

"What exactly does that mean?" she said, removing a pack of cigarettes from her purse.

"Mrs. Krueller, I'm really not supposed to talk to you. You should ask your own attorney what that means."

Debi popped a Kool between her lips and flicked open a lighter. She didn't use the disposable kind. This was a good old-fashioned, flip-top, not-even-close-to-childproof burner. It made a slight ringing sound when opened and gave off the scent of lighter fluid. "I don't think McGuckin is my lawyer. He just tells me what to say to help Les, and I don't think he cares what happens to me," she pouted.

"Well, even if there is a conflict of interest question, I know I can't be your lawyer, so we shouldn't be speaking to each other."

"Well, there's no rule against me sitting here is there?" she asked.

"No ma'am."

Debi waved at the bartender, who nodded and hollered "usual?" to which Debi nodded affirmatively. Turning back to Dixon she said, "Can we talk if we don't talk about the case?"

"Technically we probably could," Dixon said, "but under the circumstances I wouldn't feel very comfortable about it."

Debi leaned closer to Dixon and deliberately caused her leg to touch his. "Do I frighten you, Mr. Donnelly? I thought during the deposition I might have been having another effect on you."

"Mrs. Krueller, I don't want to be rude, but I'm going to have to move."

"Okay. How 'bout if I stop talking?"

"That would make it easier for me."

She pulled her upper body away but left her leg close enough to Dixon's that he could feel their pants touching. The proximity sent a shiver through him, and he realized how quickly Duke could have been overcome by her sexuality.

Dixon stared straight ahead, as if he were looking for his name on the list of recent pull-tab winners. Debi leaned forward and put her elbow on the bar. She held her cigarette with the cherry pointing to the ceiling and her thumb covering the end of the filter, as if she wanted to make sure none of the nicotine escaped. Between sips of her drink she took long draws on the cigarette and blew smoke cones toward the ceiling. Her actions seemed designed to make sure the smoke made its journey through her lungs but the smell stayed as far away from her clothes and hair as possible.

After sitting quietly for several minutes, Debi blurted out, "Y'know I really don't want to get up in court and tell the whole town about what I did with Duke. I'd do just about anything to keep that from happening." As she spoke she moved her leg and began tracing a line up Dixon's calf with the toe of her shoe.

Dixon swung his legs out of her reach. "Mrs. Krueller, I don't really have any control over that. If you want to avoid testifying, you have to bring that up with your husband or your attorney."

Apparently realizing that for once sex wasn't going to get her what she wanted, Debi pulled back. She was quiet for a long moment, but then began to cry. She put one hand over her eyes to cover the tears. She didn't wail, but after a while her shoulders began to shake. While the tears were real, Dixon wasn't convinced this wasn't simply another one of her manipulative ploys.

"Am I allowed to talk to the MacKenzies?" she asked.

"There's no restriction on that. I'm not sure they'd talk to you, but it's allowed."

"I just want to tell them how bad I feel about the whole thing," she sobbed.

"Look, Mrs. Krueller, I don't want to offend you, but I can't stay here and talk to you. I've already stayed longer than I should have, but I didn't want to be rude. I hope you get everything worked out." With that, Dixon slid off the red vinyl stool and headed out the front door. He decided to make it an early night after all.

# CHAPTER 21

DIXON WOKE EARLY the next morning. He'd upgraded to a motel outside of town, and the amenities were slightly better. The building was a large block structure devoid of architectural style or design. The guests were generally business travelers on budgets, so the ambiance was of little concern. People stayed there out of necessity, and it was not and never would be a destination.

To kill time, he walked to the lobby in a hopeless search to find the current edition of any national newspaper. He managed to find a *Duluth Gazette* and perused it for sports, comics, and anything else that might be of interest. After that lost its power to hold his attention, he checked out of the motel, making a point to tell the clerk he wasn't leaving at that instant, but wanted to settle the bill while he had the opportunity.

Dixon strolled back to his room and packed. Even though he had already accounted for everything he had come with, Dixon did a once-over, looking in drawers and closets to make sure he'd remembered everything. Finally, he flung his bag over his shoulder and headed out to the parking lot on the back side of the motel.

As the glass door of the motel closed behind him, Dixon stared in shock at what he saw—his car was covered in red. Dixon dropped his suitcase and slowly circled the car. The red substance wasn't just splashed on as though the result of a paint balloon. A swastika was smeared on the windshield and a stick figure with a noose around its neck appeared to have been finger-painted into the splotch on the side. Dixon felt a profound sense of terror. It was morning and the sun was up, but the demonic nature of the vandalism unnerved him.

He touched the substance and determined it was dry and did not have the consistency of paint. *Omigod,* Dixon thought. *Is it blood?* He obtained some paper towels from the motel and rubbed the windshield. Slowly he created an opening through which a driver could see. Having minimal luck removing anything further, he loaded his bag and headed for a car wash, drawing plenty of stares as he drove through town.

The red substance seemed to respond to the pressure hose at the self-serve car wash, but it took numerous rinses. Dixon considered whether he should have the authorities test the substance before it was all in the sewers under the streets of Hibbing. He decided there was a reasonable chance the authorities took exception to his second-guessing their police work and they'd be largely indifferent. Worse yet, it occurred to him the authorities could turn out to be the perpetrators.

Dixon was a half hour late meeting Hank. He apologized and explained what had happened.

"What the hell is that about?" Hank asked.

"I don't really know. The sheriff's office didn't seem too happy about all the questions I was asking, but how would they know what I was driving or where I was staying? McGuckin and Les Krueller aren't too fond of me, but they're such obvious suspects they'd be idiots to try something like that. Of course there's Debi. I saw her at the bar last night and she came on to me in a big way because she doesn't want to testify."

"Before you go any further, ya gotta tell me about that," Hank said.

"Not much to tell. I went down to the Boondocks to have a drink. I was minding my own business, and all of a sudden she showed up beside me. She asked me about the case and pretty soon she was rubbing up against me. When I resisted her advances, she broke down and cried."

"So, she offered her honor, but you didn't honor her offer."

"That's about the size of it. I can see how a man could fall into that pretty easy. She's not particularly classy, but she sure exudes sex."

Hank was having trouble concealing his amusement at Dixon's

encounter. "So, do you think she was offended that you wouldn't mess around and took it out on your car?"

"That doesn't seem likely. I mean, I don't know how she'd even know what I drive or where it was parked."

"Let me have a look at it, or did you get it all cleaned off?" Hank said.

"I think I got most of it, but it's hard to say." The two men circled the car looking for any remnants in a crack, on some chrome, or otherwise hiding. Dixon popped the trunk and found some red that had trickled through. "Here's some."

Hank leaned close and scratched it with his thumbnail. "Hard to say, but it looks like blood. I've had my share of deer strapped to car roofs and in pickup beds and this looks kinda like blood. On the other hand, it could be red dye number 2 for all I know."

Dixon closed the trunk. "I decided not to bother contacting the authorities. I don't really think there's much they could do, and I don't want anyone to think that I'm concerned about it."

"That's probably a good idea," Hank replied. "It was probably just some kids playin' a prank." He shrugged his shoulders to punctuate the end to the topic. "As long as we're running a little late, you wanna skip breakfast and head out to Duke's?"

"That would be fine. Should I follow you, or do you want to just give me a ride?"

"Hop in," Hank said. He drove a one-ton pickup that looked like it had escaped from a monster truck show. The sheer size of the cab and the tread on the tires made it clear this wasn't the highway ride. It was made for gravel roads or less. Hank's relatively small stature made the truck seem even larger.

Dixon swung open the cab door and took two steps up as though he was boarding a bus. "What's happened with the house since the incident? Has it been sealed off? Has anyone lived in it?"

"It was off-limits for a while. I guess they had to give Krueller's lawyer a chance to look at it before doin' too much. After that, we put it on the market. We cleaned it up quite a bit, but we left some of the furniture."

"Any buyers on the horizon?" Dixon asked.

"A couple. In fact, there's a guy who's a retired Minneapolis cop who's interested."

"Does he know what happened there?"

"Yeah, and that type of t'ing doesn't bother him. Better yet, I asked him about the whole shooting, and he said he'd be happy to help if there were any questions about procedures, the evidence, or anyt'ing else."

Dixon pressed his lips together and slowly shook his head. "Y'know, I have no doubt the local authorities did a bad job handling the matter, but I don't think we'll find anything different from the conclusions already reached."

"What happened to the attitude from that sign on your office wall? Something about doubting authority?"

"I don't think anything should be accepted at face value, but that doesn't mean the authorities are always wrong. More importantly, Hank, that's not why you hired me. My only job is to prove that Les Krueller is a bum and that he's not entitled to anything because he was the cause of his own injury."

"You're right," Hank responded. "I'm sorry I brought it up, but I just have a hard time believing Duke would kill himself."

"You don't need to apologize. I think I understand how you feel, but it puts pressure on me to think you want me to accomplish something I don't think is possible. You want answers to what happened and why Duke would do such a thing, and it's easier to believe he wouldn't have done such a thing. I don't claim to know anything about the psychology of it, but I'm sure suicide is rarely a rational act."

They had now turned off the main road and were racing along on a gravel road. A plume of dust rose behind them as they drove and hung in the air like a jet's exhaust stream on a clear winter day. Hank motored along as though he was on a highway. As they rounded curves and crested hills, Dixon could only imagine what would happen if they met oncoming traffic on the narrow road. For his part, Hank drove as though that simply never happened.

Hank slowed as they approached a turn-off. Signs were posted on either side of what appeared to be a driveway declaring "Private Property" and "No Trespassing."

"This is it," Hank announced. "Wait here while I unchain the gate."

Hank unlocked the chain that kept vehicles from entering, and they drove up the drive toward a large shed with several doors that looked like a five-car garage. Hank parked the truck, and they walked toward the house.

"That shed is where they parked Debi's car," Hank said.

"How do you know that?"

"It was still there when I got here. Deputy Halvorsen called me after the ambulance had taken Krueller to the hospital. I came right out and tried to help find Duke."

"So was Halvorsen still here when you arrived?"

"Yeah, and so was Debi Krueller."

"What did you do?"

"Well, I talked to everybody to find out what happened, and then I went out and started yelling for Duke. I wanted to let him know Krueller was gonna live and that he should turn himself in."

"How long did you do that for?"

"Oh, I don't know. I yelled for a while and then I went in the house. After the deputy left I went out again and yelled that the coast was clear. I thought about going into the woods, but this is his land so I figured I wouldn't find him if he didn't want to be found.

"So how long were you here?"

"Probably till early the next morning. I kept thinking he'd come back or that he might call for help. He left his wallet in the house, so I figured he couldn't go far."

"So, from the time the sheriff's office got here at about eleven until the next morning, someone other than the Kruellers was always here, but nobody heard a shot."

"That's right."

They had reached the house, but Hank paused like a tour guide while they finished the discussion. "You see that hill back there? I think that's where Krueller claims he went to try and look in the bedroom. See, if you go back far enough you're level with the bedroom, but between the trees and the distance you couldn't see much."

The house was more of a log cabin, or even a lodge. It was rustic in design, but the construction was relatively recent. The front of the house faced the lake and had windows extending to the top of the second story. On the second level there was a deck on one side with a sliding glass door. "That's the door that got smashed," Hank said while pointing.

They walked up to the front door and Hank dug in his pocket for a key.

"Is this the door Krueller walked through when he was here the day before?" Dixon asked.

"It would have to be. There's another door in back, but it's always locked and you can't see in through it."

"I thought Krueller said there was a screen door. This doesn't look like it was even built for one."

"I hope yer not surprised that Les Krueller might be a liar," Hank said with a grin.

"No, it just always amazes me what people will lie about."

Hank turned the key, and they entered the house. The front of the house was a great room in the true sense of the word. The ceiling was two stories high, a rock fireplace dominated one wall, and an antler chandelier hung in the middle. The log walls were decorated with hunting and fishing trophies and with antique equipment for trapping, shooting, or catching such trophies.

"So," Dixon remarked, "this must be the table where Duke and Debi were sitting when Lester showed up the first time."

"Yup. And that chair over by the fireplace is where Debi was sitting when the deputy showed up the night of the shooting."

"Let's take a look upstairs," Dixon suggested. They walked to the back of the house and ascended a circular staircase. Once on the second level, the sliding glass door was on their right. Hank unlocked it and they walked out on the deck.

"Do you see these scratch marks from where Krueller tried to pry the door open?" Hank asked.

Dixon looked close. "Actually, I don't see anything."

"That's exactly right," Hank said with a twinkling eye. "Could it be that he told another lie?"

They went back inside and walked down the hall to the first door.

"This is the bedroom," Hank said as he pushed the door open. A king-sized bed flanked by matching nightstands sat against the wall opposite the door. At the far end of the room was a large closet leading to a bathroom.

Dixon strolled around the room as though he was a crime scene investigator. He didn't really know what he was looking for, but he studied everything as if it might come to him. He looked out the window, inspected the bathroom, opened the nightstand drawers, and otherwise acted as though he had a purpose. "Well, I suppose we should get some measurements and do some reenactments," he suggested. "We'll want to impress upon the jury how close everything was and how quickly things would have happened."

Dixon pulled out a tape measure and, with Hank's assistance, began measuring the distance from the sliding glass door to the bedroom, the distance from the bedroom door to the bed, and anything else that seemed relevant.

"Should we time it?" Hank suggested.

"Good idea," Dixon responded. "Our reenactment won't be scientific enough to present as evidence, but it may help our own analysis. Go to the sliding glass door and when I say 'go,' come in here as quick as you can."

Hank obliged, and they determined that once inside the house it would take less than three seconds to get to the bedroom. "Of course, I wasn't carryin' a shovel," Hank stated.

"Good point. Furthermore, you didn't have to open the bedroom door. Why don't you go get a shovel or something equally as cumbersome and I'll close the door and we'll try again."

Hank departed. Dixon grabbed the door and swung it back and forth a few times to confirm its easy glide. He then examined the handle to see if there was a locking mechanism. He looked for a doorstop to see what effect it might have if someone threw the door open the way Krueller had claimed.

He started to turn to walk to the bed when something caught his eye. He leaned in close and froze. About five feet off the floor was a hole in one of the logs. Not a big hole, but more than one of Mother Nature's imperfections. Between the knots and everything else, it was barely perceptible. The open door usually covered it, making it even less likely to be noticed.

Hank yelled from the sliding glass door to see if Dixon was ready. "Come here a minute," Dixon called. Hank ambled into the bedroom with a snow shovel in hand. "Look at this," Dixon said, pointing.

Hank leaned in to get a closer look.

"What the hell do you think this is?" Dixon asked.

"Looks like a bullet hole," Hank replied.

"The bullet that hit Les was pulled out of his stomach, wasn't it?"

"Yeah."

"Holy shit," Dixon said in disbelief. "I don't remember reading anything about this in any police report."

"You think it's from that night?"

"I don't know what I think."

Hank was wide-eyed. "What should we do?"

"Nothing. This is a crime scene, and we don't want to be accused of disturbing the evidence."

"So ya t'ink the sheriff's office can handle this?" Hank asked.

"I think we need to talk to that retired cop who's thinking about buying the place. Let's have him look things over before we bring in the sheriff, and let's make sure we have somebody overseeing the process so we know if the sheriff's office does the right thing."

"Good idea," Hank responded.

"This might be nothing," Dixon said, "but I sure as hell want to know exactly what it is."

"I'll second that."

Dixon stared at the hole a little longer. "Why don't we go look in the woods and see if there's anything else worth noting."

Hank led Dixon down the stairs and out the door. "I wasn't here when they found the remains," Hank said, "but I think I know about where they were." They walked from the lawn into the woods. There was minimal brush, and the ground was mostly dirt. After about twenty-five yards, they came to a wall of underbrush. "The gun and part of his body were found on the other side of these bushes," Hank said. "Some of the other body parts were found nearer the lake. I don't really remember what was found where."

"And I believe you told me before that you had the remains cremated, is that right?"

"Well, there wasn't really enough left to put in a coffin. I'm planning on spreading the ashes over the Bighorn Mountains the next time I'm out there hunting."

"This spot doesn't seem very far into the woods," Dixon remarked. "Why did it take so long to find the remains?"

"The land gets real swampy if you go another twenty yards or so. We figured if Duke ran away he wouldn't go where he'd be boxed in. We looked in the opposite direction, so we didn't really look here until nothing else turned up."

"I gotta tell ya," Dixon said, "this case seemed bizarre when you first told me about it, but it keeps getting even more bizarre. Call that cop the first chance you get and see if you can get him up here."

# CHAPTER 22

IT WAS SATURDAY, and that meant date night. For a change, that was a good thing in Dixon's life. He'd suggested a movie, but Jessica had other ideas. She said she wanted to cook dinner. Dixon offered to bring his fresh catch, but she said she'd take responsibility for everything except, of course, the wine. Dixon forgot to ask what the main course would be, but covered his slip by arriving with a bottle of red and a bottle of white.

Dixon rang the bell and waited. He thought of letting himself in, but it seemed a little presumptuous at that point in the relationship.

Jessica opened the inside door and, noticing Dixon's hands were full, propped open the screen door. "Hi there," she said with a smile.

Once inside, Dixon leaned over and gave her a quick kiss on the lips. "Hi yourself."

Jessica appeared surprised by the kiss, but it was clearly a pleasant surprise.

"I brought a bottle of red and a bottle of white," he said, holding them up for display. "I wasn't sure what you were making, but I thought this would cover it either way."

"What if I told you the perfect wine for my dinner is a white zin?"

"Well, then we'll open both bottles and mix them together."

Dixon wiped his feet and noticed Jessica's shoes on the rug near the front door. Assuming that was the protocol, he removed his shoes. Looking around, he noticed the table had already been set, the stereo was playing, and everything otherwise seemed to be in place. "Can I ask what we're having?"

"Of course," she replied. "Pork tenderloin, mushroom risotto, and an asparagus dish that is sort of an asparagus au gratin."

"That sounds fabulous. Speaking of which, I can't believe how good you look. Are you sure you cooked, 'cause you don't look like you spent the afternoon in the kitchen."

Jessica smiled, but didn't respond.

Dixon followed her through the living room into the kitchen. "It smells fabulous too."

"Well, I hope everything turns out," she said. "I usually only try one new recipe at a time so I can be assured the meal isn't a total flop, but these are all new." She lifted a lid on one of the pots on the stove and stirred the contents with a wooden spoon.

Dixon walked up behind her, reached his hands around her waist, and clasped them across her stomach. He leaned his head over her shoulder and pulled her hair back with his chin. With her backside pressed against him, he kissed her neck. Jessica paused to let the electricity of his touch run the length of her body, then continued to stir the rice as if she was a woman on a mission.

Realizing that she wasn't going to turn around and throw her arms around him, Dixon released the embrace. "Should I open the red or the white?" he asked. "I mean, now that pork is 'the other white meat,' I'm not sure I know what to do."

"Either is fine with me," she said. "I usually think of white as being for the summer and red for winter, but either would be fine."

Dixon decided to uncork the merlot. "Anything else I can do?"

"Not really. Dinner won't be ready for about fifteen minutes, so I guess you can pour us each a glass."

Dixon obliged. While Jessica checked on the rest of the food, Dixon wandered back into the living room. There were several framed pictures on the mantel. He spied a small black-and-white photo of a little girl on ice skates. "Who's this little cutie with the skates?"

"Who do you think?" Jessica yelled from the kitchen. "That's yours truly, circa 1968."

"Y'know, your eyes look blue even in this black-and-white picture," Dixon remarked.

Jessica walked into the living room. "I hope you don't think flattery will get you anywhere."

"Well, it won't hurt will it?"

"No, not if it's sincere."

"Well, I'm not kidding, those eyes of yours are something else."

Jessica batted her long eyelashes and, affecting a demur southern drawl, said, "Oh, Mr. Donnelly, you do go on." As she said it she wiped away imaginary perspiration with an imaginary handkerchief.

Dixon placed a hand on her shoulder. He thought about pulling her close and kissing her, but that didn't seem to fit Jessica's schedule. This was talk time, which would be followed by dinner time, and, with any luck, followed by couch time. "Who are these people?" Dixon asked, pointing at another picture.

"Girlfriends from college. They came to see me last year in Atlanta, and we went to Savannah."

Dixon nodded and continued to examine the pictures, stopping when he had a question or thought he could make a joke. He noted to himself that none of the pictures looked like former boyfriends, and he was happy about that. He picked up a picture of a scruffy looking group standing in front of a mountain. He held it close, trying to see the faces. "What's this?"

"That was from backpacking a couple years ago. I'm a youth counselor at my church, and we went to a place called Camp Fellowship in Rocky Mountain National Park."

"Really. Did you go backpacking too, or just stay at the camp?"

Jessica gave him a penetrating look. "Yes, I went backpacking, and, believe it or not, I even carried my own pack."

"Oh, I didn't mean it like that," Dixon said apologetically. "I just didn't think of you as the camping type."

"I did it three years in a row. The last year we covered about forty miles in five days."

"Impressive. So, what religion are you?" Dixon asked.

"I was raised Lutheran. The church I belong to now, though, is nondenominational."

"How did you choose that?"

"I went to a lot of churches till I found one I liked."

"So, it had the best music, the best doughnuts, or what?"

"I think of myself as very spiritual, but I'm not looking for something dogmatic. I believe in a higher power, but I don't accept the literalism of some religions."

"What do you mean?"

"Here's an easy example. Catholic priests can't get married because they think they have to emulate Jesus and they don't think Jesus was ever married. How can anyone make a rule like that? Jesus never condemned marriage or told his followers not to get married. I mean, the Catholic Church didn't even come up with that idea until about a thousand years later."

Dixon watched in awe as she articulated her argument and her beliefs. It was exciting to him to be with a woman who seemed ready to challenge assumptions and question authority. "That's interesting," he said. "My objection to organized religion was always that people mindlessly went to church without any idea of why, and to find someone who's really dwelled on it is quite refreshing."

"Well, maybe I need to get off my soapbox," she blushed.

Dixon continued down the row, examining the pictures. Near the end, he found a snapshot of two young men and an older woman standing in front of a Christmas tree. "Family?" he asked.

"Yeah. Those are my brothers, Tom and Jeff, and that's my mom."

Next to the snapshot was a picture of a middle-aged man that appeared to have been taken by a professional photographer. "Is that your father?" Dixon asked.

"Yes. He had to have a photo taken for some lawyer award he got, and that's the picture."

The family photos were remarkable by virtue of the fact that they were the only ones that were not enlarged and only one of them was framed. Dixon wondered whether there was significance in that fact or in the fact that the picture of Jessica as a little girl was placed on the opposite side of the mantel.

"So, you and Dad are going on your Baltic Sea adventure next week. Are you looking forward to it?"

"I'm looking forward to the trip, but you know how those tours go. Several hours on a bus, walk around a church or a shrine, get back on the bus, get up the next day and start over again."

"Do you know anyone else going on the trip?"

"No. We just signed up with a tour company called Destination Tours. I just hope I'm not the youngest person in the group."

A timer dinged in the kitchen. "Looks like dinner's ready," Jessica said. "Would you help me get it on the table?"

"Of course." While he carried in the food, Jessica dimmed the lights and lit a candle. After everything was on the table, Dixon grabbed the wine bottle and topped off their glasses. He held his silverware, waiting for her to take the first bite. Once she did, he slowly sliced the pork and put it in his mouth, where he held it a moment before chewing. "Outstanding," he said. He then went around the horn on his plate and declared each item better than the last. His praise was sincere.

"Do you cook at all?" Jessica asked.

"Not really. I mean, I like food and would like to be able to cook, but I don't have the knack. Sometimes I think I have no right brain whatsoever. I can follow a recipe, but good cooks have a certain panache that makes the difference between edible and outstanding."

"So, you don't think you have a creative side?"

"I wouldn't necessarily say that, but it's creative in a very linear way. I mean, I could write a poem and make the words rhyme, but it would never be great poetry."

"Well, to paraphrase Dorothy in *The Wizard of Oz*, what would you do with a right brain if you had one?"

"You mean other than whiling away the hours conversing with the flowers?"

She smiled in appreciation that he had understood her reference. "Yes, other than that."

"I think I'd like to be able to play the piano. And not just able to read music and hit the keys. I mean understand it, compose it, and just be able to feel it."

"So what would you do with that talent? Be a concert pianist?"

"Who cares? All I know is musicians get more women than they know what to do with," he said facetiously.

"And that's what's important to you in life—getting action?"

"I was only joking. I moved past sex on Maslow's hierarchy of needs a long time ago."

"Because you had so much it was time to move on?" she asked.

"Quite the contrary, I'm afraid. The physical act of sex is satisfying on one level, but to achieve the higher levels requires the physical act of love. It seems to me that reaching self-actualization requires a state where physical love is part of the process, but it's not the kind of stuff you see on cable TV late at night."

"Are you saying sex without love is meaningless?"

"No, I think I'm saying sex without love is just sex. That doesn't mean it's bad or that it's meaningless, it just means you're operating on a lower order. If you can only connect with someone below the waist and there is no emotional or intellectual connection, you've fulfilled one need but left others unfulfilled."

"How will you know when you find someone with whom you have that connection?"

"Well, for starters, she'll laugh at my jokes."

Jessica burst out laughing and it was all she could do to keep her food in her mouth. Dixon sat back and watched her. After a moment he said, "Are you laughing at me or auditioning for the part?"

"No. I'm sorry. That just struck me as funny because we were having this deep discussion and you popped that in there."

"If you were auditioning, you did a good job."

She smiled at him. Her eyes seemed to get larger, and the candlelight caused them to sparkle even more than usual.

After a long look, Dixon said, "I don't know if it's the candlelight or the company, but you're looking a little moony-eyed tonight."

"Whatever do you mean?" she asked with a coquettish smile.

"You have a glow of something. I don't know if it's excitement, romance, or something else." Dixon wanted to say she had the glow of a woman in love, but it was a little early in the relationship for such words. "Whatever it is, it makes you even more attractive than usual and I'm hoping that I'm having something to do with that."

"You don't think it's just the wine?"

"That's possible, but I don't think so. I guess time will tell."

"Are you this charming with all your dates?" Jessica asked.

"I think I'm usually about as charming as the circumstances dictate and, candidly, I guess I haven't been that charming for a while."

"What do you mean?"

"Well, if I met a woman and only wanted to have sex with her or only wanted her to go out with me because I needed a date for a party or something like that, I would be pleasant and probably even clever, but saying nice things in order to get something is not really charming no matter how syrupy the words are. I guess it's been awhile since I was with someone that went beyond that."

"So what do you want to get from me?"

Hesitating, Dixon said, "I don't really know. Right now I don't think I want anything from you except to be with you. Sitting across from you, listening to your opinions and adventures . . . that seems to be enough." Nervous that the conversation might be sounding a little too schmaltzy, he tried to change the tone. "Of course, I guess I would like you to pass me more asparagus."

After dinner, Dixon helped clear the table. Despite what he thought was palpable sexual energy in the room, Jessica filled the sink to soak the dishes as though they were an old married couple following a routine that had lasted for decades. Dixon finally coaxed her to the couch.

"Thanks for dinner," he said softly. "It was wonderful."

"You're welcome."

Dixon slid closer and kissed her on the lips. He reached up with his right hand and clasped the back of her neck, rolling the tendons of her neck between his thumb and middle finger.

"That feels good," she said. "How would you like to give me a little shoulder rub?" she said, turning her back to him.

"That would be fine. Would you like to lie down?" Dixon asked.

"This is good enough," she said. "Just a chair massage. I get so tight between my shoulder blades."

Dixon put his thumbs on either side of her spine and began to work up and down. After a few trips up and back, he began working toward the outside of her back. "You are awfully tight in here. I hope you weren't stressed about the dinner."

"No, actually making dinner was a nice diversion. I think I'm stressed about the trip. I don't think I've ever spent that much time alone with my dad, and being in a foreign country on a hectic schedule probably won't help."

"Do you speak the language at all?"

"So far I know two things in Lithuanian: *labas,* and *vizuiti e Riga. Labas* means 'hello,' and *vizuiti e Riga* means to 'go to Riga,' which is the capital of Latvia."

"I can understand the need for *labas,* but the other phrase doesn't seem like it will come up very often."

"Actually, the other phrase is kind of a joke among Lithuanians. The literal translation is 'to go to Riga,' but it's a colloquial expression that means 'to get so drunk that you throw up on yourself.'"

"You're kidding."

"No. My dad has used that expression most of his life. It's kind of like the way people like to tell Iowa jokes."

"Does he speak the language?"

"No, not really. It's been too long. Like all good Americans, I'm sure he'll think everyone can understand English so long as he speaks it loud enough and slow enough."

"Ain't that the truth," Dixon chuckled.

Dixon looked at her soulfully and she looked back. After what seemed like forever, he leaned in and kissed her. Slowly, she lay down and, without breaking the kiss, pulled him down on top of her. His left leg was now between hers, and he slowly released his weight from his knee until his thigh was solidly resting on her pubic bone. He broke the kiss and moved down to kiss her neck. In doing so, he deliberately moved his left leg in an attempt to stimulate her, but in a way that seemed incidental. She responded and began grinding her pelvis against his leg.

He propped his elbows on either side of her so he could suspend himself over her. They kissed long and passionately until he broke for air before starting again. Dixon rolled over on his side and slid his arm under her head. "I'm really going to miss you," he whispered.

"It'll only be ten days," she said.

Dixon's left hand was now on the warm skin of her back. He was mesmerized by its softness, and traced his fingers ever so lightly until he could sense the hair on her neck standing on end. Jessica closed her eyes and laid back. Her right arm was across Dixon's chest and her feet were on the tops of Dixon's feet, as though she were a little girl dancing with her father at a wedding. Jessica flexed both feet, as if to massage the top of Dixon's arches with the pads of her toes.

"Maybe I better go along on your trip to make sure you don't get in any trouble," Dixon said softly.

"I think I'll be pretty safe," she whispered.

Dixon ran his hand higher up her back and casually across the back of her bra. He pretended like he was simply continuing her back rub, but he was really sending in the scout team to determine the latching mechanism on her bra. *Two hooks, and I'll have to do it left-handed,* he thought to himself. If he missed and looked like a novice, the entire moment could become awkward. Worse yet, it might give her a chance to object.

He was thinking about timing and how to make the move when his left hand developed a mind of its own. Before he knew it, his left hand had slid down and popped the hooks like he was opening a pop can. Jessica showed no resistance and kept kissing.

Dixon rubbed her whole back, as if his motive was simply to remove the impediment to the back rub. That only lasted so long.

Dixon's left hand was in the middle of Jessica's back. He slid it around to the front, taking care to guide it under her bra. His thumb reached the destination first, and he moved his palm slowly up the side until he was cupping her right breast. He felt the protrusion of her nipple and rubbed soft circles over it with the palm of his hand. As he did so, Jessica's kiss became more passionate. She was now gripping the hair on the back of Dixon's head and her tongue had ventured farther into his mouth.

He gently pushed her onto her back and swung his leg across so that he was straddling her hips. Sitting on top, he now had both hands inside her shirt and resting on her stomach. Dixon smiled at Jessica and leaned forward to kiss her. As his head moved forward, he moved his hands upward until he was cupping both breasts.

Dixon sat up again and began tugging at the parts of her shirt that were pinned between her body and the couch. Jessica did a partial sit-up in order to free the garment. She then raised her hands above her head, and Dixon slid the shirt and dangling bra up and over before tossing them on the side chair. Jessica lay before him in all her splendor—thin arms, large breasts, and satin skin.

Dixon rocked forward, pressing his crotch against the mound between her legs. As he did so, he began kissing her neck. He went from one side to the other and then started the descent. He kissed her neck, then drew a line with his tongue to the top of her breasts and kissed some more. Using his tongue as a guide, he moved farther south until a nipple was in his mouth. He sucked it, gently at first and then increasing the pressure.

He started to pull away and she grabbed the back of his head and pulled his mouth back to her breast. "I wasn't going far," he said, as he moved to her other breast and began the same process.

Jessica's breathing became deeper. She reached her hands under Dixon's shirt and started to raise it. Dixon broke the lip-lock he had on her nipple long enough to allow her to pull his shirt off. As soon as they were both stripped to the waist, she grabbed him and pulled him close. "Mmmm, skin on skin," she purred.

They were locked in an embrace when Dixon rolled over, pulling her on top. Jessica slid down and started kissing his neck. As she did so, she dragged her breasts across his chest. She was now straddling Dixon, and the full weight of her upper body was pressing her crotch against the bulge in Dixon's pants. She began to rock slowly, and her breasts swayed as she did. He grabbed both breasts and massaged them as she rocked. He then sat up half way and put both of her nipples in his mouth. Jessica's breathing continued to get heavier.

Dixon lay back down and reached his hands to the front of her pants and tried to unbutton them. Jessica moved her hands on top of his and pushed them away. "No, I don't choose to do that," she said. Dixon wasn't sure what that meant, but willingly moved his hands back to her breasts.

The grinding became faster and more intense. Suddenly, Jessica let out a faint yelp and collapsed on top of him. It wasn't an orgasm, or at least it didn't seem like one, yet Jessica lay on him as though some sort of climax had been achieved. Dixon just lay there and held her. After a moment, he whispered, "Did I mention how glad I am that we met?"

"You don't even know me. What can you tell about someone after a few dates?"

"Enough. I have to make judgments about people all the time, and I'm usually pretty good. I feel pretty good about my read on you."

She smiled. "Well, other than you being a man, I have a pretty high opinion of you."

"Wait a minute," Dixon blurted out. "Nobody said anything about you being a lesbian. Not that I necessarily mind, it just changes the dynamics."

"I'm not a lesbian," she retorted. "I just don't find men to be that reliable. Putting your faith in one is a fast road to heartbreak."

"That sounds like the voice of experience," Dixon said.

"Hey, I'm thirty-five. I've been around."

Dixon wasn't sure how to respond, so he didn't try. They lay arm in arm without speaking. He turned so he could see her face and stared at her while she rested. Dixon then rolled over and got on his hands and knees above her. He lowered his face within inches of hers and, starting at the upper left-hand side of her face, moved up and back as though he were a computer scanner mapping the images of her face.

"What are you doing?" she asked.

"I'm memorizing every detail of your face. I want to be able to visualize you while you're gone."

Jessica smiled warmly.

When he finished he paused and made eye contact. Then, with an impish grin, he slid down and traced comparable grid lines across her breasts. He couldn't help but burst out laughing.

"You think you're just so darn funny," she said sarcastically.

"Hey, I'm sorry, but you have really nice breasts, and I don't want to forget what they look like either."

"Keep it up and you might never see them again."

"Just like a woman. Always using sex as a weapon."

"No, it's just a matter of only doing what I choose," she said. "And I might choose not to take my shirt off in the future."

"Well, maybe I'll do that too," Dixon said.

"Nice try. Apparently you forgot you're a man."

"Can we go back to just lying here?" Dixon asked.

"That would be fine."

As passionate as the night had been, Dixon took a hint from the discussion that he shouldn't expect to spend the night even though they wouldn't be seeing each other for a couple weeks. Eventually, they both got up and got dressed. Standing by the front door, Dixon was suddenly struck by the fact that he was saying good-bye for ten days. They embraced and kissed some more. Finally, Dixon hugged her and let himself out.

# CHAPTER 23

THE WEEK CRAWLED by slowly. Dixon had no particular deadlines pending and it was hard to get motivated. He read pleadings, dictated correspondence, and made calls. He found himself pausing to reminisce about the time he'd spent with Jessica. Looking out his office window to the lakes south of downtown, he daydreamed about walking hand in hand with her. Dixon hadn't thought a ten-day separation would be a big deal, but he found himself struggling already on Monday.

On Tuesday, he received summary judgment motion papers in one of his cases. *Thank God, I'll have a purpose,* he thought. He went to the law library to review the law on shareholder disputes and began crafting a response. He couldn't help but think that people should find a better way to solve their problems than fighting in court. *Wait a minute,* he thought to himself, *all this dating bliss might be taking away my edge.*

On Friday, Hank called. "What's the good word?" Dixon asked.

Hank could barely contain himself. "I had that retired cop out to Duke's. He looked at that hole and said he thought it could be from a bullet. He had a metal detector and it rang when he put it up by the hole. He said he didn't want to dig it out 'cause, if it was evidence, he wanted the authorities to find the scene intact."

"That's interesting. Did he find anything else?"

"Not really. He said they can do other tests to see if there was blood or anything that had been cleaned up, but, other than that, he thought the crime scene was too stale."

"What did he suggest we do now?" Dixon asked.

"He said we should ask the Bureau of Criminal Apprehension to do an investigation. If we go to the sheriff they'll ignore us, but the boys from the state call their own shots and the sheriff's office will have no choice but to cooperate."

"Do I have to make a call?" Dixon asked.

"He said he'd take care of it. He's really a great guy. I think he's hoping I'll give him a better price on the property. If he only knew that the shooting makes it hard to interest any of the locals in it anyway."

"Did he tell you anything else?"

"Well," Hank paused for a moment, "he didn't think much of the investigation. He said there were other things they could have done to find out exactly what happened."

"Y'know, Hank, I want to get as much information about what happened as possible, but I'm really concerned that you think there's something else out there and I don't want you to be disappointed. I'm afraid you feel responsible in some way, so you're hoping to find anything at all that shows it wasn't suicide."

"I know I'm tempted to believe what I want to believe," Hank responded, "but there are too many unanswered questions. Those answers may lead to the same conclusion the sheriff's office reached, but at least those answers will give me peace."

Talking by phone gave Dixon the luxury of rolling his eyes without offending his client. "Maybe those questions are better left unanswered," Dixon said. "What if the evidence proves that Duke shot Krueller and then himself? Wouldn't you be better off going through life holding out hope against hope that something else happened?"

"I know what you're saying, but I'll be okay regardless. Besides, don't you think that paint job someone gave your car might suggest someone doesn't want you snoopin' around?"

Dixon liked Hank, but he sometimes got frustrated with him. "I don't have any reason to believe the paint job was anything other than a random prank. I could be wrong, but I'm not dwelling on it." His words were meant for Hank, but privately he hadn't forgotten the fear it had instilled.

They were both quiet for a moment. Dixon decided to change the subject. "Should I be there for the State investigation?"

"I think it would be a good idea for you to see exactly what they do and to ask questions as they go."

"I suppose you're right. Maybe I should get a lake place up there since I'm there so much."

"Why don't you fly up this time?" Hank said. "I feel bad for all the driving you've been doing. I'll pick you up at the airport and it'll be a snap."

"Here's the thing," Dixon said. "We have a pretrial scheduled for the middle of September. Talk to your guy and see if we can do something then. That way I can kill two birds with one stone."

"I'll do my best," Hank responded before saying good-bye.

Dixon hung up the phone and went back to pining for Jessica. He wondered whether Jessica was thinking about him. *Of course she was,* he thought to himself. *She's spending most of her time on a bus with old people. She must be missing me as much as I'm missing her.* Finally, he decided he couldn't sit still any longer.

Dixon flipped through his rolodex until he found his travel agent's number and gave her a call. "Hi Monica, it's Dixon Donnelly. I need a little favor. Destination Tours has a tour group right now on some sort of Baltic Sea adventure. Lithuania, Latvia, Estonia, that type of thing. I need an itinerary of their trip that shows hotels, dates of stay, and phone numbers."

"Is it some sort of family emergency?" she asked.

"If that's what you need to say to get it, then yes, it's a family emergency."

"Okay, but can you tell me what it's for."

"Someone that I'm dating is on that trip, and I want to let her know I miss her."

"Dixon Donnelly, you romantic, my heart's all aflutter. Give me your fax number and I'll fax you an itinerary when I get it. Just one more thing: are there anymore at home like you?"

"Sorry, they broke the mold," he quipped.

With part one of his plan in motion, he pulled out the Yellow Pages and began looking for florists offering some sort of out-of-town delivery services. He was surprised by the number of ads promising such services and began making calls. He soon learned the services had a network of affiliates and were plenty happy to deliver flowers to anyone in a major American city, but service dropped off substantially after that.

He finally located numbers for establishments promising international delivery, but that proved equally unhelpful. Some of them had no idea where the Baltic countries were located, and the best he could find was someone who would actually send flowers from the U.S. via Federal Express for a huge fee and without any assurance the flowers would survive the trip.

Dixon was disheartened. He'd been giddy when the thought first hit him and was now becoming depressed because his plan was coming undone. Making matters worse, the fax machine started ringing and Monica had, in fact, succeeded in sending an itinerary.

Dixon scanned the schedule. "Vilnius, Kaunas, Palanga, Riga, Pilsrundale, Tallinn." The most logical thing would be to find a place where Jessica would be more than one night so she could enjoy the flowers longer. The only remaining stop on the itinerary that fit that criterion was Riga, and that was the next day. Because of the time difference, however, it was already evening in Riga and, presumably, everyone was getting drunk and throwing up on themselves. Dixon decided the hotel had a reasonable chance of having employees who spoke English so, after struggling to decipher international calling codes, he gave them a ring.

After the obligatory clicking and switching, Dixon heard a low-pitched ring like something he would have imagined out of the fifties. A woman's voice answered: "Labdien, Hotel de Rome."

"I'm sorry," Dixon said, "do you by chance speak English?"

"Yes sir, how can I help you?" Her accent was discernible, but her English was very understandable.

"There is someone who will be staying at your hotel tomorrow night, and I would like to arrange to have some flowers waiting in her room when she arrives. Can you give me the number of a florist or someone who would take a credit card and make the arrangements?"

"That's very nice, monsieur. Is it a birthday or an anniversary and you are not able to be together?"

"No, I just miss her, and want her to know I'm thinking about her."

The woman let out a sigh. "Let me give you a telephone number of a nearby florist who should be able to help you. If there is a problem with the language or anything else, please make sure you call me back. My name is Annika and I will do what I can to make sure it is taken care of. Why don't you tell me the guest's name so I can confirm that she has a reservation."

Dixon obliged and the reservation was confirmed.

"One other thing," Dixon continued, "she will be checking in with her father, who is in a different room. If possible, I want to make sure she gets the key to the room with the flowers."

"I understand. Here is the phone number . . ."

Dixon dialed the florist with considerably less confidence that the keeper of a flower shop in the former Soviet Union would understand English. An old woman answered the phone, but Dixon couldn't understand anything other than "Labdien."

"I'm sorry," Dixon began, "does anyone there speak English?"

The woman said some more words that Dixon could not make out and then he could hear her yelling to someone else "something, something, English." After a moment, a woman with a middle-age sounding voice picked up the telephone and said "hello."

Dixon found himself talking slowly and loudly. "I would like to have some flowers delivered tomorrow to someone who is staying at the Hotel de Rome."

"One moment," the voice said. Dixon could hear her translating in the background. "Okay," she said coming back on the line.

"If I give you a credit card, can you handle that?"

After another brief translation session, she assured him that they could. "What kind of flowers would you like?"

"I don't really know much about flowers. Can you send something that is native to the area?"

Another translation session occurred. "What is the occasion?" the woman asked.

"I just want to let someone know I miss her," he replied.

Dixon overhead another translation session. The old woman in the background said something in Latvian that, by the melody in her voice, seemed as if it would translate as "isn't that sweet." The woman providing the translation came back on. "Yes sir, we can send a very nice bouquet. With delivery it will be ten Lats, which is about twelve American dollars."

"That sounds fabulous," Dixon said.

"Would you like to say something on the card?"

"Yes, it's kind of long, would you like me to fax it?"

"Why don't you read it to me and I'll let you know."

Dixon proceeded: "Across Lithuania, Latvia, and Estonia you roam, while I'm going to Riga without leaving home. Without you here I'm alone counting the hours, so to tell you that I miss you I'm sending you these flowers. Hurry back. Dixon."

"I think I can get that," the woman responded. "Read it back again slowly."

Dixon obliged.

"Sir, I assure you, we will take care of it and your lady friend will be very pleased."

Pleased was what Dixon was feeling. He imagined Jessica, weary from a day of bus travel with elderly tourists, finding a bouquet to brighten her day. He was proud of his initiative and couldn't wait until the moment of truth arrived the next day.

◆

Dixon ran his Saturday errands first thing in the morning and made a point to be home by eleven. Jessica probably wouldn't check in until about noon Dixon's time, and he didn't want to miss her call. He tried to imagine how she'd react or what she'd say to him. In his fantasy, she was generally clutching her heart and following it up with an effusive telephone call. Dixon thought, *This should ease her concerns about the fast road to heartbreak.*

About noon the phone rang and Dixon picked it up with anticipation. It turned out to be a telephone solicitor. The phone rang a few more times and each time was a false alarm. *"Maybe it's easier to dial into the former Soviet Union than out,"* Dixon thought to himself.

At about one o'clock, Dixon called Sandy to see if he wanted to have lunch sometime soon. He got his voice mail and left a message. At 1:30 the phone rang and he assumed it was Sandy calling back. "Hello," he said into the phone.

"How did you know how to find me?" The voice was Jessica's.

"What do you mean?" Dixon asked.

"I didn't give the itinerary to anyone, not even the people at work. In fact, I didn't even know it until I was on the plane. How did you know it?"

"Y'know," Dixon replied, "I might be an eternal optimist, but I was kind of expecting you to call and say something like 'Dixon Donnelly, you're the sweetest, kindest man I've ever known.'"

"Well, I'm not saying that's not the case, I just can't figure out how you were able to find me."

"Does it matter?"

"Yes, it does."

"Okay, I didn't want you to know, but I was concerned about all the wealthy widowers hitting on you so I hired a private investigator to follow you."

"Nice try," she responded.

Dixon tried to redirect the focus of the discussion. "So, are they nice? The woman at the flower shop assured me it would be a very nice bouquet, but it's not like I was able to pick it out."

"Yes." And for just a moment, Jessica appeared breathless. "It's a very nice arrangement."

"There wasn't any problem with the delivery, was there? I was afraid they'd hand you two keys and your dad would end up taking the room with the flowers."

"That's funny you should say that, because the woman at the desk was very emphatic about giving one key to me and one to my dad. I guess she must have been in on the deal."

"I trust you didn't need to read the card to know they were from me."

"That's funny, too. The bus driver has been kind of leering at me and when I saw the flowers I thought, 'oh no, they must be from him.' But then I read the card and was very relieved."

"Well, I'm glad you liked them. By the way," Dixon's voice became coy, "do you need to know my shirt size or anything?"

"Listen to you," she said. "All you can think about is what I might bring you."

"That's not fair," Dixon protested. "I just thought you might be thinking about bringing me something and I was just trying to be considerate by making it easy for you to know my size."

"Isn't it enough that I said 'thank you that was very nice of you'?"

"And, have you missed me?"

"It's only been like five days."

"Well, I've missed you."

"Well, if you must know, I was thinking of calling you tonight anyway."

"To tell me how much you miss me?"

"Nice try," Jessica responded. "What if I said I missed you so much I wanted you to pick me up at the airport?"

"That's more like it," he replied. "I'd love to."

She gave him the flight info and apologetically explained that her dad was waiting and she had to go.

Dixon hung up and strutted around the kitchen. Not quite the response he'd envisioned, but still he felt he had touched her even if she wouldn't admit it.

# CHAPTER 24

O N MONDAY, SANDY called and scheduled lunch. Their respective schedules had kept them from running together, and lunch would be a good opportunity to catch up. They met at noon at The Loon Cafe.

"I hope you didn't mind the walk over here," Sandy said. "I figure the summer will end soon and we'll be confined to restaurants we can reach through the skyway, so we should come here while we can."

Downtown Minneapolis is connected by a patchwork of overhead, enclosed bridges from building to building. There had never been a master plan, and the "skyways," as they were called, just started to spring up as a response to the cold weather.

"Did I ever tell you the story about the lawyer from Philadelphia and the skyways?" Dixon asked.

"I don't think so."

"This is true. I was local counsel for this guy from Philadelphia and apparently some guy from his firm had been here twenty years earlier on a similar gig. Anyway, when the other guy was here twenty years before, there had been one of those mosquito-borne encephalitis outbreaks up in the Red River Valley along the North Dakota border. You know, like we have every five or six years. Anyway, twenty years later my guy comes out here. We're walking down to court and he says, 'oh yeah, my partner told me about these skywalks; how you had to install them because of the poisonous insects that live here in the summer.'" Dixon paused for effect. "I just about split a gut when he said that."

"So this dipshit figured we lived here for the glorious winters?" Sandy cracked.

"Apparently."

"I guess that's the risk you take when you stray too far from home."

"That's the great thing about East Coast lawyers," Dixon said. "They think they're infallible, and they come here to try and talk to a jury and they look like idiots."

"Kind of like you trying a case up in Hibbing?" Sandy said.

"I know I may not exactly blend in, but I don't think I'm as out of place as you make it sound."

"Just be careful," Sandy cautioned.

A waitress stopped at the table to take their drink orders. As was the norm for The Loon, she was young and pretty. After taking Sandy's order she placed a hand on Dixon's shoulder and asked, "How about you?" Dixon smiled and repeated Sandy's Diet Coke request.

"Whoa. What was that about?" Sandy asked after the waitress was out of earshot.

"Just because she touched me you think it's a big deal?"

"Well, if it was a guy, wouldn't you have been a little creeped out about it?"

"Good point," Dixon said. "Guys on the prowl must give off a scent or something, because I seem to be in demand all of a sudden."

"Wait a minute," Sandy said, "you've got something going on other than Jessica?"

Dixon smiled. "Not exactly. I ran into Mrs. Krueller in a bar in Hibbing, and she wanted to go a couple rounds with the champ."

"Your trailer or hers?" Sandy asked.

"We didn't get quite that far. I kept asking her to leave me alone and finally I just had to leave. As is, I'm afraid she'll make up a story about it. There were a lot of witnesses, but none I could count on to back me."

The waitress returned with the drinks. She took Sandy's order and then turned to Dixon. "And what's your pleasure?"

Dixon returned her gaze. "Chinese Chicken Salad, please."

"Coming right up," she said, collecting the menus and heading for the kitchen.

"Man!" Sandy said. "She gives you a ground ball like 'what's your pleasure' and that's the best you can do?"

"What am I supposed to say?" Dixon replied. "It's lunch, she's a waitress, and neither of us has had anything to drink. Do you think I could just say, 'hey baby, what's your Sleep Number?' and we'd be off to the races?"

Sandy wasn't accepting Dixon's response. "Couldn't you have said something like, 'my pleasure would be dinner with you'?"

"I suppose I could have said that if I were in a Doris Day movie. Otherwise, that's the corniest line I've ever heard."

Sandy took a long drink from his soda. "Look, I'm just trying to help. The cat's away, I thought maybe you were looking to play."

"I'm finally dating someone I'm excited about. Why would I want to screw that up? Hell, I couldn't even cheat on Sharon."

"So, things are going well with Jessica?" Sandy asked.

"In general, yeah. I'm smitten to say the least."

"Is she?"

"I don't know. I'm confident she's not seeing anybody else, but she doesn't seem quite as head over heels as me."

"What do you mean?"

"All right," Dixon said, "I'll let you in on a little secret, but if you blab about it, so help me God, I'll beat the living snot out of you."

"Okay, assuming you could beat the living snot out of me, let's hear it."

"You know how she's traveling in Eastern Europe with her father and a bunch of senior citizens. I thought it would be a particularly nice gesture to send flowers to her hotel room in Latvia, and let me tell you that was no easy task. Everyone I talked to in order to set it up—the travel agent who gave me the itinerary, the hotel clerk who gave me a number for a florist, and the florist herself—gushed about what a sweet gesture it was. Jessica calls me up and all she can say is: 'How'd you know where I was?'"

"She didn't thank you?"

"She did eventually. Don't get me wrong. She was very nice and I could tell I touched her, but she just couldn't say it."

"Are you sure she's just not interested?"

"I don't think she'd have any trouble telling a guy she wasn't interested, but she seems to have a hard time telling a guy anything that renders her at all vulnerable. When I first called her she said some things that made me think she could accept the vulnerability of putting her trust in someone else, but I'm not even sure about that anymore."

"What do you mean?"

"Well, she said she wanted to go out with me. But, in retrospect, she didn't say she liked me, that she thought I was cute, or anything particularly flattering. Just that she wanted to go out with me. That seems to let her off the hook later because she didn't make any emotional commitment; she just made a time commitment."

"Maybe you're just imagining things."

"I doubt it. Trust me, I'm not really complaining, because it was a very nice conversation and, like I said, I could tell that I got to her. She just wouldn't admit it."

"Well, a lot of people grow up in families that aren't particularly demonstrative with their affections," Sandy offered.

"Well, I understand that, but it appears to go deeper. She seems to have a real control issue."

"Oh-oh," Sandy said. "Talk about locomotives on a collision course."

"What does that mean?" Dixon protested.

"Come on Dix, you're as big a control freak as there is."

"What makes you say that?"

"Let's see, how about, wanting a woman who's smart and beautiful, strong but demure, good in the sack but still a virgin. You want everything to fit your preconceptions and aren't happy if they don't."

"Wait a minute. I never tried to control Sharon. I'm smart enough to avoid that Pygmalion thing. I never tried to mold her into something she wasn't."

"But you hated the fact that she wasn't what you wanted."

"She's a bad example," Dixon replied. "Do you have something else to support your theory?"

"How about the woman you broke up with because she folded your morning paper inside out before you'd read it?"

"That's not why we broke up," Dixon said. "I'll admit it annoyed me, but I was willing to go to counseling to help her learn to respect my rights."

"Dixon, you're just a control guy. It's in everything you do. There's nothing wrong with that, you just have to realize it and admit it."

"I don't agree with you. I may like things a certain way, but I don't have to announce that I'm in control or otherwise have things objectively my way. I mean, with Jessica, she actually says things like, 'I'll only get naked if I choose to get naked.' I mean, it's like she has to tell me she's in control."

"Really? She verbalizes that?"

"More than once, actually," Dixon replied.

"You know what I think that is?"

"What?"

"Didn't Matt tell you she had some hard drinkers in her family?"

"Yeah. So?"

"I've heard of this 'my choice—I choose' thing. It's got something to do with treatment for alcoholism or therapy for the adult children of alcoholics."

"Y'know, you're probably right. She was talking about religion, and she referred to a belief in a 'higher power.' Isn't that the lexicon of the twelve-step program?"

"Yeah," Sandy responded, "I think so. It sounds to me like at least she's got an explanation for being a control person. What's your excuse?"

"I'm not a control person. I just don't like to be out of control."

"If you're not the control person I say you are, what's wrong with letting her have control?"

"I don't know. The problem is even if I submitted, she couldn't control whether I lost interest or started dating someone else. And without being able to control that, I don't know that she'd ever be able to surrender to the relationship. I mean, she said a few choice things about not trusting men."

"Well I don't get it," Sandy said. "You're nuts about her, but you think she may have all these issues. What's it gonna be?"

"Y'know, I've thought about what you said at the wedding. You know, your formula for the perfect woman. It really comes down to three things: physical, intellectual, and emotional."

"Wait a minute," Sandy said, "are you labeling 'making a yuck face after oral sex' as an emotional problem?"

"No, but emotional can be kind of broad and cover attitude as well."

"Perhaps. Anyway, sorry to have interrupted."

Dixon continued. "The first two are pretty much inborn. A woman either has those traits or she doesn't. The attitude/emotional component is one that a woman can make a decision on and should be within her control. I've dated beautiful women who were of average intelligence and I've dated average looking women who were quite smart. The best any of them could ever do was to satisfy two out of the three criteria, but most of them at least tried to score points in the last category to cut the deficit. Jessica is unique in that she has the first two categories nailed, but the problem is in the third category."

"Well wait a minute, nature/nurture boy. If personality is inherited like you contend, then she can't control it."

"But a person in her position believes it's a matter of socialization and their personality is forever shaped by that. I'm saying the human persona is basically good and she should have the strength to adapt to any ill effects of living with an alcoholic."

"Maybe that's what you're missing," Sandy said. "Maybe that's exactly how she's coping with it, and you just don't like the way she's doing it. At least she's out in the open about it."

The waitress came by and set down the food. "What do you think?" Sandy said to her, with a finger pointed toward Dixon. "Do you think this guy looks like a control freak?"

"Hard to say," she responded. "Does he wear those wife-beater tee shirts?"

"Wife-beater tee shirts," Sandy said incredulously. "What the heck is that?"

"You know," the waitress said, "those tank top undershirts."

"Why are they called 'wife-beaters'?"

"I don't really know where it started, but it seems like every time you see some loser getting arrested for beating his wife, he's wearing one," she said.

Dixon jumped in. "I can assure you I don't have any, so how does that affect your answer?"

"Then I'll go with 'no.' You look too gentle to be a control freak."

Not satisfied, Sandy shot back, "Before you make that your final answer you might want to consider the fact that I'm leaving the tip."

She smiled and said, "Wow, then I guess maybe he has you under his control." With that, she turned and walked away.

"Let's get back to this," Sandy said. "What has she really done that causes you to question her emotional side?"

"I think she has a fear of intimacy. There's a bright line on the limits of our physical intimacy, and that wouldn't bother me so much if she could express something verbally."

"Has it occurred to you that she doesn't want to go as fast as you do?"

"Of course that's occurred to me. But it kind of begs the question. We otherwise have a wonderful relationship. Everything about our dates is terrific. At the end of the day any normal woman would be saying: 'Omigod, I'm falling in love.' She is polite as can be, but is completely unable to be emotionally vulnerable."

"Dixon, I don't want to argue with you, because I think your points are valid. But don't you think maybe you're playing a little Pygmalion. You already said that looks and intelligence are pretty much unchangeable so, with the exception of changing hair color or having a boob job, the only thing you can try and change about a woman is her personality."

"So, Dr. Freud, what's the answer?"

"Acceptance."

"What do you mean?" Dixon asked.

"You need to decide if you need regular validation or whether you can accept the situation the way it is. Ultimately, unexpressed love is not necessarily unrequited love. You just need to decide if you have the strength to accept that."

"So I'm the problem?"

"I didn't say that," Sandy replied. "I'm saying that you can be the solution."

"I think it's about choice, but in a different way," Dixon responded. "She simply has to choose to want to live a normal life and do what normal people do."

"So, just give her an ultimatum," Sandy suggested. "Say to her: Be as nuts about me as I am about you or it's over."

Dixon paused as the waitress refilled their glasses. He gave her a big smile before turning back to Sandy. "I'm not really sure why I'm consulting you on any of this. You're not exactly the relationships expert."

"What do you mean? I've had a lot of relationships," Sandy protested. "A really lot," he said with a wry smile.

"That's just it. I should be calling you when I'm concerned about how to screw two women at once while standing in a hammock. You're an expert on sexual relationships, but a novice on emotional relationships."

"Hey," Sandy said with mock seriousness, "I resemble that remark."

"Speaking of which, are you still dating Melody?"

"Yes, but that's irrelevant because I'd much rather talk about your character flaws than mine."

"How about a truce, and we talk about something else altogether?"

Just then the waitress came by to drop off the check. "Thanks for coming in." She handed a business card to Dixon. "I've taken the liberty to write down my name and number. If you'd like to hook up sometime, give me a call."

Dixon was momentarily dumbstruck. This was the sort of thing that happened to Sandy—regularly. Not only was it remarkable that it was happening to Dixon; it was happening to Dixon in front of Sandy. "Thank you," he said with a smile. "I should tell you I'm sort of in a relationship right now, so if I don't call you immediately you shouldn't take it as a sign I'm not interested, only that I'm not sure about the timing."

"Well, I'll leave that to you," she said. "I'm not asking for a commitment. I just thought you might like to get together for a drink or something. Your girlfriend or whatever wouldn't have to know."

"Thank you," he said again. "I'll keep that in mind."

# CHAPTER 25

D IXON ARRIVED AT the airport an hour early. It wasn't that he liked to watch planes take off and land. He just wanted to be early in case there were parking problems or the flight arrived early or something else unforeseen happened. He found a discarded newspaper and passed the time rereading stories he had read earlier in the day.

At about twenty minutes past the appointed time, Jessica's plane arrived. Dixon paced nervously. For all of his excitement to see her, he realized he'd be meeting her father for the first time. In his mind, he was sure Jessica had told her father all about him, and he wanted to live up to what he assumed was the high billing she'd given him.

The jetway doors opened and the passengers began coming out. It was a trickle at first, as the first class passengers exited. The flow increased, but Jessica wasn't among them. Thereafter it came in spurts, seemingly corresponding to older or less mobile passengers who, for one reason or another, held up the flow. After what seemed like an eternity studying the sea of faces, Dixon spotted Jessica. Despite a day's worth of plane travel, she looked radiant. Following in close pursuit was a man in his late sixties wearing a gray raincoat. He didn't look nearly so fresh.

Jessica didn't scan the crowd or otherwise look for Dixon. For his part, Dixon tried to remain inconspicuous so he could watch her for as long as possible. She was almost past him when he stepped up along side her. "Can I give you a hand with that bag?"

She turned slowly at first and then did a double take upon seeing Dixon. "How did you get through security?" she asked.

"Pulled some strings. I told them I couldn't wait any longer to see you and they let me through." With that, he put an arm around her waist and attempted to pull her close.

She responded with a tenuous hug. "Thanks for coming to pick me up." She turned back to the man in the raincoat. "Dad, this is Dixon. Dixon, this is my dad—Linus Palmer."

Dixon offered a handshake and the appropriate greetings. Mr. Palmer was less intimidated by the circumstances. "Is this the poet who sent the flowers?" he asked with a smirk.

"Guilty," Dixon said.

"Let me tell you, I've known my daughter all her life, and I never saw anything like it."

"Aa-hem," Jessica cleared her throat in a manner meant to say, 'excuse me, but shut up.'

"What do you mean?" Dixon encouraged him.

"Well, this trip, it was interesting but it got long. And even longer for Jessica because she didn't really care to sit on the bus listening to stories about grandchildren. I was feeling bad for dragging her along, but after those flowers came everything was hunky dory. She spent the rest of the trip skipping around like she was chasing butterflies."

"Okay, Dad, I think we've heard about enough," Jessica interjected.

Dixon had developed an instant bond with the man he'd been nervous about meeting. "Is there any other good stuff to tell, or should we go along with her wishes?" Dixon asked.

"I'll save the rest for later," Mr. Palmer said with a wink.

"There is no 'rest,'" Jessica protested. "Why don't you tell him everything now, because there is nothing else and even what you said was fantasy. At least if you tell him in front of me, I'll know what things you made up."

Mr. Palmer smiled at Dixon. "She's a little cranky from all the travel. Don't worry about it though, she'll get over it."

They reached the end of the concourse and proceeded to the bag claim. "So tell me about the trip," Dixon said. "I've already heard about the highlight, but there must be other things to tell."

"I took a lot of pictures," Jessica said. "I'll give you a full report when they're developed. For now, I can tell you it was a good trip.

The people were very friendly, the sites were very interesting, and the Baltic Sea was very beautiful."

"How about you, Mr. Palmer, what did you think?"

"I can't believe I waited so long to go. Next time I'm not going with a tour group. It was nice to see the sights, but I'd like to go and just experience living among the locals. And another thing, next time I won't take my daughter. That way I can jump off the wagon and really live like the locals."

Jessica rolled her eyes. "That sounds like a really good idea."

Mr. Palmer excused himself to use the restroom. After he was gone, Dixon leaned over and kissed Jessica on the lips. She kissed him back, but seemed as self-conscious in front of strangers as she had appeared in front of her father. "I'm really glad to see you," Dixon said.

"Thanks," she replied. "I really appreciate you coming out here to get me."

When Mr. Palmer returned, they claimed their luggage. "Mr. Palmer, can we give you a ride somewhere?" Dixon asked.

"No thanks," he responded. "I'm staying with a friend for a couple days before going back to LaCrosse. I just talked to him on my cell phone and he's on his way."

"Well, in that case, it was nice to have met you." Dixon extended his hand.

"Nice meeting you too," Mr. Palmer responded. "And thanks again for cheering up my little girl. I hope I'll be seeing you around some more." Father and daughter hugged and Mr. Palmer departed.

Dixon turned to Jessica. "Well that was nice. I was a little uneasy about meeting your father, but he's really a charming guy."

"That's nice of you to say. Of course, with the things he was saying, you have to say nice things about him."

Dixon leaned over and rubbed the tip of his nose on her cheek and spoke softly into her ear. "I don't think we need to make a secret of the way I make you feel or the way you feel about me."

"I didn't say it had to be a secret, but I don't think we need to go public with it until we really know the answers to those questions."

That was not a response Dixon was expecting, and it wasn't one that made him particularly giddy. He decided to drop the subject rather than risk further problems.

On the way home, Jessica recounted the highs and lows of the trip. It had been a trip best described as schizophrenic, ranging from the incredibly morose visit to a KGB prison to watching a glorious sunset over the Baltic from the pier at Palanga. Dixon rested his hand on Jessica's knee as she spoke. It was not sexual; it was just a connection.

Dixon carried the luggage into Jessica's house. As soon as they entered, Jessica began making the rounds watering plants, adjusting the thermostat, and plugging in appliances. Dixon offered to help, but she seemed to be following a routine that she had rehearsed many times in her head. Dixon took a seat on the couch and simply watched.

When she finished she walked to the couch and reached out her hand. "Now for you, Mr. Donnelly, let's talk about those flowers you sent me." With that, she pulled him up and led him into her bedroom. Standing next to the bed, she wrapped her arms around his head such that her elbows were on his shoulders and her hands were entrenched in the hair on top of his head. She pulled his mouth to hers and they kissed. She tilted her head sideways so that their lips were nearly perpendicular to each other and their noses were not inhibiting their movements.

Dixon grabbed her waist and squeezed. He reached around until he was cupping both of her cheeks and pulled her groin to his. He grabbed the sides of her shirt and slipped it effortlessly over her head. She reciprocated with his shirt and then reached behind her back and unhooked her bra. After allowing Dixon an eyeful, she stepped toward him and pushed him back onto the bed. He sat on the edge, and she put her knees on either side of him and sat on his lap.

Dixon kissed her neck and clasped her breasts in an overhand position. He rubbed her nipples with his palms until they were erect and then reached his hands under her breasts and propped them up between the thumb and forefinger on each hand. He took her nipples in his mouth one at a time and sucked and licked. After a while he suggested that the whole thing would be a lot more comfortable without pants on. Jessica agreed, but made him promise that underwear would stay on.

Dixon wrapped his arms around her back and stood up. Jessica was temporarily suspended by his embrace, but unwrapped her legs and extended them to the floor. Dixon stepped back and unbuttoned her pants. He tugged at the sides until they slipped over her hips and headed toward the floor. Dixon knelt down to guide them the rest of the way off. With her hand on his shoulder, she alternately lifted her feet to facilitate the process. While Dixon had used care not to pull her panties down, he took the opposite approach as he passed her feet to make sure her socks came off with the pants.

Dixon unbuttoned and unzipped his own pants, and Jessica guided them the rest of the way to the floor. Once they were off, he picked Jessica up by the hips and told her to wrap her legs around him. She did so, and he sat back on the bed with her straddling him and her feet extending out behind him as though they were sharing a swing at the playground.

The stimulation was much greater now, as they were separated only by thin layers of cotton. Jessica was thrusting harder and harder until it felt like she would give him rug burn. Dixon put his arms around her back and clasped his hands over her shoulders. He slowly laid her back and then pulled down on her shoulders to provide even more force to their erogenous union.

Jessica's breathing became heavier and her thrusting more rapid. She seemed to build to a point and then her breathing and hip movements would return to normal. The process would repeat itself. Each time she seemed to near a precipice, she seemed to take a step back.

Dixon clasped his hands behind her back and stood up again. "Let your legs dangle this time," he whispered, and she obliged. He lay down and pulled her on top of him. Balancing her above him, he reoriented himself so they were lying lengthwise instead of across the bed. He accomplished the entire motion without any separation of their groins.

He slid his hands inside the back of her panties and gently

squeezed the bounty within. Jessica had stopped gyrating, and Dixon did nothing to encourage her. Jessica pulled her arms up along her sides and tucked them in close to her body as though she were cold. Dixon left one hand on her butt and moved the other up to caress her back. "That's nice," she said. "After a long day of travel, that feels good."

All of her weight was on him. He reached around and did his best to massage her back. She closed her eyes and purred. After a while, he rolled on his side to tip her off of him, sliding around to assume a position sitting on her rear end. He massaged more deeply, starting with his thumbs just below the line of her panties and kneading and working his way up to her shoulders and back down.

"That feels great," she said. "Would it be a little presumptuous to ask for a foot rub?"

"Well, this is sort of a special occasion," Dixon replied. "Let me check the supplies."

He got up and walked into the bathroom. He returned with some items he had retrieved from the linen closet, including body lotion. Jessica rolled onto her back, and Dixon assumed a seat at the foot of the bed. He placed her feet in his lap and squeezed out some lotion into his hand. He then began working each foot from the heel to the end of each toe, rubbing and squeezing the tension out as though he were working the last dab out of a tube of toothpaste.

"That feels so good," Jessica said. If you keep this up I'm liable to ask you to do it again and again."

"Just remember," Dixon replied, "today is your day, but some day it will be my day."

"Don't worry," she said, "I'll let you rub my feet no matter whose day it is."

"Well, now for the pièce de résistance," Dixon announced. He held up a bottle of red nail polish he'd gotten from her bathroom.

"You're going to paint your toenails red?" she joked.

"No, I'm going to paint your toenails red." He took her left foot in his left hand and started with her big toe before working down to the more delicate handiwork.

"Don't you think red toenail polish looks kind of trampy?" she asked.

"That's what I'm hoping," he said with a sly smile.

He finished one foot and held it up, blowing on her toes to dry the polish. Jessica giggled and rippled her toes in response. He picked up the other foot and attempted to match his craftsmanship.

"There's something I want to ask you," Dixon said. "What did you mean at the airport about not having to keep our relationship a secret, but not 'knowing the answers'?"

"What are you talking about?"

"When we were at the airport I said something about the way I make you feel and the way you feel about me and you said something like you didn't really know yet."

Jessica sat up on her elbows and pulled a pillow over her breasts. Dixon continued to paint as he waited for a response. She watched him, but hesitated. Finally, she spoke. "I don't know, Dixon. This is all going so fast and I'll be going back to Atlanta pretty soon. I just don't think getting emotionally involved is a very good idea."

"You don't think it's a little late to not get emotionally involved?" he said as if he were an auto mechanic carrying on a conversation while focusing intently on his work.

"I'm sorry if you think I led you on or something. I've had a good time with you and everything, but I thought we both understood this was sort of like having a summer fling."

Dixon completed the last toe and set her foot down. "I don't necessarily have a problem with flings, but I don't think that's what this is. I'm not someone that you're looking to merely for physical pleasure, because you're not the kind of person who seeks merely physical pleasure. If I thought you weren't interested in me, that would be one thing, but I think you are interested and you just don't want to admit it."

"Why wouldn't I want to admit it?"

"That's the harder question. You have a strong personality, and part of that is not wanting to be dependent or show your emotions. But don't you think real strength comes from being able to show your emotions and being willing to be vulnerable."

Jessica glared at him. "That may be, but that's not the way I am. You don't know what it's like to be me or to grow up the way I did, and if you can't accept me as is, that's your problem."

"I'm sorry, Jessica. You're right. I don't know what your life has been like, but I know what it's like when you're with me. I can tell how happy you are when we're together, but not because you ever verbalize it. So when you tell me you don't know what your feelings are, I think it's more a matter of you not wanting to admit what your feelings are, because you think you can't get hurt if you never admit to having those feelings."

Jessica sat up, still clutching the pillow as a shield. Her face had become flush and she was starting to cry. "Look, I know I don't express affection well. I've been told that before. But it's my choice. We've only dated for a couple months, and I'm going back to Atlanta soon. Why would anyone want to set themselves up for heartbreak in that situation?"

"Well, I don't really accept that whole Atlanta thing," Dixon said. "If we really had something between us we could work out a solution to that pretty quick. So, I think that's just an excuse to avoid facing the issues. As for not wanting to get hurt, I understand that desire, but it seems like I'm being made to pay for the sins of somebody else. Someone has hurt you somewhere along the way, and you're affected by that once-burned-by-the-fire-always-afraid-of-the-flame syndrome. I don't think you can go through life with a strategy of not getting hurt. It's the risk that makes life exciting."

"Maybe I'm not looking for excitement."

"Maybe not, but you're looking for love. Everybody is. And the question is whether you can ever find love without taking chances. If you want loyalty or obedience, buy a dog. If you want love, you achieve it by finding someone who excites you and hope that you have the same effect on them. The first time I called you, I was scared to death. If my life were dictated by pain avoidance, I would have never taken the chance of asking you out, because the wrong response would have hurt too much. On the other hand, when you said 'yes,' it shot a chill through me. I was so excited, I was beside myself."

"Why does it have to be that way?" she asked.

"Look. You always talk about making choices and how you want to choose what you do. That's fine. I'm just trying to influence the choices you make. I realize there's comfort in not taking risks, but I want you to choose to let yourself go and accept some vulnerability. I can't guarantee what will happen between us, but I can assure you the ride will be a lot more exciting. And, just to make it less uncomfortable for you, I'm telling you right here and now that I'm nuts about you, and I intend to do what it takes to prove it to you."

Jessica sat quiet for several seconds. "Maybe I should have ended up with your friend Sandy. I think the physical side would have been enough for him, and the last thing we'd be talking about is a relationship."

"Well, he might still be available," Dixon joked. "Should I call him?"

"No, I was just kidding. Can you do me a favor though? Can you just remember we've only dated a couple months and that I'm only here for a couple more months? I mean, why does everything have to go so fast?"

"I'm not trying to pressure you into any feelings you don't have. I'm trying to get you to acknowledge the feelings I think you do have. If I'm wrong, just tell me."

"Okay. I understand." After a pause she said, "I'm kind of beat from traveling."

"I understand," he said without hiding his disappointment.

She apparently sensed what he was feeling. "Do you want to spend the night?"

"Do I?" Dixon responded eagerly.

"Don't get too excited. I didn't say 'do you want to have sex?' I just said would you like to spend the night even though that means just sleeping together in the literal sense of the word."

"How do you know that's not what I thought you meant?"

"Mostly because you're a man," she replied. "This is just about sleeping, is that understood?"

"Yes, ma'am," he said in his best Opie Taylor. He crawled up to her side and lay down. He laid his arm across her stomach and leaned over to kiss her. "Goodnight," he whispered.

Jessica rolled onto her side with her back facing Dixon. He snuggled in close behind her. "You know they call this spooning," he said.

"So I've heard."

Dixon smiled behind her back. "Maybe when we've dated longer we can try forking."

Jessica let out an involuntary laugh, but quickly tried to act indignant.

Dixon's smile grew wider as he considered how clever he was.

After a few minutes, she rolled onto her back, and Dixon lay on his side facing her. He closed his eyes for a while, but then opened them to watch her sleep. She apparently sensed his eyes upon her, and opened hers. "What are you doing?"

"I only agreed to no sex," he said. "I didn't agree to not look."

"Don't you think you should get some sleep?" she asked.

"That will come soon enough. For now, I'm just dreaming."

# CHAPTER 26

SUMMER MADE AN unceremonious departure. Dixon and Jessica had settled into a routine. He saw her as often as he could, and rarely a day went by when they didn't at least talk on the phone. For all intents and purposes, they were a couple.

The Bureau of Criminal Apprehension was remarkably accommodating in responding to the request for an investigation of the incident. The retired cop pulled a few strings, and Dixon was on his way to Hibbing. Flying on a propjet was the price he had to pay for the shorter commute. He'd been in smaller planes on fly-in fishing trips, so he wasn't really concerned.

Upon entering the aircraft, he had to lower his head because he felt like he might hit his head on the ceiling. There was just one seat on each side. The exception was the last row, where a middle seat made for three across. Dixon thought that was the least desirable seat in the plane because it had neither a window nor an aisle, while almost every other seat had both. He soon learned there were two less desirable places to sit.

Dixon had a window seat in the last row. He didn't give it much thought until a slightly overweight man took the middle seat, trapping Dixon in the corner. The cabin was long and narrow, and appeared longer and narrower from Dixon's vantage point. He felt as though he were in the bottom of a cigar tube with no way out.

As the plane taxied onto the runway, the problem became more acute. Dixon felt himself getting light-headed, and his heart began to race. He looked out the window to distract himself, but that didn't help. He struck up a conversation with the man in the middle and that seemed to distract him. *Focus on the conversation,* he told himself. The most important thing was diverting the focus from his surroundings.

"Don't you hate these little planes?" the man in the middle asked.

"I didn't think I did until I got on board," Dixon replied.

"The extra turbulence really unnerves me," the man said.

"I think my issue is more claustrophobia than anything else. I feel so trapped back here and the main door looks so far away." Surprisingly, the discussion was helping. Not because it was therapeutic, but only because it allowed him to focus on something other than the helplessness that he felt.

Dixon sat back and closed his eyes. He tried to imagine himself on a golf course or a beach. He tried to distance himself from the thought that he was trapped in a situation where he would be totally powerless to control what would happen to him in the event of a problem.

The man in the middle looked him over and sensed his distress. "Would you like to switch seats?" he offered.

"Thank you. If you don't mind, once we're at cruising altitude, that would be great." Just the thought of a discernible end to his agony gave him hope. After a few minutes, they switched seats and Dixon found himself very much relieved. The little plane might still crash, but at least he felt like he would have a chance to do something.

The plane landed less than an hour after takeoff and Hank was waiting in the hangar. "I appreciate the gesture," Dixon said upon meeting him, "but next time I'll probably drive instead of flying in an oversized MRI machine."

"I guess you'd have had time. The investigator from the state won't be here until one. Why don't we grab some lunch before we head out?"

They drove into town and angle-parked in front of Dot's Diner. Dixon pulled the glass door open and, in doing so, rattled the sleigh bells that had been attached to the door to announce visitors. The restaurant consisted primarily of a serpentine lunch counter fronted by round disks that were each connected to the floor by a single metal bar.

As they walked to a booth, Sheriff Langaard appeared from a door that Dixon presumed was the bathroom. "José, how're ya doin'?" Hank asked.

"Good, thanks, and you?" The sheriff had not originally noticed Dixon, but now took a stride toward him. He put his hands on his hips and stood over him with a menacing countenance.

"Afternoon, sheriff," Dixon said.

Without changing his expression, the sheriff offered a curt "afternoon," and strutted out of the restaurant.

Hank and Dixon took their seats. "What's that about?" Dixon said.

Hank shrugged his shoulders. "I guess he's still a little upset about you snooping around his investigation."

"Do you think he's got something to be concerned about?" Dixon asked.

"No," Hank responded, "he wouldn't have anything to hide. I just don't think he likes outsiders."

A waitress appeared in a pink dress and a white apron. Over the din of dishes clanking in the kitchen, they both ordered the special—roast beef, mashed potatoes and gravy, and green beans. Before long, Dixon was telling Hank the Latvian florist story.

Hank smiled and chided, "I bet you didn't get much sleep when she got back."

"What do you mean?"

"I can't imagine how tired you must have been after she got done with you," Hank said.

"Well, the oddsmakers took another beating if that was the morning line."

As they spoke, Dixon spotted Perry Passieux coming in the front door. "This may save me some time," Dixon said. "I was planning to pay a visit to Mr. Passieux anyway."

Dixon gave Passieux a wave of invitation. When he arrived, Dixon asked, "How's the appeal coming?"

"Fine," Passieux responded. "They're such narrow issues that we agreed to proceed based on letter briefs. The main issue is whether the entire jury panel should have been dismissed. We argued harmless

error because the evidence raised the issue of domestic abuse anyway and, more importantly, the curative instruction was sufficient."

"Is the brief already done?" Dixon asked.

"Yes sir. Served and filed last week. Oral arguments are the end
of October."

"Perry," Dixon said, "Hank and I appreciate the work you're doing
on this case and we realize that, while it's important to us, it's certainly not the most important thing on your plate."

"Well, that doesn't mean I won't be zealous," Passieux assured
them.

"I have no doubt," Dixon said. "But I also had a thought. You're
aware that the State sometimes hires private attorneys to handle
things."

"Oh sure. In fact, I started doing prosecutions while I was in private practice. Some of the smaller municipalities can't afford to have
a city attorney or even a county attorney so they just hire someone
on a part-time basis."

"Exactly," Dixon responded. "We were thinking this Krueller case
is really only important to Hank and his family and maybe it would
be a good idea all around for you to hire me to handle it. I actually
won't charge you much of anything, or we'll arrange to have Hank
reimburse the State or something like that."

"I think there's a conflict-of-interest problem," Passieux responded.
"I realize we both have similar interests, but there's a problem with
you representing the State and the estate at the same time. I mean,
after all, you could theoretically cut a deal where you compromised
the criminal case in exchange for Les Krueller dropping the civil
claim."

"Yeah, I guess you're right," Dixon said. "Would you let me help
out at all?"

"I'd be happy to get any information from you, and I'd be happy
to share our strategy with you, but I don't think we could do anything that made you co-counsel or anything like that."

"Fair enough," Dixon replied. "Here's my card. Could you send
me copies of the briefs?"

"You betcha." Passieux spotted his lunch companion and excused himself.

After lunch, Hank and Dixon drove to Duke's place. Hank unchained the gate, and they drove up and parked outside the garage. They strolled around the yard until another car pulled in. The driver's side door opened and a blonde woman in her late twenties emerged. "Is one of you Hank MacKenzie?" she asked. "I'm Rebecca Stadsvold from the BCA."

Hank shook her hand and then introduced Dixon.

"You don't fit my preconceived notion of a criminologist," Dixon remarked.

"Is there a problem with that?" she said in a tone that made it clear she didn't interpret his statement as a compliment.

"No, not really. The key is making sure a jury is comfortable with you in that role and, up here on the Range, it might take a little extra work."

"What was your name again?" she asked.

"Dixon Donnelly."

"Well, Mr. Donnelly, I'm going to be conducting a criminal investigation here. It's not customary for civilians to be present but, under the circumstances, the Bureau decided to allow it. I can revoke that privilege if you think you're going to have a problem with my investigation."

"I'm sorry, really," he responded. "It's just that I've been going through a stretch where women seem to find everything about me to be charming and I guess I was taking things for granted. We really appreciate your being here and I'll do everything I can to stay out of your way."

As they spoke, a squad car pulled up and Deputy Halvorsen joined them. Hank led the group into the house, up the stairs, and into the bedroom. He pointed out the hole behind the door and Ms. Stadsvold began her investigation.

She took pictures, she inserted tools into the hole, and she scoured the surface with a magnifying lens. Then she scraped the inside of the hole and collected the residue in little bags. Finally, she inserted a long-nosed tool and attempted to extract whatever might be in the hole. Hank and Dixon were subconsciously leaning forward and staring in anticipation. After significant manipulating she pulled the tool from the wall. Holding it up as if she were a surgeon making a display for the operating theater, she announced, "Gentlemen, we have a bullet."

Hank's face lit up.

Agent Stadsvold held the bullet up for Deputy Halvorsen, who held out a plastic bag. After she deposited it, Halvorsen filled out a tag and affixed it to the bag.

Agent Stadsvold walked the perimeter of the room looking high and low for any other such specimens. Finding none, she turned to Deputy Halvorsen and said, "Could you grab the Luminol out of my bag?"

Halvorsen dug through the bag and produced a small bottle with a nozzle that looked like a mister for houseplants. "Is this it?" he asked.

"Yes," she replied, signaling him to bring it to her. "Where was the one victim found, the one who was shot in the stomach?" Hank pointed out the area just inside the threshold, and she aimed the bottle and squeezed the trigger. "You see that outline?" she said. "That's where the blood was before it was cleaned up."

Dixon was fascinated by the process and quick to ask questions. "Can you test it to see who it came from?"

"No. We have to find actual blood to do DNA testing. This process just shows where blood has been."

"How does it work?" Dixon asked.

"Hemoglobin contains microscopic iron ions that remain even when someone tries to clean it up."

Hank looked at Dixon. "Maybe she can test your car to see what that was."

"Good point," Dixon responded. Turning to Agent Stadsvold, he said, "My car was vandalized awhile ago. I found it covered with something red that looked like blood. Could you test it?"

"We might be able to, but looking for iron ions on a car may be more difficult because, depending on the location, iron is already present. Furthermore, even if it shows blood, that doesn't necessarily mean a crime has been committed. Hemoglobin is what carries oxygen in the blood, so all mammals have it."

"Well, I guess it's a moot point anyway," Dixon responded, "because I flew up this time." Dixon thought of making a date to have her examine it later, but thought better of it.

Agent Stadsvold directed Halvorsen to take some pictures of the Luminol's effect on the carpet. She then turned to the bullet hole in the wall. Hank and Dixon were again holding their breath. She squeezed the trigger and misted the Luminol onto the wall.

"Holy shit," Dixon said. "Is that what I think it is?"

"This shows a pattern of blood around the bullet hole," she responded. "As you can see, it's not a particularly wide pattern."

"What does that mean?" Hank asked.

Agent Stadsvold turned to address him. "The pattern of the blood suggests the bullet passed through living flesh before lodging in the wall. Also, given the size of the pattern, it occurred at fairly close range."

"So what happens now?" Hank asked.

"I'll have to run ballistics on the slug and see what we have. This bullet might not match anything and it's possible it has been here a long time. In fact, if it wasn't for the blood outline, I would have suspected this log might have taken the bullet while it was still a tree growing in the forest."

Privately, even Dixon was quick to dismiss that suggestion.

Agent Stadsvold was nothing if not thorough. She took samples from the carpeting and other locations. Then she asked to see where the remains were found. After completing that survey, she announced she was done. "I'll contact you with all of my findings and conclusions in a couple weeks."

Hank thanked her for her help. Dixon tried to be gracious, but concluded he wasn't likely to ever make inroads with Agent Stadsvold. He gave her a business card and asked her to call him with the results.

After she left, Deputy Halvorsen approached Hank. "Boy, I'm

awful sorry if I missed something out here. It's just that Les was shot and there didn't seem to be any other explanation for what happened."

"Don't worry about it," Hank said.

Dixon stepped in as well. "We don't know anything yet. There's no reason to believe the original version isn't correct."

"Do you think I should tell José?" Halvorsen asked.

Dixon shook his head. "If it's all the same to you, I don't think the Sheriff really likes me, so maybe you should hold off until there's something to report."

"Why doesn't he like you?" Halvorsen asked.

"I don't know. I was hoping maybe you could shed some light on that. Do you think he feels threatened by me or by my investigation?"

"I don't know why he would. I was responsible for the case. If something wasn't done, it was my fault."

"Did José have any part in the investigation?" Dixon asked.

"Not really. He said it was a tragedy for everyone involved, and it would be for the best if we wrapped it up quickly, but he didn't tell me what conclusions to reach or anything like that."

"Does he have any sort of a relationship with Les Krueller that you know of?" Dixon persisted.

"No. I haven't been on the force here all that long, but as far as I know the only connection is that he's been called out to break up domestic disputes at the Kruellers', so he's familiar with Les. On the other hand, Les is the last guy a sheriff could afford to take up with."

"How about Debi, is there any relationship between José and Debi?

"No," Halvorsen replied. "I think José was married when Debi first moved here and then Debi got married to Les before José got divorced. I can't imagine they had any relationship other than him breaking up fights between Les and her, and he doesn't even do that anymore now that he's sheriff."

"Well, until we get a little more information, I'd appreciate it if you'd leave the sheriff out of the loop."

"What about the county attorney?" Halvorsen continued. "My understanding is that an accused is entitled to all of the evidence against them. Shouldn't I tell Passieux so he can turn it over?"

"I don't want to tell you how to do your job," Dixon responded, "but you're only required to turn over information relating to an active case. As of right now, Krueller's already been convicted. As a result, there is no case pending."

"I guess you're right," Halvorsen replied. "Maybe just to be safe I'll ask Passieux hypothetically whether the duty to disclose evidence goes away when there is no case pending."

"I think that's a good idea," Dixon said.

Afterward, Hank drove Dixon to his motel. "Got a date with Mrs. Krueller again tonight?" he chided.

"I think I'll make it an early night. Are you going to chauffeur me around again tomorrow?"

"Sure."

"Well, the pretrial is at ten and my flight's at two. Pick me up around 9:30, and we'll go from there."

# CHAPTER 27

Pretrial conferences consist of an informal meeting between the judge and the lawyers to discuss the issues expected to be raised at trial. They are generally held in chambers and this one was no exception. Dixon rang the security buzzer to announce his presence and was let in. Predictably, he was the first to arrive. He sat in the judge's waiting area perusing the same hunting and fishing magazines that had been in the waiting room at the sheriff's office.

After a while, he overhead another voice on the intercom, and McGuckin soon joined him in the waiting area. Dixon stood and they exchanged greetings. After a few more minutes, they were joined by a third lawyer. He introduced himself as Skip Blakemore. He was the attorney for Duke's insurance company and had been summoned by the judge to participate in the meeting. The three of them were talking when the secretary announced the Judge was ready for them.

Judge Stockman's office was large and well appointed. The walls and counter space were covered with a seemingly endless array of photographs. There were the obligatory family shots, but also an overwhelming number of pictures of the judge with the famous or powerful, ranging from political leaders to entertainers. The photographs emphasized that, while Hibbing might be a small pond, Judge Stockman was a big fish in that pond.

Stockman was dressed in casual clothes. Apparently there weren't any formal proceedings expected for the day. He directed the attorneys to the chairs that were facing his desk. His secretary came in and sat at a nearby conference table. "We won't be on the record," the judge announced. "Whatever is decided here, I'll issue a written order. If anyone wants to make a record, we'll bring someone in at the end, okay?"

The lawyers nodded in agreement and took their seats. Stockman picked up a file and opened it. "We have two issues I think we need to discuss. There are three different legal proceedings, and we have to figure out how they relate to each other. First, we have to consider what effect the criminal conviction and the pending appeal have on the personal injury action. Second, we have to consider the relationship between the personal injury lawsuit and the insurance coverage dispute. Anybody got any bright ideas?"

McGuckin jumped in to claim the floor first even though it was apparent he wasn't sure what he wanted to say. "Your honor, it seems to me . . . all things considered . . . that evidence of the criminal conviction should not be allowed into evidence. If it is, we could have an entire civil lawsuit that becomes invalid if the criminal conviction is reversed. As a result, even though a conviction like this might be admissible, it becomes invalid."

"Well, your honor," Dixon piped in, "the law is pretty clear that a conviction is a conviction. The possibility of reversal on appeal is just that—a possibility. Criminal defendants are frequently sentenced and begin incarceration pending appeal. If it's final enough for that, it's final enough to be admitted into evidence in our case."

McGuckin chimed back in, "My first choice would be to wait until the issue is resolved by the Court of Appeals."

"I'm not sure we have that luxury," the judge replied. "I've slotted the civil case in on my schedule, and I don't have any openings on my calendar for six months after that. There are a few weeks I hold open for criminal matters that receive speedy trial priority, but those dates usually do fill up."

Dixon raised a finger as if he were a schoolboy wanting to be called on by the teacher. After Stockman finished, Dixon said, "My clients would like this resolved as soon as possible, so we'd rather find a solution than delay the matter. It seems to me like it's really our choice. The law is clear that it is admissible evidence. If we put it in, we take the risk of a reversal of the criminal conviction. On the other hand, we'll put in independent evidence of the assault, so the

Court would always be in a position to determine that admission of the conviction was harmless even if it turned out to be in error."

"Excuse me," McGuckin said. "I'd like you to choose. If the conviction is admitted, then there's no reason to put in other evidence of the assault. It would just be piling on. If you want to try and prove assault independently, do so, but don't put in all the evidence and then say to the jury, 'by the way, he's already been convicted for the assault.'"

"He might have a point," Stockman said to Dixon. "If you put in the conviction you're entitled to a jury instruction that the jury must presume an assault occurred, so there's no reason to put in the other evidence."

"With all due respect," Dixon responded, "whether my client acted in self-defense does require the jury to know the details of the assault."

Judge Stockman held up a hand to signal he didn't want any more comments at that time. "Let's let that one simmer for a minute. What are we going to do about the two civil trials? Mr. Donnelly, you've filed a lawsuit against the insurance company for failing to provide coverage and that seems to raise the same issues as the personal injury case. Can we consolidate them?"

McGuckin was again first to speak. "We would most strenuously object to such a course of events, your honor. As the plaintiff, we have the burden of proof and, as a result, we are allowed to make the first presentation and the last rebuttal. Primacy and recency are the hallmark of what we do. If we consolidate the cases, it'll be two on one and I don't know how you'll protect my ability to present my case."

Blakemore spoke next. "I agree with Mr. McGuckin, but not for the same reason. We would like the insurance coverage issue decided first and, that way, we may be able to avoid the expense of a protracted personal injury trial."

"All right," Stockman said. "I agree that trying those two cases together would be too confusing. But which one should we try first? And couldn't we have inconsistent verdicts if we try them separately? What if we tried the coverage case first and the jury

found self-defense or something else that invokes insurance coverage, but the jury in the second case finds no self-defense and awards
substantial damages?"

Dixon was first to speak. "Your Honor, the insurance company
has taken its chances by withdrawing its defense of the homeowner.
If we prevail in the personal injury action, I think we'll have the
right to seek an appropriate recovery."

Blakemore disagreed. "The issues are not identical, and I really
think we should decide coverage first."

"Absolutely not," Dixon said as his voice rose in anger. "By doing
so, the insurance company will be making arguments that might
be harmful to its own insured. Furthermore, at a minimum, it will
be giving the Plaintiff a practice trial. I think it's unconscionable
that the insurance company would not only not provide coverage,
but would take a legal position that may actually be harmful to its
insured." Dixon could fake outrage when needed, but his frustration
over the situation was genuine.

Stockman nodded before responding. "Mr. Donnelly, are you saying that if the jury rules in favor of the Estate in the personal injury
action, the insurance company should automatically reimburse the
estate for costs and fees, but if the jury finds against the Estate, it's on
its own and the insurance company is off the hook?"

"Basically, yes," Dixon responded. "I don't want to completely
commit to that, because there may be some nuances that come up."

"All right, gentlemen," Stockman said. "These are my thoughts
and my plans. I will put them in an Order and you can comment or
make a record once I do that. This is not easy and I want everyone
to have time to reflect and research before they tell me I'm wrong.
The first issue is whether the guilty verdict can be admitted into
evidence in the personal injury case. My preference is that the jury
not be given anything about the results of the criminal trial. Now,
Mr. McGuckin, if you try to get the burglary acquittal into evidence,
I will absolutely let the assault conviction in if anyone else wants it.
Otherwise, Mr. Donnelly, you have the right to put the assault conviction into evidence, but I'm telling you now that I will seriously
entertain any motions to limit additional testimony on the assault.

Furthermore, while I'm not predicting in advance how I will rule on issues, don't expect me to help you out if the assault conviction is overturned on appeal. So, just to be clear, you can put the conviction into evidence, but if it's not important to your case, I'd strongly recommend that you avoid doing so."

"Understood," Dixon said with a nod. "Maybe we'll have a ruling from the Court of Appeals by then anyway."

"Now, for the second issue," Stockman continued. "If a jury finds Duke MacKenzie didn't do anything wrong, then I think the insurance company should pay for the defense. I realize the law isn't completely clear on that, but if I have anything to say about it, that's the way it will be. I'm going to try the personal injury matter before the insurance coverage dispute. The reason, however, is simple. That case was the first one filed and, under our normal protocol, that one is entitled to be tried first. We'll see what happens, but if the Estate wins I think the insurance company should reimburse it. The alternative is to have another nearly identical trial, and it just doesn't make sense for the insurance company to pay its attorney to try that second case when the cost wouldn't be much different if it just paid the Estate's fees. I won't make any ruling on that until after the personal injury trial, but that's what I'm thinking will be the outcome."

McGuckin grabbed the floor again. "As always, your honor, your wisdom graces this Court and the entire county."

"Give it a rest, Earl," Stockman replied. Turning to the others, he said, "Anyone else want to gild the lily before we adjourn?"

"Would it help my case?" Dixon responded with a smile.

"Tell you what," Stockman said. "Let's save that for another day. I'll issue a proposed Order. Everyone has five business days to respond and, if nobody convinces me that I'm wrong, the Order will issue. You'll have a right to appeal regardless, but I think the Court of Appeals would be more impressed if you raised your concerns before the Order becomes final." With that, the pretrial was adjourned.

# CHAPTER 28

DIXON ROSE FROM his desk when he heard the mailman chatting with his assistant. He was always eager to see the mail and, on this occasion, he was eager to receive the package that Perry Passieux had promised to send with the appellate briefs from the criminal trial. He greeted the postal carrier and, after some small talk, a large stack of mail was deposited on the reception counter.

Dixon's assistant began sorting. "Anything in particular you're looking for?"

"I'm expecting something from the County Attorney in Hibbing," he replied.

"Well, here's something with a Hibbing postmark, but there's no return address."

Dixon took the envelope and studied it from the outside. His name and address were typed and "Dixon" was misspelled "Dickson." There were no other words or marks. "What the hell could this be?" he remarked as he slid his finger under the flap and pried it open.

He reached in and pulled out a folded magazine article. The story was about a mafia hit on an attorney, and included a picture of the corpse covered with a sheet. Dixon turned it over to see if there was anything written on the back. Finding nothing, he looked in the envelope again but found it empty.

"I think someone's sending me a message." Dixon handed the contents to his assistant. " But I'm at a loss to know what it is."

"Omigod," his assistant said. "That's creepy. Call the cops."

"I'm not sure what they can do."

"Well, find out," she pleaded.

Dixon retreated into his office. He opened his rolodex to find the number for a law school classmate who worked for the Hennepin County Attorney. He dialed the number and was lucky enough to reach him on the first attempt. "Bob, this is Dixon Donnelly, how are you?"

"Oh-oh, is it fund drive time again already?"

"No," Dixon assured him. "I have a criminal law question I was hoping you could help me with. I just received some intimidating mail. I'm sure you heard about the mob lawyer that was gunned down execution-style in Vegas. Well, I got an envelope sent to me with a magazine spread about it. No message and no return address, but the postmark is from Hibbing, and I've got a kind of contentious case going on up there. I think somebody might be trying to send me a message."

"Do you know who the somebody is?"

"I really don't. It could be one of four or five people."

"Well, I'm afraid you have a hard case. Sending those pictures might constitute making terroristic threats, but that's going to be tough when you can't identify the sender and when you can't even say for sure what the message is meant to be."

"Is there any way we can examine the stuff and figure out who sent it?" Dixon asked.

"Well, unfortunately, that high-tech, forensic stuff is usually reserved for capital crimes or at least something more than this. If there are fingerprints, that might be easy to look at, but even the most novice criminal knows enough to avoid fingerprints when given the opportunity to plan. Let me give you a name at the police station. You can make a report and deposit the evidence. I've got to be honest with you, though, the main benefit is that if something ends up happening to you, they would use that evidence to try and find the perpetrator."

"Boy, you're a real comfort," Dixon remarked.

"Sorry, but I'm just giving it to you straight."

"I think for now I'll just put it in a sealed envelope and let my assistant know what to do with it if something happens."

"Suit yourself," Bob replied.

Dixon hung up and recounted the story for his assistant.

"If it's any consolation," she said, "I think your package from the County Attorney arrived." She handed him a large manila envelope, and he took it back into his office.

He started with the "Letter Brief of Appellant Lester Krueller." Few things had gone against Krueller at trial, so there wasn't much about which he could complain. The brief contained two main arguments. First, the jury pool was "irrevocably tainted," according to McGuckin, and the only alternative after the inadvertent disclosure that Les Krueller was 'the guy who always gets drunk and beats up his wife' was to start over. Second, Krueller argued that the verdict was inconsistent because a jury could not reasonably find not guilty on the burglary charge and guilty on the subsequent assault. The brief was fifteen pages in all and, because the alleged errors were discrete questions of law, there was no need to include any of the transcript.

Passieux's brief was comparable in length. It contained all the passion of his previous oral arguments—next to none. The response to the jury pool taint was primarily to claim "harmless error" that was cured by the admonition given by the judge. As a backup, he argued that information of spousal abuse should have been admitted in any event because, even though it wasn't part of the crime charged, the evidence supported the conclusion that Krueller was attacking his wife as well. On the second issue, Passieux argued the verdicts were not inconsistent because the jury could have concluded that Krueller was not originally intending to commit a crime when he broke in, but that the situation evolved. Alternatively, he suggested that the real problem was the not guilty verdict on burglary, given those facts were undisputed. Unfortunately, it seemed apparent the jury had simply been confused by the difference between the popular conception of burglary and the statutory requirements. All in all, Dixon thought, it would be a coin flip.

Dixon strolled to the front office and poured himself a cup of coffee. "Anymore surprises in the mail?" he asked.

"Well you got a postcard from someplace I've never heard of."

It had taken three weeks for Jessica's postcard to make it to its destination. Dixon took it and looked at the picture of a beach scene showing middle-aged European men with oversized stomachs protruding over their undersized swimsuits. Jessica's message was sweet, but, in her inimitable style, somewhat less than effusive. She reported on the weather, the length of the flight, the sights, and nothing about her feelings. She signed off with the always inspiring "See ya soon!" If only she'd known how long it would take her postcard to arrive.

Dixon carried it back into his office and called Jessica on the phone. He asked whether she couldn't have sent pictures of topless women instead. She mock scolded him for expressing an interest in seeing breasts, much less breasts other than hers. That conversation continued for several minutes.

"Are we still on for dinner with Sandy and Melody on Saturday?" Dixon asked.

"Yes, but there's one other thing," she responded. "My mom has asked us to have brunch with her and her husband on Sunday, and I want to make sure you're okay with that."

"Yeah, I guess that'd be fine," he responded. "Will I like them?"

"Will you like them or will you like them more than I do?"

"There's a difference?"

"You'll probably like them more than I do. Most people like them, but I don't seem to have the smoothest relationship with either of them."

"Well, let's make the best of it, okay?"

"Fine. I'll see you Saturday night."

Dixon hung up and pondered this latest mystery. It's probably not unusual for children to resent parents who get divorced, but thirty years seemed like a long time to hold a grudge.

Dixon picked up the phone and dialed Perry Passieux. After speaking to a receptionist, he got Passieux on the line. "Perry, this is Dixon Donnelly. Thanks for sending me the briefs. Listen, do you have a minute? I want to talk to you about a strategy on the oral argument."

"Sure," he responded.

"Before I get to that, I have to ask you something else. I received a threatening package today in an unmarked envelope from Hibbing. No note or anything. Just a magazine article about a lawyer who was brutally murdered. What do you think of that?"

"You think someone up here is trying to send you a message?"

"I don't know how else to interpret it. Any thoughts?"

"Well, unless the pictures were cut out of a nudie magazine, I don't think they'd be from Les. And I can't imagine McGuckin doin' something like that, because he'd have too much to lose. Debi just isn't sophisticated enough to try something like that."

"Let me ask you this," Dixon responded. "The sheriff sure doesn't seem to be taking a shine to me. Is there any chance he's afraid I'll uncover something?"

"Boy, I can't imagine that. He's the last person who would want to help Les Krueller. A while back, Krueller filed police brutality charges against José."

"For what?"

"José was called for a domestic out at the Kruellers' house. He got there and it was pretty clear Les had popped his wife 'cause she had a bloody nose and a puffed face. José took one look at her and went postal on Les. José claimed that Les resisted arrest and there was some evidence of that, but I think José was looking for a reason to turn it up a notch."

"So what happened?"

"It was settled out of court. Les got a small payment and now José makes sure somebody else handles the domestic disputes at the Krueller abode."

"How come Deputy Halvorsen didn't know anything about it?" Dixon asked.

"It might have been before he was here. It's kind of hush-hush now."

"So is there something going on between José and Debi?"

"Not that I know of, but I s'pose it's possible. Even if there was, why would José want to discourage your investigation?"

"I don't know. Maybe he was mad because Duke beat him to Debi

Krueller. Or maybe he's afraid Debi will end up telling people about her secret relationship with the sheriff. Makes me wonder if there's something somebody doesn't want me to find out."

"Now you're starting to sound like Hank," Passieux said.

"I know, I know. But even though the evidence in this case is pretty straightforward, I just have an uneasy feeling about the whole thing."

"Well, if we win the appeal, doesn't that pretty much seal your case?"

"Maybe, but I don't know if we'll have a decision on the appeal before the civil trial. The law is clear that I can still put the conviction into evidence, but there are risks—not the least of which is that a reversal in the criminal action might then result in a new trial in the civil action."

"Well, all the same, aren't you in pretty good shape if we win the appeal?"

"Yeah, but the interplay between the criminal trial, the personal injury trial, and the coverage trial is complicated. That's what I want to talk to you about."

The pair continued to debate the interaction between the cases, the findings of the first jury, and the likely outcome of the second trial and any others thereafter. After an extended discussion, Passieux said that he would take the suggestions under advisement. Dixon asked about the date for oral argument, and it was agreed that Dixon would attend as a spectator. Things were starting to happen, and they were happening fast.

# CHAPTER 29

T HE MINNESOTA JUDICIAL CENTER houses the state's appellate courts. The Krueller case was before a three-judge panel of the Court of Appeals, which was considered the error-correcting court because its mission was primarily to determine whether the trial court had made a mistake. Issues of first impression or of particular importance went to the Minnesota Supreme Court, while issues of basic trial court review were handled by the Court of Appeals. It was a system that allowed the Supreme Court Justices to work about as much or as little as they wanted.

Dixon met Passieux in the lobby before oral arguments. "Are you ready?" Dixon asked.

"As ready as I'll ever be, I guess," he responded with a nervous smile. "I don't make many trips down here, so I never know what to expect."

"Assuming that they let you speak and don't take up all of your time with questions, do you have in mind what you're going to say?"

"Pretty much. I think the law is pretty clear, but how it applies to this case is anybody's guess. I mean, whether the trial judge committed harmless error sort of depends on a person's subjective view of the case."

"I agree," Dixon said. "Do you think we'll have a decision before the civil trial?"

"When is the civil trial?"

"About a month from now," Dixon responded. "The week after Thanksgiving."

"We might. Because of speedy trial concerns, these criminal appeals are sometimes turned around in thirty days. But I doubt it."

They spoke a few more minutes before heading up to the court-room. McGuckin was already in the courtroom seated at one of the counsel tables. He was wearing a navy blue suit, which was uncharacteristic for him. He didn't look overly debonair, but it was more appropriate than his usual garb.

After a few minutes, a clerk came out to explain the time limits and the light signals on the lectern that regulated the length of the arguments. Each side was allocated fifteen minutes. The fear among practitioners was always that the judges would start asking questions and fifteen minutes wouldn't be sufficient to complete the presentation. Running out of things to say with time to spare, however, was the real death knell.

The clerk exited and returned a few minutes later to call the Court to order. Three judges appeared in black robes and assumed their seats at the dais. The one in the middle announced the case and file number, requested an entry of appearances, and directed the arguments to begin.

Because McGuckin represented the appellant, he got the first shot. He spent the first several minutes blowing smoke up the judges' asses about the fine system of jurisprudence we enjoy in this country and the fine record of the public servants in Minnesota. He transitioned by making it clear that none of that would continue to be true if the conviction of his client was allowed to stand.

McGuckin started rambling through what was essentially his closing argument at trial. He told the judges how his client was wronged by the local rich boy and was driven by forces that would cause any man to do the same.

"Mr. McGuckin," one of the judges interrupted. "That's an argument for the jury. What we want to know is why the judge or jury made a mistake."

"Yes, yes, of course," replied McGuckin. And he proceeded to reiterate the arguments in his brief. He had, he advised them, promptly and strenuously insisted that the entire jury be dismissed when the juror prospect characterized Les Krueller as a well-known wife beater. Furthermore, the finding of not guilty on the burglary count was a finding of no criminal intent and that finding should be carried over to the assault charge as well. The yellow light came on, signaling he had only a minute left. "With the Court's permission, I'd like to save my last minute for rebuttal." McGuckin strolled from the podium back to his seat.

Now it was Passieux's turn. He sped through the facts in an effort to highlight the more egregious of those that were undisputed. "Let me turn first to the tainted jury issue. The State's position is that the real error was the decision not to allow the introduction of evidence of past domestic abuse in the first place. There is no question that Lester Krueller has a history of domestic abuse, so the juror's statement was consistent with the evidence that should have been allowed."

One of the judges interrupted him. "But there were no charges brought for assault on the wife."

"That's only because she was too afraid to cooperate," Passieux responded.

"Could you have brought the charges without her cooperation?" the same judge asked.

"Not in this case. We will bring charges without cooperation, but we have to have some other admissible evidence. In this case, the only other witness was dead, so there wasn't much we could do."

"Couldn't you just put her on the stand?"

"Well," Passieux responded, "the spousal privilege has an exception that would have allowed her to testify, but we couldn't make her testify."

"So you want us to fashion a rule that allows evidence of past spousal abuse to come in when there could have been a domestic abuse charge, even though no such charge is actually made, is that correct?"

"That's right, your honor."

"Do you have anything else to say on that subject?"

"No, your honor. If there are no questions, I'll move on to the question of the inconsistent verdict. The evidence here supports a finding of guilty on the burglary charge as a matter of law. There is no dispute that Krueller smashed the window—and that's unlawful entry—and the conviction on the assault charge shows he did, in fact, commit a crime."

"Excuse me, counsel," another member of the panel spoke up. "Are you suggesting that we can reverse the jury's finding of not guilty on the burglary conviction?"

Passieux stood silent, and appeared to be in shock. He shuffled his notes and then recovered. "Absolutely. It's clear the jury just misunderstood the instructions."

"Are you forgetting about the Constitution and the right to a trial by jury? We have no authority to overrule a finding of not guilty."

"But . . . judges overrule juries all the time," Passieux protested.

"Not when it comes to not guilty verdicts. Judges overrule juries in civil cases and overrule juries on findings of guilt, but judges have no authority to override an acquittal."

"Well they should have that authority," a desperate Passieux responded.

"Mr. Passieux," the judge in the middle said. "I don't understand what you're doing. You have some plausible arguments in your favor, but you have chosen to ignore those arguments and pursue arguments that are contrary to the plain language of the statute and hundreds of years of American jurisprudence. I see that your time is just about up. Is there anything else that you'd like to say?"

"No, your honor."

"In that case, Mr. McGuckin, would you still like your rebuttal?"

McGuckin stood up. "I will rest on my prior argument," he replied, with a confident smile.

Passieux hadn't accomplished much, but he had succeeded in keeping McGuckin from seizing an opportunity to talk.

As the Court adjourned, McGuckin tossed his notepads into his briefcase and exited. When he passed Dixon he shot him a look and commented that his case kept getting better and better. Dixon did his best to ignore him.

Passieux took a little longer to collect his things. He swung the gate open that separated the gallery from the counsel tables and came face to face with Dixon. "Well, what do you think?"

"I think we'll be working without an assault conviction during the civil trial."

# CHAPTER 30

Dixon picked Jessica up at 6:30 for their seven o'clock rendezvous with Sandy and Melody. Persian food was the choice.

"Don't tell me it's 'Persian' food," Sandy said when Dixon suggested it. "It's Iranian food and calling a duck a dog doesn't make a duck man's best friend."

"Well, it's your birthday," Dixon said. "Where do you want to go?"

"The Caspian is fine with me. Just don't tell me it's Persian food." And so they agreed to meet for dinner at the Caspian.

The restaurant surprised all of them by being white tablecloth and remarkably upscale. "What a gyp," Sandy said after the maître d' had dropped off the menus. "There's not one camel dish on the menu. And they claim this place is authentic."

"Well, if it were authentic, I don't think they'd be serving alcohol, so let's praise Allah for small favors," Dixon replied. Putting that bug in Sandy's ear soon proved to be a mistake.

When the waitress came for their orders, Sandy insisted he wanted an authentic Persian beer. When she said there weren't any, he grudgingly agreed to settle for an authentic Iranian beer. When she apologetically explained he was in no more luck with that request, he demanded a beer brewed anywhere in the Muslim world. When the beer requests went unfulfilled, he began asking for Muslim wine coolers. Finally, Melody leaned against him and said, "We get your joke, you're very funny, now please shut up."

"You know in Tehran they'd probably cut out your tongue for talking to a man that way," Sandy said.

"Yes, and they probably would have castrated a wisenheimer like you to make sure you didn't procreate." Melody had a sharp tongue and didn't mind using it to bring Sandy into line.

"There's an interesting question," Dixon interjected. "Are wisenheimers born or made? If we castrated Sandy, could we prevent him from creating other wisenheimers or would we have to kill him because of his bad influence and the possibility that he'd train another wisenheimer?"

Melody piped in, "I guess the only way to be sure is to castrate him and then kill him, is that what you're saying?"

"Not exactly," Dixon said. "I'm asking: Do you think people are born funny—or in Sandy's case thinking that he's funny—or do you think it's learned?"

"This is a hot topic for you, isn't it?" Jessica said.

"No, not really. I'm just interested to see what people have to say about the subject. I'd be happy to move on. In fact, while I have the floor, I'd like to propose a toast to the birthday boy. Thirty-five years old. Man, you're halfway to forty. Just remember, Sandy, you're not getting older . . . you're getting grayer and fatter."

They clinked glasses and sipped. Sandy picked up his napkin and pretended as if he were wiping away tears. "That was touching," he said, affecting a crack in his voice.

After the toast, Jessica spoke. "So, how long have you two been friends?"

"We met in law school," Dixon responded. "We weren't really friends until third year."

Sandy spoke next. "That's because it was dangerous to be friends with Dixon during first year."

"What does that mean?" Jessica asked.

Sandy smiled at Dixon before responding. "Dixon didn't always espouse the most popular positions."

Jessica prodded him on with a wave of her hand.

Sandy hesitated, but clearly wanted to proceed. "Well, first year you study a lot of Constitutional law issues like abortion, welfare rights, et cetera. Dixon's views didn't really qualify as mainstream."

Dixon was happy the subject had come up so he could speak his peace. "Y'know, in the sixties there were a lot of people who began expressing antiestablishment opinions, and they were hailed as revolutionaries whose provocative views sparked a new world order. Now that those people *are* the establishment, they are totally against anyone questioning the rightness of their beliefs. As far as I'm concerned, they can eat the proverbial shit and die."

Sandy could not have asked for a better response. "Do you see what I mean about it being dangerous to be friends with Dixon during first year?"

Jessica and Melody had a chuckle at that.

"Well, I had no problem looking myself in the mirror," Dixon said. "Sandy, on the other hand, couldn't open his mouth in class without first acknowledging the validity of whatever position he wasn't going to take. In fact, I think he usually just declared every sensitive issue to be a tie."

Jessica stepped in to defend Sandy. "Maybe he's just not as decided about those issues, so he's less self-righteous."

"I doubt it," Dixon said.

"Why is that so hard to accept?" she persisted.

"Because I later got to know him better."

Sandy let out a staccato laugh.

"That sounds like there's a story behind it," Jessica said.

"Yeah, there is. And that's how Sandy and I became friends."

"Well, let's hear it," she prodded.

Dixon looked at Sandy. "You or me?"

"Go ahead," Sandy replied. "I'll jump in if you screw it up."

"Fair enough," Dixon said. "I had a party during our third year of law school. I didn't really know or like Sandy enough to invite him, but the party was pretty much open to anybody, so he showed up."

"Just trying to make sure the party was a success," Sandy interjected.

"Anyway, later on the party started thinning out, and Sandy had this idea to entertain everybody. He found the personals section of the newspaper and started calling gay chat lines. Sandy Swanson, Mr. Touchy-feely, starts calling all these numbers and talking in a swishy voice. Then he started calling the gay personals and leaving my name and number."

"And that made you guys friends?" Jessica said.

"Well, I wasn't happy with incurring the phone charges," Dixon said, "but it revealed a side of Sandy that let me know he wasn't a complete wiener."

"Cut it out, Dix," Sandy said. "I'm afraid I'll start crying again."

"Anyway," Dixon continued, "it was the first time I really saw Sandy when he didn't have his political guard up."

"And you've been friends ever since?" Melody asked.

"Actually, that's not quite the end of the story," Dixon said. "The next week, I started getting return messages from some of the gay guys Sandy had called. In particular, one guy named Lance, or something like that, started leaving me messages. This guy was a real flamer and he started leaving me messages about how great I sounded, how much we had in common, and how eager he was to meet me. I didn't respond or do anything, but he kept calling back every day while I was gone. And he kept getting madder when I didn't call him back."

Sandy hung his head and held up a hand to shield his eyes as if he were embarrassed.

Dixon resumed the story. "So, after several days of messages, the phone rings one night when I'm at home and it's Lance. He starts in with 'I'm so glad I finally reached you, et cetera. When he finally let me get in a word edgewise, I tried to explain I wasn't the one who left the message and that it had been a joke. That turned out to be about the worst thing I could say."

Dixon looked at his audience to make sure they were following the story. "This guy now had hurt feelings and reacted like I'd duped him for my own amusement. He started laying into me for toying with other people's emotions. I tried to explain it was some boob that I knew from law school, and then it got even worse. In his Tinkerbell voice, he starts with 'the gay community is stronger than you think. You'll be sorry. I'm going to the law school to expose you as a gay basher and then I'm going to contact all of my gay friends at all the law firms in town and make sure they all know what kind of a savage you are.'

"Well, that scared me a little, so I start pleading with this guy to show some restraint and give me a chance to prove that I was a victim too. Of course, the word 'victim' apparently pushed another hot button, because he went ballistic about me claiming to be a victim when gay men were the real victims."

"Everybody loves a wisenheimer," Melody remarked.

"Now I'm begging him to give me a break," Dixon continued. "Finally, he agrees to reconsider if I agree to meet him and convince him of my sincerity. I agree to meet him, and then he tells me to meet him at some gay bar. At that point, I can't really object, so I agree to do it. I go down to this place, and I'm standing outside looking around to make sure I don't see anyone on the street that I know. The coast looked clear, so I headed in. Right as I pull open the door, Sandy jumps out and snaps my picture."

Jessica looked confused. "How did he know you'd be there?"

Dixon turned to her. "There never was a Lance. The whole time it was Sandy leaving the messages and pretending to be Lance on the phone."

Everybody had a laugh. Even though Sandy knew the whole story, he laughed heartily at his own mischief.

"And that's the basis for the friendship?" Jessica asked.

"Hey," Dixon said, "I have to respect anyone who would go to that much trouble for a practical joke, and I have to respect anyone who could pull one over on me." Dixon clinked his glass against Sandy's, and they both drained their beers and ordered another.

Dixon enjoyed telling the story, but it gave him a desire to tell embarrassing stories about Sandy. Before long, it was basically a contest. Each attempted to identify a story that would be embarrassing to the other. Each then tried to top the other's story. The process continued, and the alcohol continued to flow. The women laughed along in the beginning, but seemed to lose interest as the stories became bluer. Fraternity-type high jinks were rarely amusing to women.

Dixon and Sandy would switch topics and draw the women back into the conversation until, before long, one of them remembered another story he felt was worth sharing. After dinner, Jessica switched to water, while Dixon and Sandy continued on the barley train. For the last half hour, Jessica didn't really say anything. Dixon sensed she must be ready to go and they settled the tab. "I hope this was your most memorable birthday ever," Dixon said with a slap on Sandy's back.

Dixon and Jessica walked through the parking lot. "Would you like to drive?" he asked.

"No, you knew you were driving when you kept ordering drinks. You're a big boy."

He opened her door and let her in. He circled around the back and got behind the wheel. He pulled out and they rode in silence. After a couple blocks, Dixon asked, "Are you mad?"

"What makes you say that?"

"Well, for starters, you're awfully quiet."

"Can't a person be quiet without being mad?"

"Sure, but I don't think that's your nature."

They drove on in silence. They came to a stop at a signal. "If I did something wrong, I'd like the chance to respond or apologize or something," he said.

"You don't have to say anything."

After a pause, he tried to change the subject. "What did you think of the food?"

"It was fine."

"Have you ever had Persian food before?"

"No."

Exasperated by her unwillingness to help the conversation, he said, "Hey, what do you think about that conflict in the Middle East, is that nutty or what?"

Jessica looked out the side window. "Not my problem."

They drove the rest of the way in silence. When they reached her house, Dixon got out and walked her to the door. When they got to the steps he remained on the lower one the way he had on their first date. She unlocked the door and pushed it open. "What time should I pick you up tomorrow?" Dixon asked.

"Aren't you coming in?" Jessica said, with surprise.

"No, I don't think so."

"Why not?"

"Well, you're mad about something, and you don't want to talk about it so what's the point."

"So, what does this mean?"

"It doesn't mean anything. If you don't want to talk, I can't make you. But being with you right now is very uncomfortable and if that's your intention, I'm ending it. When you want to talk about it or just want to return to normal, let me know."

That response didn't please her. "Do you want to just skip tomorrow?" she asked.

"No, I don't. But that's up to you. I don't want to spend what might already be a slightly uncomfortable day and add the discomfort you're inflicting."

Jessica stood and looked at him for a long time. "Why don't you come in and we can talk about it."

"Are you sure? Because I don't want to argue, and it might be better to get a night's sleep and talk tomorrow."

"No, let's talk now," she said, grabbing his hand and pulling him inside.

Dixon walked to the couch. Jessica went into the kitchen to get a glass of water and offered him one as well. She reappeared and sat next to him. "So, what do you want to talk about?" she asked.

"I didn't say there was anything that I wanted to talk about. I said you seemed upset about something, and I wanted you to talk about it."

"Can't I just be quiet once in a while."

"Jessica, I agreed to come in so we could discuss this. If you didn't want to, you should have let me go home."

"Well, I don't know, I just . . . you and Sandy were having a grand old time, but after a while there wasn't anything in it for me other than to watch the two of you get drunker and drunker. I was ready to go long before you finally realized I wanted to go."

"So even though Sandy and I were having a good time, you wanted me to cut it short because you weren't enjoying it as much."

"You and Sandy can go out and have fun together anytime. You don't need to bring me along for that."

"Well, we tried to include you."

"Not hardly. I don't have a lot of stories about getting drunk and dancing half naked."

"Was that it? Was there something about the stories?"

"No. It's just that I'm not really comfortable being with people who are drinking that much."

"Is this about tomorrow?" Dixon asked. "Are you a little uptight about us going to see your mom and her husband?"

That seemed to hit a nerve. "Maybe, I don't know. I just wasn't comfortable after dinner and I wanted to go, and you and Sandy kept joking and laughing and you didn't notice I was ready."

Dixon was quiet for a long time as he pondered what she was saying. Finally he spoke. "Do you like being with me?" he asked.

"What do you mean? What's this about?"

"Just a question," Dixon said. "You've never really said you like me or that you like being with me. I mean you're always very polite and say you had a nice time or thank me, but you've never really expressed your feelings toward me."

"Don't you think it's pretty obvious from the time we spend together?"

"I think it is, but I'm still wondering why you can't just say it."

Jessica puffed out her lower lip and blew her breath up across her face like a locomotive releasing steam. "Yes, already. I like you and I like being with you."

"I guess I was hoping for a little more tenderness when you said it," Dixon replied.

"Well, I thought we were talking about you, and now you turn it around and have to talk about me again."

"Jessica, listen to me. I'm sorry if I seemed insensitive tonight. Maybe I should have been more considerate about the drinking, but it never seemed to be an issue before. The problem is that you make it sound like I deliberately tried to upset you."

"I didn't say you did it on purpose."

Dixon was exasperated, but tried not to show it. "So, tell me, are you a little anxious about tomorrow?"

"I guess."

"Anything we can talk about?"

"No. I don't know what it is. My mom and I just don't get along very well."

"Did she ever have an alcohol issue?" Dixon asked.

"She had a codependency issue."

"I don't know what that means."

"Basically, she took on all the traits of an alcoholic by being an enabler."

"Have you ever talked to her about it?"

"Look," Jessica said, "we talked about what was bothering me tonight. Do we have to keep talking about my personal life?"

"Your personal issues seem to have a little overflow. Since you seem to want to take things out on me, I have a vested interest."

"What do you want to do about it?"

"I don't know. I mean, I want this to work out, but sometimes it seems like I'm the only one who wants to make the effort."

"Maybe you're a little too eager for it to work out," she responded. "I feel as if I'm being rushed."

"Jessica, it's been almost five months. I think that's enough time to at least know if it's something you want to pursue."

"Maybe if I wasn't leaving so soon."

"Well, that seems like even more of a reason to make the effort."

"I don't think we're going to agree on anything tonight."

"You might be right," he said. Listen, maybe we need to spend some time apart. I can't go through life walking on eggshells, so you've got to give it some thought.

That statement didn't please her either. "Fine," she said in a tone that suggested anything but.

They said an awkward goodnight and Dixon headed home.

# CHAPTER 31

PREPARING PRETRIAL submissions was among Dixon's least favorite activities. Generating witness lists, exhibit lists, jury instructions, and related documents was among the more tedious tasks undertaken by a trial lawyer. In short, it was a process whereby each side disclosed what they expected would happen at trial. Dixon was at a loss to make any prediction in this case.

He had only minimally availed himself of pretrial discovery procedures because the facts had been played out in such detail already. McGuckin, on the other hand, took no discovery whatsoever. Under the circumstances, that wasn't surprising. But, because McGuckin never served any requests for information, Dixon was not required to disclose his theories of the case. Furthermore, Dixon wasn't required to disclose what he knew about the additional forensic evidence. That was good because Dixon hadn't determined what, if anything, it meant.

The pretrial protocol required McGuckin to submit his witness list, exhibit list, and other documents first, and Dixon could then review them and submit his. The process was designed to minimize duplication and, because the plaintiff was the one seeking relief, it was fair to require him to provide the first disclosure.

McGuckin's witness list was predictable: Lester Krueller, Debi Krueller, Deputy Halvorsen, and Krueller's treating physician—Dr. Richardson. Dixon's expected witnesses were basically the same people, though for different reasons. Dixon's witness list added Hank, Debi Krueller's daughter, and the daughter's boyfriend, and contained the statement: "In addition to the witnesses listed and those identified by Plaintiff, Defendant reserves the right to call any rebuttal witnesses deemed necessary."

The exhibit list exchange had a similar result. For simplicity or out of laziness, McGuckin had identified "The Entire Koochiching County Sheriff's Office Investigative File" as one exhibit. Krueller's medical records were a separate exhibit, and some miscellaneous documentation purporting to document his wage loss made up the balance. Dixon's exhibit list was simple: "In addition to the documents identified by Plaintiff, Defendant reserves the right to introduce any documents necessary for impeachment or for rebuttal." Dixon's responses were typical of all lawyers' responses when the objective is to preserve as many options as possible.

McGuckin's proposed jury instructions were fairly standard. There are routine instructions used in almost every case. The issue is always tailoring instructions for the specific legal claims. Jury instructions advise the jury what the law is and the issue they need to decide. They were rarely written in a manner that a layperson could really understand, but the juror's basic sense of determining right and wrong usually resulted in justice, even if it was rough justice.

The thrust of McGuckin's proposed instructions was to outline a claim for Duke MacKenzie to be held liable because he either acted intentionally, recklessly, or negligently in discharging a firearm in Les Krueller's direction. The original Complaint in the matter hadn't used the concept of "recklessly," but Minnesota was a "notice pleading" state. In short, the Complaint merely needed to lay out the thrust of the claim and didn't need to plead the evidence or circumstances with any specificity. Dixon had considered making an objection to the addition of the recklessness count, but believed his likelihood of success didn't justify the effort.

McGuckin's proposed instructions then recited the standards for causation. In short, if the jury was to find that Duke had done anything wrong, it would be asked to determine whether those actions caused the injury and whether they were the "proximate" cause, which basically meant that the actions of Duke MacKenzie were the principal cause of the injury, that the outcome was reasonably foreseeable, and that there was nothing else that either set the events in motion or acted as an intervening cause.

Dixon had a little more trouble agreeing to the jury instructions. While he tweaked the language of the instructions regarding the *actus reus,* or wrongful act, he couldn't dispute that such instructions would be given. Furthermore, he would ask the Court to use the same instructions when asking the jury to consider whether Les Krueller acted improperly and, as a result, was the cause of his own injuries and/or Duke MacKenzie's death.

The only real difference was Dixon's submission of a self-defense instruction. He quoted the statute verbatim: "A person may use deadly force against an intruder in the person's place of abode." He also submitted a separate instruction indicating the jury could consider the reflexive nature of Duke's actions in determining whether he acted intentionally, recklessly, or negligently. Thus, the jury would not be asked to make that determination separately, but it was a factor they should consider when determining if Duke had done anything wrong.

The problem in the case was in the ambiguous nature of the word "intentional." A jury was likely to find Duke's actions were intentional, but that was potentially different from saying he acted with the intent to harm Krueller. Intentionally pulling the trigger and intentionally injuring someone were different issues, but the difference wasn't easy to explain to a jury. The safest route was to ask the jury to make a finding on self-defense.

Dixon liked the instructions as they had been developed, because they didn't really box him into any particular theory of the case. Considering he didn't really know what the evidence would show or even what he would try to make it show, the instructions seemed to allow for pretty much any theory. It was like his horoscope; ultimately he could contort the words to mean whatever he needed them to mean.

Dixon's other preparation included short briefs on a variety of legal issues that might come up during trial. He'd be working away from his normal domain and wouldn't be in a position to research and write in the evenings. Thus, he tried to anticipate the disputes that might arise in order to prepare short memoranda for himself and, if necessary, the Court. He had also prepared detailed outlines of his expected cross-examination. Where appropriate, he annotated his outline with references to the depositions or exhibits. If someone said something different from the depositions or the exhibits, he wanted to be on them instantly to point out the inconsistency.

Trial itself is a dynamic process and it's rare for things to go as rehearsed. When most of the witnesses are on the other side, there is no chance to rehearse. Consequently, the only thing to do is mentally play through all of the conceivable scenarios. The key was not to decide on a course of action in advance because, inevitably, the trial wouldn't play out according to a particular scenario.

In the end, it was all about being able to think on your feet. Still, the ability to think on one's feet is aided by preparation. The more familiar an attorney is with the evidence, the more likely the attorney will catch inconsistencies in the testimony. Ultimately, cross-examination was generally about discrediting the witness. That might involve a witness who is well intentioned, but who, for example, didn't have a good view of the incident. Conversely, it might involve a witness who is comfortable making up testimony out of whole cloth. Catching a witness lying is perhaps the quickest way to win any case—even if the lie isn't related to the incident. Unfortunately, that generally only happened on television.

The preparation was over and it was time for trial. The required submissions were exchanged a couple weeks before trial, and it was for the Court to resolve any remaining issues. A pretrial was conducted on Monday, with the trial scheduled to start the following day. The Court reviewed the submissions, but made no rulings. Everything was under advisement and would be ruled upon when necessary.

## CHAPTER 32

Dixon met Hank and Margie on Monday night for dinner in order to prepare them for the case and to discuss strategy. Hank was stressed out about the trial and eager for the premeal cocktail. Dixon declined because of a stated desire to conduct some last-minute analysis and to assure sharpness the following day.

"Hank, we need to talk about a strategy tomorrow," Dixon said. "We really only need to show that Duke acted reasonably and I gotta believe any jury in these parts would condone the use of a firearm under the circumstances. In short, I think we should focus on the self-defense."

"What about the bullet and the other stuff that forensic lady from the State found?" Hank asked.

"Well, it's only relevant to the criminal charges. We don't have to prove Lester is lying about what happened that night. I'm afraid if I try and prove more than we need, we might get burned."

"I'm not sure I understand."

"If I try to prove Krueller is lying about what happened and it doesn't go well, it will be hard to switch the strategy. I'll be like that northern pike once my head's in the net. I won't be able to back up and go in a different direction."

"But you said there are no criminal charges at this time, right? If the conviction is upheld, I might never get any answers 'cause this case will be over."

"I understand," Dixon responded. "But you may not get any answers and lose this case to boot. I'm not telling you what to do. I'm just telling you what the risks are so you can make an informed decision."

"What do you t'ink happened that night?" Hank asked.

"I don't really know. I think the Krueller version of events sounds pretty plausible, but they're such unsavory people I tend to want to believe the opposite of anything they say."

"Just because you ask them other questions, it doesn't mean you can't still claim self-defense, does it?"

"No, not by any means. I'm just afraid of losing focus. If I spend too much time trying to prove things that aren't necessarily relevant to the issue, the jury and I might both lose sight of the real purpose. I think we have a strong case on self-defense, so I'm nervous about spending too much time on other things."

"I understand what you're saying, Dixon, and believe me, I won't hold you responsible if it goes bad. But I want you to go all out tomorrow. Dispute every part of their testimony even if it sounds plausible. And that includes any testimony that suggests Duke shot hisself."

"Hank, I'm happy to go to the mat for you, but we might be using a bazooka to shoot a duck. The duck might end up dead, but if we were hoping to eat it, we might have defeated the purpose."

"I understand," Hank said. "Look, we'll go along with whatever the jury says, but we want to be as thorough as possible."

As they debated the issue, Dixon realized that his personal dilemma wasn't a matter of not caring about the problems of the common man. The problem was that he cared too much. He had stayed away from emotionally-charged disputes because he couldn't be dispassionate. He internalized every problem of every client, and the stress of doing so could be substantial. While great surgeons adjusted to patients dying on the table, the comparable outcome was not acceptable to Dixon.

"Okay, we're agreed," Dixon finally said. "We'll go after it with all we've got. Now, let's talk about something else other than the case."

"I want to hear about the young lady you're seeing," Margie interjected.

"You sure you wouldn't rather talk baseball? I'm much better at that." Dixon replied.

"I'm sure you're fine at both. How's it going? If you really don't want to talk about it I'll leave it alone, but I can't figure out how such an eligible bachelor made it so long without getting married, so I'm curious to know how it's going."

"I'm not really sure what to say. I am completely infatuated with her. We generally always have a good time together, and we seem to have a lot in common. On the other hand, we have some different interests and that's maybe even better."

"So, you've waited all this time to find the perfect one and now you've found her," Margie said.

"Something like that."

"You don't sound too confident."

"There's one thing missing. I feel as if I've waited this long and found the perfect one, but she's waited just as long but doesn't necessarily act like she thinks I'm the one."

"Is she mean to you or just not that gung ho?" Margie asked.

"Neither. She's actually extremely considerate. And there's no hint of anybody else or even someone from the recent past she hasn't gotten over. It just seems she can't be in love because it means being vulnerable."

"That's a tough one," Margie said. "Some people just grow up a certain way or have things happen to them, and it's pretty hard to undo."

"If I accepted that, and I'm not sure I do, what does it take to 'undo' that learned behavior?"

"Wait a minute," Margie said. "What do you mean you don't believe she's the way she is because of things that have happened in her life?"

"I think personality is inborn. If some kid turns out wild, everyone says it's because he grew up with wild parents, but it just might be that the growing up part had nothing to do with it and the common denominator is genetics."

Margie wasn't accepting that. "Dixon, I don't want to try and tell a big-city lawyer anything when it comes to something like this, but I think you've oversimplified things. Genetics probably does have a lot to do with personality. But behavior isn't necessarily the same thing."

"What do you mean?"

"Oh, I don't know. Let me give you a bad example. Let's say you're a dog breeder and through careful picking and choosing you've managed to generate a litter of superior dogs. Well, if you sell one of those pups to someone who mistreats it, underfeeds it, and never trains it, it's not going to win any awards. It might have the genes of a champion, but it won't behave like one."

"I think I get your point, but the problem with the example is that a person has the ability to think and to understand."

"I told you it'd be a bad example, but I wanted to make a point. Now look at someone growing up in a bad family. When they're little, they're not much more sophisticated than the show dog. Little children are very vulnerable and the slightest little thing can be devastating."

"That's what I don't get," Dixon said. "Jessica didn't grow up in a trailer park. She wasn't molested by her uncles. As far as I can tell, her father used to tip a few, but her parents got divorced when she was at a relatively young age so she wasn't that exposed to him."

"Maybe that's part of the problem," Margie responded. "Maybe she felt very close to her father and then felt abandoned and, as a result, is afraid to feel close to anyone again."

"I think anything learned can be unlearned."

"Maybe that's what you're missing," Margie responded. "You think intelligence is basically genetic, don't you?"

"Yes."

"But will you admit the best time for someone to learn a different language is as a child?"

"Yeah, I guess I've read that."

"Well maybe the best time for a person to learn how to love and to trust is at that same age, so maybe she never learned that behavior."

"I have to admit, Margie, I guess I'd never really looked at it that way, but as an adult I would think one could analyze those things and get over them."

"Dixon, let me ask you this. Do you tend to have high expectations?"

"What do you mean?"

"Well, like your last girlfriend. When you started dating her were you thinking 'this could be something big' or were you thinking 'well, I've got nothing else to do?'"

"That's a bad example. With the last woman I dated, I deliberately tried to lower my expectations in order to avoid being disappointed. But you're right, I do tend to have high expectations of people and, as a result, I'm frequently disappointed."

"How does that affect you?"

"I guess it makes me a little bitter. Maybe a lot bitter."

"That's okay," she said. "You know they say a cynic is just a frustrated idealist."

"I could see that. But what's your point?"

"I think maybe Jessica is like you; someone who tends to have high expectations as well. Maybe, like you think, she was just born that way. So if you have high expectations and they're not met, it could have a strong reaction. Someone with high expectations wouldn't necessarily have to be in a horrible environment to have a strong negative reaction to something. If they had high expectations and they weren't fulfilled, it might have a very strong effect."

"So, what's the answer?"

"I don't know if there is one," Margie said. "At least not an easy one."

Dixon shook his head. "But why would anyone choose to so cloister their emotions that they never really got to live, got to feel the magic of being in love, got to walk on the wild side?"

"I think it's a pretty basic risk-reward type of deal. A person in that situation either doesn't understand or remember the reward part, but is painfully aware of the risk part. Just like you might not play golf in a thunderstorm because the risk of lightning seems to outweigh the minimal reward of playing in the rain, a person in that situation sees lots of risk and little reward."

"Were you like a psych major or something?"

"You don't think I could get all this just from watching daytime television?"

The three of them laughed. "I guess you could," Dixon said, "but you must have been taking good notes."

"I think I've just lived a little longer than you. Plus, I've seen a lot of alcoholism around here."

"So, you've identified the problem pretty well," Dixon said. "How are you at solutions?"

"Well, I can tell you what won't work, and this is a word I heard on a talk show. Looking for a 'cathartic' solution won't do you any good. Don't try to engineer some scenario where she suddenly sees the light and can love and express love with ease. If you want this girl, you have to prove to her you'll always be there. Wine and roses are nice, but whoever hurt her before probably gave her nice gifts as well. Proving your love is about a lot more than remembering birthdays and anniversaries."

"You've certainly given me a lot to think about on the eve of one of my most important trials."

"I'm sorry," she said with a laugh. "You said we should talk about something other than the trial, and I just got carried away."

"That's okay," Dixon said. "It was very helpful. In fact, it's advice I may be able to use in more ways than one."

"Let me give you one warning before we change subjects," Margie said. "You might spend a long time and never get her to be the way you want her to be. The investment may be worth it, but it might not. You need to decide if you want to take that risk."

Dixon nodded in silence. After a moment, he again tried to steer the discussion to baseball. There didn't seem to be any takers.

Hank had been relatively quiet during the relationship debate, but spoke up now. "Here's one of the joys of living in a small town." He nodded toward the front of the restaurant, where Les and Debi Krueller had just entered. The three of them were far enough back so as not to be noticed, and the Kruellers walked into the bar area without giving any indication they were aware that Dixon and the MacKenzies were in the house.

"For someone who went through treatment for booze and apparently has no willpower, a bar seems like an odd destination," Dixon commented.

"You didn't believe her when she said she was dry, did you?" Hank asked.

"Not for very long, on account of she drank the night I saw her at the Boondocks. I thought maybe it was an act for her husband, but I guess it was just a load of bullshit."

"That's a safe bet," Hank said. "Y'know, it's people like that who gave the trailer park its name."

Dixon pondered that for a moment. "What do you mean?"

"I mean, that's why we named the place the way we did."

"I don't understand," Dixon said. "'The Chateau Le Blanc Camelot,' I thought it meant something like the 'white house of royalty.'"

Hank smiled. "That's what we were counting on. Everybody calls it 'Camelot,' but it actually has an *e* on the end of it and in French it's not pronounced 'Camelot.' It's two syllables and the *t* is silent. It's pronounced 'Chateau Le Blanc *Kamlow.*'" Hank spoke the French as effortlessly as a maître d' in a French Restaurant.

Dixon stared at Hank with wide-eyed surprise. "So, what does it mean?"

"Well, you got part of it right. But, Camelote, in French, means rubbish."

"Okay."

"So, Chateau Le Blanc Camelote basically translates to 'Home of White Trash.'"

Dixon let out a laugh. "Nobody ever figured that out?"

"You didn't, and you're a lot better educated than the people who live there."

"Yeah, but you must get some French Canadians occasionally."

"Well, if anyone ever figured it out, they apparently didn't care."

"You MacKenzie boys are quite the pranksters. First the story about Duke impersonating the busboy and now this."

Margie turned to Hank. "Did you tell Dixon that story?"

"Yeah, y'know we told a lot of stories when we were fishing."

Dixon chimed in. "Thanks to Hank's expert guide service, we had plenty of time for talking."

Hank didn't take offense at the jab. "Yeah, we told a lot of stories about the old days. I guess talking about Duke was the next best thing to having him there."

"Well, tomorrow we defend his honor," Dixon announced. "Thus, even though I'd like to watch the Krueller Battle Royal if it breaks out, I'm afraid I should take my leave."

"Are you staying in the same place?" Margie asked.

"Yes, but under a false name. If someone still wants to keep me from being here, they'll have to figure out that Don Alduck is a fictitious name. Furthermore, I borrowed a pickup, so my car won't stand out."

"I'm sure you'll be fine," Hank said. "Sleep well."

"Thanks. I'll see you at the courthouse in the morning."

# CHAPTER 33

"A LL RISE!" And with a bang of a gavel the civil trial was under way.

Dixon had opted for the counsel table farthest from the gallery. There was no apparent tactical advantage to either table, given the unusual layout of the courtroom and the fact that, ultimately, the jury watched from behind. Dixon had determined, however, there were at least two reasons to choose that table. First, before jurors were put in the jury box, they would be seated in the gallery nearest the Kruellers and McGuckin, and Dixon reasoned that up close they would give off a stench, either literally or figuratively. Second, the witness stand was to the judge's left, so sitting at the table to the judge's right would allow him to sit in a way that he could see the witness, but also see the jury with just a turn of his head. McGuckin, on the other hand, sat directly between the witness and the jury and could not, therefore, look in the direction of the jury without being conspicuous.

Dixon took the seat closest to the Kruellers and McGuckin and put Hank in the seat against the wall so as to give the appearance of protecting him from the heathens. McGuckin, on the other hand, positioned his clients nearest to Dixon and sat himself near the gallery in the apparent belief that his magnetism or Old Spice would charm the juror prospects before the process even started.

"Ladies and gentlemen," Judge Stockman began, "you are here because as citizens it is your duty to participate in deciding the legal disputes that arise in this county." Stockman continued with his praise of American jurisprudence and the willingness to serve of those who couldn't come up with a good enough excuse to avoid it. "I'm going to ask all of you a few preliminary questions. After that, we will call twelve names and you will take your positions in the jury box as directed by my clerk. The attorneys will then ask additional questions. If you are not one of the first twelve called, you should not assume that you will not sit on this case, because some of the first twelve may be deemed not appropriate, in which case we will call additional names."

After explaining a few more ground rules, Stockman said, "The plaintiff in this case is Lester Krueller. Signify by raising your hand if you know Lester or his wife Debi, know of them, or think you know them." Stockman had learned from the first trial. For those who raised their hands, he was emphatic in saying, "Tell me how you know them or of them, but don't tell me what you know about them."

"Excuse me, your honor," McGuckin said, jumping to his feet. "May counsel approach the bench?"

"By all means."

Dixon pushed back his chair and followed McGuckin to the front of the large elevated desk that was the bench. McGuckin lowered his voice so as not to be heard by the juror prospects. "Your honor, I understand the care you're using to avoid what happened last time, but I'm afraid your question will cause the same problem. My client knows one of the prospective jurors because they met in jail, so, you see, your question is likely to lead to prejudice against my client."

Dixon was quick to respond. "Unlike the criminal trial, I think Mr. Krueller's past criminal record, or at least his criminal record for domestic abuse, is going to come in as a result of his claim that the incident has harmed his otherwise idyllic married life. That being said, your honor, I have no objection to rephrasing the question, provided Mr. McGuckin identifies the juror in question and he is dismissed for cause."

"Sounds fair, what do you think?" Stockman said, turning to McGuckin.

"Fine," he responded. McGuckin identified the prospect and the Court excused him.

Stockman continued his preliminary screening, occasionally

dismissing prospects. Confident that he had dismissed or at least identified everyone who might have personal knowledge, he instructed his clerk to commence the draw. She then proceeded to pull folded slips of paper from a bowl and announce the "winners" as if it were a church raffle. "Scot Yezek, Tom Dolven, Sandy Weinberger, Marc Parenteau, Amy Jo Heyman, Grady Durham, Richard Shelton . . ." Twelve names were called. In the end, they only needed six and two alternates. Each side could move to dismiss any juror if they could show good cause, and each got two peremptory challenges, which allowed them to strike prospects for any reason or no reason.

McGuckin, as counsel for the plaintiff, got first crack at interviewing the prospects. He immediately started in with the same spiel that he'd used at the criminal trial. "Would you be willing to listen to the explanation of an otherwise law-abiding citizen if he committed one indiscretion, but he had a good reason?"

Hank leaned close to Dixon. In a soft voice he asked, "Haven't we heard this horseshit before?"

"That's how he holds his fees down," Dixon responded. "He uses the same stuff over and over." Privately, Dixon thought the approach that had seemed to work in the criminal case was monumentally wrong for this matter. Asking a jury to excuse an indiscretion is a lot different from asking a jury to award money for an indiscretion. False indignation was really the only way for McGuckin to secure a large damages award.

McGuckin established his theme and provided an advance look at some of his facts, but he didn't seem to have the mastery that he'd displayed the first time. Whether it was because the approach didn't fit or because he wasn't as inspired the second time around, the jury remained for the taking.

Now it was Dixon's turn, and he wanted to overcome any negative perceptions resulting from the fact that he appeared to be the hired gun from the big city. His youthful looks certainly helped overcome the idea that he was a high-powered, high-priced hotshot, but he was still an out-of-towner. Asking if they would be prejudiced against an out-of-towner was not, however, likely to be the answer.

Aside from using the process to get jurors to prejudge the case, voir dire is supposed to root out jurors who might be particularly harmful to your position. The problem was that it was always easy to explain after the fact why a particular juror went a particular way, but it was pretty hard to work all of the angles in advance.

"How many of you either own guns or live with someone who owns guns?" Dixon asked.

Every potential juror raised a hand. Dixon then followed up with questions to confirm that none of them had an aversion to guns and, while most of them identified hunting as the reason for gun owner-ship, all of them seemed to think that protection was a good enough reason to own a gun. Maybe this would be easier than Dixon had thought.

Dixon then interviewed each prospect one at a time to determine their opinions on women working. He didn't ask it that way. Instead, he asked the married men if their wives worked, whether they approved of it, and how the chores at home were handled. He asked the others similar questions to help assure that his audience was as enlightened to women's rights as possible.

"Now this one might sound kind of peculiar," Dixon said. "You are likely to hear some fairly graphic language, and, in particular, the 'f' word. The lawyers may use it, too, and that's because it will probably be part of the testimony. Now, I know some people can't even enjoy a movie if it uses the 'f' word too much. So my question is whether you will be uncomfortable or otherwise react adversely from hearing that. Why don't we start in the back left and each of you can tell me if it will have an effect on you."

Someone trying out as a ventriloquist said a soft "fuck no," and the prospective jurors all started laughing.

"I'm sorry, what was that?" Dixon asked.

The first prospect smiled an embarrassed smile. "It wouldn't bother me. I work in the mines, and I hear it all the time."

The second prospect was an older, more professional looking man. "I was in the service for four years. I reckon I heard it enough to make me immune."

Dixon nodded and turned his focus to the woman who was

next. "Are you kidding," she said. "I work at the high school. I hear it all day."

Dixon smiled at that response. He continued the line of questioning and found little resistance. Guns and swearing were apparently the norm.

Next, Dixon had to deal with the fact that his client did, in fact, have sex with another man's wife. The issue, therefore, was rooting out prospects that might think Duke got what he deserved. Dixon asked lots of questions about taking the law into one's own hands and tried to draw a distinction between Krueller, who had other options, and Duke, who didn't. None of the prospects managed to disqualify themselves on that basis.

Dixon shifted gears. "How many of you have bumper stickers on your car?"

McGuckin rose to his feet. "Your honor, I don't think that's a proper question. Some people have political bumper stickers, and it's not proper to ask a prospective juror who he or she voted for."

"Your honor," Dixon replied, "I haven't asked anyone who they voted for. Furthermore, if someone has a political bumper sticker, it's pretty clear they're not trying to keep their political leanings a secret."

"Overruled," Stockman said.

That voir dire question was the only one Dixon borrowed from the jury consultants. The theory was that a person with a bumper sticker is the type of person who tries to force his or her opinion on others. As a result, they were potentially the most helpful or the most dangerous jurors to have.

Two jurors admitted to having "Power 92" radio station stickers, but insisted their teenage children were responsible. Another had a prounion sticker, while a fourth had something supporting the National Rifle Association. Finally, one of the women acknowledged having a bumper sticker with a prochoice message.

Dixon then asked whether the prospects were quick to make decisions or whether they could keep an open mind until all of the evidence was submitted. The need to reserve judgment was never so apparent as in this case, considering Dixon hadn't yet made a judgment as to what the facts would show.

Along the way, two of the prospects were dismissed for cause and duly replaced. Each side was then given the opportunity to remove two prospective jurors, which was done alternately starting with Plaintiff. The trick was not to use a strike on someone the other side was likely to strike anyway. Dixon determined that he wouldn't strike any of the women even though some seemed a little religious, because he assumed McGuckin would want to get rid of anybody who would have an aversion to a wife beater.

In the end, McGuckin exercised his peremptories to remove a small business owner and the woman with the prochoice bumper sticker. Dixon ousted the union member and a man who seemed unable to give concise answers to pretty simple questions. The panel ultimately consisted of five men and three women. Two of them were alternates, but only the judge would know their identities until such time as deliberations were to begin. The foreperson would not be selected until later, and selection would be done by a vote of the jurors.

With the preliminaries out of the way, Stockman recessed for ten minutes so everyone would be fresh when the real fun began.

"What do you think of our panel?" Dixon asked Hank.

"How come there are only eight of them?" he responded. "Last time there were fourteen."

"The State Constitution requires twelve for felony charges, and alternates are used so there isn't a mistrial if a juror gets sick or stops showing up. Civil cases only require six jurors plus alternates."

"Well, other than that, I think it looks good. I thought it really looked good until McGuckin struck Parenteau. He's done business with us, and I think he was trying to get picked so he could help out."

"Well," Dixon responded, "if that's the case, we're probably better off he's not on the jury, because it might have given them grounds to appeal later on."

"Who cares about later on? I want to make sure we win now, and we can worry about later on later on."

"I think we got a pretty good jury," Dixon said. "You just need people with common sense who can follow directions."

"I hope you're right."

After ten minutes, court reconvened. McGuckin stood at the portable lectern as the jury filed back in. He had used the recess to transfer his notes in an apparent effort to avoid the appearance that he needed them. Judge Stockman returned and directed McGuckin to proceed. Unlike the Court of Appeals, there was no limit on the length of time he could drone on.

"Ladies and gentlemen of the jury," McGuckin began, "this is the part of the trial called the opening statement. It's my opportunity to tell you what I expect the evidence to be and what I believe it will prove. During the trial, you will hear witnesses telling about the events in question. Testimony is presented by witnesses and not by topic. By that, I mean there are several relevant events occurring over several days. Rather than picking one event and having everybody testify and then picking the next event and repeating the process, each witness will take the stand and tell their entire story. My job at this point is to synthesize those accounts in order to make them more understandable."

McGuckin stepped out from behind the lectern and began pacing in front of the jury. "The evidence will show that Debi Krueller is a woman who means well, but is unable to resist impulses. As a result, she has a history of alcohol abuse. Furthermore, she isn't always strong willed when it comes to the sexual advances of men. This case is about what happens when somebody takes advantage of those weaknesses."

McGuckin was at the far end of the jury box with his back to the jury. He turned and raised his right index figure as if making a point of law. "The evidence will show that a relationship developed between Debi Krueller and Duane MacKenzie. Mr. MacKenzie was a pretty well-to-do fellow, and he used his charm and money to alienate Debi Krueller's affections from her husband Lester. That interloping caused stress in the marriage and led to a misunderstanding that caused Debi Krueller to vacate the homestead and flee into the all-too-eager hands of Duke MacKenzie.

"The evidence will show that Debi Krueller spent several days and nights with Duke MacKenzie, and that it all went on right in front of Les Krueller. He witnessed on more than one occasion that his wife was with MacKenzie and was with him overnight. He tried to talk about the situation, but Duke and Debi just lied to him. They told him there was nothing going on. You will hear testimony of more than one encounter where Les tried to address the matter with words but was ignored or, like I said, lied to."

Dixon was taking notes and had asked Hank to do the same. McGuckin was trying to sell his case, but trying a little too hard. During closing arguments, Dixon would remind the jury what McGuckin had promised the evidence would show and then highlight how the promise wasn't met. For example, what McGuckin characterized as Les "trying to talk about the situation" consisted of threats to "blow Duke's fucking head off." The jury would be asked to determine whether McGuckin had fairly characterized the facts and, once his credibility was in doubt, his case would be in trouble.

"You will hear how Lester Krueller was broken up about what was happening and how he feared for his wife's well-being. Just as in the Greek story *The Odyssey*, when Ulysses had to choose between Scylla and Charybdis, or as the expression is now known, between a rock and a hard place, Lester Krueller was forced to choose between two difficult alternatives." McGuckin apparently needed to remind jurors that he was better educated than they were, and it seemed to work. "You will hear how Les was overcome by emotion and faced the prospect of doing nothing and having his marriage basically end, or taking action even though it meant breaking into the house. He chose to break into the MacKenzie house to break up the adulterous affair that was going on." McGuckin paused to let those words sink in.

"Most importantly," he continued, "you will hear that Duke MacKenzie heard Les Krueller outside of his house and readied himself with a loaded pistol to use on Les Krueller. After putting that pistol in place, MacKenzie went back to defiling Les Krueller's wife while he waited for Les to appear so he could shoot him."

Dixon heard Hank taking deep breaths and appreciated the fact that he was following his advice about remaining calm.

McGuckin was now strutting back and forth in front of the jury. "Les Krueller looked for an open door or window, but when he couldn't find one he broke the only window that was big enough to allow him to enter without having to climb over a broken window-pane. Les Krueller will testify that he dropped the shovel and proceeded into the bedroom where MacKenzie was having his way with Debi Krueller. As soon as he walked in, he was shot by MacKenzie. And MacKenzie didn't bother to help him or call 911. He just swore at him and ran away. And MacKenzie had gotten Debi so liquored up that she wasn't thinking straight, so she didn't call for help either."

McGuckin strolled back to the lectern to access his notes. "As a result of this terrible act, Les Krueller suffered great pain, missed substantial work, required surgery and hours upon hours of therapy, and suffered real and substantial damage to his relationship with his wife Debi. At the conclusion of this trial, we will be asking you to award damages to Mr. Krueller for these wrongful acts in order to compensate him for the damages that he has suffered." After a short pause, McGuckin did his best to affect an earnest look and said, "Thank you."

Judge Stockman watched as McGuckin took his seat. "Mr. Donnelly."

Rising to his feet, Dixon said, "Your honor, while the defense obviously has a different view of the facts, we would like to reserve opening statement until the beginning of our case."

Deferring the opening statement was a matter of right, but it was rarely exercised. The risk was that it would be too long before the jury would hear your side of the case. On the other hand, when all of the surviving eyewitnesses are adverse parties, it's dangerous to tell the jury what the evidence will be, because there's very little control over it.

"Okay then," Stockman said. "Why don't we break for lunch." The Judge admonished the jurors about not discussing the case and court was recessed.

# CHAPTER 34

A N HOUR AND A HALF later, court was back in session. "Mr. McGuckin," Judge Stockman said, "call your first witness."

"Plaintiff calls Lester Krueller."

Lester, wearing his "good luck" leisure suit, rose from the table and worked his way to the witness stand. McGuckin spun the lectern around to face the witness. Les Krueller was sworn in, and the Fuckin' McGuckin show was off and running.

McGuckin spent an inordinate amount of time on Les's life history. From simple beginnings, to an attempt at vo-tech education, to a series of jobs focused mainly on working in the taconite mines. Then the focus was his first marriage at an early age and a divorce caused by her desire to move to the Twin Cities. "Ordinary Joe" doing his best to earn a living is how McGuckin wanted his client portrayed.

After a half hour of that, McGuckin moved to the Les and Debi courtship and marriage. If the testimony was to be believed, Debi Krueller was a woman who needed help and protection and Krueller was the white knight. She was in dire need of financial and emotional support when he "rescued" her. McGuckin never bothered to mention that Krueller got something out of the deal too—plenty of sex from a woman who was, at least physically, very appealing and substantially better looking than someone of his ilk would otherwise be expected to attract.

Krueller's testimony was past rehearsed. In fact, he had given it twice before. Unfortunately for him, that's the way it came across. Rather than speaking to the jury, he answered McGuckin's questions with an "it's like I told you before" tone. In fact, once he even said those words out loud.

The topic turned to Debi's bouts with depression, her chemical dependency, and her attempts at treatment. Les, through McGuckin's questioning, portrayed himself as a pillar of strength who wasn't prone to vices or wrongdoing. However, Les's appearance wasn't consistent with the tender side he was trying to portray, and if the jury got a glimpse of him leaving the courthouse in his pickup truck with the naked lady mud flaps, it would completely destroy the image McGuckin was trying to create.

Dixon occasionally cast fleeting glances at the jury. He kept it subtle, not wanting them to see him and feel self-conscious. The jury generally seemed attentive, though not overly piqued. "When did you first meet Duke MacKenzie?" McGuckin asked. The jury seemed to take note that the preliminaries were over and it was time to focus. McGuckin proceeded to walk Krueller through the same testimony he had given in the criminal trial and in his deposition—Duke had been doing some work around the trailer park and seemed to be taking a shine to Debi, Les had a "disagreement" with Debi that led to her seeking out Duke MacKenzie, and ultimately Debi succumbed to Duke's advances.

McGuckin seemed to be eyeing the clock. As a normal rule, the strategy is to position witnesses and testimony so opposing counsel has to present key parts of his or her case during the last hour of the day when the jury is likely to be least attentive. McGuckin wasn't able to relinquish the witness mid-story, however, so his objective was to draw out the testimony so the jury heard only from him on the first day and went home to sleep on only Les Krueller's thus far unchallenged version of events.

"So what did you do that night in the woods?" McGuckin asked.

"Started to cry."

"And then what?"

And so the questioning went. Les tried to find an unlocked door or window, tried to pry open the sliding glass door, finally smashed the window, walked in on MacKenzie and Debi, and was shot. The last time he saw Duke MacKenzie was when Duke was standing over him waving a gun in his face and swearing at him.

"Your honor," McGuckin announced, "we have another hour or so relating to Mr. Krueller's injuries and damages, but this seems like it might be a good place to break for the day."

"Any objection, Mr. Donnelly?" the judge asked.

McGuckin had succeeded in securing for himself the morning hours, when the jurors would be most alert. There was, however, no good way to raise that issue in front of the jurors without running the risk of alienating them. "The defense is happy to continue today, your honor, but we will defer to your judgment on the issue."

"Why don't we recess for the day," Stockman said. After admonishing and instructing the jury, he pounded his gavel and court was dismissed. Dixon and Hank sat down and waited for the courtroom to clear. Les Krueller gathered some things from Plaintiff's table and sneered at Dixon as he walked by. Debi Krueller followed Les out and batted her eyes at Dixon as she passed. Finally, McGuckin walked by and gave a terse "see you in the morning."

# CHAPTER 35

D AY TWO STARTED with substantially less formality than day one. Les testified about the pain, the time off work, and the problems with intimacy. For good measure, he lifted his shirt to show a beer belly with an extra belly button where the bullet had entered. In the end, between his health plan and his sick pay, it didn't appear he was out of pocket any significant amount. Furthermore, to the extent he recovered damages for some of those things, he would probably have to reimburse the insurance companies that were entitled to rights of subrogation. McGuckin introduced the evidence because it helped show the magnitude of the injury and because, in all likelihood, McGuckin had a deal with the insurance company that paid him a percentage of anything he recovered for the benefit of the insurance companies. The thrust of his case, however, was the hope for a big award for pain and suffering. McGuckin droned on for an hour before saying, "Your witness, Mr. Donnelly."

McGuckin had stood with his back to the jury. Dixon spun the lectern ninety degrees so it faced the gallery and pulled it back to make sure he was not in the sight line between the witness and any jurors. McGuckin had not directly impeded the view from the jury box, but his positioning had provided Les with somewhat of a buffer. Dixon wanted the jury to focus completely on Krueller and, in turn, for Krueller to have to look at them when he testified.

"Mr. Krueller," Dixon began, "you've previously been convicted of filing a false claim for disability benefits, isn't that right?"

"Objection, your honor," McGuckin said, jumping to his feet. "May we approach the bench?"

When they arrived, McGuckin began his plea. "Your honor, that relates to something that happened more than ten years ago. It's not relevant, it's prejudicial, and we were not given any advance notice."

"Your honor," Dixon proceeded, "I have here a certified copy of the conviction from the Gogebic County Court in the Upper Peninsula of Michigan. Under Rule 609 of the Minnesota Rules of Evidence, evidence of crimes can be offered without violating the character evidence rules if the person is testifying and the conviction is for something that involves dishonesty or a false statement."

"But you didn't give notice," McGuckin protested.

"Your honor, first of all, Mr. McGuckin didn't serve any discovery requests, so we didn't have a discovery obligation to give notice. Second, the rule only requires notice if the conviction is more than ten years old. The fact that the act itself occurred more than ten years ago is not the test and, as this certified copy shows, the conviction is not quite nine years old. I have a short memo here with the rule quoted and some of the precedents." He handed the document to the judge and a copy to McGuckin.

"Why didn't this come up in the criminal trial?" Stockman asked.

"I don't know," Dixon responded. "Either the County Attorney didn't search out-of-state records or he had the same misunderstanding of the rule that Mr. McGuckin just showed."

After Stockman scanned the memo he asked Dixon whether he needed to spend a lot of time on the issue because of the remoteness of the event.

"Your honor, I will try not to belabor the point, but under the circumstances I'm not going to just drop it and let the jury wonder about it and have them think I did something wrong. Furthermore, your honor, this isn't one of those evidence rules that require you to judge the relevance before allowing it in. In fact, I don't think there is any mechanism to exclude it."

"Very well," Stockman said. "You can elicit all of the details, but don't attempt to retry the previous claim."

Dixon resumed his spot at the lectern. "That's true, isn't it, sir?"

"That was something completely different a long time ago."

"So, you admit that you were previously convicted of a felony for submitting a false claim of employment disability?"

"Yes."

Dixon stared at Krueller with as much disdain as he could muster. "You pretended to be injured on a job that you had in Bessemer, Michigan, isn't that right?"

"Yes," Krueller responded while trying to appear exasperated.

"You decided you liked drawing disability benefits better than you liked working, so you claimed a long-term back injury, correct?"

"That's the gist of it."

"And then you were caught on videotape hunting, including hoisting up your deer?"

"Well, I wasn't really caught on videotape. We just took some videos of our hunt, and later on my girlfriend and I had a fight and she sent them tapes in."

"What was the total amount of disability you had to repay?"

"About $8,000."

"You pled guilty as well?"

"Yes."

"Did you serve any time?"

"Just a couple weekends in the workhouse."

"So, you've faked an injury before in order to collect money?"

McGuckin could be still no longer. "Your honor, that's been asked and answered already."

Judge Stockman gave Dixon a look suggesting that he'd like to move on, but overruled the objection.

"I guess that's right," was all Les could say.

Dixon took Stockman's hint and moved on. "Now, part of your claim in this lawsuit is that your relationship with your wife suffered, is that right?"

"Yes."

"And how would you characterize your relationship with Mrs. Krueller before the events giving rise to this lawsuit?"

Les shrugged his shoulders. "Pretty good. You know, all married couples have their ups and downs."

Dixon smiled and furrowed his brow for effect. "Well, it's true isn't it that your wife has filed assault charges against you on at least three occasions?"

McGuckin was on his feet again. "Objection. Can we approach?"

Judge Stockman was not impressed. "I think this information is relevant to damages, so if your objection is under either Rule 404 or 609, I'm going to overrule it. Is there something else you want to raise?"

McGuckin thought for a minute. He had to have anticipated that such evidence would be admitted, and his objection was only meant to distract the jury. "Just so my objection is noted," he said and retook his seat.

"Mr. Krueller," Dixon resumed, "do you remember the question that was pending?"

"Not really, can you ask it again?"

"Sure," Dixon responded, relishing the opportunity to repeat the damning question. "It's true isn't it that your wife has filed assault charges against you on at least three occasions?"

"Those were bogus charges, and they were always dropped," Krueller snapped.

"We'll get to the substance in a minute," Dixon said. "Right now it's just a 'yes' or 'no' question. Has your wife Debi in fact filed assault charges against you on at least three occasions?"

"I don't know for sure how many times. That sounds about right."

"What led to those charges? Was it the same thing every time or different things?"

"Different things. She'd be drunk or we'd start arguing about how she was wasting her life and she'd get mad and start throwing stuff."

"After each of these incidents, did you reconcile?"

"Yes."

"By the way," Dixon said, "were there other domestic disturbances that occurred but where she didn't file charges?"

"No."

"So if the court records here at the courthouse show two other incidents where she sought a restraining order against you, those records would not be accurate?" As Dixon spoke he held up a fist full of documents to let the witness and the jury know that his reference wasn't a bluff.

"I don't know. There might have been others. I can't really keep track."

"Well, Mr. Krueller, when I started this examination I asked you about your relationship with your wife and you said something to the effect of it being 'up and down and much the same as all married couples.' From your perspective, do you believe it's typical in a marriage for one of the parties to have called the police so many times that the other partner cannot even remember how many times the police were called?"

"Objection," McGuckin said. "Argumentative."

"Sustained," Stockman responded. Dixon paused and made a quizzical look. In Dixon's mind the question was appropriate, but Stockman apparently felt it was time to rule in McGuckin's favor on something. Given that the question had such an obvious answer, Dixon decided to move on.

"Okay, before I digressed, you said you and your wife always reconciled, correct?"

"Yes."

"And each time it happened, the charges against you ended up getting dropped, is that right?"

"Yes, because she made those things up."

"Your honor, could you please instruct the witness?" Dixon asked.

"Mr. Krueller," Judge Stockman said, "just answer the question that's put to you. If your attorney so chooses, he can ask you questions later on to let you add whatever information you want to add."

"Okay," Krueller said. "Sorry about that."

Dixon resumed. "On at least one occasion there was evidence that she'd been struck in the face. How do you account for that?"

"That whole thing is confidential," Krueller said.

"Well, sir, any settlement that might have been reached relating to that incident might be confidential, but the underlying circumstances are not. The fact that your attorney didn't make an objection is perhaps the best indication of that."

Judge Stockman spoke up. "Mr. Krueller, your attorney has not objected, and it's not your job to make the objections. Please answer the question."

"Debi just freaked out one time. She started trying to hit me, and I swung my arm up to block hers but missed and the back of my hand hit her in the nose. That was the only time there was every any blood or evidence of contact."

"So, on the other occasions there was no ... *evidence* of contact, is that what you're saying?" Dixon put emphasis on "evidence" to highlight to the jury that Krueller had not denied beating her on other occasions, but only denied that he had allowed there to be any evidence of such beatings. Krueller wasn't sharp enough to recognize the ploy.

"That's right."

Dixon glanced back at the jury and noticed they seemed quite attentive. The women on the jury seemed particularly engaged.

"Mr. Krueller, have you ever been in any kind of treatment?"

"Like for what?"

"Chemical dependency, anger management, anything like that."

"No."

"How 'bout counseling? Ever go to counseling with or without your wife?"

"Not really. Sometimes Debi's therapist wants to meet with me to talk about things, but that's mostly to tell me things about her treatment and progress."

Dixon paused and tried to look pensive. "So, is it your testimony that all of the domestic disturbances and assault charges were caused by your wife and she just made them up?"

"No, I didn't say she made up the arguments. I said she made up the parts about me assaulting her."

"Okay, but all of the arguments were started by her?"

"Yeah, one way or another. Either she'd start hollering about nothing or I'd say something to her and she'd get mad and start hollering."

"Has that been the case throughout your relationship or have there been periods where you seemed to get along okay?"

"Hard to say. Sometimes when Debi doesn't drink for a while we'll go a long time without any problems and then sometimes we'll have a lot of problems in a short period."

Having succeeded in educating the jury as to Krueller's past encounters with the criminal justice system, Dixon moved on. He spent some time reviewing the testimony relating to his employment history and highlighted a few gaps and other things that McGuckin had managed to gloss over. The truth was that Krueller had held a variety of jobs and often changed jobs under circumstances suggesting he wasn't a model employee. The information wasn't particularly relevant, but McGuckin had brought it up, so it was fair game.

"Tell me about your first wife," Dixon requested. "Were there any domestic abuse issues in that marriage?"

"Objection!" McGuckin bellowed. "Are we ever going to get to the facts of this case?"

"Your honor," Dixon said. "I didn't write the Rules of Evidence, I just live by them. Mr. Krueller opened this door when he suggested his current wife was the aggressor in all of their domestic disputes."

"I'll overrule the objection," Stockman said.

Dixon proceeded to introduce Court documents from the first marriage that suggested Krueller apparently had a habit of marrying unstable women who fabricated things to get him in trouble. Dixon enjoyed exposing Krueller for what he was, but tried to remember not to lose focus.

"Mr. Krueller, when did you first meet Duke MacKenzie?"

"The first time I remember for sure was a couple months before he shot me."

"How did the first meeting come about?"

"I think it was just a 'howdy neighbor' kind of deal."

"Isn't it true that you met Duke MacKenzie because he heard you and your wife arguing and came over to see if everything was okay?"

"Is that what he says?" Krueller taunted.

McGuckin cleared his throat to try and signal his client that such impudence wouldn't help his case.

Krueller's smirk disappeared. "No, that's not true," he said. "He stopped by one night and said he heard we were home and wanted to introduce himself."

"So you and your wife were both there at the time?"

"That's right."

"And do you know if your wife had already met him?"

"I think she had, 'cause he called her by name."

"Do you remember when I took your deposition and you told me the first time you met Duke MacKenzie was in your backyard? I can show you the transcript if you like."

"No, that's okay. I remember it. I think the first time I saw him was just a backyard kind of thing, but then I found out his name when he came over to the house."

"So, your testimony is that you and Duke had kinda waved to each other and that he had already met your wife, but the night he came over wasn't to break up an argument, it was just to introduce himself. Do I have that right?"

"That's pretty much it. He might have heard some hollering, I don't know, but we weren't having a fight, and he didn't break nothin' up."

"Your honor, may I approach the witness?"

"Go ahead," the judge said.

"I'm showing you the transcript from your deposition where I asked you questions under oath. Do you remember giving that deposition?"

"Yes."

"And do you remember swearing to tell the whole truth and nothing but the truth?"

"Yes."

"Now look at this part where I asked you when the first time Duke MacKenzie was at your house, and you said you came home one day and he was having coffee with the wife. Do you see that?"

"Yes."

"So why didn't you tell me about this other meeting where he allegedly heard you were home and dropped by?"

"I guess I just forgot about it on accounta I didn't think much of it at the time."

"Can you think of anything else that you might just kinda forgot about that you should have told me at your deposition?"

"Not right off, no."

Dixon walked back to the lectern. He didn't look directly at the jury, but smiled to let them know he was in control.

"Mr. Donnelly," Judge Stockman interjected, "whenever you get to a convenient spot, why don't we break for lunch."

"This is as good a time as any," Dixon said, and they took a break. With any luck, Dixon would keep Les on the ropes until midafternoon and force McGuckin to start his next witness in the waning hours.

# CHAPTER 36

Aᶠᵗᵉʳ ʟᵁɴᴄʜ Dixon picked up where he had left off in the chronology, working through Krueller's fishing trip and a few other details until he got to the weekend of the incident. "Now, on or about September 4, which was a Friday, you had a disagreement with your wife, is that correct?"

"Yeah, I guess."

"What was that about?"

"The usual."

"And you took all of her belongings out of the bedroom and threw them out in the yard."

"I told you before that I put those things out there after she left." Krueller was now looking down at his hands while he spoke. Whether it was because he was embarrassed by his behavior or his discomfort over the lies he was about to tell wasn't clear.

"I know what you said before, but the truth is you'd started throwing things out there before your wife left and that was why she left. Right?"

Krueller looked around as though surveying how he could get caught if he lied. "Maybe, I don't remember the exact order. After she was gone I was still putting her stuff out there."

"Because you were kicking her out of the house?"

"No, I threw the first clothes out there because we got in a fight over how much she'd just spent on new clothes. After she left, I put the rest of her stuff out there so she could get it without having to come into the house."

"Because you thought she wouldn't have her key?"

"In part. And maybe she just wouldn't want to face me because

she was so ashamed of the way she blew our money on clothes."
McGuckin had clearly counseled Les since the deposition. His story
was still not believable, but it was a little less outrageous.

"Did you go looking for Debi that night?"

"No."

"Why not?"

"She has other family in town. A sister and a daughter. I figured
she was with one of them."

"So this type of thing had happened before, where she'd spend the
night with family?"

"I don't really remember that. It mighta."

"All right," Dixon proceeded. "You get up Saturday morning and
what do you do?"

"Made a couple calls. Couldn't find her and then I talked to someone who had seen her with Duke MacKenzie the night before."

"So, what did you do?"

"Drove out to MacKenzie's house."

"How did you know where it was?"

"This is a small town. I'd been out that way before, and I had a
pretty good idea."

"You didn't call or anything, right?"

"Right."

As Dixon approached the critical facts, he switched to asking
leading questions. When the subject was basic background, he let
the witness tell a story. When he needed to make a point, he asked
leading questions. "When you got there you parked down on the
road instead of in the driveway, correct?"

"Yes."

"You then snuck up on the house, right?"

"Well, I didn't make no noise, and I didn't want to be seen until I
knew if she was there."

"Fair enough. When you got close you saw your wife sitting in
the lower level with Duke, is that right?"

"Yes."

"And you just walked up and opened the door and let yourself in?"

"The door was open. I just opened the screen door and went in."

"Okay, your testimony is that the inside door was open and you saw them and you opened the screen door and just walked in?"

"Right."

"Did you knock, ask if you could come in, or anything like that?"

"Didn't need to."

"So, the answer is 'no'?"

"Correct."

"May I approach the witness, your honor?" Dixon asked.

"Go ahead," Stockman said.

"Mr. Krueller, I have some photographs taken by the sheriff's department, and later on Deputy Halvorsen is expected to testify about taking them, but I want to show them to you and ask you a few questions."

"Okay."

"What exhibit number are we up to?" Dixon asked anyone who could help.

"Nine," the clerk responded.

"Sir, I'm showing you what's been marked as Exhibit 9. Do you recognize what's depicted in the picture?"

"Yeah, that looks like Duke's house."

"And from the angle of the picture, is it accurate that the person taking the picture would have been on the side of the house nearest the garage?"

"Yes."

"So this picture would show what it would look like for someone who approached the house from the driveway?"

"Right."

"And this was the view that you had when you approached, right?"

"Yeah, I guess."

"Is it fair to say that in this picture the person taking it would be looking at the front of the house and then the right side of the house as you face it from the front?"

Krueller stopped to try and digest the question. "Yeah, I guess so."

"Show me on the picture where the door is that you walked through."

Krueller pointed.

"So it's fair to say that the door you used is the only one you can see in this picture?"

"Yes."

Dixon took the photograph and handed it to the nearest juror. "Please take a look at this and pass it on." Returning to Krueller, Dixon said, "Look at the next picture, which we'll mark as Exhibit 10. Can you tell us what that is?"

"That's the same door, only closer up."

"Yes, it is, and do you notice something really interesting about it?"

"No."

"Take a closer look. Do you see how there is no screen door? In fact, there's not even a place where a screen door might go."

Krueller took a long look at it. Realizing that a thousand words wouldn't stand a chance against the picture, Krueller could only answer, "So?"

Dixon's voice and mannerisms became more forceful. "So, you've testified under oath that the inside door was open and you opened the screen door and let yourself in. In light of this picture, that's not accurate is it?"

"Well, if there ain't no screen door then the door was just open. That's what it was. The door was wide open so I just walked in."

"So now you're telling me that this door was just sitting open and Duke and Debi were sitting inside eating breakfast?"

"Yup."

"Doesn't that seem a little strange out there in the woods with all sorts of animals and stuff that anyone would just leave the door open like that?"

"I don't know. What animal is going to come in as long as the two of them are sitting there?" Les responded.

"Well, let's leave the animals out of it. Wouldn't there be an awful lot of mosquitoes and other insects coming in if your new version of events was correct?"

"No, we had an early frost that year."

"Excuse me?" Dixon asked incredulously.

"We had an early frost that year."

"I realize this is a little farther north than what I'm used to, but you're telling me there was a killing frost by the first weekend in September?"

"Yup."

"Fine," Dixon said, with a slight chuckle. "When you walked into the MacKenzie house that day you were angry, weren't you?"

"I was upset. I don't know if I'd say I was angry."

"You thought your wife and Duke had engaged in sexual intercourse, didn't you?"

"I didn't know. I thought they might have."

"You told Duke MacKenzie that if you caught him having sex with your wife you'd blow his fucking head off, isn't that right?"

"I don't remember nothin' like that."

"What did you say to him?"

"I don't remember. I was upset and I said something like 'I hope nothin's goin' on here,' and Duke said 'no, no, don't worry, I just gave her a place to stay.'"

"Did you threaten to take any physical action against Duke MacKenzie?"

"No."

"So, you go to all of this trouble to go out to his house, sneak up on them, and walk right through the front door just for chitchat?"

"I didn't say that. We talked about what was going on, and I told him I'd be really upset if I found out they were messing around on me."

"Come on, Mr. Krueller. You thought your wife was sleeping with another man. You can admit you were upset. That would only be natural."

McGuckin rose. "Your honor, is that a question?"

"I'll withdraw it," Dixon said, but the point had already been made.

"What did you do the rest of the day?"

"Nothin' special. Worked on my truck."

"That night you went out with some friends to a bar, isn't that right?"

"Yes."

"And you were looking to meet other women, right?"

"Just looking to unwind, hang out, like that."

"You were looking to get some action to get even with Debi, isn't that right?"

"I wouldn't say that."

"Well, you might not say it, but it's true, isn't it, that you actually met up with a woman and in the end she performed oral sex on you? Right?"

Les lowered his voice. "Yes."

"And you thought that was just fine because as far as you were concerned Debi had already been unfaithful to you, so it wasn't really like cheating?"

Les perked up at the justification Dixon offered. "Yeah, I guess that's right. I didn't do nothin' wrong, because she was already running around."

Dixon pondered whether the revelation that Les's "conquest" was his wife's sister would further tarnish Les's image. Dixon decided it wasn't necessary to sully the reputation of someone who wasn't even in the courtroom to defend herself, and he let it go.

"The next afternoon your wife came home, isn't that right?"

"Yes."

"Did you talk at all?"

"Not really."

"What had happened with her belongings? The ones you put in the front yard."

"Someone came by when I wasn't there and picked everything up."

"So, was she moving back in, stopping by to talk, or something else?"

"I don't really know. I went out for a while and when I came back, she was drinking again and I said something and she got mad and left."

"What did you do?"

"Went for a drive."

"Any particular destination, or just driving?"

"Just driving. It was a real nice day, so I was just driving around thinking about stuff."

"So, you remember what the weather was like that weekend?"

"Oh yeah. It was real nice that whole week."

"Really. So that killer frost you told us about a little while ago actually occurred in August. Wow, we really are up north."

Several snickers could be heard from the jury. Judge Stockman gave Dixon a look to advise him that his job was to ask questions and not give commentary.

Krueller seemed to have already forgotten the earlier lie he'd told and didn't understand the reference.

"Okay, while you were taking this pleasure cruise you happened upon the MacKenzie residence, isn't that right?"

"Yes."

"And Duke was there with Debi and Debi's daughter Bambi and Bambi's boyfriend Troy, right?"

"Yes."

"And you hadn't been invited, correct?"

"Right."

"And you threatened Duke again, didn't you?"

"Objection, your honor," said McGuckin, rising to his feet. "Assumes facts not in evidence. It's only conjecture that there was a prior threat and the question is the proverbial 'have you stopped beating your wife.' If Mr. Krueller says 'yes, he threatened him again' it is damning and if he says 'no, he didn't threaten him again' it suggests he did threaten him before."

"Sustained," Stockman ruled. "Mr. Donnelly, perhaps you could rephrase the question."

"Isn't it true that you told Mr. MacKenzie if you caught him with your wife you'd blow his fucking head off?"

"I don't remember that. I think I said something like you must be out of your head to be doing what you're doing."

"You're aware, aren't you, that the three other people there all gave statements to the sheriff's office that you said words to the effect of: 'Duke, you no good son of a bitch, you're banging my wife and when I catch you I'm going to blow your fucking head off'?"

"I don't know what they said. Besides, Debi's daughter doesn't like me and would do whatever she could to get me in trouble."

"Why doesn't she like you?"

"I think because I'm not her real dad, and she wishes her parents hadn't gotten divorced."

Dixon pondered whether a man who could have sex with his wife's sister might also be prone to make a pass at his stepdaughter. A cleverly asked question might plant that idea in the jurors' minds, but the ethical rules require that there be at least some factual basis for any such questions and Dixon thought better of it. Finally, he said, "Well, I expect she will testify later in this trial. What do you think she'll say is the reason she doesn't like you?"

"She's got a lot of her mom in her, so I'm sure she'll say as many rotten things as she can think of to get me in trouble."

"In any event, Mr. Krueller, how long were you at the MacKenzie place on that occasion?"

"Ten minutes or so."

"Do you remember saying anything else?"

"No."

"Throughout this process you never said anything like: 'Debi, I'm sorry—Debi, I love you—Debi, let's work this out'?"

"Not them words, no."

"And you do admit you were upset during this visit?"

"Yes."

Krueller was starting to show some fatigue. Thinking on his feet didn't come naturally to him, and the stress of focusing on every word was showing. Dixon took notice and said, "How are you doing, Mr. Krueller? Do you need some more water?"

"Yeah, that would be great." The clerk passed a pitcher and his glass was refilled. The glass shook as Krueller raised it to his lips, and he had to use his other hand to steady it.

"So, after you left you drove around some more until it got dark?"

"Yeah."

"Have anything to drink?"

"No."

"Did you go anywhere in particular?"

"Went home for a while. Got restless and went back out driving."

"You got to the MacKenzie residence around 10 P.M., is that right?"

"Something like that."

"And you were careful to be quiet again so they wouldn't hear you?"

"Right."

"Then after a while you tried to get in, so you checked the doors and windows?"

"Yes."

"And you didn't pound on the door or anything because you wanted to catch them in the act, right?"

"Yeah, 'cause up till then I didn't have no proof."

"When you got there, could you hear them having sex?"

"Not when I first got there."

"But later on, they were making enough noise that you could hear them from outside?"

"Yes."

"The windows in the back of the house were open?"

"Yes."

"Did they have screens on them?"

"Yeah, I guess so."

"Did you try and climb in them?"

"No, they were too high up."

"After a while you bumped into something and they stopped what they were doing, isn't that right?"

"Yes."

"And you were afraid they'd heard you?"

"I guess that's right."

"You didn't want them to know you were out there because you wanted to catch them in the act?"

"I just wanted to stop them and protect my wife," he protested.

"Well, yelling 'honey, I'm here' probably would have caused them to stop, wouldn't it? But you didn't do that?"

"No, I didn't."

"So you waited until you heard them start again, because you could get closer and would be able to catch them in the act?"

Lester sat silent. "Mr. Krueller," the Judge said.

"Yeah," he finally replied.

"Mr. Krueller, I'm showing you a picture that I've marked as Exhibit 11. Is that the sliding glass door through which you entered?"

"Yes."

"I'm now showing you Exhibit 12, which is a close-up picture of that door. Can you please confirm that?"

"Looks like it."

"Now you testified that you climbed up the ladder and tried to pry the door open, isn't that right?"

"Yes."

"Now, in this picture, we know it was taken after the fact because the glass is all broken, do you see that?"

"Yes."

"But there aren't any pry marks, are there?"

Lester studied the picture. "They were lower down."

"So, instead of holding the shovel at waist height and prying you got down in a crouch or on your knees to try and pry it?"

"Yeah."

"Wouldn't it make more sense to pry at the level of the lock?"

"I s'pose, but I wasn't really thinking all that clearly."

Dixon nodded his head and ignored the absurdity of the testimony. "What did you do after you smashed the glass?"

"Dropped the shovel, walked in the house, through one room, and opened the bedroom door."

"When you opened the door, what did you see?"

"Pretty much nothing. Just a flash and then I heard the shot."

"What's the first thing you remember seeing after that?"

"Duke MacKenzie came running at me with the gun in his hand and started swearing at me."

"What was he wearing?"

"Nothing."

"How about a hat, glasses, cowboy boots?"

The gallery and the jury let out a little snicker.

"No. He was naked as the day he was born."

"What happened next?"

"Duke just ran off. That's the last we ever heard from him."

"Mr. Krueller, I'm showing you Exhibit 13, which is a picture of the scene in the bedroom as Deputy Halvorsen found it, with the exception that you are no longer in it. Do you see that?"

"Yes."

"Tell me, if you dropped the shovel after you smashed the window, how did it end up in the bedroom?"

Krueller didn't hesitate to give his rehearsed response. "Duke brought it in. He musta gone out to see what I had done and then he carried it back in."

"Did he do anything with it or say anything about it?"

"No."

"Let's go back to Exhibit 12, which is the picture showing the room just inside of the sliding glass door after the incident. Do you see that?"

"Yeah."

"And is that pretty much the way it looked, with all that glass everywhere?"

"Yeah."

"So your testimony here today is that Duke MacKenzie walked barefoot through all this glass just so he could pick up the shovel and put it in the bedroom next to you?"

Dixon glanced at the jury and noticed they were enjoying the destruction of Les Krueller.

Krueller was now stammering. "Ah . . . ah . . . everything just happened so fast I guess I don't really know how it got there. Maybe Deputy Halvorsen moved it."

Dixon didn't dignify the response and moved on. "Finally, sir, you never heard any other shot other than the one that hit you, is that right?"

"That's right."

"Your honor," Dixon said, "that concludes my cross-examination. The defense reserves the right to re-call Mr. Krueller as part of its case in chief."

"That's fine," Stockman said. "Mr. McGuckin, any redirect?"

McGuckin shuffled through his notes. Krueller had been shown to be lying about virtually everything other than his name. Trying to rehabilitate his testimony would be a monumental task and would have the unfortunate effect of leaving him on display even longer. "Plaintiff reserves the right to re-call Mr. Krueller for rebuttal, but we have nothing further at this time."

"Fine," Stockman said. "Let's recess for ten minutes and then Plaintiff can call the next witness.

"Your honor," McGuckin said, "I've got Doc Richardson sort of on standby because he couldn't just sit here all day. It may take a little longer for him to get here, but I think it would be better than calling someone else at this time."

"That's fine, just let me know if there is a problem," Stockman said.

Judge and jury left the courtroom. Dixon saw Skip Blakemore from Home Protection Insurance in the gallery and sought him out. "What did you think?" Dixon asked.

"I thought you nailed the bastard. That thing with the shovel was a classic."

"Maybe your client should kick in a little something for the effort," Dixon said.

"Hey, just 'cause it's self-defense doesn't mean it's covered by insurance."

"Be careful," Dixon said, "I might take the coverage issue up to the Supreme Court, and then you'd have a bad precedent out there."

"Look, if you win this case I can probably get the insurance company to pay for something that would approximate what it would cost to try a coverage action."

"Maybe you should make that a bona fide offer right now."

"What's the rush?" he asked.

"Well, I might end up showing facts that entitle my guy to full reimbursement. Maybe you should settle now and see if you can get it for less."

"Considering you have basically no witnesses on your side, I can't imagine how that could happen."

"That's true," Dixon said. "But in my experience it seems like every case involves things falling into place that you didn't think would fall into place. Krueller telling such blatant lies was a good example. I wasn't surprised by his lies, but it sure helped with the jury."

"You might be right," Blakemore said. "As far as I'm concerned, you've already won this case."

"Don't say that," Dixon said. "There's nothing worse than having a case that people think you can't lose. I'd rather have an unwinnable case, because you can only do better than the expectations."

Blakemore patted Dixon on the shoulder. "Okay, I'll just say that you've handled this about as well as it could be handled, and it's gone about as well as anyone could have expected."

"Thanks," Dixon said. "I appreciate that."

While they were speaking, McGuckin advised that Doc Richardson was on his way, but it would be more than ten minutes. There were at least two hours of court time left, so that was probably plenty. At 2:50, Doc Richardson was sworn in and McGuckin began his examination.

The testimony was very clinical. Richardson described the wound, the surgery to remove the bullet, the therapy that was required, and the long-term expected consequences. He wasn't Plaintiffs' expert per se. Rather, he was the treating physician and testified as such. He didn't appear to slant his testimony in any particular way, and merely reported the facts as he saw them. The most important thing Richardson did for McGuckin's case was to establish that Les wasn't just a whiner—his injuries were real and substantial, albeit short-term, and discomfort would be expected.

McGuckin succeeded in turning the witness over to Dixon for the dreaded final hour. "Your honor, because of Dr. Richardson's responsibilities, I would like to conduct my cross-examination and also conduct direct examination as part of my main case," Dixon said.

Ordinarily, a witness can only be cross-examined on topics that were brought up during the direct examination, but it was customary to allow such accommodations for witnesses with special circumstances. From the jury's standpoint, it made no apparent difference.

There were subtle impacts on things the judge might order or do, but even those issues rarely came up. Stockman solicited McGuckin's concurrence and then permitted Dixon to proceed as indicated.

"Dr. Richardson," Dixon began, "you weren't the treating physician on the evening of the shooting, is that right?"

"That's right. The EMTs and other hospital personnel were responsible for cleaning the wound, stabilizing the patient, and otherwise tending to his well-being. We didn't remove the bullet until the next morning."

"So, by the time you saw Mr. Krueller, he was prepped for surgery?"

"Yes."

"You never examined his clothes to see if there were bullet holes or anything like that, correct?"

"That's right."

McGuckin stirred. "Your Honor, Dr. Richardson is really a neutral witness, and I don't think Mr. Donnelly should be allowed to ask leading questions."

Judge Stockman replied, "You might be right, Mr. McGuckin, but so far we are just in the preliminaries. Object later on and I'll give it some thought."

"Did you ever examine his skin for powder burns?" Dixon continued.

"No. Anything like that should have been cleaned off before I got to him."

"Do you know if anyone made such an examination?"

"Not to my knowledge."

"If gun powder was present, what would it show?"

"That usually means the gun was fired in close proximity to the victim."

"As far as you knew, how far away was the gun from Les Krueller when he was shot?"

"Well, the story was that he was shot from across a bedroom, which would probably mean fifteen or twenty feet. Based on the wound, that could have been the case, but it probably could have been closer and still consistent with the injury."

"Have you ever seen a case where someone tried to inflict their own gunshot wound to make it look like they were a victim of a crime and not a perpetrator?"

Like a jack-in-the-box, McGuckin was on his feet. "Your honor, I object. Where is this going?"

"Forgive me, your honor, but I have no living witnesses to this event. I guess I'd like a little latitude."

"I'll overrule the objection for now," Stockman said.

"I've heard of such situations," Richardson replied. "I don't think I've ever handled one."

"What typically happens in those situations?"

"Frequently the perpetrator ends up dying."

"I'm sorry, doctor, I meant where do they inflict the injury?"

"Well, that's the problem. People think the stomach will seem the most realistic, but that can lead to tragedy because you never know what you might hit."

"Just so we're clear, you didn't make any determination about where the bullet was fired from or whether it could have been either self-inflicted or inflicted by an accomplice?"

"Correct."

"What is your opinion of Les Krueller's current medical condition?"

"He's basically recovered. He indicates that he still has some discomfort and that would be normal. I don't think he will have any other long-term effects other than anything psychological, and I'm a medical doctor so I don't have an opinion about that."

"Dr. Richardson, you are also the coroner in this town, is that right?"

"Yes, sir."

"Let me ask you some things about that. You examined the remains they found of Duke MacKenzie, correct?"

"That's right."

"Were you able to make a positive identification?"

"We were. The dental records were a match. We took some DNA in case there was a question in the future, but we didn't run DNA tests because they're expensive and there was no apparent need."

"Dr. Richardson, as I understand it, the identification was made based upon the upper jaw, and the lower was not found?"

"That's right."

"And the upper jaw was intact?"

"More or less. They recovered the skull, but not the lower half."

"Did that surprise you in a case like this?"

"Why would it?"

"Well, sir, you've ruled this a suicide, but don't people who commit suicide with a pistol typically either shoot through a temple or shoot through the roof of their mouth into their brain pan?"

"How else would you do it?" the doctor asked.

"Well, that's sort of the question. Duke's gunshot wound was through the back of his head, right?"

"Yes."

"Could you tell whether the bullet was fired from the front to the back or from the back, execution style?"

"I believed it to be front to back."

"What did you base that on?"

"First, there was no apparent damage to the front side of his skull. Now that could be explained as the bullet simply exiting through his mouth or some other soft tissue, but that doesn't seem that likely. Second, the hole in the skull indicated the impact was from inside to out. In other words, the diameter of the hole gets bigger as you go from inside to out, which indicates that was the flight of the bullet. If we had obtained the remains sooner we could have reached that conclusion with more certainty, but I'm still quite confident."

"Okay. Because the bullet went through the back of the head, the gun must have been held approximately level when it was discharged, right?"

"Assuming the victim was standing, yes, that makes sense."

"If someone is going to commit suicide, wouldn't it be risky to put a gun in their mouth and shoot through the back of their head? And by risky I mean isn't there a risk they won't kill themselves but might hit the spinal cord and be paralyzed."

"As a doctor I can say that. I can't tell you what someone who attempts suicide is thinking."

"Let me show you one other thing. If I'm holding a gun parallel to the ground and stick it in my own mouth it gets awfully contorted and I don't have much leverage to pull the trigger." As Dixon spoke, he made a gun with his thumb and index finger and put it in his mouth to demonstrate. "Now, if I was going to shoot someone else through the mouth, it would be hard to shoot through that upper palate, because the butt of the gun hits the chin." Dixon did his best to demonstrate that as well. "But if I'm going to shoot myself, the easiest way is to just hold the gun up like I'm shushing someone and then put it inside my mouth and shoot straight up into my brain. Am I right?"

"Maybe. But what happens if you turn the gun so that it's upside down and parallel to the ground?"

Dixon proceeded as he directed. "That might be possible, but there's a similar leverage problem. The trigger pulls easiest when the gun is in a vertical position."

"Excuse me," McGuckin said. "Who's asking the questions here and who's answering them?"

Dixon had to acknowledge the appropriateness of the objection. "Fair enough," Dixon said. "But just to be clear, no analysis like that was done at the time?"

"You're correct. I'd also have to admit it didn't occur to me until now that the location of the bullet wound was a little unusual for a suicide."

"Thank you, doctor, I have nothing further."

McGuckin rose for redirect. He didn't go to the lectern, but asked questions from his table, as if the testimony just elicited by Dixon didn't warrant the effort. "The cause of death that you reported on the death certificate was suicide, correct?"

"Yes."

"And you have not seen fit to change the death certificate, have you?"

"Correct."

"Thank you," McGuckin said. Court was adjourned and day two was in the books.

# CHAPTER 37

THE COUNTY ATTORNEY's office was located in the lower level
of the courthouse. Dixon arrived early on Thursday so he could
visit with Perry Passieux. When Dixon entered, Passieux looked up
from his work. "How's your trial going?"

"Going fine," Dixon said. "Each day promises more fireworks
than the day before."

Passieux lifted himself just off his seat and pointed to a chair
across from him. "I wanted to stop by last night to talk to you but I
got held up. We received notice that the Court of Appeals has ruled
on the criminal appeal."

"Really. What did they say?" Dixon asked.

"I don't know. That's why I didn't break my neck to reach you.
We got notice that a decision was reached and drafts are being cir-
culated among the judges. The parties will receive advance copies
tomorrow, and they'll be released to the public on Monday."

"Does McGuckin know?"

"He might. I got a notice in the mail to alert me to the advance
copy. I guess the idea is that the parties shouldn't have to hear about
their case from the newspapers."

"Makes sense," Dixon said. "So we'll know on Friday?"

"Yeah. Do you think you can you draw your case out that long?"

"Maybe. I wonder if McGuckin will try to hurry up and finish
before then. Can you do me a favor?" Dixon asked. "Tomorrow
when you get it, would you bring it to the courtroom or have someone walk it down?"

"Sure. Maybe I'll spend a little time watching the action while
I'm there."

"Hopefully, there'll still be something to see." Dixon shook Passieux's hand and left. The walk to the courtroom took him down the hallway past the sheriff's office, and he stepped gingerly, hoping not to encounter Sheriff José. He succeeded.

Dixon found the courtroom door locked, so he proceeded to the coffee shop in the basement. A couple of jurors had already arrived and were in the corner drinking coffee. Deliberate contact with jurors was taboo, but it wouldn't hurt to leave a good impression. As a result, Dixon was particularly talkative with the counter help. He wanted to appear happy and upbeat so the jurors would think he was pleased with the way the trial was going. In fact, it was going as well as could be expected, so it wasn't much of an act.

Hank arrived and the bon vivant continued. They chatted about the weather, football, and everything else that would be the last thing on the mind of someone concerned about the outcome of the trial. On a certain level, it also helped Dixon to put the events ahead into his subconscious and allow him to analyze the evidence in the background while he carried on other conversations.

Soon, Les and Debi showed up as well. Neither looked as if they'd gotten enough sleep. There were so many possible explanations for that fact that neither Dixon nor Hank tried to speculate. Appearance was another level upon which a case could be won. The tired Kruellers lacked any air of self-assurance, and a jury would be more likely to believe someone who appeared confident.

When they were done, Dixon and Hank crumpled their paper coffee cups and threw them in the basket. They walked out of the coffee shop, using care not to look anyone directly in the eye. Dixon made a point, however, of opening the door out of respect for his elder. They were on the side of good, and Dixon wanted that to resonate in everything the jury saw him do.

The participants slowly assembled in the courtroom, except for the jurors, who were directed to meet in the jury room. By tradition, the jurors all entered the courtroom together. It gave the appearance of them having been sequestered somewhere together, even though that practice had largely fallen out of favor, except in the most unusual circumstances.

On cue, the clerk banged the gavel and day three was under way. McGuckin stood at the lectern and waited for everyone to take their seats. "Plaintiff calls Deputy Halvorsen," he announced.

Deputy Halvorsen carried a redrope file, which he handed to McGuckin as he passed him. Halvorsen's testimony didn't appear to be strictly necessary to McGuckin's case, but his investigation and conclusions would put the official imprimatur on the Kruellers' story.

McGuckin hooked a thumb in his suspenders and addressed the witness. "Deputy Halvorsen, for the benefit of the jury and everyone else, please tell us what is in the redrope folder that you handed to me before taking the stand."

"That is the full investigative file of the Koochiching County Sheriff's office relative to this proceeding. You subpoenaed it for this case, and I delivered it personally because we don't like to give up custody of our investigative files."

"Thank you, sir." McGuckin proceeded to interrogate Halvorsen on his training, his experience, and his time with the Koochiching County Sheriff's office. McGuckin wanted to make it clear that Halvorsen was competent and had reached the appropriate conclusions.

He walked Halvorsen through the incident, starting with the dispatch and then proceeding with the scene when he arrived, the condition of Les Krueller, the search for Duke MacKenzie, and the gruesome discovery. McGuckin had done the same drill at the criminal trial, and he used the same exhibits. "And on October 15 of that year, you filed a report indicating the investigation was concluded and Les Krueller was the victim of a gunshot fired by Duke MacKenzie, correct?"

"That's not exactly how I would characterize it. We didn't make affirmative findings like that. What we said was the victim reported being shot by Duke MacKenzie and that version of events was consistent with the evidence we had gathered."

"Understood," McGuckin responded. It had only been about an hour, but McGuckin was done with the witness. "Your honor, I move that the Investigative File be admitted into evidence."

"No objection," Dixon responded eagerly, and it was admitted. McGuckin gathered his notes and turned the witness over to Dixon.

"Deputy Halvorsen, I'm going to cover some of the same things as Mr. McGuckin, but I will have a few extra questions along the way. Tell me first whether you had any prior experience with the Kruellers."

"Yeah, I've been out to break up disturbances at their house more than once."

"And did you know Duke MacKenzie?"

"I knew who he was. I don't recall having any official business with him."

"Had you been to his house before?"

"Not to the house itself. There's a boat landing not far from his house, so I knew where he lived."

"The night of the incident, were you the first one on the scene?"

"Yes."

"Did you wait for backup or did you go in by yourself?"

"We determined that backup would take at least fifteen minutes and it didn't appear there was any imminent danger, so I proceeded in by myself."

"Deputy Halvorsen, for the benefit of the jury, I'd like you to describe the layout of the property, okay?"

"Sure. In fact, one of my reports has a little schematic in it."

"Precisely. I've blown it up for our purposes." Dixon placed a tagboard drawing on an easel. "Do you recognize this?"

"Yes, that looks like the map I made before."

The highway extended across the bottom of the map, with the property above it. The driveway ran up the west side and the house was east of where the driveway terminated. The lake extended across the top and on the right. Duke had sort of a corner lot, with the lake on the north and east.

"Which side is the front of the house?" Dixon asked.

"The north," Halvorsen responded.

Dixon put the pointer on that part of the house. "So, if you're sitting in the front of the house, can you see the lake?"

"Yes."

"And how far across is it?"

"The part that's straight north is kind of a bay. I s'pose it's about a hundred yards across."

"What do you see if you're at the front of the house and look to the right?"

"Woods."

"So, you can't see the main lake from there?"

"Not really."

"How about if you look to the left?"

"Woods."

Dixon made his best attempt at drawing trees in the respective locations. "When you approached the house that night by coming up this way on the driveway, did you see anybody?"

"No."

"At some point you went out and called around or looked for Duke, is that right?"

"A little bit, yeah."

"What direction did you go?"

"I don't remember the exact order I did things, but I remember trying to go to the east through the woods, but a little ways past the woods it was all swamp, so I figured that wasn't very likely where he was."

Dixon drew an *S* on the map just to the east of the eastern woods and south and west of the lake. "About here?"

"Yes."

"What did you do then?"

"Well, I figured Duke must have gone toward the west or else he was hiding in the shed or something. I hollered a couple times, but it was night and my backup wasn't there, so I wasn't eager to go scouting around."

"So what happened then?"

Deputy Halvorsen proceeded to explain the scene as he found it, including the battling Kruellers.

Dixon interrupted him. "We heard the 911 tape the other day. When you were dispatched, were you advised that Les Krueller was claiming his wife had been having sexual relations with Duke MacKenzie?"

Deputy Halvorsen hesitated for a moment. "Les certainly didn't use those words." That drew a laugh from the jury.

"Did you do any investigation or reach any conclusions about whether Mr. Krueller's accusations were true?"

"Kind of."

"Tell us."

"Debi was sitting downstairs when I arrived and, after I checked on Les, I went down and asked her what had happened. She said she didn't know and that she'd just been sitting there reading when she heard some commotion upstairs and Duke ran out. I asked her if she was sure that was what happened, and she swore it was the truth."

"Okay. Then what?"

"I went upstairs and found a pair of women's blue jeans and panties laying on the bedroom floor. I carried them down and told her I found them and asked her if she wanted to change her story, but she stuck to it. Finally, I reached in the pocket and pulled out a big key ring with the name 'Debi' written on it. At that point she claimed the pants were hers, but the panties weren't."

"What did you conclude?"

"Well, I hadn't had much doubt that she must've been having sex with Duke, but she later admitted it anyway."

"If her pants were upstairs, what was she wearing when you arrived?"

"She was wearing what looked like a man's flannel shirt and a pair of sweat pants."

"How about shoes?"

"No, she was barefoot."

"Did you ask her if she'd been outside that night?"

"Not that I remember."

"That night, did you do any incident reconstruction or anything else to try and verify what Les and Debi were telling you?"

"Not really. I got their stories. There wasn't much other evidence to be gathered. We impounded all of the firearms on the premises so we could try and match one to the bullet we expected to get out of Les sometime later."

"Were you involved in the subsequent search for Duke MacKenzie?"

"Yes."

"What did that consist of?"

"We started at the house and fanned out and worked our way west looking for any clues or evidence."

"Where were his remains ultimately found?"

"East of the house, toward the swamp."

"Were they in the swamp or somewhere else?"

"They were in the woods. Remember I told you there was a little woods when you went to the east before you got to the swamp. That's where we found most of him."

"For the benefit of the jury, although I'm not sure if 'benefit' is the right word in this situation, what do you mean you found 'most of him'?"

"We believe Duke was eaten by wild animals. The bones were gnawed on, and we found them scattered all around."

Dixon peered at the jury and noticed more than one grimace. "This place that you just identified as the location where you found most of him. Did you determine whether animals had dragged him there or had dragged parts away from there?"

"We think his body parts were dragged away from there, because that was where the largest concentration was located."

"How about the gun, where did you find it?"

"Same place."

"Based upon your investigation, was there anyplace for Duke to go if he went east from the house?"

"Not as far as I could tell. There was a big marsh and once you got through that you were in the lake."

"How about if he went straight north, was that marsh?"

"No, that was just the regular lake, the bay I told you about."

"As a stranger to the property, you didn't originally realize the swamp was to the east, is that right?"

"Yes."

"But someone familiar with the property would know about the swamp?"

"Objection," McGuckin barked. "Calls for speculation."

"Sustained."

Dixon continued unfazed. "Were you ever able to come up with any explanation or theory as to why Duke MacKenzie would have gone that way? I mean, was there a boat or another shed or anything that would explain why he went in a direction that was a dead end?" Dixon was aware of the pun the moment it left his lips, but decided against making light of it in front of Hank.

"No. There was a canoe in the garage, but nothing that we saw on the shore."

"How far into the woods was the body?"

"Not very. There are a few trees with the brush cleared out and then there's about twenty yards of brush before you get to the swamp. We found him about five yards into the brush."

"We heard yesterday that the bullet went through his skull. Did you look in the woods for the bullet?"

"We looked around, but didn't find anything."

"How about footprints? Were there any other than Duke's?"

"There were other footprints, but it was about ten days before we found him so we couldn't really tell when they were made. For that matter, we had some of our own footprints from looking."

"Just to be clear, though, this area was dirt, so there would be footprints?"

"Could be."

McGuckin had been squirming for a long time. Finally he rose to his feet. "Your honor, I fail to see the relevance of the circumstances surrounding the search and recovery of Duke MacKenzie's remains. I think this whole thing is just a ploy to make the jury feel bad for Duke and that he suffered enough."

"Your honor," Dixon responded, "Mr. McGuckin has tried to cloak his version of events in the official report of the sheriff's office, and I think I'm entitled to explore everything that was and wasn't

done in order to allow the jury to decide whether to accept the conclusions of the sheriff's office."

"Mr. Donnelly," Judge Stockman said, "I agree with that, but I
don't see how this is relevant."

"I expect to tie it all together shortly and would ask for the
Court's indulgence."

"Okay. I'll overrule," Stockman said.

"The evening of the incident, did you find any evidence of a gun
being fired in the house?"

"Just Lester Krueller's bleeding stomach."

"Did you examine the wound to see if there were any powder
burns on it?"

"I did not."

"Did you search to see if there were any other shots fired in the
house that night?"

"Not originally."

"Did you subsequently do another search at the house?"

"Yes."

"When was that?"

"About two months ago."

"And what did you find?"

"Objection!" McGuckin yelled. "Can we approach?"

After they arrived at the bench, McGuckin pleaded, "I was never
advised of any subsequent investigation."

"I'm surprised to hear that," Dixon said, "because about a half hour
ago you successfully moved the admission of the entire investigative
file into evidence. Perhaps you should have examined it first."

"Why wasn't I given notice of this?" McGuckin demanded.

"As I said before, I never gave you notice because you never served
me with any discovery."

"What about the County Attorney?" McGuckin pleaded.

"Well, I'll let him speak for himself, but the government's disclosure requirements don't arise in connection with investigations.
That's only required in connection with trial preparation. There is
no pending criminal prosecution. Your client was already acquitted
on one count and convicted on another."

Judge Stockman broke the tension. "Let's take a recess so Mr. McGuckin can look at the documents he put in the record. It doesn't sound like there's much you can do about it now, Earl, but I'll give you a chance to make a record outside the presence of the jury." Stockman raised his head to address the jury. "We have some legal matters that we need to discuss. I'm going to give you about a twenty-minute recess and then we'll resume."

After dismissing the jury, the judge exited and McGuckin furiously examined the contents of the file. Deputy Halvorsen excused himself to the restroom, but Dixon didn't want to let the investigative file out of his sight. McGuckin located the most recent report and tried to digest it. After ten minutes the clerk poked her head out from the chambers door to ask if McGuckin was ready to proceed. He asked for an additional minute, and she acquiesced.

Stockman returned, but the jury was kept waiting. "Mr. McGuckin, do you have anything to say?"

"Yes, your honor. I object to the introduction of any new evidence. Civil trials aren't supposed to be about surprises and, regardless of whether I served discovery, I think Mr. Donnelly had an obligation to advise me of this new investigation. Furthermore, and equally important, I have reviewed the report and it doesn't change the conclusion previously reached. I think, therefore, it is just an attempt to confuse the jury. My clients testified they only remember hearing one shot, and now this evidence suggests Duke might have fired two shots. Well, if that's the case, it's even greater evidence it wasn't self-defense."

"Anything else?" Stockman asked.

"That, and I reserve the right to object to anything else Deputy Halvorsen testifies to relating to the investigation."

"All right," Stockman said. "Your objections are noted, but your motion is denied. It seems to me you are trying to blame others when you simply made a mistake. I'm not sure I would have done anything different in your shoes, but that's not the issue." He turned to his clerk and told her to summon the jury.

Back in place, Dixon resumed. "What were the circumstances that caused you to renew your investigation?"

"We were called in by the Minnesota Bureau of Criminal Apprehension, who wanted to conduct some additional investigation. I believe that was as a result of a request either by you or Hank MacKenzie."

"Who participated in that investigation?"

"I did, as well as Agent Stensvold from the BCA. You and Hank were there to let us into the house."

"What did you find?"

"The main thing we found was a bullet hole behind the bedroom door."

The jury was refreshed from the break, and this disclosure caused them to become even more attentive.

"Deputy Halvorsen, did you take any photographs?"

"Yes, sir."

After getting permission to approach the witness, Dixon asked, "Can you identify this picture?"

"Yes, that's the picture I took of the bullet hole."

"How did you know it was a bullet hole?"

"Well, I guess I should say we found a hole that looked like it could be from a bullet. On further examination, we determined that it was, in fact, a bullet."

"Had you looked for other bullet marks the night of the incident?"

"No. We were only told about one shot, and we were pretty confident the corresponding bullet was in Les Krueller's stomach."

"Was this bullet hole in the wall in plain sight?"

"Not really. It was behind the door. If you were in the bedroom with the door closed it was visible, but the night of the incident the door was open, and I don't think anybody bothered to look behind it."

"How high off the ground was the hole?"

"About five feet."

"Could you tell the angle at which it was shot?"

"The line was pretty much parallel with the floor, meaning the shooter held the gun at about the same height that the bullet entered the wall. The shooter wasn't necessarily standing perpendicular to the wall, however. The path of the bullet was moving slightly from left to right."

"Did you do any ballistics testing on the slug?"

"Yes. It matched the one removed from Les Krueller, and both matched the gun recovered near Duke MacKenzie's body."

"Did you draw any conclusions from that?"

"Only the obvious one—that both bullets had been fired from the gun found near Duke's body."

"What else did you do as part of the investigation?"

"I was mostly just helping the BCA agent, but the next thing done was to examine the scene with Luminol."

"How does that work?"

"Well, a cleaning agent only eliminates the part of the blood that makes it red. There are other remnants that remain, and spraying the area with Luminol allows us to see where blood was."

"Was anything found?"

"Yes, the bullet hole behind the door was surrounded by a pattern of blood."

"How did the pattern look in normal light?"

"There was no pattern in normal light. It just looked like a log cabin wall."

"How about with the Luminol. How did it look then?"

"There was a pattern about four inches in diameter."

"What did it look like?"

"It just sort of looked like a white shirt when you're in a dark room with a black light. It kind of glows."

Dixon dug through the investigative file. "Could you tell us what is depicted in this picture?"

"That's a picture I took of the wall when the Luminol was sprayed on it. It doesn't come out very good in a photograph, but you can see the outline."

"From a forensic standpoint, what did that indicate to you?"

"The bullet passed through flesh that was close to the wall at the time of the shot. In other words, as the bullet exited there would be an explosion of sorts on the epidermis, and blood would shoot onto the wall."

"Could the blood be tested for DNA?"

"No. Most cleaning solutions render the blood untestable. We weren't able to recover any blood. Just evidence there had been blood."

"Did you find any other blood at the scene?"

"Yes, we found blood on the carpeting below the spot on the wall."

"Was that using Luminol as well?"

"Yes, but blood was there the night of the incident because that's basically where Les was hit, so I didn't think at the time it was a big deal."

"You said 'at the time you didn't think it was a big deal.' What do you mean?"

"When I think back, Les wasn't really bleeding that much, so there wouldn't necessarily have been much blood."

"What time did you arrive on the scene?"

"My report says 10:30."

"When did you leave?"

"About 2 A.M."

"You never heard a shot during that time, is that right?"

"Yes, that's right."

"When you left, who was there?"

"I guess just Hank."

"Were you ever able to determine a time of death for Duke?"

"No. I mean it had to have been the night of the incident or not long thereafter based on everything we found, but there's no way to pinpoint it anymore than that."

Dixon turned to Judge Stockman. "Your honor, I believe that's all the questions I have at this time. Unlike Doc Richardson, however, I may call this witness again as part of my case if necessary."

"Fine," Stockman said. "Mr. McGuckin, do you have any redirect?"

"Yes, thank you, your honor. Deputy Halvorsen, is there any way to know whether the bullet found in the wall was fired before or after the one found in Les Krueller?"

"Not that I know of."

"So this second shot could have been fired anytime thereafter, even after you left the premises?"

"Sure."

"In fact, it could have been fired shortly before your recent visit?"

"No, sir, that wouldn't be possible."

"Why not?"

"Because we took the gun into custody as soon as we found it, and we've had custody of it ever since." McGuckin was learning the perils of cross-examining a witness without knowing the answers in advance.

"This second bullet, how far behind the door was it? I mean, if the door was open and it was blocking the hole, would the hole be about in the middle or more to one side?"

"Pretty much the middle."

"Based upon the trajectory of the second bullet and the evidence you had about the one that hit my client, is it possible that Duke MacKenzie fired two shots and the first just missed?"

"No, because there was no hole in the door."

"But what if the first shot was fired while the door was still closed, say, for example, because Duke knew someone was coming in, and then he fired the second shot after the door was opened?"

"Based only on the trajectory that would probably have been possible, but, based on the blood splatter on the wall, I don't think I could say that the first shot missed."

"You didn't reopen this case because you had any doubts about your original conclusions, did you?"

"That's right. It's like I said, the BCA wanted to do a further investigation."

"And as far as you know that's because either Hank MacKenzie or Mr. Donnelly asked them to do it?"

"That's right."

"I have nothing further for this witness," McGuckin announced.

Judge Stockman decided to break a little early for lunch rather than start a new witness and break after fifteen minutes.

McGuckin walked back to the table where his clients were sitting. "We'll start you right after lunch," he said to Debi.

Looking somewhat distraught, she said in a loud whisper, "You said I might not have to testify."

"I know what I said, but I didn't expect some of this stuff, so you have to set the record straight."

Debi looked around to see who could hear her. She tried to lower her voice some more, but the excitement caused her voice to carry. "I don't want to testify. I can't testify. You can't make me do this."

McGuckin tried to calm her down. "Let's talk about it outside, where we can have some privacy."

Dixon and Hank watched them depart. "I wonder what that's about," Dixon said.

"I don't," Hank responded. "You've made everybody look silly on cross-examination, even the ones that were helpful to us. Given her checkered history and the fact that she rarely tells the truth, she probably knows you're going to destroy her on the stand, and nobody really likes being made to look like a fool."

"I didn't make the friendly witnesses look silly, just Krueller," Dixon protested.

"Not the way I saw it. Your questions made it clear what a crummy investigation was done the first time around. I doubt anyone resents you for it, but the way you asked the questions made it seem like they failed to do some pretty basic things."

"Well, I'm just following my client's orders," Dixon said, with a smile.

"And doing a fine job of it, I might add."

"You're too kind."

"When we first met, I told you I needed the best lawyer money could buy, and I think I'm getting my money's worth."

"Please, stop. My head will get so big I won't be able to get out of the courtroom."

As they exited, they saw McGuckin in a far corner talking with his clients. Harmony didn't seem to be the theme. Debi appeared to have been crying and Lester was agitated about something. She was really the only one who could testify as to what Duke was doing immediately before and during the shooting, and she didn't appear comfortable in that role.

♦

At lunch, Hank asked, "What's all this about bringing back witnesses as part of your case?"

"It's simple," Dixon responded. "The plaintiff goes first and presents his case, but I get to cross-examine the witnesses about every subject the plaintiff raises. When they're all done, I get to present our case, and I can use the same witnesses and ask them anything I want."

"Haven't you pretty much asked everything you needed during the cross-examination?"

"As it happens, I probably have, but I want to reserve the opportunity to call someone back in case I've missed something."

"So, what will you do for our case?"

"As of now, probably just call you, Debi's daughter, and the daughter's boyfriend. I don't see any reason to call anyone else back. In fact, I might not even give an opening statement."

After lunch, Dixon and Hank spotted McGuckin sitting with Debi Krueller, having a conversation in low tones. She was quite pale, and even from a distance they could see her trembling. A few minutes later, a smug looking Lester Krueller walked out of the men's room with a toothpick cocked in the corner of his mouth. He was in charge and she was going to testify.

Court resumed and Debi was the first witness called. She nervously took the stand, red eyes and all. McGuckin tried to take her through the preliminaries of name, address, and whatnot, but had to ask her to speak up on several occasions. After he got going, she tended to keep her voice up, but she wasn't testifying with much confidence. Lester was either oblivious to her suffering or overjoyed by it, as he made no effort to ease her pain.

McGuckin walked her through her life history, her relationship with her husband, and finally the events of the weekend of the incident. Her story was substantially the same rehearsed rendition she'd given at her deposition. Essentially, everything was her fault, and

Lester was a saint for putting up with her. Those weren't the words, but that was the message.

On the critical issues, she was deliberately vague. "It all happened too fast," or "I was so upset at the time I might have said anything to get Les in trouble." Her prior statements to the sheriff generally exonerated Duke from any suggestion that Duke was lying in wait, and telling a diametrically opposed story at this juncture would probably do more harm than good. She had no trouble, however, stating that Duke got the gun out because he believed Les was outside and she had no trouble claiming that, at the moment of truth, she yelled "Don't shoot, it's Les." The apparent implication was that a responsible homeowner would have done something to prevent the illegal entry from ever happening, whereas Duke went back to having sex, secure in the knowledge that he could just shoot the intruder.

After an hour and a half, McGuckin announced he was done. Dixon collected several files of ammunition and carried them up to the lectern. Mrs. Krueller's testimony was fraught with problems. The jury had already watched Dixon decimate Les Krueller on the stand. The anticipation of what was to befall Debi Krueller was palpable.

As Dixon arranged his exhibits, Debi Krueller began to shake. "Your honor, I can't stay. I have to make a phone call."

"What?" Stockman asked.

"I can't do this now. I have to see my therapist."

"Mrs. Krueller, we have a trial going on here," Stockman said. "We have a jury impaneled, and you just gave testimony. You can't be excused."

"Please, I can't do this. Just let me make a call."

Neither McGuckin nor Lester did anything to offer any comfort or refuge. Finally, Dixon spoke up. "Your honor, perhaps this would be a good time to take our afternoon recess."

"Okay," Stockman said. "Let's take fifteen minutes."

The gavel slammed and Debi Krueller made a beeline for a pay phone. Dixon wandered over to counsel table to talk to Hank. "I've occasionally made people cry on the stand, but I've never had someone start to cry before I even started the process."

"Like I said," Hank responded, "the best lawyer money can buy."

"I think we have to be careful with this," Dixon said. "If I go too hard on her, I'll look like as big of a creep as her husband and her husband's lawyer."

"Yeah, I can't really blame her for what happened," Hank responded. "But I think we need to find a way to make her comfortable and get the facts out."

After the recess, Debi Krueller took her place back on the witness stand. The jury was led back in and the judge took the bench. He nodded and Dixon proceeded. "Mrs. Krueller, did you get your problem resolved?" Dixon asked.

"No, I couldn't reach him." Even those few words caused her to break down.

"Are you prepared to proceed?" Dixon asked.

Eyes now filled with tears, she turned to the judge and pleaded to be excused. Judge Stockman would have none of it. McGuckin and Krueller could have offered to drop the lawsuit and probably ended her misery right there. Neither seemed concerned with anything other than her testimony holding up.

Dixon addressed her again. "If we take some other testimony this afternoon, do you think you could come back tomorrow and testify?"

"That would probably be better," she whimpered.

"Your honor," Dixon said, "the defense has no objection to conducting the cross-examination tomorrow."

Stockman raised his eyes in surprise. "Mr. McGuckin, what else do you have left?"

"Nothing," he said.

"Do you have any objection to Mr. Donnelly's proposal?"

McGuckin let out a heavy sigh. "I guess not."

Stockman turned back to Dixon. "Are you prepared to proceed?"

"I think so. Two of my witnesses weren't expected to testify until tomorrow, but I can send for them while I put on the testimony of Hank MacKenzie."

Judge Stockman excused Debi Krueller but sternly advised her that her presence the following morning was mandatory. She nodded an acknowledgement and hurried out of the courtroom. Neither her husband nor her lawyer made any attempt to stop her or follow her.

Dixon called Hank MacKenzie to the stand. There was no compelling reason for calling him, but he was likable and it was as close as Dixon could come to calling Duke as a witness. Hopefully, the jurors would equate the two and ascribe only good characteristics to the deceased.

Hank established that Duke was an excellent marksman and that, if he had been lying in wait, Les would now be dead. If Duke shot Les, therefore, it had to have been in haste, in the dark, or something else.

Dixon then asked about Duke's propensity for peacefulness and how he had always found ways to avoid fights. McGuckin objected because evidence of such traits is generally inadmissible except in limited criminal contexts. Dixon persuaded the judge that this was a civil case about an event with criminal implications, and the testimony was allowed.

Dixon then called the daughter and her boyfriend. Both showed little hesitation when asked about Les's threats to blow Duke's "fucking head off." McGuckin tried to discredit them based on their animosity toward Les, but the boyfriend had since become an ex-boyfriend and there was no basis to establish any bias. He was the otherwise All-American boy who momentarily got caught up with the wrong family, and there was no reason to doubt his word.

By the end of the day, the only thing left was the cross-examination of Debi Krueller and closing arguments. It appeared that the jury would get the case before the weekend.

# CHAPTER 38

O N THE FIRST DAY of trial, Dixon had worn an olive suit with the hope that the warm tone would help his interaction with the jury. On days two and three, he'd worn power suits in an attempt to appear intimidating or authoritative. On Friday, he showed up in a sport coat with leather patches on the elbows. If decorum had allowed it, he would have shown up in a sweater and emulated Mr. Rogers. This was a day to look nonthreatening.

Dixon arrived before anyone else and moved the lectern from the jury's left, where he had originally placed it, to the jury's right. The move would put him much closer to the witness and would put him between the witness and everybody else, including Les Krueller. However, he didn't move his mountain of ammunition. That was left on counsel table, out of Debi's sight line.

The appointed time arrived, but McGuckin and his clients had yet to make an appearance. Dixon positioned himself firmly at the lectern, as if he was on guard against anyone who would move it back. The clerk came in to announce that McGuckin was in the building, but Mrs. Krueller was still having difficulty pulling herself together. Finally, at 8:35, McGuckin entered with his clients and court was convened.

Debi Krueller was directed to take the stand, and she did so, although without much spring in her step. Before she could be seated, McGuckin was up, making a production about the new position of the lectern. "Your honor, what's with the new location of the lectern?"

"Your honor," Dixon responded, "in Minnesota state courts there is no requirement that attorneys even use a lectern. I can sit at counsel table, roam around, or do pretty much whatever I like. Yesterday, Mrs. Krueller had some difficulty projecting her voice, so I want to make sure I hear everything she says, and then I will make sure the critical information is repeated loud enough for the jury to hear."

"But your honor," McGuckin responded, "we're entitled to a view of the witness."

"Your honor," Dixon replied, "I've pulled the lectern as far to the side as I can. They can see fine."

Stockman listened and then spoke. "Mr. McGuckin, if that's intended as an objection, it's overruled. If there comes a time when you can't see, speak up and we'll address it then." Stockman then turned to Debi Krueller and said, "Mrs. Krueller, you are still under oath."

Debi Krueller nodded her understanding and took the stand. She wasn't comfortable, but appeared more in control than the day before.

"Mrs. Krueller," Dixon began, "I realize this isn't your first choice for what you'd like to do on a Friday morning, but are you going to be able to testify?"

"Yes, I think so," she said in a soft voice that belied her words.

"Before we start, I need to ask you if you've been given any medication to help you deal with the stress or anything else."

"I was given Prozac by my therapist."

"Did you ask him whether it would affect your ability to testify? By that, I mean would it impair your memory, cause you to disregard your oath to tell the truth, or anything like that?"

"No. He said it would calm me down and make me be able to testify better."

"Okay," Dixon said in as warm a voice as he could muster without sounding corny. "If you feel like you need to take a break to use the bathroom, or collect your thoughts, or just regroup, please speak up and we'll see what we can do to accommodate you. Okay?"

"Yes. Thank you."

Dixon nodded his head slowly as she answered. He never looked down at his legal pad, and instead kept his eyes on her. He wasn't staring or trying to intimidate. He was trying to engage her and let her know that her welfare was important to him. "Mrs. Krueller," he said in a slow, soft voice, "we've got a lot of information to cover here and, while I know it's not that comfortable discussing your private life in front of a room full of people, that's the situation in which we find ourselves. Part of this case is about the damages your husband allegedly suffered with respect to his personal and married life, so we have to talk about that to get a sense for what effects, if any, these events had on your personal life."

She nodded her understanding, but it was already clear she didn't have much of a personal life and probably never did.

"You and Les have had some arguments in the past that resulted in visits to your house by the sheriff's office, isn't that right?"

"Yeah, but that was always my fault." The McGuckin directive had already kicked in. She was told to say something and wanted to get it out before she forgot.

"Let's slow down a little," Dixon said. "We might talk about the reasons for the arguments later, but now I just want to talk about the fact that they occurred, okay?"

"Fine," she said, shrugging her shoulders to suggest he was wasting his time, but he could waste it if he wanted to.

"Is it fair to say that the sheriff's office has been out to your house at least ten times since you and Les have been married?"

"I dunno. I don't count."

"Is it fair to say that the two of you sometimes argue, but nobody calls the sheriff?"

She let out a nervous laugh. "Yeah, that's very fair to say."

"So, if the records show ten separate visits by the sheriff's office, it's fair to assume that there were other times when you argued, but nobody called the authorities?"

"Yeah, I guess."

"How often do you argue and not call the sheriff?"

"Depends on what you consider an argument."

"Is it fair to say you and your husband argue a lot?"

"I s'pose, but it's always my fault."

"You were married before, correct?"

"Yes."

"Did you have similar issues during that marriage?"

McGuckin was on his feet. "Your honor, we object to this line of questioning. The witness's life story isn't relevant to these proceedings."

"Your honor," Dixon responded, "loss of consortium damages are a funny thing because I don't really know how you can ever monetize them. That being said, there is a claim that this incident has driven some sort of wedge between the plaintiff and his wife, and I think I'm entitled to explore everything that might be the cause of any so-called wedge."

"Overruled," Stockman said. "Mr. Donnelly, I trust you will keep it tasteful."

"I'll do my best, your honor." Turning back to the witness, Dixon reiterated, "Mrs. Krueller, did you have similar issues with your first husband?"

She sat quiet for a moment before speaking. "Yes."

"Prior to that, had you been in any other relationships that had similar issues?" Dixon wanted to characterize the "issues" as domestic abuse, but wanted to keep McGuckin in his seat for a while.

"No, not really."

"I'm including while growing up. When you were young, did your parents have the same types of problems that you have with Les?"

"Not really, 'cause my mom was too scared to call the cops."

"So your parents did argue?"

"All the time."

"Was there an alcohol-abuse issue?"

Debi rolled her eyes to emphasize the magnitude. "Yes."

"Was it one of your parents or both?"

"I guess both. Mostly my dad, but then my mom would drink to feel better about it."

"Was that the situation for as long as you can remember, or did it start after you reached a certain age?"

"Pretty much for as long as I can remember."

"How did that affect you?"

"I don't know. It was a pretty crappy way to grow up, but I don't know what difference it made in how I turned out."

Dixon had thrown the rules of cross-examination out the window. He had no real idea what her answers would be, and his questions were open-ended to let her speak without feeling pressured. "Well, how did it make you feel?"

"Not very good. I felt afraid whenever they fought."

"Afraid for what?"

"Afraid he might hurt her. Afraid they might get divorced. Afraid the child welfare department would take me and put me in a foster home."

"Have you ever been through treatment for chemical dependency?"

"Yes."

"What did you learn through that process?"

"Drinking is bad," was all she could say.

"Did they tell you about the feeling of powerlessness?"

"They didn't have to tell me about that. I knew it."

Dixon continued with a methodical, nonthreatening attempt to draw her out. After several questions designed to imitate therapy, his litigation instinct told him that many more questions on this topic would likely draw an objection or an admonition from the judge, so he moved back to Les. "I've reviewed the sheriff's files from the calls out to your house when you and Les had problems, and it appears that, in the end, you always asked to have the charges dropped. Is that accurate?"

"Like I said, those arguments were always my fault, so after I sobered up and thought about it, I always set the record straight." This time she had a little less conviction in her voice as she claimed the blame.

"That usually took a couple days, didn't it?"

"Yeah, I guess."

"And in the meantime, Les would always call you and tell you that you shouldn't go through with the charges, isn't that right?"

"He wouldn't always call. Sometimes he'd come over."

"Would he say something like 'let's drop this and make up,' or would he say 'if you don't drop this, bad things are going to happen to you'?"

"Some of each, I guess. Usually, he'd start with the sweet and, if I didn't go for it, he'd become a little more threatening. But he never did nothin' to cause them fights. It was always all my fault, so I figured I shouldn't get him in trouble."

"So, on all of those occasions, it was never you making an independent choice to drop the charges? You always agreed to do what Les wanted you to do?"

"Well, he brought it up first, but I chose to do it 'cause I thought it was right."

"Was that the way it happened with your first husband as well?"

"Not really. He was more violent and usually just threatened me."

"Was it always your fault then, too?"

She paused as though trying to recall the events. After apparently running a series of encounters through her head, she responded. "Mostly, yeah."

"Was it always your mother's fault when your father argued with her?"

"Your honor," McGuckin pleaded. "I think this goes beyond anything relevant to this case."

Dixon continued to hold Debi's gaze, and the jury now saw McGuckin as not even willing to allow Debi Krueller to explore the demons that haunted her.

"Sustained," Stockman said.

Dixon was disappointed in the ruling, but the question was really all that mattered. His eyes were locked with hers, and he could sense her response. "You say that with Les the arguments were always your fault. Are you telling me he is completely blameless?"

"Pretty much. I mean he always tells me he wouldn't have reacted the way he did if I hadn't done something wrong."

"What kind of things have you done wrong?"

"I don't know. All sorts of bad things."

"Well, I read some of the reports. Wasn't he mad once because he thought you spent too much time on the phone with your sister and he thought he'd missed an important call?"

"Yeah, I guess that was part of it."

"Another time you told him you were too tired to cook dinner and he pushed you into the kitchen and told you not to come out until dinner was ready?"

"That's what I told the sheriff at the time."

"Did you want him to push you into the kitchen?"

"No."

"So that wasn't your choice?"

"No."

"How about the time he bloodied your nose, what had you done wrong that time?"

"I don't remember. I think I was at a bar and I stayed too late and he was worried about me."

"So, because he was worried about you, he bloodied your nose and blackened your eye?"

Debi looked at her husband and McGuckin with desperate eyes. They offered no relief and she had no choice but to answer. "Yes."

"The Friday before the incident, he threw you out of the house, isn't that right?"

"I don't know that. He put my clothes outside, but I don't know what he meant by that."

"You don't know what message he was trying to send?"

"No."

Dixon broke his stare for the first time and walked to the stack on his counsel table. He removed a couple papers and walked back to the lectern. "Mrs. Krueller, isn't it true that the sheriff's office was previously called to your house because Les did something very similar with respect to your daughter? Isn't it true that he removed all her things from the house, and the whole time he kept yelling: 'I want that fucking whore out of here'?"

She paused for a long time and looked around nervously. Her eyelids were fluttering like hummingbird wings. Finally, she quietly responded, "Yes."

"So, while he threw her clothes and belongings in the yard, he yelled that he wanted her out, correct?"

"Yes."

"That's a pretty good indication that when he threw your things out he wanted you out of the house, isn't it?"

She started to answer, but the words weren't there. She raised a hand to her face as though wiping perspiration from her forehead. "I don't know."

"After he threw your daughter's clothes out, you and Les had an argument about it, right?"

"Yes."

"So that wasn't your fault, was it? You were just an innocent bystander to an argument between Les and your daughter."

"I guess."

"Regardless of what you did, do you think there's ever a justification for a man hitting his wife or behaving that way?"

Dixon had her back in his gaze and, with his eyes, implored her to look deep for the answer.

After a few deep breaths, she said, "No." It had seemed to take forever, but Debi had finally taken the first step. She had said out loud that maybe it wasn't just about her being bad.

Dixon's mission now was to keep her from looking at Les or, at a minimum, to keep her from being intimidated by him. "When did you first meet Duke MacKenzie?"

"A year ago last summer."

"That was because you moved into the Chateau Le Blanc Camelot, and Duke was doing some work around the property?"

"Yes."

"How did Duke treat you?"

"I don't know."

"Did you ever have any arguments with him?"

"We weren't together very long."

"Did the two of you ever discuss the arguments you had with Les?"

"Well, he sort of broke one of them up."

"What happened when he did that? Did Les get mad?"

"I don't think he really knew what to do. He was just surprised when Duke showed up. After Duke left, Les thought about it and got mad."

"Let's go back to my question. Did you and Duke ever talk about your fights with Les?"

"Yes."

"What was said?"

"Duke said I was too good for Les and he'd protect me from him."

"How did you respond?"

"Well, for starters, I had sex with him." That response drew a titter from the jury box.

"Was that because you were attracted to him or because you felt like you owed him?"

"I don't know. Some of each maybe." After answering, she was overcome by a brief rush of tears.

"Are you okay?" Dixon asked.

"Yeah, I'll be all right."

Dixon paused to let Debi compose herself. "The night he threw you out of the house . . ."

"Objection," McGuckin spouted. "Assumes facts not in evidence."

Before the judge could respond, Dixon withdrew the question and rephrased. "After having thought about what happened and the fact that Les had previously thrown your daughter's belongings on the lawn, do you now have an understanding of the message Les was trying to send you the night he put your belongings in the yard?"

She paused and finished wiping away the tears. "I understood he was throwing me out of the house."

"Okay. On that night, what did you do?"

"Went to a bar and called Duke."

"Okay, so you previously said you ran into him at the bar, but you actually called him?"

"Yes."

"Why did you call him?"

"I wanted to talk to him."

"About anything in particular?"

"Whether I should stay with him."

"What was there to discuss?"

"Well, we had sneaked around and had sex, but if I went and stayed at his place, Les was likely to find out, so I didn't want to go if it was just a fling and was going to piss Les off."

"What happened next?"

"Duke came to the bar. We talked for a long time, and I followed him home."

"Did you spend the night together?"

"Yes."

"What happened in the morning?"

"I got up, made breakfast, and had some coffee."

"What happened then?"

"Les showed up."

"What did he say?"

"He said something like 'what's going on here, are you having an affair or something?'"

"Were those his exact words?"

Debi quietly stared at her hands. Finally, she responded. "No."

"Did someone tell you that was what you should say today when I asked that question?"

"Objection," McGuckin said. "That question seeks to invade the attorney-client privilege."

"Your honor," Dixon responded, "there's no privilege to suborn perjury even if you are acting as an attorney. If that's what happened, it's not privileged. If that didn't happen, then there was no privileged communication to object to."

"Overruled," Stockman said. "Mrs. Krueller, you can answer."

"That's what Les told me I should say."

Dixon gave her an earnest look and again softened his voice. "Well, I'd like to hear what you have to say."

Debi returned his gaze as she pondered the question. "Les said he thought we were having an affair, and when he caught us he'd blow Duke's head off."

"Were those his precise words?"

Debi had to come clean. "Okay, he said he'd blow his *fucking* head off."

"Did Les say anything threatening to you?"

She hung her head and remained quiet.

"Mrs. Krueller, did you hear the question?"

She nodded a response and hesitantly proceeded. "He said I didn't have to worry because killing me would be too good for me, and that he'd rather torture me for the rest of my life."

Dixon was taken by surprise by the answer and paused to let it sink in with the jury. "Was there any physical contact between any-body at that time?"

"No. Duke just stood there and let Les rant and rave until he left."

"That night you and Duke left town?"

"We went to Duluth."

"What did you do there?"

"Went to a bar. Went to the casino. Went to a hotel."

"Did you have sex?"

"Yes."

"The next day you went back to your house and Les was there, is that right?"

"Yes."

"Why did you go home?"

"I don't know. I was scared about the whole Duke thing."

"Why?"

"If it turned out he only wanted me for one thing, I wouldn't have nowhere to go."

"So you were thinking about reconciling with Les?"

"I don't know. I was just so confused."

"You and Les had another argument?"

"Yes."

"What was that about?"

"Mostly about the fact that I hadn't been home the two nights before."

"What did you say?"

"I said I was really sorry, and that Duke and I hadn't had sex. That I just stayed with him because I didn't have anyplace else to go."

"What was his response?"

"I don't remember. Something like I shoulda stayed with my sister instead."

"So it was your fault again?"

"Yes."

"So, you called Duke again, is that right?"

"Yeah. I called and he invited me and my daughter and her boy-friend over for a barbecue."

"Mr. Donnelly," Judge Stockman interrupted. "We've been going for quite awhile. If this is a good place, I'd like to give the jury a short recess."

Dixon was concerned that any break might upset the momentum, but he had little choice. "That would be fine."

During the break, Debi went out the back with Les and McGuckin. Dixon walked over to Hank. "That Prozac works like truth serum," he said. "Plus it's taken away her attitude."

"I don't t'ink it has anyt'ing to do with the drug," Hank replied. "I may be a country bumpkin, but the way you softened your voice and acted like her therapist is a stroke of genius. She's saying a lot of stuff I think she's wanted to say for a long time."

"Don't give me too much credit. I thought a lot about what Margie said the other night. Maybe my belief in nature over nurture is something that needed to be challenged. I consider Debi to be a congenital liar, but maybe it is a learned skill that can be overcome."

"Well, she probably doesn't lie to her therapist," Hank said. "I'm watching from back here and it seems like there's a connection between the two of you and she just wants to tell you everything. I bet the jury can see it too."

"Well, so far she hasn't told us anything we didn't know," Dixon said. "I mean, she denied some of those things before, but she looked stupid when she did. Her testimony on the threats was helpful, though. I think it was already pretty clear that Les had made the threats, but it solidifies the self-defense issue."

"Stop being so humble," Hank chided. "Take credit where credit is due."

"I'm afraid I've seen too many of these to rest easy. It's going good now, but I'm not declaring victory just yet."

Dixon got quiet when he saw the Kruellers walk back into the courtroom. Debi was in front and was in a huff. It appeared they'd had a "discussion" during the break. If she was suddenly uncooperative, Dixon could bring out the probable influence by Les, and the jury would have little choice but to react adversely to Les and such tactics.

Debi resumed her seat and the court was called to order. Dixon looked at her for a long time in an attempt to project some empathy. "When we left off, you were having a barbecue at Duke's, do you remember that?"

"Yes."

"Les showed up again, is that right?"

"Yes."

"What did he say?"

"I don't remember."

"Do you remember just generally whether the discussions were cordial, threatening, or something else?"

"I think Les said Duke was out of his head to hang around with me, or something like that."

"You don't remember him saying something like he had said before. Something like 'if I catch you having sex with my wife I'll blow your fucking head off'?"

"Not really, no."

Dixon was stunned by her sudden change of course. Either Les or McGuckin had gotten to her, but it was so transparent that even the simplest juror had to be cognizant of what had happened.

Dixon slowed his speech and tried to focus her attention on happy thoughts. He asked a lot of unnecessary questions about the weather, the lake, the food. He thought about asking her what Les had said to her outside the courtroom, but this time she'd probably have a lie to cover it. Giving her a chance to deny it might be just enough for one juror to hang a proverbial hat on.

"Mrs. Krueller, you indicated before that you see a therapist, is that right?"

"Yes."

"Now, what you say to your therapist is confidential, and I don't want you to tell me that. I do, though, want to know how long you've been seeing your therapist."

"Three years, on and off."

"How often do you go?"

"Once a week. Sometimes more."

"Does that help?"

"Well, I'm still going. I don't know if that means it's not helping because I'm still going, or if it means it is helping because I still go."

Dixon continued the therapy discussion, and it seemed to put her back in the therapy mode. He had previously worked through the chronology to the critical events and it was time to go back. "Mrs. Krueller, what time did your daughter and her boyfriend leave on the evening in question?"

"I don't remember for sure. Probably about nine."

"You and Duke then went upstairs to the bedroom, correct?"

"Eventually, yes."

"And you proceeded to have sex?"

"Yes."

"Somewhere during that process, you thought you heard a noise outside, isn't that right?"

"Yes."

"So you stopped what you were doing and looked out the window?"

"I don't think we were doing anything except maybe smoking cigarettes."

"Okay. Did you see anything?"

"Duke thought he did, but I thought he was just being paranoid."

"After that you started having sex again, correct?"

"Yes."

"You were having sex when the sliding glass door was smashed, isn't that right?"

"I don't remember."

Dixon's voice became calm, but stern. "Mrs. Krueller, think about it. We discussed this at your deposition. My only question to you here today is whether you were in the act of having sex."

Debi Krueller had seen other witnesses impeached with prior inconsistent testimony. Her choice was to say yes and hope he moved on, or say no and have the transcript about the unconventional sex read in open court. Dixon was giving her an easy way out and she grabbed the opportunity. "Yes, we were having sex at the time."

"Thank you," Dixon said. "Now, your testimony is that everything happened very quickly and you yelled 'don't shoot, it's Les,' but Duke shot anyway?"

"Right."

"And that Duke ran off and was never seen alive again?"

"Yes."

"And that's what your husband told you to say under oath, isn't it?"

"Well, if he did, that's only because it's true."

"You never heard a second shot, did you?"

"I might have, I don't know."

"Isn't it true that you gave two prior reports to the police and gave a deposition under oath and on all three occasions you said you didn't remember hearing a second shot?"

"Maybe, I don't know."

"And the reason for that is Les hadn't told you what to say on that issue so you were afraid to say anything because you might say something wrong and then Les would be mad, right?"

She glanced around with a look of panic. "Yes ... I mean no. I mean, I don't understand the question."

"You were in the courtroom for the testimony of Deputy Halvorsen, weren't you?"

She nodded her head. Dixon turned an ear toward her as a signal that he needed to hear her answer, and she responded. "Yes, I was here."

"Deputy Halvorsen testified there was another shot fired from the same gun, and he also testified a slug from that gun was taken out of the wall behind the door. Do you recall that testimony?"

"Yes."

"And the bullet hole in the wall was approximately five feet from the ground. Now, how tall would you say Duke MacKenzie was?"

"I don't know. I guess about five feet, six inches."

"So if a pistol was shoved in his mouth and the trigger was pulled, the bullet would be about five feet off the ground?"

Debi looked at Dixon, but looked confused. "I guess."

"Mrs. Krueller, that second bullet—the one found in the wall—was actually the first bullet, wasn't it?" Dixon spoke slowly, but his words were becoming sharper.

"What do you mean?"

"I mean your husband made good on his promise to blow Duke's fucking head off and then, for good measure, Les shot himself in the stomach?"

McGuckin was up in an instant. "Objection! Assumes facts not in evidence."

Dixon did not wait for the judge to respond. "That's the point of the question. To get the facts into evidence."

Stockman agreed. "Overruled."

"Mrs. Krueller," Dixon resumed, "Les shot Duke and then faked his own injury like he faked his disability claim, isn't that right?"

Debi Krueller was starting to tremble. "No, that's not what happened."

Dixon sensed there was something she was wanting to tell, and his intensity increased as he pursued it. "Did Les have you shoot him in the stomach?"

"No, of course not."

"You heard the testimony about where Duke's remains were found, didn't you?"

"Yes."

"And nobody familiar with the property would have run that way, would they?"

"I . . . I don't know." She was becoming increasingly upset.

"Somebody unfamiliar with the property might go that way in order to dump a body though?"

She was dabbing tears again. "I don't know anything about that," she protested.

"And you had to help?"

"That's what you say. You're trying to put words in my mouth."

"No. Lester put words in your mouth because he told you what to say here under oath. Isn't that right?"

"No." She was squirming in her chair. "I don't know."

"Mrs. Krueller, Les's gunshot wound was self-inflicted, wasn't it?"

"No, that one was fired by Duke, I swear it."

Dixon stopped to ponder her words. "When you say 'that one was fired by Duke,' you mean as opposed to the other one that was fired by someone else?"

"I . . . I don't know."

"Yes you do, Mrs. Krueller. The other shot was fired by someone else, wasn't it?"

Debi Krueller looked around desperately and her eyes welled up again. "I don't remember. It all happened too fast."

"Mrs. Krueller," Dixon said slowly. "A man is dead. We want to know what happened, and we want you to tell us."

She was now crying profusely. "It all happened so fast. I don't know."

"Mrs. Krueller, you're under oath. Tell us what happened."

She was still teary-eyed, but trying to compose herself. "We . . . we heard a big smash and then Les was at the door and Duke grabbed the gun and shot. He didn't want to, he just had to. He said he'd protect me and here was Les, and there wasn't anything else Duke could do. And then after Duke shot Les, he was all upset because it was the last thing Duke wanted to do."

"Okay. Then what happened?"

Debi's voice got higher as her emotions overtook her. "Duke swore at Les. He said 'goddamnit, you son of a bitch, what didja hafta make me go and do that for?' Les was hurt, but it wasn't real bad or nothin' and Duke went to help him." She paused as shivers passed through her.

Dixon waited to see if she would continue on her own. When she remained silent, he prompted her. "What happened next?"

"Duke set the gun down on a table or something. He helped Les up and then Les grabbed the gun and said 'I've got you now, you sonofabitch. I . . . I told you I'd blow your fucking head off.' Then Les stuck the gun in Duke's mouth and pulled the trigger. I screamed. I was going crazy." She broke down and began sobbing again.

Les Krueller was on his feet. "What the hell are you talking about?! You better shut your goddamn mouth this instant!"

McGuckin pulled his client down while rising himself and shout-
ing, "Your honor, this woman is by her own admission under the
influence of drugs. This testimony must be stricken from the record."

The collective whispering and shuffling of the rest of the courtroom created a minor din. Judge Stockman seemed as transfixed as
everybody else, but then pounded his gavel to call the Court back to
order. "Overruled," he said. "You can explore that subject on redirect,
but it's not a basis to exclude the testimony."

McGuckin retook his seat, but his beet red face continued to
dominate the room.

Dixon was as stunned as everybody else. Debi Krueller's head
was now in her hands. Dixon finally continued. "Okay, then what
happened?"

Her voice was quieter and halting at times. "Les made me put a
garbage bag around Duke's head to keep blood from getting all over,
and then we dragged the body outside. Les was hurt, but he could
still get around. We dragged the body across the grass, but when
we got to the dirt Les didn't want any drag marks so we had to pick
him up. With Les being hurt, we couldn't carry the body very far.
We threw him in the woods and threw the gun next to him. Then
I had to go back because Les had forgot to wipe the prints off the
gun. Then we went back in the house and Les made me clean up the
blood on the wall and rinse the blood off the plastic bag. Les came
up with this story about Duke just running off, and he thought it
would look better if we were fighting because it wouldn't look like
we were in cahoots."

"Why did you go along with it?"

"What else could I do? I was scared of Les and had no place else
to go, with Duke being dead."

"So then Les called 911?"

"Yes."

"And the two of you have been telling this lie ever since?"

"Yes."

Dixon was terrified of asking one too many questions, but hesitant to finish his examination if there was something he missed. He
looked at Hank, who could barely hide his emotions from the jury.

He looked at the jury, and they all seemed satisfied. He swung around another ninety degrees and saw Sheriff José and Perry Passieux in the gallery. Neither of them looked as if anything was left unanswered. "Your honor," Dixon said. "I have nothing further for this witness."

McGuckin was now in the unenviable position of trying to discredit his own witness. The perspiration was starting to mat down his comb-over. He desperately shuffled papers as though he were looking for something, but there was nothing there. He asked questions about the drugs she was on and the dosage. He asked questions about her screwed up personal life and the lies she had told before to get Les in trouble. He asked about how much she had drunk the night of the incident. In short, he pulled out all the stops to undo what Debi had just done. For her part, she answered the questions and stuck to her story. McGuckin became more and more abusive in his manner, but her story didn't change.

McGuckin, who had once tried to discredit the sheriff's reports, was now trying to establish that her early recollections were the more reliable. The problem was that her early recollections were substantially the same as what she had just said in court—right up until the moment Les grabbed the gun. Debi had previously excluded that incident from her recollection.

McGuckin finally gave up. The more he attacked her, the worse he looked. When McGuckin concluded, Dixon asked to approach the bench and suggested to the judge that Debi be escorted out after the jury was dismissed. Stockman thought that was a good idea, and asked Sheriff José to take responsibility. The judge then declared a recess so McGuckin could assess what to do.

McGuckin and Krueller exited to the outer corridor. Dixon walked over to Passieux, who was wearing a broad smile that kept getting broader. "What did you think of that?" Dixon asked.

"That was something," Passieux replied. "There was circumstantial evidence that Les might have pulled the trigger, but I never really believed he did it. Her testimony was huge. Unfortunately for McGuckin, he doesn't yet know how huge."

"You mean . . ."

"That's right," Passieux said, with a smile. "The Court of Appeals decision came in." Passieux raised his fists like he was cheering at a sporting event. "We lost! The assault conviction has been vacated."

"That's awesome," Dixon said. "So, what's the plan now?"

"Well, since there's no double jeopardy if we charge him again, we'll charge him for attacking his wife, and now we can charge him with murder and manslaughter based on the testimony Debi just gave."

"That's great," said Dixon. "Good job."

"Thanks, but it's hard to call taking a dive in front of the Court of Appeals a good job."

"Well, you achieved the desired outcome. Who could ask for more?"

Passieux was still beaming. "Ordinarily, I call opposing counsel to congratulate them when they beat me, but I'm not sure I could do that in this case."

"What will happen now?" Dixon asked.

"We won't get the case file back till next week, but we'll move as quickly as possible."

"That's fabulous," Dixon said. "Let me go tell my client."

◆

$525,600. That was the amount the jury awarded to the estate of Duane "Duke" MacKenzie. Dixon had not really prepared for the possibility that he might actually recover something on the wrongful death claim, so he hadn't prepared any testimony or exhibits. In Minnesota, wrongful death damages are calculated primarily as the monetary value of the amounts the deceased would have been expected to provide to his or her dependents. Thus, the price for killing a single man with no minor children is pretty much zero.

As a result of Debi's courtroom disclosure, Dixon was allowed to add a claim for punitive damages. $525,600 represented one dollar for every minute of one year. Dixon had been at a loss as to how to rationalize any other amount, and Hank later chided him for failing to use a leap year in calculating the amount because that cost the estate almost $1,500. All things considered, very little of it would probably be collectable anyway.

The importance of the verdict was that the jury cleared Duke of any liability, and the testimony provided a basis to charge Les Krueller with substantially more than assault. Furthermore, after the verdict came in, the insurance company lawyer congratulated Dixon and Hank and promised he'd get the insurance company to pony up. He reasoned that the testimony made the shooting of Les Krueller seem to be fairly reflexive and, in any event, the particular facts might make it a bad test case. He also said the last thing he ever wanted to do was face Dixon in trial.

# CHAPTER 39

The adrenaline had kept Dixon in high gear during the trial, but he was exhausted shortly after the verdict had been returned. Hank and Dixon had agreed that Dixon would return for Les Krueller's criminal trial and that they'd have a proper celebration then. For now, Dixon was anxious to get back and see Jessica. Her assignment in Minneapolis was nearing an end and Dixon intended to make the best use of their remaining time together.

About an hour from town, he called her on his cell phone. After several rings, a soft, sleepy voice said "hello."

"Hey, it's me," Dixon said. "I didn't wake you, did I?"

"Not really. I'm afraid I have the flu and was just kind of napping on the couch."

"I'm sorry to hear that."

"How's your trial going?" she asked.

"We're done. We won. In fact, we won more than I ever thought we could win."

"How could that happen?"

"I'd really like to see you. How about if I tell you about it when I get there. Will you still be up in an hour?"

"I'll be up, but I'm a wreck. I haven't washed my hair or put in my contact lenses. You don't want to see me."

"Let me assure you," Dixon said softly, "there's nothing I want to do more than see you."

"Well, I should still be up if you're sure you want to come over. Maybe you could pick up some 7 Up on the way."

"Will do. See you soon."

Dixon clicked the disconnect button and pushed a little harder on the accelerator. Between the time-out and the trial, he hadn't seen her for two weeks, and he was eager for that to change.

Dixon tried to call Sandy to tell him about the trial, but it was Saturday night and he didn't answer his phone. The minutes were speeding by like hours. Finally, he found a basketball game on the radio and that proved to be a suitable distraction.

When he arrived, he knocked gently on Jessica's door. He fully intended to wake her if need be, but didn't want to startle her. After a few moments, she appeared and opened the door. "Come on in," she said softly, as she turned and walked away in an apparent effort to keep him from seeing her. She was wearing pajamas and a bathrobe. Her hair hung somewhat limp, and she wore wire-rimmed glasses that were so far out of style it suggested she never wore them in public and, as a result, had never updated the frames.

"How are you doing?" Dixon asked.

"Well, I look like hell," she responded.

Dixon walked over and took a place on the couch next to her. He stared at her for a long moment. "I'm flattered you want to look nice for me. It makes me feel good you want to do that. But I think you're beautiful no matter what." He paused until she returned eye contact. "You're obviously not feeling well, but your eyes still sparkle, and you still have a glow about you."

Jessica stared back. After a pause, she smiled and said, "Thank you."

"Now com'ere," he said, as he wrapped his arms around her shoulders and pulled her next to him.

Jessica stiffened to his embrace. "You don't want to catch this from me."

"I'm not planning on exchanging bodily fluids with you, but I missed you and I want to hold you for a while." She relented and wrapped her arms behind his back and they hugged for a long time. Dixon then guided her until she was lying on the couch with her back to him. Dixon lay behind her and draped one arm around her waist. They were still for several minutes.

Finally he spoke. "During trial, things were so hectic I didn't have time to think about anything else. But every night, I thought about being with you, just like this."

"Did I look this bad in your mind's eye?"

"Well, I know you weren't wearing the glasses, because I've never seen them before."

"If I'd known you were coming, maybe I would have tried not to get sick."

"Did you think about us at all while we were apart?"

She didn't answer immediately. "Yeah, I guess."

"Any epiphanies?"

"No. I mean, I thought about it, but if you're expecting me to just say 'I'm sorry, it's my fault, I'll change,' I don't think that's going to happen."

Dixon respected her resolve, but was disappointed in her response. "How about if we just lie here awhile longer and enjoy the moment?"

After several minutes, Jessica got up for the 7 Up. As she walked back from the kitchen she announced that she'd managed to get her old apartment back in Atlanta. She seemed pleased, but it was about the last thing Dixon wanted to think about.

"Starting when?" he played along.

"First of the year. The person who had taken it was going to school, but apparently decided to drop out or transfer."

"That's great, I guess. Aren't you going to miss the Minnesota winter?"

"Hardly."

"Aren't you going to miss your Minnesota boyfriend?"

She stopped to ponder the question. "You can come and visit me sometime."

"I don't think that would make it any easier. If I'm going to have to quit you, I'll probably be better off doing it cold turkey."

That response didn't sit well with her. "Well, if you don't want to see me again, fine."

"That's not what I said and you know it. I want very much to see you again, but if we're just a fling it might be easier on me to just move on and try to get over you."

"I've only got about a month left here. Are you saying it would be easier if we stopped seeing each other now?"

"That's not something I want," he responded. "It might be easier in the long run, but I'd prefer to spend as much time together as possible."

Jessica accepted that. She didn't provide any encouragement that the long-term future was going to be any different, but she was willing to go with the short-term plan.

Jessica took a long drink of her 7 Up. All of a sudden, her eyes got wide and the soda came up as fast as it had gone down. That was quickly followed by the more substantial contents of her stomach. She jumped up to run for the bathroom, but another eruption occurred halfway there. Dixon, who had narrowly missed having the first load deposited on him, got up and followed her. She reached the toilet and the onslaught continued.

When it stopped, Dixon asked if she was okay.

"I feel okay right now, but just let me sit here a minute."

Dixon left and went to the kitchen to find a towel and a bucket. He soaked the towel and returned to the living room to start the cleanup. He blotted up most of the larger puddle and used the towel to scoop the pieces. He rinsed the towel and had started over on the second splash when Jessica came out of the bathroom.

"What are you doing?" she asked.

"I'm cleaning up."

"You don't have to clean up my vomit."

"Well, you don't want to lose your damage deposit, do you?"

"No, but I can clean it up."

"Just relax, Jessica. You're not feeling well. I'll take care of it."

She smiled before going to the kitchen to enlist some additional weapons against the mess she'd made. Together they blotted up the contents and then took fresh towels and soaked the stains. "Aren't you glad you came over?" she joked.

"I'm not complaining," he said.

They finished the task and resumed their spots on the couch. "I'm going to go pretty soon," Dixon said, "but I want to hold you a little longer before I do. Just keep pointing that puke cannon away from me."

"You really didn't have to clean it up," she said again.

"Yeah, so?"

"I mean, that's gross. Why would you do that?"

"Jessica, look. I know we haven't known each other very long and I know it's kind of early in our relationship, but we have some unique circumstances so I have to explain something to you. I didn't clean it up because I felt like I had to. I cleaned it up because I wanted to. I wanted to help you and I wanted to be there for you. I cleaned it up because I would want and hope that you would be there for me."

Jessica appeared to be at a loss for words.

"Look," Dixon continued, "I don't want to make you uncomfortable, but we don't have that much time left together, so there's something I have to tell you. I know you don't want to get emotionally attached because you're leaving soon and, in your words, that's a fast lane to heartbreak. Well, I wasn't that smart. I didn't plan it well enough, because I'm already in the fast lane to heartbreak. I have never felt this way about anyone before. The fact of the matter is I love you and I'm in love with you and doing things to make you happy or to ease your suffering is reason enough for me to do something."

He paused to give her an opportunity to respond. He didn't expect her to say anything, and his expectation proved to be correct. Finally, he spoke. "I'm sorry to lay that on you like that, but I felt like it was something that had to be said."

Jessica's eyes became blurred by the tears she was trying to hold back. "I don't know if I planned so well either," she said. "I did think about you while we were apart. I think I'm going to miss you, but I don't know what I can do about it."

"I think the first thing you have to do is decide we're not just a fling. You don't have to make any other commitment to what the relationship is, but we have to remove the artificial time clock we've been operating under and look at this as though we might have a future together. We need to start with the possible and then see where it goes from there."

"What if it doesn't?"

"There's never any guarantees, and I don't want you to feel pressured. I just want you to give it a chance."

"I know what you're saying, but I'm just not sure. Couples have enough problems and our geographic distance is just one more. Maybe it would be easier not to pursue this."

"There's no question it would be easier," he responded, "but that's not the point. Love isn't about easy. The obstacles people overcome are part of what makes love what it is."

"Dixon, you have me so confused."

"Just think about what I said. You don't need to make any quick decisions. I just want to make sure you understand exactly how I feel."

They lay in each other's arms for several more minutes. Dixon finally said he'd let her get some sleep and went home. Jessica walked him to the door and looked at him longingly. In the end, she didn't say anything. She just hugged him again.

# CHAPTER 40

IT ONLY TOOK SIX WEEKS for Lester Krueller to be back in court. Upon receiving the remand of the criminal case, Judge Stockman notified Passieux and McGuckin that one of his weeks reserved for criminal proceedings was open and about a month away.

"A month isn't much time to prepare for a murder trial," McGuckin had protested.

Judge Stockman was of a different mind. "You've already tried most of this case twice. I realize you might need some time to get an expert and explore the new forensic issues, but you've got almost a month. If you have a problem with the expert stuff, come back and see me and if I think you've been diligent I'll give it some thought. Your client's out on bail, however, and, now that the charge is murder, I might need to consider whether the extra time creates a flight risk." That was Judge Stockman's gentle way of telling McGuckin that the trial would proceed or else.

As planned, Dixon made his triumphant return to Hibbing. He drove up the morning of trial, as he was content to skip jury selection this time around. He met Hank for lunch beforehand.

"I don't think I can sit through this trial again," Dixon said. "I've already seen this show twice. I liked the ending once and hated it once."

"Will this be the last of it?" Hank asked.

"That's hard to say. The time hasn't run for McGuckin to appeal our verdict, so there's a chance we could retry that case. Furthermore, Home Protection looks like they're going to pay the insurance claim, but, until we get the check, there's always the possibility that we'd go to trial against them."

"What happens if Passieux isn't as good as you and Debi goes back to her first story?"

"That's a great question. If she says something different, Passieux will trot out the transcript from the last time. The problem is that the transcript isn't as convincing because it's just cold words on a page and the emotion won't be there."

"Could it affect our case?" Hank asked. "I mean, could the judge go back and say 'well, I guess maybe Les didn't do the shooting after all, so I'm going to throw out the other verdict?'"

"Not on his own initiative. I suppose McGuckin could make a motion that key testimony was false, so Lester should get a new trial, but I don't see that happening. Judge Stockman saw Debi testify, and it was pretty clear that she was finally telling the whole truth."

"As much as I like you, Dixon, I'd sure like to start seeing you a little less. At least under these circumstances."

"I don't blame you for that. As much as I like the commute to the Iron Range, it was more fun in the summer when I didn't have to contend with the winter driving conditions."

A few minutes of silence passed while they tended to their meals. "How've you been otherwise?" Hank asked. "Did you have a good holiday?"

"I think the only word for it would be 'bittersweet,'" Dixon responded. "I've apparently spent two Christmases now with Jessica—first and last."

"That's too bad. What . . . did you have a fight?"

"No. Everything about it was splendid. We spent Christmas Eve together. We made dinner and exchanged gifts. After that we walked around the lake and it started to snow. It was like in the movies."

"Sounds nice," Hank said.

"That's the problem. She moved back to Atlanta a week later. We didn't even get to spend New Year's Eve together because she had to get back in order to unpack and everything."

"So is that it? You're just done?"

"I guess. I might try and visit her this spring, but I'm afraid that would just prolong my misery."

"Have you talked at all since she's been gone?"

"She called me two weeks ago when she first got there to let me know she arrived safe and everything. I wasn't going to call her, but I finally broke down and tried her a couple days ago. I got her machine, and I think she was gone for the weekend, 'cause I haven't heard from her."

"Any of that stuff Margie said do any good?"

"Well, it worked with Debi Krueller, but I'm afraid it wasn't enough for Jessica Palmer. If we'd had more time together it might have happened, but I just couldn't move her."

"Can't you date long-distance?"

"Of course we could, but it's the emotional distance that's the problem. If she would have made some commitment to the relation-ship, we could have found a solution to the proximity issue."

"Sounds like maybe you're better off. I mean I could tell she meant a lot to you, but maybe it's like Margie said and you'd be chasing a dream forever."

"That's what I keep telling myself."

"Maybe you should move up here. I'm sure we could find you a nice gal to settle down with."

Dixon smiled. "I'll sure keep that in mind. For now, I think I'll stick with what I have. I realize it isn't much, but I think I'll try and make the best of it."

The check came and Hank insisted on paying it. "I can still charge this to the estate as administration fees," he said, with a wink. Dixon was happy to defer.

They crossed the street to the courthouse. When they got to the courtroom, it was empty. There were files and notepads on the tables, but no one in sight. They went around to where the intercom was situated for entry into chambers. Before they could buzz it, Stockman's clerk came through the door.

"What's up with the Krueller trial?" Dixon asked.

"They picked the jury first thing, and we just had opening state-ments. The judge sent everyone to lunch, and I think we're going to have some motions first thing after we reconvene."

"Motions?" Dixon said. "About what?"

"Debi Krueller wasn't in court this morning, and it's not clear what's going to happen with that." The clerk gave a curt smile and hustled off.

"There's one we didn't think of," Hank remarked. "What does that mean?"

"I don't really know. I'm sure she's not eager to testify again, and I'm not sure Les is that eager to have her up on the stand either. But her testimony is critical."

"I tell ya, Dixon, when this is all over you should write a book. This is about the wildest ride I've ever been on."

"I think the story might be too hard to believe."

Hank laughed. "You might be right. Starting with that damn bear eating Duke." After a pause, Hank said, "Sounds like we got some time to kill."

"I think you're right. I'm gonna run up to the law library and check this out. I'm not sure what happens in a criminal trial when a witness doesn't show up."

"Can't they just read the transcript to the jury?"

"That's what I don't know offhand. Any out-of-court statement is subject to the hearsay rules. I just don't know what the exceptions are off the top of my head."

Hank decided to run some errands while Dixon researched. They agreed to meet back at the courtroom at two.

♦

As they arrived back at the courtroom, Stockman was already taking the bench. Dixon and Hank took a place in the gallery. Stockman addressed the lawyers. "I've told the jury to take some extra time so we can discuss the issues. Mr. Passieux, please proceed."

"Thank you, your honor. We served Debra Krueller with a subpoena two weeks ago. I have the Affidavit of Service right here, and I can have the deputy who served it testify if necessary. The subpoena commands her presence here today, but she's not here and the defense won't tell me whether she will be in attendance."

Judge Stockman turned to the defense. "Mr. McGuckin, it seems like Mr. Passieux is at least entitled to an answer to the question of whether she will appear."

"Your honor," McGuckin said, rising to his feet, "her presence is unnecessary because we are going to assert the marital privilege against her being compelled to testify against her spouse."

"Hasn't she already waived that privilege by testifying at the civil trial?" Stockman asked.

"No, your honor, because she took the stand in order to testify in favor of her spouse. It just turned out the testimony didn't come out too favorable. In this case, it's clear she is being called to testify against her spouse and so she is asserting that privilege."

Passieux jumped in. "She's claiming privilege or you're claiming it for her?"

McGuckin responded, "It doesn't really matter. The privilege can be asserted by either spouse."

"Your honor," Passieux pleaded, "one of the exceptions to the privilege is a case involving domestic abuse. The Complaint now includes an assault count related to the threats made against Debi Krueller."

McGuckin wasn't fazed. "Even if she could be compelled to testify against him on the claim that he assaulted her, that shouldn't open the door for her to testify about every other thing under the sun."

Judge Stockman had heard as much as he needed. "I think we need to talk to Mrs. Krueller to see what she thinks. I don't know if the husband can assert the privilege on a wife's behalf in a domestic abuse case, so I'd like to talk to her. Will that be possible?"

"Actually," McGuckin said, "probably not."

"Why is that?" Stockman asked.

"As far as we can tell, she's in chemical dependency treatment."

Stockman turned to Passieux. "What's your position on that?"

"We'll have to get a reader to read her part and we'll use the transcript from the civil trial."

"You can't do that," McGuckin snapped. "That's hearsay. Out-of-court statements are hearsay and can't be put in the record."

"It might be hearsay," Passieux responded, "but it qualifies for a hearsay exception." Passieux had anticipated the argument and flipped open his rulebook. "Rule 804 of the Rules of Evidence states there is an exception to the hearsay rule when a witness is unavailable as follows, and I quote: 'Testimony given as a witness at another hearing of the same or a different proceeding, or in a deposition taken in compliance with law in the course of the same or another proceeding, if the party against whom the testimony is now offered, had an opportunity and similar motive to develop the testimony by direct, cross, or redirect examination.'" Passieux clapped the book closed. "This witness is unavailable because one of the accepted reasons for unavailability is not being able to testify because of a mental infirmity. Consequently, the exception applies."

"But it would still violate the spousal privilege," McGuckin stated.

Passieux was well armed. "Actually, Mr. McGuckin is not right about that. Putting aside that I think the privilege was waived when she took the stand, regardless of what testimony was expected, Rule 804 specifically goes on to define 'unavailable' to include a situation where a person is ruled to be exempt from testifying because of a privilege. In other words, even if she showed up and even if your honor ruled that, no, in fact, she didn't have to testify, the prior testimony is still admissible."

Stockman had opened his own rulebook and was following along. He nodded in agreement. "That's the way it looks to me. Mr. McGuckin, would you like a little time to do some research. I want to be fair to you, but I can't see a reason not to let the transcript into evidence."

"But, your honor, her testimony was so unreliable. It conflicts with her deposition and all of the other reports she gave to the sheriff's office. You can't let it in."

"Mr. McGuckin, you will be free to put in the inconsistent deposition testimony. Frankly, I witnessed the testimony in question, and I think it might have been the only reliable evidence she ever gave. If we were in a larger community, you might now be in front of a different judge who would not have that perspective. But, as it happens, I'm the same judge and I don't think there's a reason to exclude it as unreliable."

"But, your honor," McGuckin continued, "her testimony came as a surprise last time, and I didn't have the same motive or opportunity to attack the testimony."

"That's not the way I remember it," Stockman said. "You did an excellent job trying to discredit the testimony. In the end, you just didn't succeed."

Hank leaned over to Dixon. "Who's right on this?"

"The judge is. I was looking up the same rule Passieux is quoting. If she isn't here, the transcript goes in. Has there been any scuttle-butt around town about those two? Are they still together?"

"I haven't heard, but no one has seen her around town for a while."

Stockman now turned to Passieux. "Had you planned to call her today?"

"Probably not. And since I'll have to get a reader, for sure it will be tomorrow."

"Okay," Stockman said. "Then here's my ruling. If she shows up tomorrow, it will be up to her or the defendant to decide if the spousal privilege is being invoked. If it is, I'll decide the issue at that time. If she doesn't show up, the transcript can go in." Passieux's face was aglow, as he appeared to have the upper hand on McGuckin for the first time in a long time.

"Is that everything then?" the judge asked. Hearing nothing, the judge summoned the jury and the testimony began. Deputy Halvorsen strolled to the stand to tell his story for the third time.

Hank and Dixon suffered through the afternoon in silence.

# CHAPTER 41

SLEEP WAS NOT a commodity in oversupply in Dixon's room that evening. The anticipation of how Debi would testify had been great, but somehow the anticipation of whether she would even show up was greater. Without her, there would be little chance to seriously undermine her prior testimony. While she had told lies before, under the circumstances her absence seemed like it was probably driven by Les's brutish behavior. As a result, he was getting exactly what he deserved.

The phone rang in Dixon's motel room at seven. It was Passieux. "I didn't wake you, did I?"

"No, I've been up for a while. What's going on?"

"Can you and Hank be at the courthouse by eight? McGuckin called me last night and wants to talk about a plea bargain. Strictly speaking, it's my call, but I want to be able to consult you if we can come up with something."

"That should be fine. I was meeting Hank for breakfast anyway, so we'll come straight over."

Dixon met Hank and told him what was transpiring. "What kind of plea agreement?" Hank asked, with equal parts anger and exasperation.

"I have no idea. I assume he'll want to plead to manslaughter or something like that in exchange for Passieux dropping the rest."

"Do you t'ink a plea agreement is a good idea from our side?" Hank asked.

"Depending on the deal, I think it could be a good idea. Remember, in our trial we only had to prove guilt by a preponderance of the evidence. This time the standard is beyond a reasonable doubt.

I think the most important thing is that Krueller gets some real jail time."

"That's for damn sure. I sure as hell don't want him just going to the workhouse and then thumbin' his nose around town at me."

Dixon and Hank arrived at the County Attorney's office. From the waiting area they could see Passieux in a conference room with McGuckin and Krueller. No Debi Krueller in sight.

Passieux noticed Dixon and Hank and gave them a half wave. He came out and directed them into his office. "McGuckin wants to plead to assault if we drop the murder and manslaughter charges."

"What do you think?" Dixon asked Passieux.

"Well, we have some problems with the murder charge anyway. I mean, it was basically what's known as a 'felony murder' charge, which means that somebody died while Krueller was committing a felony. The problem is that he was acquitted of the burglary charge, so it's not clear that we really have an independent felony."

"What about the manslaughter charge?" Dixon asked.

"That's as solid as Debi Krueller's testimony," Passieux responded.

Hank spoke up. "That seems pretty clear to me. Her testimony was great and, if she's not here, so much the better."

"What kind of a sentence would he be looking at?" Dixon asked.

"The sentencing guidelines with his record would be about twelve to eighteen months."

"I don't think that's enough," Dixon said. "With good behavior and whatnot, he might be out in six months. I mean, the son of a bitch killed a man."

"I'll propose manslaughter two, that's about three to five years," Passieux said.

"How can it only be manslaughter?" Dixon protested. "He swore that he'd kill Duke and he did."

Passieux appeared a little impatient at having to justify his actions. "Yeah, but with Duke's gun. If Les had carried his own piece it would be easy. In this case, it looks like the opportunity presented itself and the act was spontaneous."

"Don't you think he would have attacked him with the shovel?" Dixon persisted.

"Let me try for manslaughter one," Passieux replied.

Dixon and Hank both reluctantly approved and Passieux departed. After several minutes he returned. "McGuckin says Debi has told too many stories to be believed. He acknowledges a jury could find his client guilty, but that doesn't seem to matter. Any homicide on his record would screw him up for the rest of his life. He'll admit that Les broke in with the intent to harm and he carried the shovel in with the intent of using it as a weapon. He'll plead to aggravated assault against Duke and aggravated domestic assault against Debi. The sentencing range on that is twenty-six to forty months, and he wants us to agree to recommend thirty months with five years probation after that."

Hank responded first. "So, we have all this evidence and now he's willing to be punished for the t'ings everyone always knew he did anyway?"

"That's about the size of it," Passieux responded. "But we get the certainty of knowing he actually will be punished."

Hank shook his head in disgust. "This is really horseshit."

"Can I have a moment with my client?" Dixon asked. After Passieux departed, Dixon put his hand on Hank's shoulder. "I think it's time for me to give you what other lawyers call the 'come-to-Jesus' speech. Ordinarily, my job is just to get at the truth. If clients want to compromise, that's their decision, but I always want to fight the fight. This case is a little different because I'm just here as your friend, and it won't be my responsibility to get the conviction. It's your decision, but there are some things I'd like you to consider."

"I'm listening," Hank responded.

"The legal process is all about timing. Every case of any duration will have shifts in momentum. Right when everything seems to be going your way, the momentum can shift. We've already seen that in this case. Krueller was on top of the world after the first criminal trial and figured things could only get better. He filed the appeal because he thought he could do no wrong. Well, look at how the momentum has changed. He should have quit while he was ahead. He could have walked away a virtual winner, but he sought an all-out victory and now look where he stands. I don't want you to make the same mistake."

"What do you mean?"

"Right now you have a chance to choose an outcome that grants you certainty and punishes the man who killed your brother. If you push too hard, something might happen and you'll miss the chance. Who knows, Debi Krueller might still show up and then all bets are off."

Hank listened, but he didn't appear too happy. "So ya t'ink I should okay the deal?"

"I think Passieux might do the deal regardless of what we say. You could be angry about that and act bitter for the rest of your life, or you can embrace the deal and enjoy the fact that it was primarily your persistence and a lot of luck that got us to this point."

Hank nodded and appeared to reluctantly agree with Dixon's words.

"Besides," Dixon continued, "do you really want to go through another trial and the anxiety of more jury deliberations?"

"I guess not," Hank replied. "But this just seems like we're giving in."

"I don't want to sound trite, but sometimes discretion is the better part of valor. Even if Passieux gets the manslaughter conviction, there will be another appeal and Les will most likely continue to remain free on bail pending that. I think the momentum has shifted completely your way, and you should take advantage of it before it shifts back."

"I understand," Hank said. "Let's tell Passieux it's okay."

Dixon called Passieux back into the room. Hank was the first to speak. "Perry, I guess that's okay. But if that's what you're going to do, at least promise me they'll haul his ass away soon so that I won't have to see him around town."

"I'll do what I can," Passieux assured him. "Why don't you guys head up to the courtroom and we'll be up in a minute."

There wasn't much to see, but Dixon and Hank wanted to witness the nightmare coming to an end. They perched themselves in the back. McGuckin and Krueller walked in without any of the swagger they had been affecting before. Passieux had called the judge to announce the development, and the jury was kept waiting, pending the conclusion.

Passieux ran through the drill of reading the charges, taking the pleas, asking Krueller to admit that he understood the charges and was, in fact, guilty. The deal was explained to the judge and read into the record. Stockman accepted the plea and indicated the sentencing recommendation was acceptable, but that he couldn't impose sentence until the presentencing report was completed.

"Mr. Krueller," Passieux said. "You've agreed to be incarcerated. Many defendants prefer to begin serving their sentences as soon as possible in order to get it over with. If you like, we can start the incarceration in the next week or so and then formally sentence you once the report comes back. Otherwise, you can wait around a couple months until we get the report."

"I guess the sooner the better," Krueller said. "I just need some time to get things in order."

"That's what we'll do then," Stockman said. "Mr. Passieux will notify you of a time and place to report. We will pass sentence when we receive the report, and you will retain all rights to appeal the sentence. Now, if there's nothing else, this Court stands adjourned." Stockman banged his gavel and the saga ended. McGuckin and Krueller skulked out as beaten men.

Hank put one arm around Dixon's shoulder and shook his hand. "Thanks for everything, Dixon. I gotta tell ya, this whole t'ing's been a livin' hell, but I felt better about it from the moment you started on the case."

# CHAPTER 42

THE SIDE LAKE SUPPER CLUB didn't ordinarily keep champagne on hand. It was only two weeks after New Year's Eve, however, so the waitress was able to round up a bottle. Hank raised his glass. "To Dixon Donnelly. The finest lawyer money can buy." Hank, Margie, and Dixon clinked glasses and sipped.

"You're too kind," Dixon said.

Hank was beaming. "When I first came to see you, I asked you to handle everything, including the criminal trial. According to Passieux, this is the first time he's ever heard of a private attorney essentially getting a criminal conviction because of a civil trial."

"Well, I'll admit this appears to be one for the ages. In that regard, I have a toast as well." Dixon raised his glass. "To Hank MacKenzie. The truest test of character is a person's ability to deal with adversity, and he set an example for all the world to follow."

Hank smiled with embarrassment, but joined the toast. As the waitress refilled their glasses, she offered to put another bottle on ice. The jubilant trio assured her they'd switch to the hard stuff after the bubbly was gone.

Margie MacKenzie was next. "To Debi Krueller, whose testimony came just in the nick of time."

"Well, Margie," Dixon piped in, "I think we have you to thank for that testimony. My normal routine is to crucify witnesses, and I don't think she'd have given up her testimony if I hadn't taken the approach I did."

"I wasn't telling you how to deal with Debi," Margie responded. "I was telling you how to deal with Jessica."

An unhappy smile crossed Dixon's face. "Well, it didn't work with Jessica, but it sure worked with Debi Krueller."

"Time will tell," Margie said. "Don't give up too soon."

They completed the toast and sat quietly enjoying the moment. After a pause, Hank turned to Dixon. "What will you do now that this is all over?"

"I've got a little vacation coming up, but otherwise it will just be back to the grind. I'll get to go to depositions and ask people about the 'obsolescence assumptions' that were made in valuing the inventory of a company they bought instead of asking them what their favorite sexual position is."

"Maybe this could be the start of a new niche practice," Margie said.

Dixon chuckled at the thought. "I think I could safely claim that I'm the only lawyer in the state who handles claims against homeowners who have sex with the neighbor's wife and are then wrongly accused of shooting the neighbor when he breaks in. I'm just not sure how wide my target market is."

"Maybe you should do criminal law," she persisted.

"Criminal law is interesting," Dixon responded, "but your clients are generally criminals. This case was a rare opportunity to have criminal-law issues, but I got to represent honest, decent people. I mean, who would want McGuckin's practice? All he deals with are the dregs of society."

"It's paid his bills," Hank said.

"I don't know how he's going to get paid in this one," Dixon said. "Considering what happened, I'm not sure he deserves to get paid. I can't believe he did what he did knowing Les and Debi were hiding a secret like that."

"I t'ink maybe you're being too hard on old Earl," Hank said. "I don't t'ink he had any idea what Debi was going to testify to."

Dixon paused to reflect. "You might be right, but if that's the case, this is the clearest example of what happens when you don't tell your lawyer everything. I guess Les has no one to blame but himself."

"I'm not sure about that either," Hank replied.

"What do you mean?"

"I'm not sure Les knew about it either."

"How could Les not know about it? He pulled the trigger. We were just lucky we found the bullet."

Hank took a long drink until his champagne was gone. "You mean the bullet that the BCA pulled out of the wall?"

"Of course I mean that bullet."

Hank was now smiling a coprophagous smile. "Les wasn't there when that shot was fired."

Dixon set down his glass and stared at Hank. "What are you talking about?"

"Remember when I told you what a great marksman Duke was and how he used to shoot turtles off of logs while sitting on his porch?"

"Yeah."

"Well, a couple years ago a bat got into Duke's house. Duke was drunk, so he just pulled his pistol out of the nightstand and shot it. He was embarrassed about it, but, because the hole was behind the door, he never did nothin' about it."

Dixon was suddenly indignant. "Are you telling me that bullet from behind the door had nothing to do with the incident?"

Hank was slow and deliberate with his response. "That's what I'm telling you."

"And you knew it all along?

"I'm afraid so."

Dixon was now incredulous, and it showed in the tightening muscles in his face. "Is that why you arranged to have me find it, so I'd get more excited about the discovery?"

Hank was now chuckling. "Yeah. I would have pointed it out eventually if you hadn't seen it, but once I put the bait in front of your nose, you pretty much took it."

"But, what about the blood spot around the hole?"

"Bats have blood," Hank said. "That retired cop told me they probably wouldn't be able to analyze any blood that had been cleaned up and I figured, even if they did, it was worth taking a shot.

I mean, we didn't tell anyone there was blood there. We just let them discover it and make their own conclusions."

Dixon was now cross-examining his own client. "But the bullet and the blood were just part of it. I mean, the location of Duke's wound, the location of the body. I mean, why did Duke run east when there was nowhere to go?"

"Actually, that's the exact direction I woulda expected him to go. He's got a deer stand across the bay that's well hidden and well supplied. He coulda stayed there several days if he wanted to. I t'ink the problem was the canoe. It was usually sitting right there on the shore, but we found it up in the garage. Duke probably ran down to the shore and got frustrated when he couldn't find it."

"How come nobody heard a second shot?"

"I don't know. Maybe the sirens were on. That would make sense, because Duke might have panicked when he heard them."

Dixon shook his head and gazed into the distance as though he was trying to see something from the past. "I just thought of something else. Does this mean that you're the son of a bitch who put the blood all over my car and sent me that gruesome news article?"

Hank lowered his head in embarrassment. "Sorry about that. I didn't want to do anything to damage your car or anything, but I had to do something to get you suspicious."

"Jesus, you really had me spooked for a while," Dixon said.

"I hope you can forgive me. It's just that it is Les Krueller's fault that Duke is dead. When you told me the only way Krueller could be held accountable for Duke's death was if the evidence showed he actually pulled the trigger, I went looking for some evidence that he actually did pull the trigger. I couldn't really take it directly to the authorities, because they thought I was too personally involved to think rationally. So I needed to have a third party, namely you, get excited about the evidence."

Dixon's initial anger was starting to subside. "I feel so used."

"Sorry about that. But if I'd let you in earlier, you wouldn't have been quite so zealous. In fact, remember that stuff you told me about a lawyer can't knowingly introduce false evidence, but if he had a 'pure heart' he has no ethical issue if he later finds out that the evidence was false."

"Yeah, I remember that."

"By not telling you about it, I protected you. You were zealous—and believe me, Dixon, you were zealous—and the fact that the evidence actually didn't support the murder theory is irrelevant."

"That's all fine and good, but what about Debi's testimony? How could you have arranged that?"

"I didn't. That was just divine intervention or something. I thought the evidence would support murder and, because she's such a liar, the jury would just go with the opposite of whatever she said. Nobody was more surprised than me when she testified the way she did."

"Why do you think she did it, then? I mean she had something to gain if Les recovered money."

"I have two theories on that. First, she might have actually taken to your attempt to build her up and to convince her she didn't have to take abuse, and then, when she saw where the testimony was going and everything, she just found a good story and went with it. Second, Debi was always lying to get Les in trouble and I t'ink she was mad that she had to testify." Hank shrugged his shoulders. "Who knows. Maybe it was a little of each."

Dixon narrowed his eyes and stared at Hank. "Are you sure *somebody* at this table didn't have *something* to do with her testimony?"

"Now, why would you ask me that?" Hank said, with a shake of his head. "Are you sure you want to know the answer?"

"If my client broke the law, I think I should know it."

"Don't worry, I didn't do nothin' illegal. I didn't go see her, I didn't egg her on or anything like that. On the other hand, if she came to see me and I told her that I thought Les should be charged with murder, but that my high-priced, big-city lawyer told me the only way that could happen was if there was evidence that Les actually pulled the trigger . . . well, that's all true. I can't help it if she decides to make up a story."

"So, what do you think did happen that night?" Dixon asked.

Hank shrugged his shoulders. "I don't know for sure. It's possible

Les actually did shoot Duke. If I had to guess, though, I'd say it happened exactly like the sheriff's office said."

"What if they figure it out or Debi changes her mind? I mean I agree that you did an excellent job of protecting me, but aren't you afraid it will give them a basis to get a new trial or an early release?"

"Not really," Hank responded. "I'm not the expert, but in the end Krueller pleaded guilty to exactly what everyone knows he did. So his only argument would be that he pleaded guilty because of the threat of a claim that didn't have any actual basis. It seems to me prosecutors always negotiate based upon the possibility of bringing more serious charges that have less of a chance to succeed. The evidence in question has nothing to do with the charges for which he is being imprisoned."

"So it was all an act at the County Attorney's office? You acted upset that he wasn't pleading guilty to murder, but you knew we were better off with the plea?"

"That wasn't really an act. I did want him to plead to murder, but your advice about timing changed my mind. Les got what he deserved, and I guess I'm satisfied."

Dixon paused to reflect on Hank's words. "You're right that Les got what he deserved, but somehow the truth seems to have been trampled in the process."

"Dixon," Hank said, "your problem is that you believe truth is justice. I believe justice is justice. I'm not going to lose any sleep over Lester Krueller and neither should you."

Dixon nodded in agreement. "Well, this certainly is one for the books. I guess you're not the rube I took you for when you first came to my office."

"High praise indeed," Hank responded, with a grin.

"I don't even want to know what you thought of me," Margie said.

Dixon leaned back in his chair and held up his glass. "Whatever I thought isn't really important. All that matters is what I think now, and I want to tell you that it's been an honor and an education representing you."

♦

Hank dropped Dixon off at his motel. Dixon was somewhat intoxicated, but the events of the evening meant he was far from tired. He packed some things so he'd be ready to go in the morning. Before retiring, he decided to check his voice mail.

"Dixon, hi, this is Jessica. Sorry I didn't return your call, but I was gone. Give me a call when you get a chance." Dixon felt a gentle rush at the sound of her voice, but, on reflection, was saddened. After the click, Dixon erased it and moved to the next message.

It was Sandy wanting to know if Dixon was still running outside in the cold and whether they could do so together. Dixon smiled as he thought of all the things he'd have to tell Sandy the next time they were together. The twists and turns of the legal proceedings had made Dixon look a lot less smart than he thought he was. On the other hand, his nature-over-nurture hypothesis had been vindicated with the revelation that Debi Krueller had merely continued an inborn pattern of lying. Dixon saved the message so he'd remember to return the call at a more appropriate time.

Message number three came on. "Hi, Dixon, it's me again." The voice was Jessica's, and she was more nervous than on the previous message. "I wanted to talk to you, but maybe it would be easier for me to talk to the machine right now . . . I've been thinking a lot about you and what you said. Dixon, I . . . I miss you very much. And I realize that . . . you are very important to me and I don't want to be without you." After another pause, she continued. "Anyway, the company I was consulting for in Minneapolis has offered me a full-time job, and I want to talk to you because I'd like to take the position, but I need to talk to you because I have to make sure you still want me. Please call me when you get this, and please tell me everything you said before is still true."

# To order additional copies of *Liars Dice*:

Web: www.itascabooks.com

Phone: 1-800-901-3480

Fax: Copy and fill out the form below with credit card information. Fax to 651-603-9263.

Mail: Copy and fill out the form below. Mail with check or credit card information to:

Syren Book Company
c/o BookMobile
2402 University Avenue West
Saint Paul, Minnesota 55114

## Order Form

| Copies | Title / Editors | Price | Totals | |
|--------|-----------------|-------|--------|----|
| | **Liars Dice / Bob Gust** | $24.00 | $ | |
| | Subtotal | | $ | |
| | 7% sales tax (MN only) | | $ | |
| | Shipping and handling, first copy | | $ | 4.00 |
| | Shipping and handling, ___ add'l copies @$1.00 ea. | | $ | |
| | TOTAL TO REMIT | | $ | |

## Payment Information:

| __ Check Enclosed __ Visa/MasterCard | | |
|---|---|---|
| Card number: | Expiration date: | |
| Name on card: | | |
| Billing address: | | |
| | | |
| City: | State: | Zip: |
| Signature : | Date: | |

## Shipping Information:

| __ Same as billing address __ Other (enter below) | | |
|---|---|---|
| Name: | | |
| Address: | | |
| | | |
| City: | State: | Zip: |